DEAD LEVEL

ALSO BY DAMIEN BOYD

As the Crow Flies

Head in the Sand

Kickback

Swansong

DAMIEN BOYD

DEAD LEVEL

This is a work of fiction. Names, characters, organizations, places, events, and incidents are either products of the author's imagination or are used fictitiously.

Published by Thomas & Mercer, Seattle
www.apub.com

ISBN-13: 9781503933095
ISBN-10: 1503933091

Cover design by bürosüd° München, www.buerosued.de

Printed in the United States of America

For Monica

Prologue

It was a form of OCD. He'd been told that enough times by enough people.

It was mild and it didn't come with all the paranoia that he'd seen on the telly, but it was definitely obsessive compulsive disorder. Jars and tins with their labels facing front; shampoo and shower gel too. Curtains; right over left. And shoes? He grimaced. If she left them the wrong way round again . . .

He was the same about his car, he knew that. It was spotless, inside and out. Not a speck of dust on the dashboard; not a CD in sight. He shuddered at the thought of scratches. He went through a bottle of T-Cut a week and the bloke with the ChipsAway franchise did very well out of him.

His motorcycle, on the other hand, was untouchable. Immaculate. It had the garage to itself and was polished daily. Sometimes twice. That was his routine.

His ritual.

His first job when he got home tonight would be to polish it. Again. He'd only done it that morning but country lanes were terrible for mud and he'd been waiting in this sodding field gateway for hours now. A muddy field gateway. He couldn't imagine anything worse.

And it was cold. Bloody cold.

He wiped the condensation from his visor and peered into the night. The bright moonlight was reflected by the wet road surface; a light grey strip, framed by the hedges shrouded in darkness on either side.

What the bloody hell are you doing in there?

It was supposed to be a quick job. In and out. He looked at his watch. There was still time. Plenty of time. These long dark winter nights have their uses.

Was that an engine?

He stepped back behind the hedge, took off his helmet and listened. Yes, it was an engine. Idling. He waited for the lights but saw none.

Seconds later a small white van crept past the gateway. A flame lit up the passenger compartment and he watched the driver lighting up, not easy when both lighter and cigarette are shaking like that. Otherwise, there was still no light.

He opened the gate, stepped out into the lane behind the van and listened to the sound of the engine fading away into the distance. He waited, staring into the darkness. Suddenly, tail lights came on and the van accelerated away.

Now to work.

He left his helmet and gauntlets on his motorcycle and walked along the lane towards the cottage. An upstairs light was on and the front door was standing ajar, a narrow beam of light illuminating the garden path.

He stopped at the front gate and put on a pair of disposable latex gloves, then a pair of elasticated latex overshoes over his boots. He had come prepared and knew exactly what had to be done.

He pushed the front door open with his elbow and listened.

Nothing.

He checked the ground floor rooms; broken glass on the kitchen floor just inside the back door. Amateur.

Then he crept up the stairs.

She was lying face down on the landing in a pool of blood that was getting larger by the second. There were several stab wounds to her neck and back. And she was naked.

He reached into his jacket pocket and took out a small plastic bag. He held it up to the light. Then he opened it and emptied a cigarette butt onto the landing next to her body. Two more bags left. In and out in under sixty seconds. It was going like clockwork.

He was halfway down the stairs when she gasped and her body heaved.

You useless . . .

You're gonna pay for this . . .

He watched her fighting for shallow breaths.

She may bleed out. She may not. He couldn't take that chance. And after all, he wasn't going to take the fall for it.

He fetched a knife from the kitchen and stood over her, careful to avoid treading in the blood that was now trickling down the wood panelling and soaking into the hall carpet below.

He picked a stab wound in the left side of her upper back and inserted the knife slowly. Then he pressed down, sending it deeper into her chest cavity. He held it there until her breathing stopped before he pulled it out and put it in the empty plastic bag.

Time to go.

He paused in the garden to empty a small bag of vomit onto the lawn and then two more cigarette butts in the lane opposite the cottage.

Then it was home to clean his motorbike.

He was a creature of habit.

Chapter One

To the untrained eye, the water looked deep. Very deep. The drainage ditches on either side were submerged under murky water that met in the middle of the country road, creating a long, narrow lake with high hedges on both sides. The road rose out of the water, perhaps seventy yards ahead. But how deep was it in the middle?

The fields, visible through gaps in the hedges, were under water too. There was a rusting cattle feeder in the field to the right, the water lapping at the bars, but that was thirty yards away and not much use as a depth gauge. In the far corner of the same field a herd of twenty or so cows was standing on the only dry land available to them, pulling the last bits of greenery from the hedge.

Nick Dixon crept forward in his old Land Rover Defender, watching the bow wave either side wash through the hedge and across the field beyond, each ripple flickering in the low winter sun. He wound down the window and looked at the water level beneath him. It was almost up to the doors now and no doubt over the exhaust pipe too. Much deeper and it would reach the air intake. Fatal for a diesel engine. And very expensive.

He looked in his rear view mirror but his view was blocked by a large white Staffordshire terrier standing up at the back window and staring at the dry land behind them.

'All right, Monty, I get the message.'

Dixon reversed slowly, keeping the revs up to blow the water out of the exhaust. He looked for the white line in the middle of the road but the water was too deep to see it.

Pick a line midway between the two hedges and stay straight, for God's sake.

Once clear of the flood he revved the engine several times and then switched it off.

'I should have bought myself a Portuguese water spaniel,' he muttered, balancing on one foot while he tipped a tennis ball out of his wellington boot.

It was eerily quiet, except for the click of his hazard lights and the sound of the water lapping along the road in front of the Land Rover. Dixon pulled a dead branch out of the hedge and then began edging into the water, testing the depth in front of him with the branch as he went. After only a few paces he was in up to the level of his boots so he leaned forward as far as he could to test the depth further ahead. The road seemed to level off so he decided to keep going. What was the worst that could happen?

He looked back when he heard Monty barking and saw him standing on the front seat of the Land Rover with his paws up on the steering wheel.

He was now more than halfway through the water and both of his feet were wet. Either he had a leak in his boots or water had got in over the top. He threw the branch into the hedge and began wading along the road. The water reached the tops of his knees before shallowing off and he was soon looking back at his Land Rover from dry land, although it hardly felt like it with wellington boots full of water.

He looked down at his trousers. The tide mark was halfway up his thighs, which would take it up to the wheel arches on the Land Rover, perhaps, but it would still be below the air intake. He would need to take it slowly to keep the bow wave down but otherwise it should be fine. And he was insured, after all.

Dixon waded back to his car, stopped to empty the water out of his boots, and then climbed into the driver's seat.

'Let's get this over with then, old son, before I change my mind.'

Dixon crept forward, keeping the revs up and controlling the speed with the clutch. He watched the bow wave rise up in front of the Land Rover and slowed to a crawl so that it stayed below the level of the bonnet. He glanced down. Water was trickling in under the door but it was still six inches below the air intake. There was no going back now.

Monty was standing on the front seat barking at the water bubbling up under the passenger door.

'You're not helping, matey,' said Dixon.

He was starting to wonder whether he had done the right thing when he felt the Land Rover rising up and noticed the water level dropping away beneath him. He opened the driver's door and looked down. The water was no more than six inches deep now so he accelerated out onto dry road and then stopped to watch a Mazda MX5 in his rear view mirror. It had arrived at the same puddle and Dixon was relieved when the driver thought better of it and reversed back to the junction.

Dixon reached over and took a photograph album out of the glove compartment. He glanced at the warning that some kind soul had written on the cover in bright red ink: 'Do not open unless you have a strong stomach.' Then he read the address out loud.

'Stickland Barn, Muchelney.'

Dixon turned left off the main road on the approach to Muchelney, following a lane past a row of terraced cottages with sandbags at the front doors and 'Dredge the Rivers!' signs in the windows. He glanced up at the sky. It was clear blue, for a change, criss-crossed only by vapour trails, and no doubt the residents were praying it stayed that way.

Stickland Barn was the last building on the left as Dixon drove out of the village, and he slowed as he drove past it. Set sideways onto the road and built of grey stone, it had ornate carved stone mullion windows and an oak front door. Dormer windows on the first floor were set into a thatched roof that had seen better days. Dixon spotted the odd patch here and there. He also noticed a For Sale board. He was not going to be popular, but then he had long since given up worrying about that.

He parked on the grass verge a little way beyond Stickland Barn, he hoped hidden from the house by the orchard behind it. Better still, there would be no one at home. Then he followed the track that ran along the back of the orchard towards a five bar gate. He was flicking through the photograph album as he walked and had found the photo he was looking for by the time he reached the gate.

Whoever had written the warning on the front cover of the photograph album had been right, but then a strong stomach was an essential requirement for a police officer. And if you lacked one to begin with, you pretty soon developed one. Dixon grimaced. He had seen the photograph for the first time earlier that day but it had lost none of its power. He leaned on the gate and held it up in front of him, trying to focus on the crime scene rather than the victim. An elderly woman, according to the file, lying in a puddle just inside the gateway.

The small timber field shelter against the hedge on the right in the photograph was now a much bigger block of three stables to

Dixon's left. It had a tack or feed room set at right angles at the far end with a concrete plinth in front, all fenced in to create a small stable yard. The line of leylandii behind it was new too, presumably to give added protection from the prevailing wind, which raced across the Somerset Levels in winter.

The field itself was the same size, although there was now a steel five bar gate on the far side. It looked a recent addition and Dixon guessed that new residents had been able to buy the adjacent field off the farmer to improve the grazing. That might explain the increase from two Shetland ponies to the three large horses visible in the far field and the lack of mud in such a small paddock.

'Can I help you?'

Dixon spun round, snapping the photograph album shut.

'Detective Inspector Dixon, Avon and Somerset Police,' he said, holding up his warrant card.

The woman leaned forward and peered at it for several seconds before looking up.

'Never seen one of those before,' she said.

'And you are?' asked Dixon.

'Julia Woodgates. Mrs.'

'And these are your horses?' The Mountain Horse jacket, jodhpurs and wellington boots were a bit of a giveaway.

'Yes.'

'Do you live in the house?'

'No, I just rent the stables and paddocks. The house belonged to Mrs Harber but she's gone into a care home so it's being sold. Are you buying?'

'Sadly not.'

'What are you doing then?'

'I'm investigating the death of Wendy Gibson. She . . .'

'Really?'

'You sound surprised,' said Dixon.

'No, it's just . . . that was years ago.'

'You know about it?'

'Everybody round here does.'

'And what do they know?'

'Well, just that she was shot dead and they never found out who did it.'

'Were you living here at the time?'

'No, I moved here in 2001. When was it?' asked Mrs Woodgates.

'1994,' replied Dixon.

'I was in Peterborough then.'

'What does the village rumour mill say?'

'How d'you know there is one?'

'There always is.'

'Not a lot,' replied Mrs Woodgates, shrugging her shoulders. 'There was a story going round that she'd been a spy and it was something to do with that.'

'A spy?'

'Oh, and a concentration camp guard, but that was years ago.'

Dixon sighed.

'I know, I know,' said Mrs Woodgates, shaking her head.

'Mind if I have a look around while I'm here?' asked Dixon.

'No, you carry on.'

Dixon handed her his business card. 'If you hear of anything . . .'

Julia Woodgates put the card in her pocket. She was looking down at Dixon's wet trousers.

'You found the deep puddle on the Langport road, I see.'

'Er, yes.'

'Go back through the village to the main road and turn left. You can still get out via Martock.'

'Thanks.'

'What's the point of it?' she asked, opening and then closing the gate behind her. 'I mean, after all these years. Surely, if you've not caught who did it before, you're not going to catch them now, are you?'

'Not necessarily,' replied Dixon. 'Forensic science has moved on a bit since the early nineties.'

'I suppose it has.'

Dixon watched her trudge across the field to the far side. She untied two of the head collars that were looped over the steel five bar gate and then climbed over it into the far field, before disappearing behind the hedge.

'What time d'you call this?'

'Eh?'

'Ages I slaved over that curry.'

'Sorry!'

'You could've phoned.'

'I said I was sorry.'

'It's on a plate in the oven.'

'Thanks.'

'You're lucky it's not in the dog.'

'Is there any mango chutney?'

'In the fridge. Top shelf.'

Detective Constable Jane Winter walked into the living room of the cottage she shared with Dixon. She was carrying a tray and stood in front of the television looking down at him. He was stretched out on the sofa with Monty curled up on his lap and a can of beer on the floor next to him.

'Shift over then.'

Dixon pushed Monty onto the floor, swung his legs off the sofa and sat up. Jane sat down next to him.

'Open that for me,' she said, passing him the jar of mango chutney. 'You eaten?'

'I had mine earlier,' replied Dixon. 'Because of the diabetes.'

'I know, I know,' replied Jane. 'Regular meal times. How'd you get on then?'

'Suspended on full pay.'

'Full pay? Sounds like a paid holiday to me.'

'Not quite. I've been assigned to the Cold Case Unit at Portishead, reporting to a retired DCI old enough to be my grandfather, investigating murders that took place before I was born.'

'And your interview?'

'Tomorrow at ten.'

Jane nodded. 'When's the disciplinary hearing?'

'In the New Year.'

'Tell me about your cold case then.'

'Shotgun blast to the face at point blank range. Both barrels . . .'

Jane winced.

'It was a four ten rather than a twelve bore so it's not as bad as it could've been,' continued Dixon, 'but the photos are pretty grim.'

'When was it?'

'March '94.'

'That's not before you were born . . .'

'Sadly, not,' said Dixon, smiling. 'Anyway, she was found in the paddock behind her house with her two Shetland ponies.'

'Who was she?'

'Mrs Wendy Gibson. Lived alone. No family.'

'Where?'

'Muchelney. Out on the Levels, near Langport.'

'I know it.'

'I popped over there today for a look around and only just got through. Much more rain and I'll have to get a snorkel for the old bus.'

'That explains the wellies in the kitchen.'

'It does.'

'See anything interesting?'

'Not really. There were flowers on her grave and no one knows who puts them there. Not even the vicar.'

'What are you going to do?'

'No idea,' said Dixon. 'What about you?'

'Shoplifting,' replied Jane.

'You go steady.'

'I've had enough excitement lately, thank you. And I'm looking forward to a quiet Christmas.' Jane looked at the television. 'What's this?'

'*The Deer Hunter*.'

'How many times have you seen that before?'

'*Master and Commander* has just started on Film 4.'

'You could try switching it off,' said Jane.

'Nope, you've lost me there,' replied Dixon, shaking his head.

'What else have you been up to?' asked Jane, through a mouthful of chicken curry.

'Not a lot. Monty got a walk on the beach. Then no sooner had we got home than the Tory candidate was knocking on the door asking for my vote.'

'What'd you tell him?'

'That I'd only just moved in. Not on the electoral roll yet.'

'Is that true?'

'No,' replied Dixon, smiling.

'He'd know that was bollocks, though, wouldn't he?'

'If he bothers to check.'

'What constituency are we here?'

'Bridgwater and North Somerset.'

'This by-election's going to be a pain. When is it?'

'End of January.'

'Weeks of it,' said Jane, shaking her head. 'Well, he's wasting his time with me. I'm still registered at my parents' in Worle, so that'll be Weston, won't it?'

'Good excuse. Shall we hire that van and move your furniture over this weekend?'

'Why not?'

'What are you up to next week?' asked Dixon.

'I've got Christmas off,' replied Jane.

'Me too. There's no overtime on the Cold Case Unit. Shall we get a tree?'

'A real one?'

'Of course.'

'You got any decorations?' asked Jane.

Chapter Two

Just before 10 a.m. the following morning Dixon parked in the visitors' car park at Sandy Padgett House, the new Bridgwater Police Centre on Express Park. He had spent the previous week or so based there, until he had been shunted off to Portishead, and had a staff pass, but he still felt like a visitor. Even more so today, the day of his interview with Professional Standards.

'What are you going to tell them?' Jane had asked, over breakfast.

'The truth.'

'Really?'

'You're confusing me with someone who gives a shit.'

Dixon smiled. Jane had not been impressed with that line.

'Don't be ridiculous. D'you want to spend the rest of your life watching CCTV at Tesco?'

And she was right, of course. He did care. The prospect of a career in supermarket security would no doubt keep him awake at night until the disciplinary hearing. That, and the only thing he feared more. Being returned to uniform.

He was sitting in the reception area watching the strip lights suspended from the ceiling in the atrium. There were three of them and they were swinging from side to side on long cables like pendulums, the arc becoming longer each time the front doors opened.

The designer needs his arse kicking.

The lights reminded Dixon of a Newton's cradle and he wondered how strong the wind would need to be before they crashed into each other. He hoped he was not sitting underneath them when they did.

'They make quite a feature, don't they?'

'Yes, Sir,' said Dixon, standing up to face Detective Chief Inspector Lewis.

'Your big day, I gather?'

Dixon nodded.

'Don't say anything stupid, and leave the rest to me. All right?'

'Er, yes, Sir.'

DCI Lewis winked at Dixon, turned and disappeared through a security door adjacent to the reception desk.

Dixon smiled. Maybe he would live to fight another day, after all.

Two hours later Dixon was sitting in the staff canteen on the first floor, staring into the bottom of an empty coffee cup, when he felt a tap on his shoulder. He stood up when he recognised Chief Inspector Bateman.

'DCI Lewis tells me you've got a bit of time on your hands, Dixon?'

'Yes, Sir.'

'Good. Make yourself useful and show the Conservative candidate around the station, will you?'

'Me?'

'He's here for a guided tour and I bloody well forgot, didn't I! He's down in reception.'

'But, I've only been here a week and hardly . . .'

'Well, you'll just have to wing it then, won't you,' said Bateman, turning to leave. 'His name's Perry.'

I know that. I met him yesterday.

Dixon shrugged his shoulders and trudged over to the stairs. Once on the ground floor he looked in the open plan offices on either side of the lobby and counted at least twenty officers sitting at workstations, all of whom could have been picked on by Bateman. Having said that, they all looked as though they had better things to do.

Dixon opened the security door and peered into the reception area. He spotted Tom Perry sitting at the far end. He was wearing a jacket and tie and appeared to be mesmerised by the swinging strip lights above him. This was going to be embarrassing.

'Mr Perry?'

'That's me,' said Perry, jumping up and greeting Dixon with a smile and an outstretched hand. He was in his late thirties and well over six feet tall, with short blonde hair and rugby player's ears.

'Detective Inspector Nick Dixon.' They shook hands.

'We met yesterday,' said Perry.

'I was hoping you wouldn't remember that.'

'You were very polite.'

'Thank you,' replied Dixon.

'I get a lot worse. You'd be surprised how many words the great British public can get to rhyme with Tory when they really put their backs into it.'

Dixon laughed. Perhaps this wasn't going to be too bad, after all.

'You enjoy parachuting, I gather?'

'That's my opponents,' replied Perry, smiling. 'Their candidate is local, so they like to portray me as the London architect, parachuted into the constituency. But then you knew that?'

'I did.'

'I am local. Well, localish. My family is from Taunton.'

'That's near enough,' said Dixon.

'You'd have thought so. We've rented a cottage in the constituency, over at Northmoor Green.'

'We?'

'My wife, Elizabeth, and me.'

Moving from London, renting a cottage. It was all sounding familiar.

'Splendid set of lights,' said Perry, looking up. 'I was waiting for the trapeze artist to appear.'

'Follow me,' said Dixon, gesturing towards the security door. 'The less time we spend underneath them, the better.'

'Agreed.'

It took Dixon over an hour to show Tom Perry around the station, although he avoided the Professional Standards Department on the second floor. Perry was particularly impressed with the custody suite and the psychedelic lockers in the mixed changing rooms.

'What's with the bright colours?'

'No idea,' replied Dixon.

'And mixed? I bet that took some getting used to?'

'It's one advantage of being a detective,' Dixon replied. 'No need to get changed.' It was another reason Dixon was dreading being sent back to uniform, but Perry didn't need to know that.

The layout of the interview rooms, with the interviewing officer and suspect sitting side by side, also took Perry by surprise. Dixon was unable to explain that either, recalling many occasions when he had been grateful for the table between him and the suspect.

'Designed by someone who has never conducted a police interview.'

Perry had agreed.

'How are you finding working here?' was a question Dixon struggled with. He thought Perry deserved better than 'I've only been here a week', so he rambled on about the challenges of working in an open plan office and 'hot desking' at workstations. Dixon was used to his own office, with his own desk and a door that he could shut and a window he could open. Perry appeared to understand the point.

The only difficult moment came when Perry asked how many officers were working at the station. Dixon's reply, 'not as many as there were', appeared to hit home and Perry had quickly changed the subject. No doubt he would be trying to keep police budget cuts off the by-election agenda too.

By 1.30 p.m. they were outside the front entrance for the obligatory photo opportunity when Dixon's phone bleeped.

'It's just a text,' said Dixon, smiling for the camera.

He reached into his jacket pocket and took out his phone as he watched Perry driving out of Express Park, his car windows plastered with blue 'Vote Conservative' posters.

Where are you? Got the afternoon off. Shall we get the Xmas tree? J x

As weekends go, it didn't get much better than this. Or at least, it hadn't for a very long time. Dixon watched Jane sipping a gin and tonic. She had kicked off her shoes and her feet were resting on Monty, who was stretched out on the floor in front of the fire in the Red Cow.

They had bought a Christmas tree on Friday afternoon and spent several hours decorating it on Saturday morning, all thoughts of furniture removals postponed until the New Year. That was followed by a walk on the beach and a curry in the Zalshah. Breakfast in bed, twice, had taken Jane by surprise and now, here they were, in the Red Cow, their Sunday afternoon walk on Brean Down having been abandoned due to the torrential rain. Monty had taken one look out of the back door of the cottage and gone back to bed.

Dixon smiled. All he needed now was a pipe and slippers.

'You still haven't told me about your interview,' said Jane, breaking the silence.

'I did.'

'You're gonna have to do a bit better than "yeah, fine", if you don't . . .'

'All right, all right,' said Dixon, holding up his hands in mock surrender. 'It was going OK until the last question, really.'

'Well?'

'"Faced with the same set of circumstances, would you do the same again?"'

'And you said yes, I suppose?'

'I did.'

Jane shook her head.

'They'd have known I was lying if I'd said no.'

'Did they ask about me?'

'I said it was all your idea.'

'Stop mucking about,' said Jane, digging Dixon in the ribs.

'No, I told them you knew nothing about it. That I'd kept you in the dark.'

'Thank you.'

'You'll be fine.'

'Anything else?' asked Jane.

'I saw DCI Lewis on the way in. He winked at me.'

'That's a good sign, surely?'

'I thought he had something in his eye.'

⁂

They went their separate ways just before 8 a.m. the following morning. Jane left for Express Park and Dixon headed north on the M5 to Portishead. One day to get through and then it was Christmas Eve.

He had felt very conspicuous on his last visit to HQ, particularly having been assigned to the Cold Case Unit. It was rather like driving around in a sign written courtesy car from an accident repair centre. Everybody knew he was in trouble, the only thing they didn't know was just how deep.

He spent the day sitting at a vacant workstation in the Criminal Investigation Department, going through the box of files on the murder of Wendy Gibson. He started with the post mortem report, which documented catastrophic injuries to her head and neck. She had been all but obliterated, but he had seen that for himself in the photographs.

The weapon had been identified from the size and spread of the shot as a four ten with the barrels over and under rather than side by side, and the killer had been standing no more than six feet away when both barrels had been fired. It seemed an extravagant way to kill a sixty year old widow. Her estimated height was no more than five feet five inches and she weighed a shade under eight stone. Add to that her crippling arthritis and a burglar could have just pushed her over or hit her with the gun butt, perhaps. So, why blow her head off?

Maybe the killer had panicked? That was possible. But why shoot her in the face? Dixon reached for his notepad and wrote down two words.

Obliterated. Why?

Next he turned to the witness statements. The police evidence confirmed that nothing whatsoever had been stolen and her house had not been broken into, which didn't necessarily rule out a burglary gone wrong because the suspect would have no doubt fled the scene empty handed after the shooting. If theft had been the plan, of course.

Two of her nearest neighbours reported hearing a shotgun blast at around 6.30 p.m. One said it was just before and one just after but there was unlikely to be anything sinister in that. Both said it was not unusual to hear gunfire at or around dusk, with people out 'lamping' for rabbits. Dixon checked the date. The murder took place on Friday 25 March 1994 and so it would have been just before the clocks went forward for British Summer Time. A quick search of the Internet confirmed that sunset would have been at 6.20 p.m. or so.

Otherwise, Mrs Gibson kept herself to herself, had no living relatives, rarely had any visitors and spent most of her time looking after her two Shetland ponies. Dixon was pleased to note that they had been taken in by Horseworld, or the Friends of Bristol Horses as it then was.

The two witnesses, Albert Higgins and Sonia Spencer, still lived in Muchelney and readily agreed to meet with Dixon after Christmas to go over their witness statements yet again. They had been expecting a call, they said, it being common knowledge that the case had been reopened. Dixon thought about his visit to Muchelney the previous Thursday. As well as a village rumour mill, there also appeared to be a very effective grapevine.

Forensic evidence was non-existent and it was obvious that no suspect had ever been identified. The investigation had lacked any clear direction from the start.

'And still does,' muttered Dixon, dropping the file back into the box.

He checked the time. It was almost 4 p.m., giving him just enough time to get home and take Monty for a walk before it got pitch dark.

Dixon was lying in bed trying to work out what Wendy Gibson's killer had been intending when he or she went to Stickland Barn on that rainy afternoon in March 1994. Had they been intending to commit a burglary or a murder? The original investigation had not arrived at a conclusion either way, nor had any subsequent review, although the assumption had always been that it was a burglary gone wrong.

He was also wondering whether Jane could cook anything else apart from spaghetti bolognese. It was lovely, as it had been last time and the time before that, but he hoped her repertoire extended to roast turkey, because his certainly didn't. Still, there was always Google.

He was listening to the sound of Monty snoring in his bed on the floor next to him when the mobile phone rang on Jane's bedside table.

'What time is it?' asked Jane, from under the duvet.

'Sevenish,' replied Dixon.

Jane sat up and picked up her phone.

'Jane Winter . . . you are kidding me? It's Christmas Eve . . . who is it? . . . yes, yes, I'm on my way.'

She rang off and dropped the phone onto the bed.

'Gotta go. Sorry.'

'What is it?' asked Dixon.

'We've got a body,' replied Jane, swinging her legs out of the bed and sitting up.

'Where?'

'Northmoor Green. A cottage down by the river. Multiple stab wounds.'

'Who is it?'

'Elizabeth Perry.'

'Not Tom Perry's wife?'

Jane turned to look at Dixon and sighed.

'Tom Perry's pregnant wife.'

Chapter Three

It was still dark when Jane turned into the staff car park at Express Park in her brand new red VW Golf. The insurance company had been surprisingly generous with the settlement on her old one and a loan had topped it up. Still, she could afford it, or at least she would be able to now that she had found a tenant for her flat.

She waved her pass in front of the sensor and looked up at the station while she waited for the huge steel gates to open. All concrete and glass, Nick had said, and he was right. Lights were on everywhere and most of the workstations on the first floor, visible through the vast windows, were occupied. She recognised Detective Constables Dave Harding and Mark Pearce sitting at computers. And the unmistakeable figure of Detective Sergeant Harry Unwin, standing with his back to the windows, a mug of coffee in his hand.

She remembered Dixon pinning Harry by the throat to the vending machine in the CID Room at the old Bridgwater Police Station only a few short weeks ago. Harry was not to be trusted, if Dixon was right. And he usually was.

Jane closed her eyes.

Please don't let me be teamed up with Harry.

The open plan CID area was all but deserted by the time Jane arrived on the first floor. She spotted a bald head behind a computer screen on the far side of the workstations.

'Where is everyone?'

'Meeting room two.'

Jane sighed. Gone were the days of crowding around the whiteboard in the CID Room.

Nick will hate it.

She opened the door, crept in and sat down on an empty chair between Dave Harding and newly appointed DI Janice Courtenay.

'Glad you could make it, Jane,' said DCI Lewis.

'Thank you, Sir.'

Jane glanced across at Janice. They had worked together some years before when they had both been detective constables, Janice having been more aggressive in her pursuit of promotion since then. Their paths had crossed again more recently, when Janice had shared an office with Dixon at the old Bridgwater Police Station.

It would be her first murder as senior investigating officer and Janice looked nervous. Not a good start. Jane looked around the table and wondered whether anyone else had spotted it.

'Elizabeth Perry. Multiple stab wounds. Found by the milkman just before six this morning. That's about as far as we'd got. All right?' said DCI Lewis.

'Yes, Sir,' replied Jane, trying to shrug off all thoughts of deep ends and sinking or swimming.

'Scientific Services are on scene,' continued Lewis. 'Did someone get the pathologist out of bed?'

'Roger Poland is on his way over there now, Sir,' said Janice.

'Good.'

'What about the husband?' asked Dave Harding.

'Thomas Perry. He's the parliamentary candidate for the Conservative Party and, as we know, we're right in the middle of a by-election.'

'Surely that'll be called off now?'

'I doubt it. Nominations haven't closed yet. He may stand down, in which case the Tories will have to select another candidate, but the election will go ahead.'

'Seems a bit harsh,' said Pearce.

'And having your wife murdered isn't, I suppose,' said Janice.

'No, I meant . . .'

'We know what you meant, Mark,' said Lewis. 'The fact is that's incidental as far as we're concerned.'

'Yes, Sir.'

'Unless it becomes relevant to the investigation, of course. And keep your politics to yourselves. A woman's been murdered and no one's interested in how you vote. All right?'

'Where is he?' asked Janice.

'London. He was working yesterday and driving down this morning, apparently. I've been on to the Met and someone from family liaison is with him now. He'll be brought straight here later today. As soon as he's fit to travel, that is.'

'Was he on his own last night?' asked Harding.

'To be confirmed,' replied Lewis. 'I know where you're going with that though, Dave, and we're gonna do this one by the book. OK?'

'He could've . . .'

'Of course he could. So we check.'

'Yes, Sir.'

'While I think about it,' said Lewis, turning to Janice, 'check his bank statements. If he did drive from London to Bridgwater and back in one night, chances are he'll have stopped for petrol.'

Janice rolled her eyes.

'Teaching you to suck eggs, I know. Sorry,' said Lewis.

'It's fine, Sir,' replied Janice.

'Right, let's talk about the press. There's usually bugger all to report on at this time of year, except the Queen's speech, and we've got the by-election angle so they're going to be all over this story. The nationals too.'

'It's going to be a nightmare,' said Janice.

'It is,' replied Lewis. 'I suggest we meet with the press officer, Janice. I'll set it up for this afternoon, when you've got more of a handle on what's going on.'

'Yes, Sir.'

'In the meantime, no one says anything to anyone. Is that clear?'

'Yes, Sir.'

The phone rang on the sideboard behind Dave Harding. He leaned back on his chair and answered it.

'Chief constable's here, Sir,' he said, replacing the handset.

'Well, I'll leave you to it,' said Lewis, standing up and walking towards the door. 'Let me know when Perry gets here and ring me if you get anything in the meantime.'

'Yes, Sir,' replied Janice.

She waited for DCI Lewis to close the door behind him.

'OK. Dave, I want a full background check on Mrs Perry. Mark, you take the husband. Business dealings, bank accounts, mobile phone records, everything. Friends, known associates. I want to know everything about them before I speak to the husband.'

Dave and Mark reminded Jane of nodding dogs on the parcel shelf of a car.

'Harry, you liaise with the house to house team. I want a complete timeline of their movements for the last forty-eight hours to begin with. We may have to go back further but we'll see. All right?'

'What time does it start?'

'Nine, but there aren't that many doors to knock on so it shouldn't take too long.'

'Good.'

'I'm going over there now,' said Janice. 'Jane, you're with me.'

Thank God for that.

'How's Nick?'

Jane was sitting in the passenger seat of Janice's car as they drove over the M5 at Huntworth, over the canal and on towards Moorland. She was watching the windscreen wiper and thought it odd that Janice's car only had one. It was working twice as hard to do the same job, much like being a police officer after the latest round of budget cuts, but she decided to keep that thought to herself.

'He's fine.'

'How did his interview go?'

'OK, I think,' replied Jane. She looked at her watch. It was just before 8.30 a.m. and no doubt Dixon was still in bed.

'We'd all have done the same thing in his shoes,' said Janice. 'And I preferred sharing an office with him to this open plan crap any day.'

They arrived in Moorland to find the left turn to Northmoor Green closed opposite the church. A patrol car was parked across the road, blocking the junction. Janice waved her warrant card at the uniformed officers sitting in the patrol car, but neither of them seemed keen to get wet. Next she tried improvised sign language and a yell of 'Shift!', which appeared to do the trick.

Jane used the opportunity to read the road signs: 'Northmoor Green, No Through Road'; 'Unsuitable for HGVs'; 'No Turning Area'; and last but not least, a homemade 'SAT NAV WRONG, DEAD END'. Then she noticed that all of the bungalows either side of the junction had 'Dredge the Rivers!' signs in their windows.

'The cottage is down at the far end,' said Janice, waiting for the patrol car to pull forward. 'Waterside Cottage, so I imagine it's by the river.'

'That explains the signs,' replied Jane.

They followed the lane, the red brick bungalows on either side giving way to traditional stone cottages, a line of new houses and then to open fields. Another patrol car was blocking the road further ahead, just beyond the entrance to a farmyard, which contained two more patrol cars, two Scientific Services vans and Roger Poland's Volvo.

'Looks like we go the rest of the way on foot,' said Janice, turning into the yard.

They walked along the lane, sheltering under Janice's umbrella, although it needed both of them to hold onto to it in the wind. Waterside Cottage was at the far end, just where the road finished at a steel barrier, forming a T junction with the gravel track that followed the River Parrett. The cottage was facing the lane on the left and sideways on to the river. It was painted white, with what looked like terracotta roof tiles, and a timber framed entrance porch, which was just visible behind the tent that Scientific Services had set up to cover the garden path. Another tent had been set up in the lane outside.

Jane peered into the tent covering the lane.

'Wait there!'

Janice put her umbrella back up and stepped back into rain.

'Best do as we're told, I suppose.'

'Right, you can come in now.'

Once inside the tent they were greeted by Donald Watson, the senior scientific services officer. He was holding two sets of white overalls and blue disposable overshoes.

'Put these on,' he said, handing one set of each to Jane and Janice. 'You've got your own gloves?'

'Yes.'

Janice finished first. 'What've we got then?' she asked.

'Two cigarette butts over there,' replied Watson, pointing to an area on the far side of the tent cordoned off with tape. Two small red flags had been stuck in the mud on the edge of the grass verge. 'They look fresh so we'll check them out.'

Janice nodded.

'Follow me,' continued Watson. 'And stick to the approach path.'

They followed him along the line of metal plates that had been placed on the ground like stepping stones, through the garden gate and into the adjacent tent. The front door and porch of the cottage were glazed with stained glass windows and a wisteria was now visible growing along the front of the cottage. It was the sort of place that you might take a photograph of in different circumstances.

'There was a small pile of vomit there,' said Watson, gesturing to a small area on the lawn off to the right of the path. 'We'll see what we can get from it, but it's been raining since threeish. The same applies to the fag butts in the road.'

The sickly sweet smell of congealed blood overpowered them as soon as they stepped into the porch. Janice turned away. Her hand was over her mouth, with her nose clamped between her index finger and thumb.

'Are you . . . ?'

'I'm all right, I'm all right.'

'Do you want a mask?' asked Watson.

'No, really.'

Jane looked into the hallway. There was a large bloodstain on the carpet and a red line down the white painted wood panelling above it, where the blood had trickled down from the landing at the top of the stairs. She looked up and recognised Roger Poland kneeling next to the body. He was peering at Mrs Perry's upper arms and mumbling into a Dictaphone.

'Came in through the kitchen,' said Watson, following the steel plates along the hall, 'We've got a broken pane of glass but no fingerprints, sadly.'

'Any footprints?' asked Janice.

'Two sets in the back garden but nothing after that.'

'Tyre tracks?'

'We've got some in a field gateway about seventy yards down the lane, but that's it.'

Watson stopped just inside the kitchen door. Jane was standing in the doorway, peering over Janice's shoulder. They watched a scientific services officer crouching down by the back door picking up bits of glass and placing them in evidence bags.

'Seen enough?'

Janice nodded.

'Up the stairs then,' said Watson.

They retraced their steps back along the hall. It was an old cottage with low ceilings, which made for a short flight of stairs. Jane counted twelve. She hesitated at the bottom.

'Can we go up?'

'Yes, there's nothing on the stairs,' said Watson. 'Keep to the plastic though.'

Jane was standing on the top step before Poland noticed her. He was still kneeling over the body, with his back to the stairs.

'Hello, Jane,' he said, looking over his shoulder.

'Hi, Roger,' replied Jane. She stepped over his legs and onto a steel plate on the landing. 'D'you know DI Janice Courtenay?'

'No,' replied Roger, rocking back onto the balls of his feet and standing up.

Janice nodded without looking up. She was now standing on the top step, staring at the naked body of Elizabeth Perry lying face down on the landing. Her hands had been wrapped in plastic bags, sealed at the wrists, but it was the knife wounds that Janice was staring at. Two in the side of the neck and four in her back. A trail of congealed blood led across the wooden floor to the bannister and off the edge of the landing.

'They missed the carotid artery in the neck,' said Roger, 'so this looks like the fatal one.' He was pointing at a stab wound in the left side of Mrs Perry's upper back. 'Probably straight through to the heart but I'll need to open her up to confirm.'

Janice turned, pushed past Donald Watson and ran back down the stairs. Then she followed the approach path back out into the lane, her heels clicking on the metal plates.

'Give me a minute,' said Jane.

She caught up with Janice in the car park. Janice was leaning on the bonnet of her car with her left hand and vomiting into the undergrowth.

'I'll be fine, I'll be fine.'

'What's up then?' asked Jane.

Janice vomited again.

'You must have seen a body before?'

'And more besides,' replied Janice. 'I dunno. I wasn't feeling well before we came out.'

'You're not pregnant, are you?'

'Don't be so bloody stupid.'

'Out on the piss last night?'

'Not really,' replied Janice, shaking her head. 'I just felt a bit sick, that's all.'

Jane sighed.

'Look, it's my first murder as a DI. All right?'

'But . . .'

'And it would have to be this one. We've even got the chief constable turning up. Not to mention every journalist within a three hundred mile radius.'

'You're doing fine. Stop worrying,' said Jane. 'Now, let's get back in there. We'll tell 'em you've got a hangover.'

Jane took a packet of mints out of her handbag and passed it to Janice.

'Here, have one of these. Dog breath.'

'Thanks!'

They walked back along the lane and Janice stopped outside the tent.

'You won't . . .'

'Of course, I won't,' replied Jane.

'Sorry, bit of a hangover,' said Janice, walking back up the stairs. Jane was following behind her.

'Christmas piss up, was it?' asked Watson.

'Something like that.'

'I'm almost ready to move her,' said Poland, standing up. 'Sometime between midnight and 2 a.m. is the answer to your question, but I'll confirm that.'

'Anything else?' asked Janice.

'No defensive injuries but there's bruising on her upper arms, so it looks as though she was restrained at some point. There are some fibres under her fingernails too.'

'Where was she killed?'

'There's blood spatter in the bedroom,' replied Watson. 'It's on the wall by the door. From the height, she was stabbed in the neck in there and then came out here and collapsed.'

'She was still alive here, there's no doubt about that,' said Poland. 'So, she came out here, collapsed, and then was stabbed in the back four times.' Poland turned to Jane. 'For good measure, as Nick would say.'

Jane rolled her eyes.

'All this is to be confirmed, of course,' continued Poland.

Watson turned around and pointed to a small circle of spray paint on the wooden floor behind him.

'We found another cigarette butt there,' he said, 'Same brand. And some ash.'

'Let's have a look in the bedroom,' said Janice.

'Follow me,' said Watson.

They managed to squeeze past Roger Poland's large frame and into the bedroom. It was a small room with a low ceiling and a double bed that had only been slept in on one side.

'See the blood spatter?' asked Watson, pointing to the wall just inside the door. 'Looks like she got out of bed and met her attacker in the doorway.' Watson looked up. 'There's lighter spray on the ceiling, possibly from the knife as it was thrust . . .'

'We get the picture,' said Janice.

Jane looked out of the window at the back garden. A scientific services officer was looking in the shed at the bottom of the garden and another was photographing one of the panels in the wooden fence that ran along the right hand boundary. An area of flowerbed in front of him had been taped off. On the other side of the fence was a gravel track and then the River Parrett. It looked much narrower than Jane remembered it and was certainly narrower than it was in the middle of Bridgwater, which explained the 'Dredge the Rivers!' signs, perhaps.

'We found this on the bedside table,' said Watson.

Jane looked back to see him handing a black and white photograph to Janice. It was a snapshot of an ultrasound scan. Janice looked at it and handed it back.

'Roger will confirm if she was pregnant,' said Watson.

'Has anything been stolen?' asked Janice, looking around the room.

'Not as far as we can tell,' replied Watson. 'Her handbag's on the floor in the living room. Her purse is still in it and her watch is there, look, just sitting on the bedside table.'

'She's still got her rings on,' said Jane.

Janice nodded.

'Your van's here, Mr Poland.' The shout came from downstairs.

'We'll wait outside while they move her,' said Janice.

The lane outside was blocked by a black van when they got outside so Jane ducked back inside the tent. 'Can we get out that way?' she asked, pointing to the far wall.

'Er, yes.'

Watson unzipped a door in the wall of the tent and Jane stepped out on the far side. Janice followed.

'Where are you going?'

Jane walked up the slope to the gravel track and looked at the steel barrier. It was padlocked in the open position and was wide enough for a lorry, let alone a car.

'National cycle network,' said Jane, reading from the sign on the gatepost. Then she walked across to the river and looked down at the water. It was racing past the cottage, swirling as it went, and was getting perilously close to the top of the bank.

'Tide must be in,' said Janice.

They both turned, looked back at the cottage from the top of the riverbank and then back at the river.

'Is it me or is the water level higher than the cottage?' asked Jane.

'It's higher,' replied Janice.

'And what do you notice about that fence?' Jane was pointing to the back of the cottage.

Janice shook her head. 'What?'

'It's the wrong way round. Those horizontal struts should be on the inside, surely?'

'I see what you mean.'

'It's like a ladder. My granny could get over that.'

They watched two mortuary staff carrying the body of Elizabeth Perry to the back of the van on a stretcher.

'You drive down here at the dead of night,' continued Jane. 'No street lighting. Turn, possibly, but leave your car up here, hidden behind these trees, and then hop over the garden fence. Then when you're done, it's out through the front door, puke up in the garden, in the car and gone.'

Janice turned and looked at a farm on the other side of the river. 'We'd better make sure the house to house team gets over there.'

Jane watched the uniformed officers going from house to house as Janice drove back along the lane towards the church.

'There's Harry,' said Jane, pointing to a car parked across the entrance to the church.

Janice pulled up alongside it and wound down the passenger window. She waited several seconds before giving the horn a loud blast. DS Unwin dropped his phone and looked up. Then he wound down the passenger window of his car and leaned across the empty seat.

'What's up?'

'There's a farm on the other side of the river about fifty yards upstream, Harry. Make sure someone gets up there. All right?' said Janice.

'Will do.'

'Anything from the house to house?'

'Not yet.'

'Well, keep me posted.'

Janice kept her finger on the electric window button as she drove out of Moorland and back towards Bridgwater.

'At least we should have some DNA to work with,' she said.

'The fag butt on the landing is the best bet,' replied Jane.

Janice nodded.

They were driving back over the M5 when Jane fished her phone out of her handbag and sent Dixon a text message.

Where are you J x

The reply arrived within seconds.

On the beach ☺

Chapter Four

'What've we got then?' asked Janice, dropping her handbag onto a vacant workstation.

'Plenty of information about the husband,' replied Pearce. 'He's even got his own website, votetomperry.co.uk.'

'Well?'

'He's an architect in Richmond but his family is from Taunton. Went to Huish's then Reading University. He played rugby for Kingston before he had to give it up when he broke a bone in his neck. That seems to be when he got involved in politics.'

'When was that?'

'Four years ago. He stood for the council in Kingston a couple of times, unsuccessfully, before getting on the list of approved parliamentary candidates at the beginning of last year. Then he gets himself selected for Bridgwater and North Somerset last summer when the sitting MP announced he was standing down at the next general election.'

'Why the by-election then?' asked Harding.

'The Right Honourable Kenneth Anderson, QC, MP. He was standing down due to ill health, only it turned out he was iller than he thought he was. Died last November,' replied Pearce.

'Anything else?'

'Not known to police but then we never really thought he would be, did we?'

'No.'

'There's a photo of Perry here with his wife, usual happy couple stuff. They got married two years ago and are hoping to start a family and bring up their children in beautiful North Somerset, it says here.'

'Did she work?'

'She was an accountant but gave it up when he got selected and they moved down here.'

'What about him?'

'He's an architect. He's still working in Richmond during the week but will give it up if he gets elected. Wait a minute,' said Pearce, his eyes scanning the computer screen. 'Here it is, "If I am elected your member of parliament then I will immediately resign from my job and devote myself full time to the constituency".'

'Resign from one well paid job to take up another one,' said Harding. 'Life's a bitch, isn't it.'

'And then your wife's murdered,' said Janice. 'I reckon if you asked him, he'd say life was a bitch, don't you think?'

'Sorry,' said Harding, ducking down behind his computer.

Janice turned her back on him and spoke to Mark Pearce.

'Anything about the cottage in Northmoor Green?'

'They rented it last summer, after he was selected and they let out their flat in Kingston. According to the Met, he stays with her parents when he's in London now.'

'Her parents?' asked Janice.

'Yes, they live in Putney.'

'Are they there now?'

'No, they've gone to stay with their son for Christmas.'

'Where?'

'Poole. He's a marine based there.'

'Bank statements?'

'The request's gone in but it's Christmas Eve, don't forget.'

Janice rolled her eyes.

'Same for the wife,' said Harding.

'And the phone records,' said Pearce.

'Well, we've got a time frame now, so let's check all the traffic cameras between midnight and 4 a.m. We can widen it from there if nothing comes up. Look for anything out of the ordinary. Both of you. All right?'

'OK.'

'Is the husband on his way?'

'Be here about threeish,' replied Pearce.

Jane looked at her watch. It was nearly midday. She had been listening to the conversation from a vacant workstation in the far corner of the CID area, where she had been looking at Northmoor Green and the River Parrett on Google Earth. The satellite images were recent and the river was visible as a grey strip weaving in and out of the fields. Jane zoomed in and looked at the banks adjacent to Waterside Cottage, where the river seemed to narrow still further and the grass on the banks either side gave way to large silt deposits.

Silt had long been a political issue for residents living on the Somerset Levels. That and the failure of the Environment Agency to dredge the rivers, as evidenced by the abundance of signs Jane had seen demanding they do just that.

Then she had checked the long range weather forecast. Neither looked good.

She was still staring at the satellite picture, dragging the image with her mouse so that she could follow the gravel track south-east along the river, when her phone rang.

'Jane Winter.'

'Jane, it's Donald Watson. Janice isn't answering her phone.'

Jane looked up from her desk. Janice's handbag was on the corner of a workstation but Janice was nowhere to be seen.

'She was here a minute ago . . .'

'Not to worry,' said Watson. 'I'll tell you. I've had a look in the victim's purse. We've got a petrol receipt from the Shell garage on the A39 at 11.32 a.m. and a till receipt from the Greendale Farm Shop at 12.01 p.m.'

'What about her cards?'

'Still there. Even the cash. Sixty quid. Looks like she picked up the turkey. Then nothing.'

'Is that it?'

'From the purse, yes. There are some text messages on her phone throughout the afternoon and evening. All to and from her husband. Looks like he went to the office Christmas party, I think. The last one was sent at 11.17 p.m. and says, "Leaving now. See you in the morning. Kiss, kiss." I'll put it all in an email for you.'

'Thanks.'

Jane rang off. Office party on the Monday then driving home on Christmas Eve morning. It all sounded perfectly normal. How many other people would have done that very thing?

She went back to following the riverside path to the south-east, dragging the satellite image across the screen and waiting each time for the picture to resolve. The track turned away from the river and across a field beyond the next bend, continuing along the riverbank only as a narrow footpath, before joining a tarmac road at a farm further down. It certainly offered a way out, albeit on foot, and would need to be checked out.

'What're you looking at?'

Jane recognised Janice's voice behind her.

'I'm just following the river in both directions,' replied Jane, without turning away from the screen. 'See where the paths go.'

'And where do they go?'

'Through a farm to the north and you can get out on foot to the south.

'We'd better get someone to follow it and have a look.'

'Will do.'

'Anything from Harry yet?' asked Janice.

'Not yet.'

'Probably asleep in his car,' replied Janice. 'I'll ring him.'

Jane listened to Janice's side of the conversation.

'What have you . . . ?'

'Two?'

'What time?'

'Which bit of let me know immediately did you not under . . .'

'All right. Wait for me by the church.'

Janice rang off and snatched her handbag off the workstation in front of Jane.

'C'mon. We've got time before Perry gets here. Two people heard an engine in the early hours so let's see what they say. We can look in at the cottage too.'

Harry Unwin was waiting for them by the church when Janice and Jane arrived in Moorland. It had taken them longer than expected to drive the short distance from Bridgwater because the narrow lanes had been jammed with farmers moving their livestock out of the area and lorries bringing vast quantities of mud in.

'What the bloody hell's going on?' shouted Janice, trying to make herself heard over the rain hammering on the roof of the car.

'They're building a dyke around a house back there,' replied Unwin, pointing to a lane behind him. 'To keep the water out.'

'What water?' asked Janice.

Jane noticed several residents placing sandbags across the front doors of their bungalows. Then she remembered the weather forecast and the silted up River Parrett.

That water.

'Where are these witnesses then?' shouted Janice.

'Park on the corner over there. That's the house,' replied Unwin, pointing to the first bungalow on the left in the lane leading down to Waterside Cottage. It was right on the junction. 'A Mr Albert Grafton. Says he heard an engine pulling away from the junction at about twoish. He can't be too sure of the time though.'

'You wait here,' said Janice. She turned the car around and parked across the drive of Mr Grafton's bungalow.

Jane jumped out of the car and ran around the front, sheltering under her handbag. She was grateful that there was room enough for them both to huddle under the porch.

'Your mascara isn't waterproof,' said Jane, shaking her head.

Janice wiped under her eyes with her index fingers while Jane rang the doorbell.

'D'you think they know something we don't?' asked Janice, looking at the sandbags piled up at her feet.

A figure, hunched over and moving slowly, appeared behind the frosted glass of the front door. Janice leaned over and shouted through the letter box.

'Police to see you, Mr Grafton.'

'I know, I know.'

Jane counted two locks, a chain and two bolts before Mr Grafton finally opened the door. He was still wearing his pyjamas and dressing gown, even though it was nearly lunchtime.

'I'm Detective Insp . . .'

'Never mind that,' said Grafton, 'you're letting all the heat out. Can you step over these things?'

'Yes, I think so,' replied Janice.

'My neighbour did it for me. Waste of bloody time. Won't do any good if it comes to it.'

'Nice of him though,' said Jane, stepping over the sandbags and thanking her lucky stars she'd thrown on a trouser suit that morning.

'Suppose so.'

They followed Grafton into the lounge and sat down side by side on the sofa. Grafton sat down on an old armchair next to an even older gas fire. The middle one of three burners glowed bright orange and hissed, but it didn't appear to be giving out much heat.

'You heard something in the early hours, I'm told, Mr Grafton,' said Janice.

'An engine. Outside.'

'What time was it?'

'I can't be sure. Twoish, perhaps.'

'What were you doing up at that time of night?'

'I take diuretics to stop fluid building up on my lungs. Heart trouble, you see. Anyway, it keeps me up all night, peeing. Up and down like a bloody yo-yo, I am.'

'Is there a Mrs Grafton?' asked Jane.

'Died two year since.'

'And you think it was about 2 a.m.?' continued Janice.

'There or thereabouts.'

'Where were you when you heard it?'

'In the loo.'

'And what exactly did you hear?'

'An engine. It came along the lane and turned right towards Bridgwater. Going slow, it was.'

'Did you look out of the window?'

'No. I didn't think anything of it, really. Until one of your lot knocked on my door this morning.'

'What did you do after you heard this engine?'

'Nothing,' replied Grafton. 'I just went back to bed.'

'What sort of engine was it?' asked Jane.

'What d'you mean?'

'Car or motorbike, perhaps?'

'Car, or possibly a small van.'

'Petrol or diesel?'

'Now you've asked me,' said Grafton, rubbing his grey stubble with his right hand. 'D'you know, I think it was a diesel.'

'Did you hear it again,' asked Janice.

'No.'

'What happened then?'

'I went back to sleep. Until the next time, about fourish,' replied Grafton, shaking his head. 'Bloody martyr to my bladder, I am.'

Harry Unwin was standing under an umbrella, enjoying a cigarette and watching a large cattle truck trying to reverse in the narrow lane to allow three tipper lorries through, when Janice and Jane came out of Grafton's bungalow. They ran across the road and sheltered under the lychgate. Harry saw them and walked over.

'Anything interesting?' he asked.

'Small car or van, possibly a diesel. That's it, really.' replied Janice.

'Shouldn't we get some traffic officers down here?' asked Jane, looking down the lane.

'They'll sort themselves out,' replied Unwin.

'Where next then?'

'Edna Freeman. Moorland House. It's the last one on the left down the lane.'

'How far?'

'About two hundred yards.'

'We'll drive down,' replied Janice, looking at Jane. 'Anyone get to that farm on the other side of the river, Harry?'

'I'll send someone over there now.'

'Go yourself. It's the nearest property to Waterside Cottage and the most important.'

'OK.'

Janice took her car keys out of her handbag, pointed them at her car in the lane opposite and pressed the button on the key fob.

'Did that open?'

'Couldn't hear a thing,' replied Jane.

Janice pressed it again and this time the hazard lights flashed. 'That's it.' She then ran across the road and jumped in. Jane followed.

'Lazy bugger,' said Janice. 'I thought I'd give him something to do instead of standing around watching the world go by.'

Jane smiled. Janice appeared to have got the measure of Harry.

They drove along the lane and turned into the gravel drive of Moorland House. It was a large red brick house with sandbags across the front door and the double garage. Jane pressed the doorbell, noticing a small grey box mounted on the wall next to it.

'A key safe. She has carers in by the looks of it.'

Janice nodded. She was leaning in towards the door, trying to shelter under the small canopy above it. They waited, looking for any sign of movement behind the frosted glass in the front door.

'Try it again,' said Janice.

Jane rang the bell again. Janice stepped back into the rain and looked up.

'No lights on upstairs.'

Then she walked across the lawn and peered in through the front window.

'Oh, shit.'

Janice ran back to the front door and tried the handle. The door swung open.

'What's up?' asked Jane.

'I think she's dead.'

Janice stepped over the sandbags into the hall. Jane followed. They peered into the lounge and saw Mrs Freeman slumped in her chair, her head tipped back and her mouth open. Jane walked over and leaned in close to her. Then she touched her on the back of the hand.

'Mrs Freeman?'

'Is she all right?' asked Janice.

'She's asleep, you twit.'

'Oh, for f . . .' Janice was stopped mid-sentence by Mrs Freeman stirring.

'Sorry, dear, I . . . I must have nodded off.'

'That's OK,' replied Jane. 'We're police officers. We've come to have a word with you. Are you all right?'

'Yes, fine. Would you like a cup of tea?' asked Mrs Freeman. She pressed the button on her remote control chair, which tipped her forward slowly into the standing position.

Jane frowned at Janice.

'Yes, please.'

'Let's go and sit at the kitchen table.'

They followed Mrs Freeman as she shuffled along the hall to the kitchen at the back of the house. Janice sat down and watched her struggling to hold the kettle under the tap.

'Here, let me,' said Jane.

'Thank you, dear.'

Mrs Freeman sat down at the head of the table, while Jane finished filling the kettle.

'The mugs are in the cupboard in front of you.'

'I understand you heard something last night, Mrs Freeman,' said Janice.

'A motorcycle, dear,' replied Mrs Freeman.

'What time was it?'

'A bit after two perhaps.'

'And what were you doing up at that time?'

'I wasn't. I was lying in bed.'

'Upstairs?'

'No, I sleep in the dining room now, dear. I can't do the stairs anymore.'

'What about a stair lift?' asked Jane.

'Over my dead bod . . .' Mrs Freeman stopped mid-sentence. 'Sorry, that sounds awful.'

'And the dining room is at the front of the house?' asked Janice.

'Yes.'

'Did you have your hearing aid in?' asked Jane.

Janice looked at her and raised her eyebrows.

'No, I take them out at night.'

Jane placed a mug of tea in front of Mrs Freeman and then passed another mug to Janice.

'How much can you hear without them?' asked Janice.

'I get by. They're more to help me filter out background noise.'

'So, you're lying in bed without your hearing aids in. It's a bit after two and you hear a motorcycle in the road outside.'

'That's right, dear.'

'How d'you know it was a motorcycle?'

Mrs Freeman stood up and shuffled back down the hall. Jane watched her disappear into what she assumed had once been the dining room and was now her bedroom. Janice leaned across the table.

'How'd you know about the hearing aids?'

'There's a letter on the hall table from Hidden Hearing.'

Mrs Freeman reappeared shuffling along the hall, this time using a Zimmer frame with what looked like a photo frame in a net slung from the handles. She paused next to Janice and handed the photograph to her. Janice looked at it and then passed it to Jane.

It was an old black and white photograph of a motorcycle display team riding in a pyramid. Jane counted fifteen men riding five motorbikes.

'That's my husband on top,' she said, smiling. 'Twelve years he was in the Royal Artillery motorcycle display team. They rode the BSA 500 back then. That photo was taken in 1961.'

'Is he . . . ?'

'He died eight years ago. But I know the sound of a motorbike, dear.' Her eyes filled with tears. 'I know the sound of a motorbike.'

Janice turned left out of Mrs Freeman's drive and continued along the lane towards Waterside Cottage. The police car blocking the lane beyond the farmyard on the right had gone, as had the tents in the road and front garden, although the lane was blocked at the far end by a Scientific Services van parked outside the cottage. Janice parked behind it. Jane jumped out of the car, ducked under the police tape and ran up the garden path.

'Don't come in.'

She recognised Donald Watson's voice coming from behind the front door and waited in the porch, watching the rain running down the stained glass windows.

'All right.'

Jane pushed open the front door and peered inside. Watson was kneeling on an approach plate in the hall.

'What've you got?' asked Jane.

'Lots of blood but it looks like it's all hers. The usual fibres and hairs, but they're likely to be hers too, or the husband's. The only really useful stuff is the vomit and cigarette butts. They've gone off to PGL.'

'PGL? Why not our own labs?'

'Closed for Christmas. We'll hold the rest of the samples for them but the vomit and fag butts were urgent. I checked with DCI Lewis.'

'Anything else?'

'No.'

'How much longer will you be?'

'We'll be gone by 4 p.m.'

'OK.'

'Happy Christmas.'

The words took Jane by surprise. She had forgotten it was Christmas Eve. Maybe it would be happy for some, but not for others, and certainly not for Tom Perry. For her, it would be a working Christmas. That was the best that could be said for it. But that was the luck of the draw, and it could be worse. It could always be worse.

'Yeah, right. You too,' she said, closing the front door behind her.

Janice was having an animated telephone conversation in the car, and the rain had eased off, so Jane squeezed past the van and walked up onto the riverbank. The water was almost up to the top of the bank and swirling as it roared past the cottage, but the far bank seemed lower so if it burst its banks it would flood the fields on the opposite side first, surely? Jane looked upstream, past the farm on the far bank, to the bend. It had been impossible to tell the height of the banks further upstream from the satellite images on Google Earth. She thought about Mrs Freeman and Mr Grafton, with their sandbags.

The sound of the car horn brought her back to the present.

'Who was that on the phone?' she asked, putting her seatbelt on.

'My husband,' replied Janice.

Jane watched in the wing mirror as Janice reversed back along the lane to the farmyard.

'At least Nick's in the job so he'll understand.'

'He will,' replied Jane, imagining Dixon sitting by the fire in the Red Cow.

Chapter Five

Janice and Jane arrived back at Express Park just after 2 p.m. to find DCI Lewis waiting for them just inside the staff entrance. They took the lift to the first floor and he waited for the doors to close.

'Well?'

'You know about the vomit and cigarette butts?' asked Janice.

'I do.'

'They're on their way to PGL. In the meantime, we've got two residents who heard a vehicle of some sort at about twoish.'

'Who are they?'

'An elderly man living on the corner who was up having a pee. He says it may have been a car or van and possibly a diesel. Then we've got an old bird further along the lane. She didn't have her hearing aids in but swears blind she heard a motorbike.'

'Timing?'

'About the same.'

'There's ten minutes or so between them, assuming they're both right about the time,' said Jane.

'Which is unlikely,' continued Janice.

The lift doors opened and they stepped out onto the landing.

'So you think they both heard the same vehicle?' asked Lewis.

'Must have done,' replied Janice. 'But the DNA will soon tell us.'

'Perry will be arriving in the next half an hour or so and his parents are waiting down in reception.'

'Shall I go down and see them?' asked Janice.

'I've done it,' replied Lewis. 'And I've spoken to Vicky Thomas in PR. The press haven't got hold of it yet and we're gonna say nothing until they do. I'm hoping we'll have a DNA match by then and can tell 'em we've made an arrest.'

'What about the post mortem?' asked Janice.

'Poland's doing that this afternoon.' Lewis looked at his watch. 'Now, actually.'

Jane left Janice talking to DCI Lewis and walked over to the gallery overlooking the reception area. She looked down at an elderly couple holding hands. They were sitting with their backs to the window and the woman was crying. At their feet was a black holdall containing a change of clothes for their son, no doubt. Jane shook her head. Another couple for whom it would not be a happy Christmas.

'Jane.'

She spun round to see Janice standing at a workstation on the far side of the CID area, waving her over.

'What's up?'

'Perry's here. They're bringing him in the back way.'

'The back way?' said Jane.

'Anything else we need to know, Mark? Dave?' asked Janice.

'Not really. It's difficult to find anyone who has anything bad to say about either of them. Even his political opponents seem to like him, from what I can see,' replied Pearce. 'I've only searched the web though, so far.'

'He drives a Honda Civic and I checked the cameras on junction 24 for an hour or so either side of 2 a.m. Came up with nothing,' said Harding. 'If he did drive down, he didn't use the M5.'

'He didn't use junction 24, Dave,' said Janice.

'I suppose so.'

'He could have got off at junction 23 and gone across country from there.'

'D'you want me to check?'

'Not yet. Let's see what he's got to say first.'

'OK.'

'Where's Harry?'

'Not back yet.'

Janice looked at Jane and raised her eyebrows.

'C'mon, Jane, let's not keep Perry waiting.'

'This is not going to be easy,' said Jane.

'These ones never are,' replied Janice, grimacing.

Jane stepped back and watched Janice take a deep breath and then open the door of the interview room. Tom Perry was sitting with his back to the door, rocking backwards and forwards on his chair, his chest heaving. He was crying but making no sound. Jane looked at the uniformed officer standing just inside the door. He looked at her and shook his head.

'Mr Perry,' said Janice.

He turned around on his chair. His eyes were bloodshot and tears were streaming down his face.

'I'm Detective Inspector Janice Courtenay and this is Detective Constable Jane Winter. We're investigating the death of your wife . . .'

'Murder. The murder of my wife.'

'Yes, Sir.'

'I've had my clothes taken, my DNA taken, they've even scraped under my bloody fingernails.'

'It's standard . . .'

'You think I did it, don't you?' screamed Perry, jumping up from his chair. 'Why? Why would I kill her?'

'Sit down, sir,' shouted the uniformed officer, stepping forward.

'She was carrying my child, for God's sake.'

'Please sit down, sir,' said Janice. 'We don't think . . . nobody thinks . . .'

We have questions we have to ask, boxes we have to tick. That was Dixon's standard line in this situation. Jane stepped forward.

'We have questions we have to ask, boxes we have to tick. I'm sure you understand, sir.'

Perry glared at Jane. He took several deep breaths.

'Yes, of course, you do,' he replied, sitting down.

Jane sat down on the seat next to him. She reminded him that he was not under arrest and that he was free to leave at any time.

'I'm just helping you with your enquiries, am I?'

'You are.'

Perry nodded.

'You've declined a solicitor?' asked Jane.

'I don't need one.'

'OK. Let's start with the difficult question. You'll understand I have to ask it.'

'I went to the office Christmas party. I got home at about eleven thirty. I sent my wife a text message then went to bed. I was woken up this morning by your lot.'

'Was there . . . ?'

'I was in the house alone. My wife's parents are in Poole.'

'How much did you have to drink at the party?'

'Too much to drive, if that's what you're asking. Several people on my table can vouch for that.'

'OK. Can you think of anyone who might want to hurt Elizabeth?'

'No.'

'Tell me about her.'

'She was the sweetest person you could ever hope to meet. She . . .' Perry stopped mid-sentence and began to sob again.

'Let's get his parents,' said Jane.

Janice turned to the uniformed officer and nodded.

'Tom.'

Perry looked up at Jane.

'Someone's gone to get your parents. All right?'

Perry nodded.

'They'll be here in a minute.'

'We will catch whoever did this, Mr Perry,' said Janice.

They sat in silence, watching Perry sobbing in front of them. He threw his head back and screamed but no sound came out. Jane closed her eyes.

'Would you like to see the doctor, Tom?' asked Janice.

Perry shook his head.

Jane stood up when she heard voices outside the interview room.

'Wait here, Tom.'

She opened the door and stepped out into the corridor. A custody officer was talking to the elderly couple who had been waiting in reception.

'May we see our son now, please?' asked the elderly man, turning to Jane.

'Yes, of course. You'll understand that he's in shock. We asked him if he wanted to see the doctor but he said no.'

'Is he all right?' asked the woman.

'He's very distressed and agitated, Mrs Perry,' replied Jane. 'Not only is he having to deal with the loss of his wife but there are questions and tests we . . .'

'You surely can't think he did it?'

'No, we don't. But we have to ask, do the tests.'

Mr Perry sighed. 'Can we go in now?'

Mrs Perry pushed past Jane as she opened the door and threw her arms around her son.

Jane turned to Janice and the uniformed officer. 'Let's leave them to it, shall we?'

'I'm gonna head back upstairs,' whispered Janice, closing the door behind her. 'Can you sort them out?'

Jane nodded.

The uniformed officer looked at her and tipped his head to one side.

'Yes, yes, you go too,' said Jane. 'I'll see them out.'

Then she took her phone out of her pocket and sent Dixon a text message.

What are you up to? J x

She waited several minutes for a reply, checking the signal and shaking the phone several times, but none came. Then she knocked on the interview room door.

'Come in.'

Tom Perry had changed into the clothes that his parents had brought and the overalls were lying on the floor in the corner.

'Can I go now?' he asked.

'Yes, you can. I'm assuming you'll be staying with your parents?'

'Can't I go to the cottage?'

'No, I'm sorry. It's a crime scene and it's likely to be a few days before . . .'

'But I need clothes.'

'You can make do, Tom,' said Mrs Perry. 'There are still some at home.'

'If you let me have a list of the stuff you need, then I can . . .'

'Forget it,' said Tom, shaking his head.

'So, what happens now?' asked his father.

'We do have several lines of enquiry. I'll know more when the forensic teams have finished, but a family liaison officer will be in touch and they'll keep you informed.'

'Where is she?' asked Tom.

'Musgrove Park Hospital,' replied Jane.

'Can I see her?'

'Not yet, I'm afraid. We . . .'

'I must see her,' said Tom, jumping up and towering above Jane. Tears were streaming down his cheeks.

'Let's get out of here,' said his father, stepping in between them. 'There's nothing we can do now. Let's go home, Tom.'

Mrs Perry put her hand on her son's shoulder and turned him towards her. Then she put her arms around him. Jane watched his huge frame heaving as he sobbed.

'Have the papers got hold of it yet?' asked his father.

'No,' replied Jane. 'But it's just a matter of time before they do.'

Mr Perry gritted his teeth. 'Vultures.'

'We'll be doing everything we can to keep it out of the press as long as we can,' said Jane.

'And there's the election,' said Mrs Perry. 'Oh, God.'

'C'mon, let's get you home.'

'No,' replied Tom. 'I have to go to Poole.'

'Let someone else tell them, Tom,' said Mrs Perry.

'No. They never thought I was good enough for Lizzie and I'm not going to let them think it now.'

Jane watched from the windows on the first floor of the police station as Mr and Mrs Perry drove their son out of Express Park. The street lights lit up the inside of the car and she could see him sitting in the rear passenger seat, his head in his hands. Then she thought about Elizabeth Perry's parents and brother, who still had an hour or so of Christmas left to enjoy. She was watching the tail lights of the Perrys' car disappear into the distance when her phone rang.

'How's it going?' asked Dixon.

'Don't ask.'

'Got anything?'

'Some cigarette butts and vomit have gone off to the lab.'

'Any witnesses?'

'Not really.'

'What's happening now?'

'Not a lot. Janice is still here but the others have all gone, I think. We can't do a lot now until we get the results. What time is it anyway?'

'Just after five,' replied Dixon. 'I'm assuming Roger's doing the PM. I had a text from him cancelling our curry.'

'Yes. He's doing it now, I think.'

Jane spotted Janice waving at her from the other side of the CID area.

'I'll call you back,' she said.

'Who was that?' asked Janice.

'Nick. Just wondering where I was.'

'Has Perry gone?'

'Yes. They're going down to Poole to tell her family.'

Janice shook her head. 'Well, there's not a lot we can do here. I've sent the others home.'

'Anything from the farm on the other side of the river?' asked Jane.

'Harry never came back. Useless tosser's probably gone straight home.'

'What about Scientific?'

'They've finished and secured the property. We'll get a call if they find anything.'

'And the post mortem?'

'Poland's doing that now, so we'll get his report tomorrow, I expect.'

'You going?'

'No. She was stabbed. It'll be down to the forensics, this one. We've just got to hope they find some DNA in that puke or on the cigarettes. In the meantime, I'm going home before I end up in the divorce courts and I suggest you do the same.'

'When will we get the test results?'

'They've been expedited so possibly tomorrow or Boxing Day. Depends on their staffing at the lab, I suppose.'

'What about the murder weapon?'

'If he didn't take it with him, it'll be in the river and there's no way we can get divers in there at the moment.'

'It just doesn't seem right somehow,' said Jane.

'What? Going home?'

'Yes.'

'Look, it's all under control, Jane. And there's nothing else we can do now anyway. So go home and relax for a bit. Mark will be here until midnight and Dave's back on at six in the morning so we'll get a call if anything crops up.'

'I suppose so.'

'Anyway, I'm off,' said Janice, slinging her handbag over her shoulder. 'Happy Chris . . . no, perhaps not.'

Jane rang Dixon back. She watched Janice walking towards the lift and turned away when Dixon answered.

'Everyone's gone home,' she said.

'No one's gone to the PM?'

'No.'

'You'd better go then,' said Dixon. 'Just look in and see if Roger's found anything interesting. Give me a buzz when you're on your way and I'll put the supper on.'

'You'll make someone a lovely wife,' said Jane.

'Don't just sit there. You know the drill,' said Poland.

Jane closed her eyes. For a moment there she thought she might have got away with it but Poland had spotted her sitting in the anteroom. She opened the door and walked into the pathology lab.

'That's better. You won't see anything skulking about in there.'

'Thanks, Roger,' said Jane, rolling her eyes.

'Janice not here?'

'Gone home. It was either that or divorce, I think.'

'I keep forgetting it's Christmas Eve. Hardly feels like it, does it?'

'No.'

Jane looked down at Elizabeth Perry lying on the slab. A large incision ran the full length of her torso and abdomen. It had been stapled up so Jane had missed the internal examination. She breathed a silent sigh of relief.

'Was she pregnant?'

'Three months.'

'And the time of death?'

'Early hours of this morning. Say between midnight and 3 a.m.'

Jane stood at the end of the slab, looking down at Elizabeth Perry. Her brown hair was swept back and her eyes closed. There was bruising on her upper arms and some lighter bruising was now visible just above her wrists.

'What d'you think happened then, Roger?'

'An attempt at restraint first. That's the bruising. Then she was stabbed in the neck.'

'She survived that?'

'It missed the carotid artery so she would have been able to walk the few steps out onto the landing.'

'Where she collapsed . . .'

'Yes. Then she was stabbed in the back.'

'Cold blooded.'

'Very,' replied Poland. 'A determined effort to finish her off.'

'Why?'

'That's your department.'

'And the murder weapon?'

'There were two knives . . .'

'Two?'

'The first one penetrated to a depth of about six centimetres. The blade's two centimetres wide at the base and coated in pink paint. There are tiny deposits left behind where it hit bone. I'll get them off to the lab after Christmas.'

'Pink paint?'

'Yes. I had a quick look online and you can get pink kitchen knives, believe it or not,' replied Poland.

'And the second knife?'

'Longer and thinner. It was inserted into the wound in the left side of her back and then pushed down into her heart. You can see where the incision changes shape as it goes deeper and the sharp edge switches sides too.'

'So, he used a second knife to make sure?'

'Looks like it.'

'Anything else?'

'She's lost a fair bit of blood too, so there would have been a few minutes while her heart was still pumping. Between the initial flurry and the fatal injury.'

'Why?'

'That's your . . .'

'I know, that's my department.'

'That's about it, really,' said Poland. 'How was the husband?'

'Not good.'

'Poor sod.'

'Well, hopefully, we'll have a result for him pretty quick,' replied Jane, walking towards the door. 'Assuming we get a DNA match.'

'Tell Nick I'm sorry about the curry but I'm gonna be another couple of hours here.'

'I will. Happy Christmas, Roger.'

'You too.'

Jane turned up the collar on her coat and stepped out into the darkness of the small staff car park behind the pathology lab. She had run a few paces before she noticed that it wasn't raining so she took out her phone and tapped out a text message as she walked, hitting the 'Send' button just as she reached her car.

On way J x

She listened to the music drifting across from the houses on the far side of the car park. 'Santa Claus Is Comin' to Town.'

Maybe he was. But she didn't feel terribly festive, all the same.

Chapter Six

It had been a nice evening. Nice. It was an odd word. She remembered her old English teacher telling her never, ever to use it. 'What does it mean? What does it really mean?' Her reply, 'Nice means, er well, nice', had not gone down well. Still, she knew what it meant and it applied to last night. Her English teacher could just get stuffed.

Nick had done his best. It had been a nice meal, with a nice bottle of wine and even her choice of film. He had been making a real effort and she had done her best not to let on that she wasn't really in the mood. She'd rather have gone to the Red Cow and got drunk.

She had been lying awake since just after 5 a.m. listening to Monty snoring and was dozing when she thought she heard a car in the road outside the cottage. It was confirmed when Monty woke up and started barking.

'What's going on?' asked Dixon.

'Someone outside.'

'What time is it?'

Jane looked at her phone. 'Nearly seven,' she said, jumping out of bed and peering out through a gap in the curtains. 'It's Janice.'

She threw on her dressing gown and ran downstairs, opening the front door just as Janice was reaching up to knock on it.

'It's Christmas Day, Janice.'

'It is. And we've got a match.'

'Come in.'

Janice stepped into the cottage and Jane closed the door behind her.

'He's fine,' said Jane, as Monty came tearing down the stairs.

'We've met before,' replied Janice.

Dixon appeared at the top of the stairs. He had thrown on a pair of jeans and was pulling a polo shirt over his head.

'Hi, Jan.'

'Happy Christmas, Nick.'

'I thought you were supposed to come down the chimney?'

'Very funny.'

'Tell me about this profile,' said Jane.

'It's off the fag butt on the landing. They got nothing off the cigarettes in the lane and there was too much acid in the vomit, apparently.'

'Who is it?'

'John Stanniland. Previous convictions for burglary and possession with intent to supply. Class A. And according to DVLA he drives a Vauxhall Astra van. A diesel. We're on our way to pick him up now.'

'Where does he live?' asked Jane.

'He's got a flat in Bristol. Apsley Road. It's off Whiteladies Road.'

'Nice part of town.'

'It is.'

'Why don't we just get the Bristol lot to pick him up then?'

'No way. This is my case and I'm making the arrest.'

'But . . .'

'They're watching the flat now. Harry's picking up Mark and we're gonna meet them up there.'

'I'll get changed,' said Jane, walking over to the stairs.

'Coffee, Jan?' asked Dixon.

'No. Thanks.'

'You've got stab vests?'

'In the car.'

Dixon nodded.

'Well, good luck.'

'Thanks,' replied Janice. 'I'll turn the car round, while I'm waiting.'

'OK.'

Jane came down the stairs to find Dixon peering through a gap in the lounge curtains. He was watching Janice doing a three point turn in the road outside the cottage.

'I'd better go,' said Jane.

'Janice is turning the car round.'

Jane put her arms round Dixon and kissed him. 'Happy Christmas.'

'Wear your stab vest and be careful,' replied Dixon.

'Yes, Sir.'

Dixon pulled Jane towards him and kissed her.

'I'll see you when I see you,' she said, picking up her coat.

'Text me.'

'I will.'

Dixon watched the door slam and listened for the sound of the car accelerating away. Then he knelt on the floor next to Monty.

'Well, it's just you and me, old son. I hope you like turkey.'

The M5 had been all but deserted and Janice had got her old car up to over one hundred miles an hour coming down the Avonmouth

Bridge. Jane felt sure that she saw the flash of a speed camera but thought it best not to say anything. The sun had been flickering on the railings and she could have been wrong.

Jane had spent the journey north looking at Apsley Road on her iPhone. Number 67 was a four storey Georgian end terraced property with a balcony on the first floor. It was built of yellow sandstone and judging by the four grey rubbish bins lined up on the pavement outside, had been converted into flats at some point. She followed Google Street View along the full length of Apsley Road and then back again. It looked a nice area. Far too nice for the likes of John Stanniland.

It was just after 8 a.m. when Janice turned into Apsley Road. Jane spotted two marked police cars parked behind a van about one hundred yards along Apsley Road. A dog van was parked on the nearside, just inside the junction, and she could see several officers, all wearing stab vests, gathered around a police van, which was parked on the pavement outside number 67. More worrying still was the ambulance parked in the middle of the road with its lights flashing.

'What the fuck's going on?' asked Janice.

'They've gone in already,' said Jane.

'They'd bloody well better not have done.'

Janice parked on the wide pavement opposite number 67 and got out of the car, just as Mark Pearce appeared from behind the overgrown vegetation in the front garden.

'What the hell's going on?' shouted Janice.

'Harry said we couldn't wait any longer . . .'

'Where is he?'

'In the garden. A paramedic's seeing to him.'

'Where's Stanniland?'

'In the van.'

Janice wrenched open the back door of the van. Stanniland was wearing black jeans, an orange fleece and a pair of Crocs. He had clearly dressed in a hurry. He was sitting in the back of the van with his left eye closed, prodding a dressing on the left side of his forehead.

'Resisting arrest,' said Pearce, grinning.

'Forensics?'

'On their way. There's no sign of his van. He says it was stolen on Monday.'

Janice slammed the door and marched across to number 67. Jane followed.

Harry Unwin was sitting on a low wall in the front garden watching a paramedic dabbing the back of his right hand with cotton wool. He looked up.

'I thought I told you to wait until I got here,' shouted Janice.

'We couldn't wait all day, Jan.'

Janice took a sharp intake of breath but Jane took hold of her elbow and pulled her away.

'Can I have a word, please, Jan.'

Janice followed Jane back out onto the pavement.

'Take a deep breath, count to ten. Not here, not now. All right?'

Janice was biting her top lip. She took a deep breath through her nose, nodded, then turned and walked back into the front garden.

'What happened?'

'The local lads had another shout to go to and we were about to lose the van and the dog. I thought we'd better go in while we had the chance.'

'I told you . . .'

'It might have been hours before they could get back. And what if Stanniland tried to go out in the meantime? We'd have had to take him on our own.'

'You should've rung me.'

'I didn't have time.'

'Was he armed?'

'No.'

'No sign of the knife?'

'No.'

'So, why'd you hit him?'

'Self defence.'

'Anyone see it?'

'No. Look, I'm not the one being arrested for murder here, Jan. It wasn't my DNA at the scene remember. I went in there, he took a swing at me, I hit him. Job done. All right.'

'No bones broken,' said the paramedic. 'You'll be fine.'

'Thanks,' replied Unwin, clenching his fist.

'Don't do that, you'll have the dressing off.'

'Sorry.'

Jane tapped Janice on the elbow.

'Let's go and have a look in the flat.'

'Has Stanniland been checked over?' asked Janice.

'Yes, he's fine,' replied the paramedic.

'Let's get him transferred down to Bridgwater. And I will be interviewing him. Is that clear, Harry?'

Unwin nodded, without looking up.

Jane followed Janice into number 67 Apsley Road. Stanniland had the ground floor flat and the door was open at the bottom of the stairs. Jane looked up.

'Anyone spoken to the neighbours, I wonder?'

'Mark can organise that.'

Jane stood in the doorway of the flat, peering over Janice's shoulder, neither of them too keen to venture further in. The door opened into the lounge and the floor was strewn with rubbish; empty beer cans, pizza boxes and other takeaway debris. A glance through the door to the left confirmed that the bedroom was in much the same state. There were piles of newspapers and magazines along the walls and rugs pinned up at the windows.

'What's that smell?' asked Janice.

'Cat shit.'

'Where's the cat?'

'Probably moved out. I would.'

'I have never understood how people can live like this.'

'Scientific Services are going to earn their money with this one,' replied Jane, squeezing past Janice and following a narrow path through the debris towards the kitchen. She reached into her handbag and took out a pair of latex gloves as she tiptoed across the floor.

'Holy shit.'

'What?' asked Janice.

'You won't believe this kitchen.'

'What are you looking for?'

'Pink knives,' replied Jane, pulling open the kitchen drawers one by one. She shook her head. 'There aren't any.'

'What did you expect to find? A set with one missing?'

'Yes,' replied Jane, with an exaggerated shrug of her shoulders.

'Not even Stanniland's that stupid.'

They walked back out into Apsley Road to find that the ambulance had left and been replaced by a Scientific Services van. The police van that Stanniland had been sitting in had also gone.

'Where's . . . ?'

'On the way to Bridgwater,' replied Pearce. 'Harry's gone with them.'

'What about his car?' asked Jane.

'I said I'd drive that back.'

'Before you go, check if he reported his van stolen and see if it's turned up anywhere. All right?'

'Will do.'

'Morning all, or should I say Happy Christmas.'

Jane and Janice spun round to find Donald Watson standing behind them. He was dressed in white overalls and was carrying a large briefcase.

'What're you doing up here?' asked Janice.

'It was either that or sit at home on my own all day. Thought I might be of some use here.'

'On your own?'

'Long story.'

'I may be on my own next year at this rate,' said Janice.

'Oh, and ring Lewis,' said Watson. 'The press have got hold of it and he needs something for the evening news.'

Jane glanced across at Brent Knoll as they sped south on the M5. There were several tiny figures on the top of the hill and she wondered whether one of them was Dixon, taking a lunchtime stroll with Monty. More likely they were on the beach, stuffed full of turkey, no doubt. She took out her phone and sent him a text message.

Got him. On way to Bridgwater J x

Her phone buzzed before she could put it back in her handbag.

Weel don

Jane smiled. Dixon had made an early start on the beer.

'Get everyone lined up for a meeting,' said Janice, looking at her watch. 'Room two, twenty minutes.'

'OK.'

Jane was tapping out a text message when she was distracted by the smell of concentrated screenwash and the clunk of Janice's windscreen wiper.

'That came in quick.'

'It did,' said Janice, switching on her headlights.

Jane looked up at the sky ahead. It was a mass of thick grey cloud, swirling much as the water in the River Parrett had been doing yesterday and was no doubt still doing today. She clicked 'Send' on the text message and then checked the weather on her phone. A small black cloud with two raindrops underneath it denoting heavy rain was forecast for the rest of Christmas Day and Boxing Day. She scrolled down. The forecast was the same right through to New Year's Eve.

'It's going to be pissing down for days.'

'Well, we're not going to be out in it, are we?' replied Janice.

Jane looked down at the King's Sedgemoor Drain from the elevated motorway roundabout at junction 23. The usually still and clear water was chocolate brown in colour and flowing fast.

'I've never seen that before.'

Janice leaned over in her seat and peered out of the passenger window.

'They must have the sluice gates open at Dunball.'

It was just after 1 p.m. when they turned into Express Park.

'There'll be plenty of spaces on the ground floor,' said Jane. 'And we'll be under cover.'

'Good thinking.'

Working on Christmas Day had its advantages. And no shortage of parking spaces in the staff car park was one of them. It was also just about the only positive thing she could think of when it came to the budget cuts.

The station was eerily quiet, except for the CID area on the first floor. As she headed over to the coffee machine, Jane spotted Harry Unwin, Dave Harding and Mark Pearce, all engaged in an animated conversation with DCI Lewis. She also recognised the press officer, Vicky Thomas.

'Well done, Janice,' said DCI Lewis.

'Thank you, Sir.'

'We've got a press conference lined up for 6 p.m.'

'Has someone told the husband?' asked Janice.

Jane was listening from the coffee machine.

'Family liaison are with him now.'

'Good. Well, let's make a start.'

Jane followed Janice across the landing to meeting room two and placed a coffee on the table in front of her.

'Right, let's start with the forensics. What evidence have we got placing him at the scene?' asked Janice.

'We've got a DNA profile off the cigarette butt on the landing,' replied Harding. 'It's clear and it matches John Stanniland on the database.'

'And there's ash on her body and on the congealed blood . . .' said DCI Lewis.

'So, we can prove it came after the murder.'

'We can,' replied Lewis.

'Anything else?'

'No. The cigarettes in the lane are the same brand, but that's it,' replied Harding.

'And nothing from the vomit?'

'No.'

'What about trace DNA?'

'Plenty from her husband and from her, of course. Hair, skin, saliva. Nothing else though,' replied Harding.

'What about under her fingernails?'

'To be confirmed.'

'So, we can assume no one else was there then,' said Janice.

'Possibly,' replied Lewis.

'What about the footprints in the back garden?'

'We've got imprints off them but they don't match any of his shoes. Right size, but that's it.'

'He's probably got rid of them,' said Pearce.

'Same for his clothes,' said Harding.

'What about the van?' asked Janice.

'Reported stolen yesterday at 5.32 p.m. Not turned up yet though.'

'When was it stolen?'

'Sometime in the previous forty-eight hours. That's all he could say, apparently.'

'Anything on the traffic cameras?'

'We've got a white van getting on the M5 at junction 24 and going north at 2.12 a.m. but there's no number plate visible.'

'Why not?'

'Covered with mud, I expect. Either deliberately or . . .' replied Harding. 'We're getting it enhanced now.'

'So, he headed south to go north?'

'Avoids all the cameras in the town,' said Lewis.

'What about further north?'

'We've got him getting off at 21 then nothing after that,' replied Harding.

'What about his neighbours?'

'Fully paid up members of the "see no evil, hear no evil" brigade,' said Pearce.

'Don't they know this is a murder investigation?' asked Janice.

'Saw nothing, heard nothing. And they gave that answer before they even heard the question.'

'Gits,' said Harding.

'What about the murder weapons?' asked Janice.

'Murder weapon,' said Lewis.

'There were two knives, Sir. One made the visible injuries and then a longer knife was inserted into a wound in her back. That's the one that went into the heart and killed her.'

'Have we had Poland's report then?' asked Lewis.

'Not yet,' replied Janice. 'Jane went to the post mortem last night.'

Lewis looked at Jane and nodded.

'What do we think happened then?' he asked.

'His knife wasn't long enough so he got another from the kitchen, perhaps?' asked Jane.

'He could have just cut her throat, surely?'

'He'd stabbed her twice in the neck and it had made him sick, don't forget.'

'He's not got a strong stomach, has he?'

'No, Sir.'

'What about motive?' asked Lewis.

'We'll need to speak to the husband again. See if their paths have ever crossed but, apart from that, we don't have one,' replied Janice.

'Burglary gone wrong,' said Pearce.

'There's always that possibility,' said Lewis. 'Drives out to a rural area, picks a remote cottage he thinks is empty . . .'

'Surely he'd take the cash out of her purse?' asked Jane.

'Not necessarily, if he's smart,' replied Janice. 'Stolen goods might connect him to the murder and cash can be traced from serial numbers.'

'Does he look smart to you?' asked Jane.

'No, but let's go and find out, shall we?'

'Well?'

'No comment,' replied Janice, throwing her empty coffee cup in the bin. 'No bloody comment to every single question.'

DCI Lewis sighed, loudly.

'He didn't even offer an alibi?'

'No.'

'Who was his solicitor?'

'Duty solicitor from Taunton. Harrison. It was a bit of a struggle to get him to come out at all, until he found out it was a murder.'

'Twat.'

'A fair assessment,' replied Janice.

'Was there any reaction to anything?'

'Not really . . .'

'Only when we asked him about the two knives,' interrupted Jane. 'He looked . . .' she hesitated.

'What?' asked Lewis.

'Surprised.'

'That we knew or that there were two knives?'

'I couldn't tell,' replied Jane, shaking her head.

She noticed Mark Pearce standing behind Janice, so she nodded in his direction. Janice turned round.

'What?'

'They've found his van.'

'Where is it?'

'In a field off,' Pearce looked down at a piece of paper, 'East Dundry Lane. It's south of the city.'

'Burnt out, I suppose?'

'Incinerated is probably a more accurate description. They're emailing over some photos now though.'

'We'll get nothing off that then,' said Janice.

'Did they find anything at his flat?' asked Lewis.

'No, Sir,' replied Pearce.

'So, have we got enough to charge him?' Jane and Janice recognised the rhetorical question. They waited. 'We can place him at the scene,' continued Lewis, 'standing over the body on the landing and smoking a cigarette. We've got a white van matching the description of Stanniland's getting on the M5 at junction 24 and heading north. At or near the time of death . . .' his voice tailed off.

'And we've got a suspect who's offered no alibi,' said Janice.

Lewis grimaced.

'We need more, I think. Let's get an extension and see what else we can find. We've got time,' said Lewis. 'Then we'll do the press conference, Janice. All right?'

'Yes, Sir.'

'I'll ring the husband now.'

Jane was standing in the large windows on the first floor at Express Park, looking down at DCI Lewis. He was flanked by Janice and Vicky Thomas, who were holding umbrellas, and was talking to a group of reporters. Some were holding Dictaphones in front of him while others were pointing television cameras at him. Several flashes were also going off at regular intervals. The press conference, such as it was, did not last long, the agreed script having been short and to the point.

A forty-one year old Bristol man had been arrested that morning on suspicion of the murder of Mrs Elizabeth Perry, who had been killed by an intruder at home in the early hours of Christmas Eve. A more detailed statement would follow in due course and, in the meantime, the members of the press were asked to respect the family's request for privacy at this difficult time.

Fat chance.

She could just about make out muffled shouts from below and guessed from the animated gestures of some of the reporters that they were now firing questions at DCI Lewis. Jane watched him turn and walk back into the station. Then she watched a male reporter standing under an umbrella talking into a television camera. She recognised none of them, but then she rarely watched the news.

'C'mon, Jane. I'll give you a lift home.'

'Thanks, Jan.'

'Let's go and see what's left of Christmas, shall we?'

Jane hesitated on the pavement outside the cottage, watching the rain bounce off the roof of Janice's car as she drove off. She looked across at the Red Cow. It was closed, so Dixon must be at home, although it struck her as odd that Monty was quiet. He usually barked at the slightest noise outside.

She wondered if Dixon had got her text message telling him she was on her way, but then he was probably fast asleep on the sofa with Monty curled up on his lap. It was just before 7 p.m. and too early for them to have gone to bed, surely?

Jane inserted her key in the lock, turned it and the door swung open. It took her a moment to recognise that it was Monty standing in front of her. Perhaps it was the pair of reindeer antlers he was wearing? He looked none too pleased about it either.

'There you are,' said Dixon, thrusting a tumbler into her hand before she had even closed the front door behind her. The bottle of Bombay Sapphire in his other hand confirmed the glass contained a gin and tonic.

'You've got twenty minutes till supper,' he said.

'You've cooked?'

'Roast turkey and all the trimmings. With a little help from Aunt Bessie,' replied Dixon, grinning.

Jane smiled. She could get used to this. She could even overlook the frozen roast potatoes.

'I thought you'd be legless by now.'

'I've been waiting for you.'

'Only your text message was a bit garbled.'

'That was my gloves.'

'I thought you'd had a few.'

'We went up the hill for a change. Then it started pissing down so we had to shelter in the Red Cow.'

'Of course, you did.'

'You got him then?'

'Yes.'

'Who made the arrest?'

'Harry Un . . .' Jane stopped mid-sentence. She had not told Dixon that Harry was involved in the investigation.

'Harry Unwin? Harry bloody Unwin?' shouted Dixon, from the kitchen.

'Yes.'

'You never said he was on the team.'

'I knew how you'd react.'

'There's a gang of Albanians who know where we live thanks to that prick.'

'You can't prove that.'

'I can't, but if I could . . . let me rephrase that. When I can . . .'

'Look, this is a separate investigation. And besides, I'm working with Janice.'

'Keep it that way.'

'I will.'

Dixon appeared in the doorway of the kitchen. He was carrying a large spoon and a jug.

'D'you like bread sauce?'

A hot shower and a gin and tonic later and Jane tiptoed down the stairs wearing a pair of jeans and one of Dixon's shirts. She squeezed between the sofa and the Christmas tree, which was far too big but Dixon had insisted, and placed her empty glass on the side in the kitchen with a bang. Dixon started refilling it right on cue.

'What's on telly tonight?' she asked.

'You choose.'

Chapter Seven

Jane arrived at Express Park just before 8 a.m. the following morning. There were a few more cars in the car park but she was still able to get a space on the ground level. The skeleton staff on for Boxing Day was bigger than the day before but not that big.

She glanced through the window of the staff canteen as she walked past and spotted Janice sitting alone in the corner, so she poked her head around the door.

'Are you all right, Jan?'

'Yeah fine.' She replied without looking up from her coffee, so Jane walked over and sat down next to her.

'Everything all right at home?'

'He did at least wait until the children went to bed, I suppose. How about you?'

'Fine. Look, he married a police officer. What the bloody hell does he expect?'

'You try telling him that.'

'Gladly.'

Janice shook her head.

'He was just disappointed, I think, but I could've done without all the histrionics. He was drunk too, which didn't help.'

'He didn't hit you, did he?'

'God, no.'

'Twat.'

'We'll get through it. Tell me about your evening.'

'Nick had cooked roast turkey,' replied Jane.

'Detective Inspector Dixon cooked?'

'He did. Then we sat and watched a film and polished off a bottle of Bombay Sapphire.'

'Sounds lovely.'

'It was. Till Monty was sick on the carpet. Too much turkey, I think.'

Janice laughed.

'Which reminds me,' continued Jane, 'have we had SOCO's report yet?'

'No. I asked Watson. He's dictated it and it'll be typed up today. We'll get the post mortem report tomorrow too.'

'What about the lab report?'

'We've got PGL's. That's how we made the match with Stanniland.'

'What does it say about the vomit?'

'Too much stomach acid and rainwater to get a decent profile, apparently. But the cigarette's a good match. It'll be in your email.'

'When are our labs open again?'

'Tomorrow.'

'And Stanniland?'

'Special sitting of the mags later this morning. We'll get another twenty-four hours to hold him.'

'What's the plan for this morning then?' asked Jane.

'We need to have another word with the husband, I think. Then her parents.'

It would have been easy for Jane to have got lost in the maze of new bungalows on the outskirts of Trull, a small village to the south-west of Taunton, had it not been for the four large vans with satellite dishes mounted on top parked outside one particular property. She counted at least six camera crews and several other journalists waiting patiently in the road outside the bungalow, all of them standing under umbrellas and most of them smoking.

Jane turned into the cul-de-sac and hooted at the journalists gathered at the gate. They moved to the side, allowing her to park in the drive. She looked up at the bungalow. It was small, possibly two or three bedrooms at most, with bay windows either side of the front door. Roses had been planted in large tubs on either side and a small tree, possibly a magnolia although it was difficult to tell at this time of year, grew in the middle of the lawn. The bungalow itself was built of red brick and looked no more than a few years old.

'Let's get this over with,' said Janice, sitting in the passenger seat of Jane's car.

They had telephoned ahead and the Perry family were expecting them so they jumped out of the car and made the short dash down the side of the bungalow to the back door without bothering with umbrellas and ignoring the shouted questions from the journalists at the gate. The back door opened as they stepped into the porch.

'Come in.'

'Thank you,' replied Janice, looking up to see Tom Perry's father standing in the doorway.

'Leave your coats over those chairs,' he said. 'Tom's in the living room. Down the hall, on the left.'

Jane left her coat over the back of a kitchen chair and followed the hallway towards the front of the property. She pushed open the door on the left and peered into the room. The curtains were closed and there was only one small lamp, making the room all but dark. She recognised Tom Perry sitting in an armchair by the fire. He was wearing jeans and a green sweatshirt with 'Exeter, probably the best university in the world' written on it. To his right was his mother, sitting on the sofa, and next to her was the family liaison officer, Karen Marsden.

'Let me make some tea,' said Karen. 'Tom?'

'Yes, please.'

Jane and Janice sat down on the sofa either side of Mrs Perry. Jane sat nearest to Tom Perry.

'Hello, Tom,' she said.

He nodded.

'I gather DCI Lewis has spoken to you?'

'He has. And Karen's been great.'

'Good,' replied Jane. 'We need to know if either of you ever met John Stanniland before.'

Tom Perry shook his head.

'It's very important, Tom.'

Janice took a photograph out of her handbag and passed it to Jane. Mrs Perry craned her neck to see it as it was passed in front of her.

'Is that him?' she hissed.

'Yes,' replied Jane, holding the photo in front of Tom Perry.

'Do you know him, Tom?'

He stared at the photograph for several seconds before shaking his head.

'I've never seen him before.'

'What about online? Has he ever got in touch with you over the Internet? About politics perhaps?'

'No.'

'Are you sure?'

'Where does he live?' asked Perry.

'Bristol.'

'That's not even in the constituency.'

'What about Elizabeth? Did she know him?' asked Jane.

'Not as far as I know.'

'She never mentioned his name?'

'No.'

'I thought you went to Reading University, Tom?'

'Lizzie went to Exeter.'

'You called her Lizzie. I'm sorry, I didn't know,' said Jane.

'That's OK.'

'What about that lot out there?' asked Janice, gesturing to the front of the bungalow.

'They'll have to wait,' said Mrs Perry. 'They remind me of . . .'

'That's enough, Mum.'

'We've even had his constituency chairman on the phone already, would you believe it?' said Tom Perry's father, walking into the room and standing behind his son's chair.

'What did you tell him, Tom?'

'I didn't speak to her. My father did.'

'I told her he'd got more important things to worry about at the moment and they'd have to wait.'

'Will they?'

'I don't know, I can't think . . .' Tom Perry's voice tailed off as he buried his face in his hands. His father leaned forward and put his hand on his son's shoulder.

Suddenly, Perry looked up.

'I want to know why he killed her.'

'We'll find out, Tom,' replied Jane.

'Why her, why now?'

'It may have been a burglary gone wrong,' said Janice.

'I need to know whether it was something I did. Whether there was anything I could have done to stop it.'

'We'll keep you informed, Tom.'

'Then, one day, Stanniland and I are going to meet.'

The drive to Poole took nearly an hour and a half and much of the journey was spent in silence. Jane guessed that Janice was not in the mood for conversation and so kept her thoughts to herself, although Janice was clearly thinking about the case, judging by the questions she blurted out from time to time.

'Was she insured?'

'What?' asked Jane.

'Life insurance. Was there any?'

Next came a real belter.

'They're doing a DNA test on the child, aren't they?'

'Yes, they are.'

That was followed by 'Have we had the bank statements yet?'

'No.'

'Were they in debt, d'you think?'

'We'll soon find out,' replied Jane.

'What about his reaction? Genuine, do you think? Or put on?'

'I thought he was genuine.'

Janice had sighed at regular intervals, shaken her head and even grimaced. Eventually, Jane lost patience.

'You don't seriously think Tom Perry was behind it, do you?'

'It's possible,' replied Janice. 'He could have paid Stanniland.'

'Right in the middle of a by-election? Do me a favour, Jan.'

'Depends what she was gonna reveal about him, perhaps? Have you thought of that?'

Jane hesitated. Stanniland being paid to kill Elizabeth Perry would explain a great deal.

'All right. I'm with you up to a point,' said Jane. 'Someone coming out of Bristol looking for a remote house to burgle is unlikely to drive all the way to Bridgwater, is he? It also explains why nothing was taken. Where you've lost me is Tom Perry.'

Janice took her phone out of her handbag and began tapping out a text message. Jane leaned across and tried to read it.

'I'm telling Mark to chase up the bank statements. Stanniland's and Perry's.'

'Waste of time,' said Jane. 'Stanniland'll have been paid cash.'

Janice began tapping out a second message, reading it aloud as she did so.

'Ask Watson if he found any cash in Stanniland's flat.'

'It'll be stashed somewhere else,' said Jane. 'Well hidden.'

'I suppose so. It's hardly going to be under his mattress, is it?'

The Antelope was just behind the quay in Poole and proved easy to find, once Jane had got the hang of the one way system. She parked on the pavement outside an empty shop and directly opposite the hotel, placing one of her Avon and Somerset Police business cards on the dashboard in the hope that an officer from the Dorset Constabulary might not give her a ticket.

'You'd have thought they'd have gone home, wouldn't you?' asked Janice, looking up at the antelope on a plinth above the front door.

'Maybe they wanted to be with their son?'

'Maybe.'

Jane followed Janice into the hotel and waited behind her while the receptionist rang Mr and Mrs King in their room.

'They're expecting you. Room seven. Through that door, up the stairs, then follow the corridor around to the right.'

'Thanks.'

'Another one that's not going to be easy,' said Jane.

'They never are.'

Janice knocked on the door and waited.

'Yes.'

The man was young, perhaps late twenties or early thirties, with short dark hair that was shaved at the sides of his head. He was very tanned and wore a polo shirt, open at the neck, and a pair of chinos.

'Er, we're here to see Mr and Mrs King,' said Janice.

'Let them in, Simon.' It was a woman's voice, coming from behind the door.

Jane followed Janice into the middle of the large room and listened while Janice made the introductions. Mrs King was sitting on a purple sofa behind the door and her husband, Charles, was pacing up and down in the bay window.

'This is our son, Simon. He's based at RM Poole and on standby so he can't get away,' said Mrs King.

'What do you do there?' asked Janice, turning to Simon King.

'I'm not allowed to talk about it.'

'Do sit down.'

There were two small chairs either side of a chest of drawers, which Simon carried into the middle of the room.

'Thank you,' said Jane.

'We're really sorry to . . .'

Mrs King raised her hand, stopping Janice in mid-sentence.

'We know. We just want to know what you're doing about it,' said Mrs King. She was fighting to keep her composure and winning. Just.

'A forty-one year old man from Bristol has been arrested and charged with the murder of your daughter, Mrs King. At the moment we're looking for any connection between them to give us a . . .'

'Motive,' interrupted Charles King.

'He's a barrister,' said Mrs King.

'Well, yes, then,' said Janice. 'We're looking for a motive.'

'So, what have you got? DNA at the scene?'

'The arrest is the result of forensic . . .'

'So, he's miles from home. But what's he doing there? That's the question, isn't it?'

'Mr King, we have boxes we have to tick, questions we have to ask,' said Jane.

'Well, you'd best get on with it, hadn't you?' snapped Mrs King.

'How would you describe your daughter's relationship with her husband?' asked Janice.

'You don't seriously think he's behind it, do you?' asked Mr King.

'It's a question . . .'

'You have to ask. I get it.'

'No, definitely not,' said Mrs King. 'They were devoted to each other.'

'Had she ever said anything that might have given you cause for concern?'

'No.'

'Or that Tom might have been unfaithful, perhaps?'

'No. Look, they were planning to start a family, for God's sake.'

'Mrs King, your daughter was . . .'

'Did they have any money worries?' interrupted Jane. 'Were they in debt?'

'Not that we knew of,' replied Mr King.

'And if they did we'd have helped them out,' said Mrs King.

'What about her previous boyfriends?'

'She only had one. That lad at Exeter.' Mrs King shook her head. 'What was his name, Simon?'

'James somebody. Bryce, I think. Something like that. It was years ago.'

Jane was making notes.

'What did Elizabeth study at Exeter?'

'Economics. Then she trained as an accountant.'

'And James Bryce?'

'Chemistry, from memory,' replied Simon.

'Have you ever heard her mention the name John Stanniland?'

'Is that him?' asked Simon. 'Her killer.'

Jane nodded.

'Where is he now?'

'He's in custody.'

'Have you charged him?' asked Mr King.

'Not yet,' replied Janice.

'I've never heard that name,' said Mrs King. 'Have you, Charles?'

'No.'

'Where did Tom and Elizabeth meet?'

'At the wedding of a mutual friend. We knew it was serious before she did. Well, I did anyway,' replied Mrs King. 'He's a good lad is Tom. Or at least he was until he got involved in politics. Whatever possessed him . . . Lizzie was never cut out to be an MP's wife. She was supposed to have her own career. Her own life . . . but she threw it all away to support Tom . . .' Her voice tailed off.

Charles King sat down next to his wife on the sofa and put his arm around her.

'Anyway, I refuse to believe he could've . . . would've . . .' she buried her face in her hands and began to sob.

'Did you interview Stanniland?' asked Charles King.

'We did,' replied Janice.

'And what did he say?'

'We can't divulge . . .'

'My daughter has been murdered, Inspector, and I would like to know whether her killer offered any explanation as to why he killed her.'

'He said nothing,' replied Jane.

'No comment?'

'Every question.'

'Was he advised?'

'He had the duty solicitor.'

'What happens now?'

'We're waiting for the forensic and post mortem reports and trying to build a picture of their lives together. It remains possible that it was purely random . . .'

'Random? You're joking surely?' said Simon.

'It's possible,' replied Janice.

'Bollocks.'

'What my son means is that Elizabeth died for a reason and we want to know what it was,' said Mr King.

Don't we all.

Jane peeled the parking ticket off her windscreen and jumped into the driver's seat.

'I wasn't expecting a bloody cross-examination,' said Janice.

'At least they were quite clear about Tom.'

'And thanks for stopping me. I nearly put my foot in it, didn't I?'

'Odd they didn't know she was pregnant though, don't you think?' asked Jane.

'Possibly.'

'I mean, she was three months gone and they'd had a scan too. You'd have thought she'd have told her mother by then?'

'Maybe they were going to tell them at Christmas?' asked Janice.

'Yes, that might be it.'

'What d'you make of Simon?'

'A grieving and angry brother.'

'I'd love to know what he does at RM Poole.'

Jane took her phone out of her handbag and opened a web browser.

'Here it is.' She was reading from the screen. 'Wikipedia. Ah, that explains it.'

'What?'

'Special Boat Section.'

'What's that?'

'Think SAS but with boats instead of wings.'

'He's on standby to go overseas then, I suppose, which explains why they've stayed in Poole.'

'It does.'

'Let's get back. Then I want to go right through Elizabeth's past and see if we can't find John Stanniland cropping up somewhere.'

'And Tom's?'

'Yes, and Tom's.'

Jane was filling up with petrol at the Shell station at the entrance to Express Park when four police cars and a van came screaming down the service road from the back of the police station. They turned left at the roundabout, and then sped north towards the motorway roundabout, turning their sirens on as they accelerated away from Bridgwater.

'What the hell's going on?' asked Janice. She was standing behind Jane, swigging from a bottle of Diet Coke.

'God knows.'

'I'll walk in from here. See what all the fuss is about.'

'I'll catch you up,' replied Jane, replacing the nozzle on the pump.

Jane watched from the queue in the petrol station as Janice walked along the pavement towards the police centre. She had always cut a confident figure had Janice, but somehow seemed just a little bit out of her depth this time. Or maybe Jane had just got used to working with Dixon, who oozed confidence even when he had no real idea what was going on at all. Not that he would ever admit it, of course, at least not to anyone else except her.

She sent him a text message, *where are u J x*, wondering whether the reply would be *in the pub* or *on the beach*. She looked across the garage forecourt. Vehicles were turning in with their headlights on now and it had been raining hard for most of the day. Yes, it would be *in the pub*, she felt sure of that.

Jane was parking her car on the top floor of the car park when the reply came.

watching tv x

'Tosser,' muttered Jane, rolling her eyes. Then she jumped out of her car and ran across to the staff entrance, sidestepping the large puddles as she went. Janice opened the door for her from the inside.

'What's up, Jan?'

'The Parrett's burst its banks.'

Jane looked back and watched the rain falling in the lights on the far side of the car park. She listened to the water running along the gutter in front of her and the sound of the raindrops hammering on the parked cars. It was difficult to tell which was louder. Then she thought about Mr Grafton and Mrs Freeman, with sandbags across their front doors.

'Muchelney's cut off,' continued Janice. 'And they're evacuating Moorland and Northmoor Green.'

Chapter Eight

'What're you up to this morning?' asked Jane.

'I'm gonna pop down to Landroverman and see if they've got a snorkel,' replied Dixon. 'Then I'll have a go at fitting it.'

'You?'

'What's wrong with that? There's a video on YouTube that shows you how to do it.'

'Still, if it falls to bits you'll have to get a new car.'

'Fat chance. How about you?'

'Still looking for a connection between Elizabeth Perry and her killer.'

'What's his name?' asked Dixon.

'Stanniland.'

'Any ideas?'

'None.'

'There may be no connection, of course.'

'I thought you said there was no such thing as a random murder?' asked Jane.

'There isn't. So, look for a connection between Tom Perry and Stanniland.'

'We are.'

'Or with the person who paid him.'

'We are.'

'I'll shut my face then,' replied Dixon, smiling.

'What about your cold case?'

'I was supposed to be seeing the witnesses next week but they'll have been evacuated, I expect. Muchelney's flooded, isn't it?'

'Yes.'

'I've got mobile numbers so I'll catch up with them on Monday.'

Jane followed Dixon south on the M5, getting off at junction 23. She slowed as she crossed the motorway and watched the back of his Land Rover disappearing into the distance as he continued south. Monty was sitting in the rear window staring at the cars behind them. She thought about her conversation with Dixon over breakfast and the little white lie she had told. Look for a connection with the person who paid Stanniland. That had been Dixon's advice and she had replied 'we are' when what she really meant was 'we will be'. But where to begin?

She arrived at Express Park just as the morning briefing was finishing. Janice, Dave Harding, Mark Pearce and Harry Unwin were gathered around a workstation in the CID area on the first floor and Jane caught the tail end of the discussion. Dave was to focus on the Bridgwater end, while Harry and Mark were to concentrate on Bristol, building a complete picture of Stanniland's movements for the forty-eight hours leading up to the murder, profiles of his known associates, CCTV and traffic cameras, and his van. They had their work cut out.

'Jane, you're with me,' said Janice, picking up her handbag and walking over to a workstation in the vast windows of the police centre. 'We need to find a connection between Stanniland and the Perrys. All right?'

'What if they're not connected? What if the connection is with someone else, and that person paid Stanniland, possibly?'

'That'll have to be stage two, if we find nothing directly connecting them, and let's hope it doesn't come to that.'

'I'll drink to that,' said Jane. 'Coffee?'

'Yes, please. You take Elizabeth and I'll take Tom. OK?'

It was just after 4 p.m. by the time Jane looked up from her computer. She had spent much of the day on the phone and the rest staring at her screen. Her eyes felt dry and hot, so she rubbed them and peered out into the gloom. The street lights were already on and it was still raining. Hard.

She turned back to her computer, opened a web browser and went to BBC News.

'Oh, shit,' she said, scanning the news headlines. 'You seen this, Jan?'

'What?' Janice was sitting at the next workstation and spoke without looking away from her screen.

'A major incident has been declared by Somerset County Council and Sedgemoor District Council. An amber flood warning is in place and they're expecting another inch of rain in the next twenty-four hours.'

Janice looked up.

'And listen to this,' continued Jane, reading from her screen. 'Experts tell the public to be prepared for further flooding.'

'I could've told them that,' said Janice.

'And look at this,' said Jane.

Janice jumped up from her chair and stood behind Jane.

'Where the hell is that?'

'Muchelney,' replied Jane.

They were staring at a photograph of the roof of a silver car, water gently lapping against the top of the windows.

'That must be four feet deep,' said Janice.

'Find anything in Tom's past connecting him with Stanniland?' asked Jane.

'No. What about Elizabeth?'

'Straight "A" student at every turn. Gap year working for charity in Malawi. There's lots on Facebook but nothing sinister. Not even amongst her friends. I can't find anyone who has a bad word to say about her. And as for her path crossing with a drug dealer? No chance.'

Janice shook her head.

'What now then?' asked Jane.

Janice was about to reply when they were both distracted by the sound of a door slamming at the far end of the first floor. They listened to heavy footsteps marching along the landing and watched the end of the canteen to see who would appear around the corner.

DCI Lewis was flushed and Jane could see that he was gritting his teeth, even from twenty yards away. He stopped on the far side of the workstations and looked across at Jane and Janice.

'Meeting room two. Now.'

They followed DCI Lewis across the landing and into meeting room two. He slammed the door behind them and spoke without sitting down.

'Well?'

'Nothing, Sir,' replied Janice.

'Nothing?'

'Not yet, anyway. We've been looking for a connection between the Perrys and Stanniland. The next step is to proceed on the basis that Stanniland was paid by a person or persons unknown.'

DCI Lewis shook his head.

'We've got the DNA, don't forget, Sir,' said Janice.

'Well, that's just the point, isn't it,' replied Lewis. 'We haven't got the DNA, have we? At least, not anymore.'

'What's happened?' asked Jane.

'PGL fucked it up,' replied Lewis.

'What d'you . . . ?'

'What was the term they used?' replied Lewis, shaking his head. '"Investigator mediated contamination".'

Janice pulled a chair out from under the table and slumped into it.

'It was a skeleton staff on over Christmas, so they retested the sample this morning,' continued Lewis. 'A matter of routine, apparently.'

'And?'

'They got a different result. A stack of plastic trays from a robotic unit was reused when it shouldn't have been and it's contaminated the whole bloody lot.'

'But that's all we had.'

'Exactly.'

'They got nothing from the vomit or the cigarettes in the lane,' said Jane.

'So, what've we got left?' asked Lewis.

'Not enough,' replied Janice.

'There's his van on the traffic camera,' said Jane, 'if High Tech can enhance the footage so we can see the number plate.'

'And what does that prove?'

'On its own, nothing,' replied Janice.

'That's what we've got then, isn't it? Nothing.'

DCI Lewis saw Dave Harding waiting outside the meeting room door and opened it.

'What's up, Dave?'

'We've lost the crime scene, Sir.'

'What d'you mean "lost it"?'

'It's under twelve feet of water.'

'It just gets better and better,' said Lewis, sitting down on a chair he had kicked out from under the table. He closed his eyes and sat in silence, breathing slowly through his nose. Dave Harding used the opportunity to back out of the room, closing the door behind him. Janice and Jane waited.

'We'll never get another extension to hold him based on what we've got,' said Lewis. 'The reason we got the last extension has gone now and we sure as hell haven't got enough left to charge him.'

'No, Sir,' replied Janice.

'I'll speak to the chief constable. And Vicky Thomas. Our press officer's going to earn her bloody money this time.'

Jane followed Janice out into the rain and stood holding an umbrella over her while she smoked a cigarette that she had scrounged off Harry Unwin.

'It's not your fault, Jan.'

'You and I both know that . . .'

'And Lewis knows it too.'

'Maybe, but that's not how it's going to look. Is it?' replied Janice, blowing the smoke out through her nose.

Jane watched a large black Jaguar turning into the staff car park. She recognised the driver.

'That's the assistant chief constable, Jan. We'd better go.'

'Well, we haven't exactly covered ourselves in glory, have we?' said David Charlesworth. He was sitting at the head of the table, dressed casually and chewing an earpiece of his black horn rimmed spectacles.

'The fault rests with PGL, Sir,' said Lewis.

'An inevitable consequence of the privatisation of the Forensic Science Service, I suppose?'

'Yes, Sir.'

'Well, you're probably right. But how do we explain that to the Perry family?'

'And to the press,' said Vicky Thomas.

'It's not as if we've come up with anything else, is it?

'No, Sir.'

'Have the family been told?'

'Not yet, Sir,' replied Lewis.

'When can we hold him until?'

'We've got a Warrant of Further Detention but it expires tomorrow morning.'

'And the DNA was the basis upon which we got it?'

'Yes, Sir.'

'Where is he?'

'In custody here, Sir.'

'Have forensics finished in his flat?'

'Yes, Sir.'

'What did they find?'

'Nothing.'

'Nothing off the van either, I suppose?'

'No, Sir.'

'And the crime scene is flooded, I gather?'

'It's under twelve feet of water.'

'He's been very lucky then, hasn't he? This . . . what's his name?'

'Stanniland, Sir.'

David Charlesworth shook his head.

'I don't see we have any real alternative, do you? We have to release him. But for God's sake, keep a tail on him.'

'What about the family?' asked Lewis.

'I'll tell them,' replied Charlesworth. 'Although God alone knows what I'm going to say.'

Jane arrived home just after 7.30 p.m. The cottage was dark and there was no barking when she put her key in the door, so she walked over to the Red Cow to find Dixon standing at the bar, paying for a pint. Monty saw her first and ran across to greet her, his lead trailing on the floor.

'Just in time,' said Dixon. 'Gin and tonic?'

'Make it a double,' replied Jane.

Dixon shrugged his shoulders and turned to the barman.

'I've got it,' said Rob.

They sat down at the table by the fire and Monty took up his usual position, stretched out on the floor as close as he could get to the hearth.

'Bad day?'

'You could say that,' replied Jane, taking a large swig of her drink.

'What's happened?'

'The lab mucked up the DNA sample. Contaminated it. That was all we had so we've had to let him go.'

'Let him go?'

'No choice. Four o'clock this afternoon.'

Jane spent the next twenty minutes bringing Dixon up to date with the investigation, which involved starting from scratch, given that she hadn't really told him anything about it before. What she chose not to tell him was that DCI Lewis had taken her to one side after the meeting with the assistant chief constable and asked her to brief Dixon. Lewis had tapped the side of his nose with his index finger leaving Jane in no doubt that she wasn't to let on. But he had definitely used the word 'brief'. It sounded formal.

Dixon had listened intently and finished his beer before he spoke again.

'What's Janice doing about it?'

'Thrashing around, I think. I'm not sure she knows what to do, to be honest.'

Dixon was sucking his teeth. Jane recognised the signs and waited.

'So, you've got three DNA profiles?' asked Dixon.

'We *had* three DNA profiles.'

'The usual you'd expect from Tom and Elizabeth and then Stanniland's?'

'Yes.'

'So that means no one else was there?'

'Right.'

'Wrong,' said Dixon, picking up his glass. 'Fancy another drink?'

Dixon placed a fresh gin and tonic in front of Jane and sat down next to her.

'What d'you mean "wrong"?' she asked.

'Let's start at the beginning. What is trace DNA?'

'Well, it's proof of . . .'

'No, it isn't. It's evidence. That's all. Hair, saliva, skin cells. And it needs to be interpreted just like any other piece of evidence.' Dixon took a swig of beer. 'It's often misinterpreted too.'

'Anyone would think you knew what you were talking about,' said Jane.

'Thank you.'

'It's good evidence then?'

'Sometimes, but not always.'

'So, what if there's no profile?' asked Jane.

'That doesn't mean someone wasn't there. Just that they left no DNA behind,' replied Dixon. 'Absence of evidence is not evidence of absence.'

'Who said that?'

'Lots of people. It's an aphorism. But it's quoted by Professor Peter Gill. Twenty-six years with the Forensic Science Service, so he should know,' replied Dixon. 'I've got his book at home. You should read it.'

'But . . .'

'Have you ever stopped to think that Grafton and the old bird might both be right?'

'Mrs Freeman?'

Dixon nodded.

'No,' said Jane.

'Try it,' said Dixon. 'You eaten?'

Dixon was standing in the kitchen window, watching the first light of dawn spread across the fields behind his cottage. It had stopped raining by the time they had left the pub the previous night and a clear sky had made for a hard frost, as evidenced by the thick layer of ice coating his Land Rover. At least the snorkel hadn't fallen off.

He heard footsteps behind him and turned to find Jane standing in the doorway. She was leaning against the door frame with her eyes closed.

'Can I smell coffee?'

'You can,' replied Dixon, flicking the switch on the kettle. 'Want some?'

'Yes, please.' Jane was rubbing her eyes. 'What time is it?'

'Eightish.'

Dixon watched her yawn.

'What time are you due in?' he asked.

'Whenever I get there.'

'And what time did you finish reading last night?'

'Two or so.'

'You go and sit down, I'll bring your coffee in.'

Dixon was handing a mug of coffee to Jane when they heard the bleep of a text message arriving on a phone in the bedroom.

'Was that you or me?' asked Jane.

'You probably. I'll go and have a look.'

It took Dixon a minute to find her phone, which was being used as a bookmark in his copy of *Misleading DNA Evidence* by Professor Peter Gill.

'It's you,' he said, walking down the stairs.

He took a swig of coffee while he watched Jane open the text message and read it.

'I just don't f . . .'

'What's happened?' asked Dixon.

'You wouldn't believe me if I told you.'

'Try me.'

'Stanniland's disappeared.'

'You said there was a tail on him.'

'I thought there was,' replied Jane. She held her phone out in front of her and read from the screen.

Stanniland not on train. Never arrived Bristol Temple Meads yesterday. Jan

'They put him on a train?' asked Dixon.

'Looks like it,' replied Jane. 'I'd better go.'

Jane arrived at Express Park just as Janice was leaving, at speed. She screeched to a halt and wound her window down.

'There's a body in the water off Brean Down,' shouted Janice. 'It fits the description of Stanniland. Dump your car in the visitors' car park and get in.'

Jane turned into the visitors' car park and left her car in the first space, while Janice reversed back to the entrance. Jane then ran over and jumped in the passenger seat of Janice's car.

'You said he was on a train?'

'Yes. He was put on the 4.02 p.m. to Temple Meads and they were going to pick him up at the other end. But he never got there, did he?'

'Whose bloody stupid idea was that?' asked Jane.

'Mine.'

'What about his flat?'

'Never turned up there either.'

Janice accelerated up to ninety miles an hour on the dual carriageway out towards the motorway roundabout.

'What's the rush?' asked Jane.

'Tide's going out,' replied Janice. 'It brought the body in and if we don't hurry up it's going to take it back out again.'

'Lifeboat?'

'On the way.'

'I'll ring Nick,' said Jane. 'He'll be on the beach with Monty by now.'

Chapter Nine

Dixon had watched Jane leave for Bridgwater and then bundled Monty into the back of the Land Rover. The tide would be turning in an hour or so and, if it was too high, he could always park in front of the Sundowner Cafe, instead of on the beach. It was worth a look.

The wooden bollards designed to stop you parking too close to the sand dunes meant that parking on the beach was impossible, even with a snorkel, so Dixon reversed back along the beach access road. He left the Land Rover outside the Sundowner and then followed Monty towards Brean Down.

He thought about Janice, who seemed to be jinxed. After all, it was not her fault that PGL had contaminated the DNA sample, nor was it her fault that the crime scene was flooded. And as for Stanniland's disappearance, it would have happened sooner or later no doubt, even with a tail on him.

Dixon was walking along the base of the cliffs at Brean Down, wondering who DCI Lewis would get to sort the mess out, and thanking his lucky stars he was suspended, when his phone rang in his pocket.

'Hi, Jane, what's up?'

'Where are you?'

'Brean Down.'

'Thank God for that.'

Dixon could hear a car engine in the background.

'What's going on?'

'There's a body in the water on the far side of Brean Down. It fits the description of Stanniland so we got the shout. We're leaving now. The RNLI have been called out. Can you get over there and see if you can spot it?'

'Whereabouts?'

'About a third of the way along on the north side. Two men are fishing off the terraces.'

'OK.'

'Look, the tide's turning and if the Axe takes it out into the main channel we'll never find it.'

'All right, I'm on my way now.'

Dixon rang off and started running towards the gap in the sea wall. Monty chased after him, thinking it was a game, no doubt. They ran along the path between the bungalows and then followed the track towards the steps that would take them to the top of Brean Down from the south side. Dixon stopped at the bottom to put Monty on his lead and then began the climb.

Dixon was familiar with these steps. He used to run up and down them when training for climbing trips to the Alps, but that was many years ago now, or at least it felt like it. He remembered throwing up his breakfast at the top the first time he had done it and hoped he wouldn't do the same again today.

He arrived at the terrace, less than halfway up, and stopped for a rest. His legs were burning and he was leaning on a fence post, breathing hard. He could hear sirens in the distance but could not tell how many there were, nor could he see any blue lights. He looked to the south, hoping to see the lifeboat coming, but there was nothing. Yet.

Dixon looked at Monty, who was panting hard.

'You and me,' said Dixon, gasping for breath. 'New Year's resolution. Diet. All right?' Then they started running up the steps again.

Dixon stopped at the top with his hands on his knees, trying to get his breathing under control, if only so he could stuff a handful of fruit pastilles into his mouth. Managing his blood sugar levels had become second nature now. Weston pier was visible in the distance but the old fort at the western end of Brean Down was out of view, around the corner.

Dixon looked up and saw a man standing on the tarmac road about two hundred yards away. He was waving both arms above his head and shouting, but any sound was being carried away on the wind.

The River Axe swept past the base of the cliffs on the north side of Brean Down and it was beginning to swirl as the tide turned. Jane was right. If the body was caught by the River Axe, it would meet the outgoing tide on the rivers Parrett and Brue before being taken out still further into the main Bristol Channel.

Dixon sprinted down towards the man standing on the service road, which ran along the clifftops on the north side. As he approached, he could hear the man shouting.

'Have you got a phone? My battery's gone.'

Dixon stopped in front of him.

'Detective Inspector Dixon, Avon and Somerset Police. Help's on the way.'

'Oh, thank God. The body's in the water and the tide's going out,' said the man, pointing to a narrow path leading down through the dense undergrowth towards the clifftop.

'What's your name?' asked Dixon.

'Colin Wright.'

'Got ID?'

'Er, yes,' replied Wright, fumbling in his back pocket. 'What d'you need my ID for?'

'I need to know who I'm leaving my dog with,' replied Dixon. He looked at the photocard driving licence and then handed Monty's lead to Wright.

'You'll have to hang on tight.'

'Right.'

Dixon set off down the muddy track through the brambles. It was steep and slippery, with nothing to hang on to on either side, but it was no worse than some of the descent chutes he had navigated in his old climbing days. And at least this time he wasn't weighed down with climbing equipment.

Suddenly, the track opened out and Dixon found himself in a clearing at the top of the cliffs. Another man was standing there, peering into the bottom of a deep cleft in the rocks. Four fishing rods were leaning against a large boulder just below the top.

'I don't suppose you've got a rope?' shouted Dixon, trying to make himself heard over the noise of the wind and the waves.

'No, sorry.'

'Hold this.' Dixon handed the man his phone.

'You're not going down there?'

Dixon smiled and then began scrambling down to the fishing ledges. The rock was slippery and sloped towards the water, which focussed his mind, but he made short work of it and was soon standing on the lowest of three ledges. Then he shuffled to his left until he was able to look directly over the ledge and see the water below him.

The body was floating face down at the bottom of a deep cleft in the cliffs, being carried in and out on the waves. It was male and so could perhaps be Jane's missing suspect. Then Dixon noticed that the feet were bound, with a length of rope trailing behind the body. He knew the signs. The trademark. An old saying about playing with fire and expecting to get burnt flashed across his mind, although he couldn't remember the exact words.

The rock was wet and coated in black slime just a few feet below the ledge he was standing on, and the body was no more than ten feet below that. Seaweed was washing in the current of muddy brown water that was surging into the cleft and back out again.

Dixon thought it might be fun to catch fish off these ledges, but eating it was out of the question.

Suddenly, he heard a dog barking and looked up to see Monty running backwards and forwards along the clifftop above him, his lead trailing behind him.

'Get hold of my dog, will you?' shouted Dixon, to the man watching his every move.

The current seemed to be getting stronger and it would not be long before it took the body out with it. Then it would be out into the main channel and gone.

He took a deep breath and began climbing down. He turned to face the cliff and picked his hand and foot holds with precision, making sure he had three points of solid contact with the rock before he moved. The band of black slime was the high tide mark and beneath that it gave way to smelly brown slime, although no more than a foot had been revealed by the outgoing tide so far. Dixon hoped that it was mud and silt but either way, holding on to that rock was out of the question.

He shuffled along a narrow ramp that descended towards the water. At the bottom was a narrow crack, perhaps four inches wide, from which he would be able to reach the body. Whether he would be able to hang onto it long enough was another matter, but he would cross that bridge when he got to it.

From a standing position at the bottom of the small and narrow ramp, he lowered himself down into the water up to his waist. He was feeling around with his feet, trying to find footholds to steady himself. Then he jammed his right hand in the crack in front of him, clenched his fist and twisted it.

The waves were crashing into the rocks all around him and he was soon soaked to the skin. He was trying to breathe through his nose, having decided that swallowing a mouthful of seawater was not an option, but it was far from easy with the water splashing up into his face on each surge.

Timing was everything. An incoming wave would bring the dead man close enough to catch. Then all Dixon had to do was hang on. He waited for the next wave, took a deep breath and turned. The body was surging towards him so Dixon reached out with his left hand and took hold of it by the belt.

Then the wave raced back out of the cleft. The man rolled over and Dixon could see that his hands had been tied in front of him using cable ties, which were biting deep into the flesh of his wrists. Dixon grimaced. It took all of his strength to hold on to him with his left hand and keep his right wedged in the crack, but he was able to do it. Just.

Now he had to do it again. And again.

Each wave that surged in twisted the body behind Dixon, turning him away from the sanctuary of the rock and showering his face and head with muddy brown water. There was no escaping it, no matter which way he turned his head. He tried to hold his breath and breathe only with each outgoing wave, but he was starting to swallow seawater now.

He had lost all feeling in his legs and was shivering violently. Much longer and he would have to let go. Either that or he would risk being sucked out into the main channel himself.

Dixon closed his eyes and tried to imagine himself walking along the beach in the heat of the midday sun on an August bank holiday. It didn't work.

He had lost all track of time and had given up trying to count the tidal surges. It was far easier to count the bouts of vomiting now: five, six. Then he heard a shout from above. PC Cole was standing on the clifftop above, pointing out to sea. Dixon turned his head and looked out towards the main channel.

It was the inshore lifeboat, no more than fifty yards away, engines racing to hold station in the current.

The lifeboat sped upstream, out of sight, before turning in a loop and coming in closer this time, no more than ten yards from the rocks. The noise of the engines, the wind and the waves made it impossible for Dixon to hear the instructions being shouted by the helmsman, but he peered around the rocks and watched the crewman in the bows drop the anchor over the front of the boat just a few yards upstream of his cleft in the rocks.

The boat then began reversing back towards the rocks, both of the large engines screaming in protest as it tensioned against the anchor chain. The backwash was immense, churning the sea into a boiling mass of foam and bubbles under the boat. The anchor slipped and the boat jerked back. Then it held.

A crewman at the back of the boat was leaning over the side, testing the depth with a pole as the boat inched back towards the rocks. Dixon watched the helmsman fighting the current and gunning the engines, trying to hold the boat straight across the current. Dixon was resisting the temptation to put his hands over his ears. It would mean losing his grip on the body and the crack in the rock in front of him, although that was just a matter of minutes away anyway.

The boat was getting close enough for Dixon to hear the shouts of the crew.

'One metre.'

The anchor chain had given way to rope now and the crewman in the bows fed another metre over the front, allowing the boat to tension back still further.

The crewman at the back was testing the depth with the pole.

'Clear.'

'One metre.' The helmsman again.

'Clear.'

The boat was upstream of the cleft but close enough now that Dixon could almost reach out and touch it. He looked at the gap and wondered whether he could make it across before the current swept him away.

'Stay where you are!'

Dixon looked up. The clifftop, no more than thirty feet above, was lined with people, looking down at him. He spotted Jane, holding Monty. She shouted something but it was lost on the wind.

Suddenly, Dixon heard the engines ease off and the lifeboat began drifting downstream towards him. Then the crewman at the back dropped the pole into the boat, tilted one of the engines clear of the water and jumped over the side. He was in the cleft in a flash and took hold of the body. Dixon let go. At last.

'What's your name?'

'Nick Dixon.' His teeth were chattering as he spoke and he was shivering violently.

'Police?'

'Yes.'

The crewman rolled the body over. Dixon got his first look at the face, which was almost unrecognisable as one, were it not for the eyes, one of which was almost out of its smashed socket. The rocks and the tide had seen to that.

'He's dead,' said Dixon. 'Look at his hands and feet.'

'You first then,' said the crewman.

'No chance. Get him out of here first.'

'You've got hypothermia . . .'

'I'll be fine,' replied Dixon.

The crewman turned the body and passed it up to a second crewman who was leaning over the back corner of the boat. Together they manhandled it up and over the side of the boat. The backwash from the single engine on the nearside of the boat was keeping the waves down and it was Dixon's first respite for God knows how long. It felt like an age, as he vomited again into the water in front of him.

The water was now no more than waist deep and was quickly becoming too shallow for the inshore lifeboat, with its large outboard engines. The crewman in the water with Dixon shouted into a waterproof radio on his life jacket.

'Too shallow.'

The helmsman eased off the power, allowing the boat to drift away from the rocks downstream of the anchor. The second crewman in the boat tilted the other engine back into the water and then went to the bow to retrieve the anchor.

The boat surged forward to a position upstream of the anchor, pulled it in, and then sped off in a loop to take up position fifty yards away.

Dixon looked at the crewman with him in the cleft. He had his arms around Dixon, holding him up.

'The water's too shallow now for the big boat. Can you climb out?'

Dixon shook his head.

'My legs have gone.'

'Not to worry, here comes the Puffin,' said the crewman, smiling despite another wave crashing over them.

Dixon looked back out into the open water and spotted a smaller inflatable boat speeding towards them. It was heading straight for the cleft and slowed at the last minute, coming in bow first, right up to them.

'It's all right. You can let go now.'

Dixon unclenched his fist and slid his hand out of the crack. He felt himself slump back into the crewman, who held him up. Then he was lifted out of the water and into the boat in one movement. A life jacket was put on him and a space blanket wrapped around his shoulders.

'There's an ambulance on the beach the other side.'

Dixon watched the crewman climb into the boat and then it reversed back out of the cleft, before turning across the current and back out into the main channel.

'I'll be fine,' said Dixon.

'Have you inhaled any seawater?'

'Swallowed a lot, but not breathed it in,' replied Dixon. He turned and vomited over the side of the boat.

'Good.'

He looked up at the cliffs and the old fort as the boat sped around the end of Brean Down and, once round to the south side, the larger inshore lifeboat turned in towards the beach where a small orange hovercraft was waiting on the mudflats. It would take the body to the ambulance that was waiting on the beach still further in the distance.

'Are you sure?'

'Yes. I just need a cup of tea.'

The crewman who had jumped into the water was sitting opposite Dixon.

'What's your name?'

'Matt.'

'Thank you, Matt,' said Dixon, shaking his hand.

'My pleasure.'

Familiar landmarks raced past as the boat sped towards Burnham. The receding tide meant that they stayed well out to sea on the way back but the two yellow buoys marking the wreck of the SS Nornen were just visible bouncing around in the surf, and the lighthouse, of course, with several dog walkers on the beach behind it. Dixon hoped that the next time he saw it he would be walking his dog.

He was helped out of the lifeboat onto the jetty at Burnham. The larger boat had caught them up after dropping off the body and was being backed onto a trailer that had been reversed into the water by a giant tractor on the beach. Not easy in a strong cross wind. A smaller trailer was waiting alongside to retrieve the Puffin.

He looked up at the sea wall, which was lined with spectators. Several photographers were standing at the top of the jetty.

'C'mon, let's get you out of those wet clothes,' said Matt.

Dixon was sitting in the corner of the Burnham lifeboat station, watching the steam rising from a mug of hot, sweet tea that someone had thrust into his hands. He was wearing an RNLI thermal fleece undersuit and had a coat wrapped around his shoulders. His own clothes were lying in a sodden heap on the floor at his feet.

The lifeboats, now back on their trailers, were parked outside, being hosed down before the tractors reversed them into the shed.

'Are you sure you don't want to go to hospital?'

'No, thanks, I'll be fine.'

Dixon smiled and went back to watching the steam rising from his mug of tea. Drinking it was not an option, for fear of bringing it back up again, but just holding it was warming him up.

'I'm looking for Inspector Dixon.'

He recognised the voice.

'He's in there.'

'Thanks.'

Dixon listened to the sound of footsteps approaching and claws scrabbling on the concrete floor.

'There you are,' said Jane. She was being pulled along by Monty, before deciding it would be far easier just to let him go.

'Have you got my phone?' asked Dixon. He was trying to fend off Monty without spilling his tea.

'You were just supposed to spot the body. Not go in after it.'

Dixon shrugged his shoulders.

'Idiot,' said Jane, handing over his phone.

'Was it Stanniland?'

'Yes.'

'Where are they taking him?'

'Weston,' replied Jane. 'How're you feeling?'

'I'll be OK. I threw up most of the seawater I swallowed on the way in.'

'Good.'

'Where is he?' The voice was loud and came from outside.

'Oh shit, that's Lewis,' said Jane. 'I'll go and see what he wants.'

Dixon put down his mug of tea and began fishing his wallet, keys and warrant card from the pile of wet clothes at his feet.

'Have a nice swim?'

He looked up to find DCI Lewis standing in front of him.

'Yes, Sir.'

'Bloody good job you were there. Well done.'

'Thank you, Sir,' replied Dixon. 'You know what this means? A body dumped in the Bristol Channel . . .'

'I do,' said Lewis, 'And it'll be your job to prove it.'

'What about Janice?'

'She's going to take a few days off, then go on a training course.'

'But . . .'

'It's out of my hands,' continued Lewis, shaking his head. 'Let's just leave it at that, shall we?'

Lewis reached into the inside pocket of his coat, pulled out an envelope and handed it to Dixon.

'These are the papers for your misconduct meeting. Witness statements, documents, that sort of stuff.'

Dixon looked at the envelope and then dropped it onto the chair next to him.

'I take it you agree to waive the twenty day notice period?'

'Yes, Sir,' replied Dixon.

'Good.'

Lewis reached into his other pocket and took out a smaller envelope, which he handed to Dixon.

'This is notice of your misconduct meeting. Monday morning at 10 a.m. Portishead.'

'That's the day after tomorrow?'

'It is. Smile sweetly, speak when you're spoken to and tell 'em what they want to hear. Otherwise, keep your trap shut.'

Dixon nodded.

'Then get yourself down to Express Park as soon as it's over. All right?'

'What's going to . . . ?'

'Management advice. You'll be reminded to disclose personal connections in future and a letter will be placed on your file to that effect.'

'Is that it?'

'Yes. And you're being assigned to the Major Investigation Team.'

Dixon smiled.

'Is that a promotion?' he asked.

'Of sorts. They could hardly give you a commendation, could they?' replied Lewis. 'And you'd best hand back that cold case too.'

'No chance.'

'Have it your own way.'

'Has he gone?' asked Jane, peering around the door.

'Yes, you're quite safe.'

'What'd he say?'

'I'll tell you later.'

'D'you need a lift back to your car?'

'I'll get Cole to drop me back, don't worry,' replied Dixon.

'I'll head back with Jan then.'

'Wait a sec.'

'What?'

'Can you remember what was in the vomit?' asked Dixon. 'The pile outside the cottage.'

'Lamb, rice and yoghurt, I think. Why?'

'Doesn't matter. Just be careful. All right?'

'OK,' said Jane, shaking her head.

Dixon waited until she had gone and then opened a web browser on his phone. He typed 'lamb rice yoghurt' into Google and looked at the first search result, which came from saveur.com.

'We meet again,' he muttered, from behind a wry smile.

He was looking at a recipe for tavë kosi, otherwise known as Albanian baked lamb and rice with yoghurt.

Chapter Ten

Dixon was asleep on the sofa by the time Jane arrived home just after 7 p.m. He had spent the morning in the bath and the afternoon sitting on the edge of it, vomiting at regular intervals into the lavatory, and was exhausted. He had at least remembered to put his clothes in the washing machine first though.

He woke to find Jane standing over him.

'You all right?'

He rubbed his eyes and sat up.

'Yes, a bit better, I think.'

'Have you had anything to eat?'

'God, no.'

'What about your blood sugar levels?'

'Let's try a cup of tea with a sugar in it first then. See if I can keep that down.'

'Like that, is it?' asked Jane.

'You could say that.'

'Have you fed Monty?'

'Not yet.'

'I'll do it.'

'Have they done the post mortem?' asked Dixon.

'Drowning. He was alive when he went into the water.'

Dixon shook his head. 'You'd have thought they'd have put a bullet in the back of his head first, wouldn't you?'

'Who?' shouted Jane, from the kitchen.

'Do you remember that chief super from Bristol in the sharp suit?' asked Dixon.

'He came to the hospital after our early morning visit from the Albanians,' replied Jane.

'That's right. Do you remember what he said?'

Jane was standing in front of Dixon holding a mug of tea in each hand.

'If they'd wanted you dead,' continued Dixon, 'you'd be at the bottom of the Bristol Channel by now.'

'He did.'

'Those were his exact words.'

'D'you think the Albanians are involved?'

'Google lamb, rice and yoghurt.'

Dixon watched Jane tapping the words into a web browser on her phone and waited for her reaction.

'Oh, shit.'

'I couldn't have put it better myself.'

'So, what d'you think happened?' asked Jane.

'Either Stanniland was framed for Elizabeth's murder or someone went in after he killed her to make damn sure he got caught. The latter would explain the van and the motorbike, wouldn't it? And the different knife.'

'If you assume Grafton and Mrs Freeman are right.'

'And why wouldn't they be? Just because they're old?'

'I didn't mean it like that.'

'Then, when Stanniland walks free, what better way to close the whole thing off than to make him disappear? We'd have been chasing his shadow for months until the file was quietly closed.'

'Why though?' asked Jane.

'No idea,' replied Dixon. 'Yet.'

'I'm assuming you're taking over the investigation then?'

'I am.'

'That explains this,' said Jane, handing Dixon the file that had been tucked under her arm. 'And Janice's holiday. Poor sod. It's hardly her fault, is it?'

'She'll bounce back,' said Dixon.

'What about your disciplinary?' asked Jane.

'Monday morning.'

'It's been fixed?'

'I'm not sure fixed is the right word. At least I hope it isn't.'

'A reprimand?' asked Jane.

'Management advice.'

'You lucky sod.'

'And I've been assigned to the MIT.'

'That's based at Portishead,' said Jane, frowning.

'Yes, but it only assembles when there's a major investigation, don't forget.'

'Some people always come up smelling of roses.'

'Well, I bloody well didn't this morning,' said Dixon, smiling.

'No, you didn't,' said Jane, sniffing the air. 'I'd suggest another bath.'

Dixon tiptoed down the stairs. He had a towel wrapped around his waist and another draped over his shoulders.

'What's this you're watching?' he asked, dropping onto the sofa next to Jane.

'*Long Lost Family*. It's where they reunite parents with children given up for adoption. Happy ending stuff.'

'Always?'

'Seems to be. Although they probably don't show those where it goes wrong.'

'I bet they don't.'

'I'm adopted, you know.'

'Really? You never said.'

'Came as a bit of a relief, to be honest. My parents are mad as hatters, aren't they?' asked Jane, grinning.

'No, they're not,' replied Dixon. 'Well . . .'

Jane elbowed him in the ribs.

'Are you really adopted?'

'Yes.'

'Have you ever tried to find your real parents?'

'No. Never.'

'Why not?'

'I've thought about it sometimes, but mostly I think of them as dead. It's the only way I can deal with it. And it's easier. Full stop.'

Dixon thought it best not to press the point. Jane would look for them if and when she was ready. Both parties must want to be found for it to work, no doubt. Otherwise, who knows what might happen.

'What's her story then?' asked Dixon, gesturing towards the screen.

'Single mother in the 1960s. She was sixteen. Things were different back then.'

'That they were,' said Dixon, nodding. 'Fancy something to eat? I think I could keep it down now.'

Dixon had spent the Sunday with his feet up, reading the file of papers that Lewis had sent via Jane. It contained a copy of Elizabeth

Perry's post mortem, the forensic reports on both Waterside Cottage and Stanniland's flat, the witness statements, such as they were, and, lastly, the DNA reports from PGL, which had made grim reading. It had been an otherwise pleasant day, best described as the calm before the storm and, now, as he sped south on the M5, Dixon reflected on his misconduct meeting.

It had lasted all of ten minutes.

'You admit that you should have disclosed your personal connection to the case from the outset?'

'The possible connection, yes.'

Dixon had resisted the temptation to smile sweetly and hoped DCI Lewis would forgive him.

'Do you have anything to add before this tribunal arrives at a decision?'

'No.'

'Very well. There will be a finding that your conduct failed to meet the requisite Standards of Professional Behaviour. However, I find that it was at the lower end of the scale and propose to deal with it by a reminder to disclose personal connections in future. You will receive a letter to this effect and a copy will be placed on your file. Do you understand?'

'Yes, Sir.'

'You will receive written notice of the outcome of these proceedings within five days and have seven days from receipt of that notice in which to appeal, if you wish to do so.'

'I don't.'

'Then that concludes these misconduct proceedings,' said the officer, standing up. Then he had walked around the side of the table and stood in front of Dixon, with his hand outstretched.

'Thank you, Sir,' said Dixon, shaking his hand.

The officer had smiled and nodded, but had said nothing more.

Dixon turned off the M5 at Burnham-on-Sea and went home. He was standing in the field behind his cottage, watching Monty sniffing along the hedge, when his phone rang.

'How'd it go?' asked Jane.

'Ten minutes.'

'Where are you now?'

'Just giving Monty a quick run in the field.'

'Well, you'd better get here sharpish. There's a rumour Tom Perry is a suspect in Stanniland's murder and the press have got hold of it. They're crawling all over the place and Perry's downstairs kicking up a helluva stink.'

Dixon arrived at Express Park twenty minutes later and parked in the staff car park. It had taken him several loud blasts of his horn to clear a way through the journalists and TV crews and he watched them milling around outside the police centre while he waited for the huge steel gate to open.

He parked on the top floor. Jane was waiting for him.

'Lewis wants to see you. Now.'

'Where is he?'

'Meeting room two.'

Dixon winced. Still, the open plan office was likely to be the least of his worries.

They could hear the shouting as they stepped out of the lift on the first floor and looked across to the meeting room. Lewis was visible through the glass, waving his arms at Harry Unwin, who was standing with his back to the window.

'Aren't they supposed to be soundproofed, those meeting rooms?' asked Dixon.

'Yes.'

'More like a bloody echo chamber.'

Lewis looked across the landing and saw Dixon watching.

'Just get out,' he said, to Unwin. Then he waved at Dixon to come in.

Dixon was blocking the door and waited for Unwin to open it from the inside. Dixon glared at Unwin, who looked away and stepped back to allow him into the room. Lewis waited until Unwin closed the door behind him.

'Jane's filled you in?'

'She has.'

'What d'you need?'

'Rid of Harry, for a start.'

'Leave it to me,' replied Lewis. 'What about a replacement?'

'Can I have Louise Willmott?'

'Fine. Anything else?'

'What about Jane?' asked Dixon. 'We're living together now.'

'She'd better stay on the team,' replied Lewis. 'But I'd suggest you work with Louise and put Jane with one of the others. All right?'

'Have you spoken to Tom Perry?' asked Dixon.

'Not yet. Vicky Thomas is on her way to deal with the press.'

'I'll go and see him now.'

'Did you read the file?'

'Yes.'

'What d'you make of it?'

'Person or persons unknown paid the Albanians to arrange the murder of Elizabeth Perry. Stanniland was the fall guy, the Lee Harvey Oswald of the piece, so when we mucked up the DNA and had to release him, they needed to tidy up.'

'And you can prove that?'

'Not yet. The vomit at the scene, possibly Albanian baked lamb. It's a bit of a leap but it makes sense. And the Bristol Channel's their trademark, don't forget. My guess is that someone went into the cottage after him. He or she delivered the fatal stab wound and dropped the cigarette butts for us to find too. That would explain the van and motorbike.'

'I still don't understand why we got no DNA from the vomit,' said Lewis.

'Have we got the PM report on Stanniland yet?'

'Yes.'

'That should tell us,' replied Dixon.

Lewis shook his head. 'Well, you've got your work cut out. Keep me posted.'

Dixon opened the interview room door and walked in. Tom Perry was sitting with his back to the door and turned to face him. He was flushed, which was visible even through several days of stubble.

'You?'

'I'm taking over your wife's murder, Mr Perry.'

'I thought you were suspended?'

'You're well informed.'

'One of our members is on the civilian staff here.'

Dixon nodded. 'My hearing was this morning and I got off with a warning.'

'What did you do?' asked Perry.

Dixon sat down opposite him.

'Seventeen years ago my fiancée was murdered. I got the chance to catch her killer but to do so I had to keep quiet about my connection to the case. I failed to disclose my personal involvement.'

'Did you catch him?'

'I did.'

'Then it was worth it.'

'Yes, it was.'

'So, what the hell's going on?' asked Perry. 'The press seem to think I killed Stanniland.'

'I'll deal with that.'

'I bloody well wish I had killed him.'

'No, you don't. Not really.'

'Has there been a leak?'

'We've had a few changes of personnel,' replied Dixon.

'About bloody time.'

'You are not a suspect in the murder of John Stanniland and I will make that clear to the media.'

'Are they here?'

'I'm afraid so.'

'Wankers.'

'Mr Perry, it's my belief that your wife was killed to get to you. Can you think of anyone who might wish to do that?'

'You mean it wasn't a burglary that went wrong?'

'No.'

'That makes it my fault, doesn't it?'

Perry slid his wedding band off his ring finger and stared at it in the palm of his hand.

'Tom?' Dixon could hear him breathing deeply. 'Listen to me, Tom.'

Perry looked up.

'What campaigns have you been involved in?'

'Recently?'

'Yes.'

'Hinkley C, the new reactor at Hinkley Point. There's a wind farm over at East Huntspill. But who's gonna kill my wife over a few wind turbines?'

'What about planning applications?'

'I was helping residents oppose one on the edge of Burtle and another at Berrow, but that's it.'

'Were they big developments?'

'Not really. But why kill my wife and not me, if that's it?'

'I'm exploring all possibilities at the moment. Look, I want you to think about this, carefully, and if you come up with anything else, you let me know immediately. All right?'

'I will.'

'Are you carrying on with the election?' asked Dixon.

'I haven't decided yet. I think so,' replied Perry. 'It's what Lizzie would have wanted me to do, I know that much.'

'I've got some more digging to do and then we'll have another chat. All right?'

'Fine.'

'Where's your car?'

'Out the front.'

'I'll get someone to bring it round the back.'

'This is the one bit of the job I dread,' said Dixon, looking out of the huge windows on the first floor at the journalists gathered below.

'You'll be fine,' replied Jane. 'Vicky Thomas has told you what to say, hasn't she?'

'Fat lot of bloody good she is.'

'You know what not to say?'

'I do. And it doesn't leave a lot else,' replied Dixon, straightening his tie.

He went downstairs in the lift and stepped out into the glare of the flashbulbs and spot lamps in front of the police centre. It was just after midday and overcast.

'My name is Detective Inspector Nick Dixon. I am the senior investigating officer in the murders of Elizabeth Perry and John Stanniland. I will make a short statement and then take questions, but you will appreciate that I am limited in what I can say at the present time.'

Dixon waited for the clicking of cameras to subside.

'Mrs Elizabeth Perry was, as you know, stabbed to death in the early hours of Christmas Eve. John Stanniland was a suspect in her murder. He was released on police bail pending further enquiries on the afternoon of Friday 27 December. His body was found in the Bristol Channel to the north of Brean Down on the morning of Saturday 28 December. He too had been murdered.'

'Has Tom Perry been arrested for the murder of John Stanniland, Inspector?' The shouted question came from the back of the crowd of journalists.

'No, he has not. Mr Perry is not a suspect in either murder. He is a husband whose wife has been murdered and I would reiterate the family's request for privacy at this time.'

'Do you have a suspect?'

'Our enquiries into both murders are ongoing. That is all I can say at this stage, although I would ask anyone with any information to contact the incident room, anonymously if needs be, by dialling 101 and asking for Bridgwater CID. All calls will be treated in the strictest confidence.'

'Is Tom Perry going to stand in the election?'

'That is a matter for Mr Perry,' replied Dixon.

'What would you say to members of the Conservative Party moving to deselect him?' The question came from a reporter at the front of the crowd. She was holding a microphone at full stretch in front of Dixon.

'It is not for me, as a police officer, to comment on the internal affairs of the Conservative Party. But, as a voter in the North Somerset constituency, I will just say this. I think I would take a dim view of any political party that chose to kick their candidate when he or she was down. Tom Perry needs their support at this difficult time.

Not to face moves behind the scenes to get rid of him. And I suspect many voters in the constituency would feel the same.'

Dixon was momentarily blinded the camera flashes going off all around him. Then he turned on his heels and walked back into the police centre.

Dixon walked back up to the CID area on the first floor. Louise Willmott was standing by Jane's workstation, following Jane's finger as she pointed at her computer screen. Dave Harding and Mark Pearce were standing by the kettle, waiting for it to boil.

'Meeting room two, twenty minutes,' said Dixon, sitting down at a vacant desk. 'Louise?'

'Yes, Sir.'

'We need to get out to the crime scene. Get on to the underwater search team and see if they can take us out there in their boat, will you?'

'Yes, Sir.'

'The Burnham Area Rescue Boat is out there, Sir,' said Dave. 'Ferrying people around, that sort of thing.'

'We won't worry them with it, Dave. They've got better things to do.'

'OK.'

Dixon switched on the computer on the desk in front of him and logged in. Then he scrolled down through his emails until he reached the one attaching Stanniland's post mortem report.

'If I send this to print, where will it go?'

'The printer's over there, Sir,' said Mark, pointing to a line of printers against the far wall.

'I used to have one in my office,' muttered Dixon. Then he sighed loudly. 'And what the hell's this?' He sat back in his chair and folded his arms.

'What's up?' asked Jane.

'What on earth possesses them to spend millions of pounds on a shiny new police station and then stick the old computers in it? I've got a bloody egg timer now.'

'Calm down.'

'All I want to do is print this report,' said Dixon, clicking the mouse over and over again.

'And stop clicking,' said Jane.

'I know what I want on my gravestone. Here lies Nick Dixon, brackets, not responding, close brackets.'

Louise laughed.

'Don't encourage him,' said Jane.

'Nice to have things back to normal though, isn't it?' said Louise.

'I suppose it is,' replied Jane, smiling.

Dixon was standing by the printer when Louise shouted across to him. She had her hand over the mouthpiece of her phone.

'Will the inflatable do, Sir, or do you want the big one?'

'The inflatable's fine.'

'What time?'

'An hour. On the Moorland road, as near as we can get to the village without getting our feet wet.'

'OK.'

Dixon sat down on the edge of the printer table, speed reading Stanniland's post mortem report, and quickly found what he was looking for. Stanniland's stomach was full of seawater, making an assessment of the pH levels impossible, but he did have advanced Barrett's oesophagus.

'Right. Let's get on with it,' said Dixon.

Chapter Eleven

'There's two ways of looking at this thing,' said Dixon. 'The first and obvious conclusion is that Stanniland broke into Waterside Cottage to get some money for his next fix, was confronted by Elizabeth Perry, killed her and then fled the scene, torching his van on the outskirts of Bristol. He stood over the body and smoked a cigarette, vomited on the lawn and then drove off, heard by Mr Grafton, as we know.'

'It all fits,' said Harding.

'Does it?' replied Dixon. 'Even ignoring Stanniland's subsequent murder, which we discovered by pure chance, there are still gaping holes.'

'Like what?'

'All right. Let's start with the vomit. You'd expect to get some DNA off that, wouldn't you? Let's assume he puked up at about 2 a.m. and the sample was found and collected at, what, let's say 8 a.m. That's six hours, being rained on for five of them. That shouldn't destroy any DNA trace, should it?'

'No, Sir.'

'But there was nothing?'

'Right.'

'We know from Stanniland's post mortem that he had advanced Barrett's oesophagus. That's a thickening of the lining of the gullet just above the stomach caused by persistent acid reflux, what you and I would call heartburn. It can lead to cancer, but it tells us that Stanniland had high levels of acid in his stomach.'

'And the acid would have destroyed any profile?' asked Louise.

'Over time, yes,' replied Dixon. 'Remember, we're looking at abnormally high stomach acid levels here.'

'That would take longer than five or six hours, surely?' asked Harding.

'Yes, it would. Not least because the acid was being diluted by the rainwater, wasn't it?'

'So, what are you saying?' asked Jane.

'I'm saying that Stanniland vomited hours earlier, possibly days, and it was collected, bagged up and then deposited by someone at the scene. Someone riding a motorbike.'

Silence.

Dixon looked around the room. All but Dave Harding were smiling.

'So, Mrs Freeman was right about the motorbike?' asked Harding.

'Well, let's assume she was right, for a minute. It explains the vomit and the cigarettes, which I'll come onto in a minute, and the second knife wound.'

'What about the cigarettes?'

'The two in the lane are the same brand. That's it. So, they could have been bought, lit and allowed to burn down to the filter, then dropped in the lane to make it look as though Stanniland waited outside the cottage, perhaps until Elizabeth went to bed. There was no DNA on them at all, so it was either washed away by the rainwater, which is unlikely, or the cigarettes never touched anyone's lips.'

'And the one on the landing?'

'Smoked by Stanniland at the same time as he ate his Albanian baked lamb and rice with yoghurt. They call it tavë kosi. It's a national dish.'

'Was the lamb baked?' asked Louise.

'There's your first job. Find out.'

'Yes, Sir.'

'So, he eats his tavë kosi and smokes a cigarette,' continued Dixon. 'Then he's punched in the stomach and pukes up. The vomit is collected for later use by our motorcyclist and the cigarette butt is bagged up to be dropped at the scene.'

'The Albanians again,' said Pearce.

'Stanniland's murder is their style, as we know,' replied Dixon. 'And he would have done as he was told, no doubt.'

'Why kill him though?' asked Pearce.

'Once we'd released him it was the obvious way of tidying up the loose end. If he'd just disappeared we'd have chased our tails for a few months and then closed the file.'

'Why didn't we pick this up before?' asked Harding.

'The assumption was made that Grafton and Mrs Freeman heard the same vehicle so no one was looking for it,' replied Dixon. 'It becomes clearer if you assume they were both right about what they heard. We also now have Stanniland's murder, don't forget, and that puts the whole thing in an entirely different light.'

'Is there anything else?' asked Jane.

'There is. What brand of cigarettes was it?'

'Marlboro Lights,' replied Pearce.

'Right. The ash that was recovered from the landing, let's get it tested. My guess is it'll come from several different brands.'

'Why?'

'Because it was taken from an ashtray.'

'Can you tell from ash?' asked Louise.

'Sherlock Holmes can tell the difference between one hundred and forty different types of tobacco just by sniffing it so I'm damn sure our lab can do it. Jane?'

'I'll sort it.'

'Then we come onto the second knife wound, the fatal one, which we know from the blood loss came several minutes later. What do we make of that?'

'Stanniland realises he hasn't killed her. Perhaps his knife isn't long enough. So, he goes to the kitchen to get a longer knife and then stabs her again.'

'That's possible, Jane,' replied Dixon. 'There's only one thing I don't like about it. He's stabbed her umpteen times already, so why would he take the time and trouble to insert the knife into an existing wound? He'd just stab her again surely?'

'Possibly.'

'My reading of Poland's report is that time and care was taken to insert the blade into a wound in her back. To hide it, as far as possible. After all, it was only visible internally on close inspection of the heart and surrounding tissue.'

'So, you're saying the motorcyclist did it?'

'I am. This is a real professional we're dealing with here. Make no mistake about it. There's no trace he or she was there whatsoever.'

'Absence of evidence is not evidence of absence,' said Jane.

'It isn't. And when he gets in there he finds Elizabeth still alive.'

'And he finishes the job,' said Pearce.

'He does. Clean and clinical,' replied Dixon.

'Bastard.'

'There's a lot of guesswork in there . . .' said Harding.

'There is, Dave. So, it's our job to prove it. Louise, you were going to check the vomit.'

'Yes, Sir.'

'And Jane, the ash?'

Jane nodded.

'Dave, I know you've looked at the traffic cameras going north. Look at them again, north and south this time, for a motorbike.

Harding bowed his head and sighed.

'It's a pain in the arse, I know, but it's got to be done.'

'They may have gone cross country,' said Pearce.

'Possibly, but their plates will almost certainly be fake so they're likely to be a bit more relaxed about cameras. Let's hope so, anyway.'

'OK.'

'I'd like to speak to Mrs Freeman again, so if we could find out where she's been evacuated to?' asked Dixon.

'Leave it to me, Sir,' said Louise.

'Thanks.'

'Why though, Sir?' asked Pearce. 'What's the motive?'

'That's for you and Jane to find out, Mark. We've got a professional killing dressed up to look like a drug induced burglary gone wrong. Someone has gone to a lot of trouble to kill Elizabeth Perry and the reason is going to be hidden in Tom Perry's political life. Somewhere.'

'Politics?' asked Jane.

'Think about it. They're just a perfectly normal young couple expecting their first child. He's an architect and she's a housewife. What's the one thing that sets them apart, makes them stand out?'

'Puts them in conflict with others,' said Louise.

'It does. We've got the expansion of Hinkley Point Nuclear Power Station, wind farms, housing developments. He's getting involved in stuff where millions of pounds is at stake.'

'But why her and not him?' asked Pearce.

'That's what we've got to find out, isn't it? replied Dixon. 'I want you two to look at the campaigns he's been involved in recently. Look at who stands to lose if his campaign is successful. And I want detailed profiles on the local Conservative Association. Start with the chairman and work down. Who are these people and who are they connected to?'

'Shame we've lost our best witness,' said Harding.

'Stanniland and our mysterious motorbike rider are just the foot soldiers, Dave. Expendable. They knew nothing. The Albanians were paid to arrange it. What we need to do is find the money behind it and Tom Perry's our best witness, only he doesn't know it yet.'

'I never got to thank you properly. For what you did,' said Dixon, as he drove over the M5.

'It's fine, Sir, really,' replied Louise. 'You'd have done the same for me.'

'That's not the point. Thank you.'

'I'm assuming your disciplinary went well?'

'It did,' said Dixon. He leaned forward, over the steering wheel and looked up. 'I don't like the look of these clouds.'

'There's another storm front coming in off the Atlantic, apparently. Three days of rain.'

'Marvellous.'

Dixon stopped on the railway bridge and looked to his right.

'What the f . . .' His voice tailed off.

The small hill of Burrow Mump, with its church on top, was visible in the distance, perhaps six miles away at Burrowbridge. But the land in between was under water. Murky, brown water. Lines of trees and hedges marked the boundaries of the fields and smaller hedges and fencing, the gardens of the houses in Moorland. All of them flooded.

'You've seen it on the telly, Sir?' asked Louise.

'Yes, but nothing prepares you for the scale of it, does it?' replied Dixon. 'And look at that!'

He was looking at a train in the middle distance, perhaps a mile or so away. It was stationary in the midst of the floodwater that had almost reached the level of the tracks. A bright blue First Great Western InterCity 125 brought to a standstill by water.

'We'll see that on the evening news, I bet,' said Louise, pointing at a helicopter that was hovering above the train.

'That embankment must be eight feet high.'

'It's flooded to eighteen and a half feet further up,' replied Louise.

Dixon shook his head. Maybe his snorkel had been a waste of time, after all.

The road took a sharp turn to the right and then followed the River Parrett. There was a short section of stone wall on the nearside and then a steep earth bank on top of it. Much of the vegetation on the bank had been flattened so Dixon guessed that the water had been over the bank here as well, perhaps at high tide.

The road itself was under several inches of water but it appeared to be draining away into the culvert on the other side. Dixon kept going.

Around the next bend he spotted several vehicles and trailers parked in a farm gateway on the right. The Burnham Area Search and Rescue vehicle was there, with an empty trailer behind it. There was also a large six wheel drive Mercedes that looked like a giant version of his Land Rover. It had a bright orange inflatable boat on the roof and was sign written Avon and Somerset Police Underwater Search Unit. Dixon parked next to the Mercedes.

'Are you Inspector Dixon?'

'Yes.'

'Sergeant Watts, Sir. I hope you've got some wellies.'

'I have. What about you, Louise?'

'No.'

'We've got some in the van, don't worry. And put these on,' said Watts, handing Dixon and Louise a bright red life jacket each.

They watched two of the dive team lift the boat off the roof and then carry it along the road until it was sitting in a foot of water.

'When you're ready,' said Watts. 'We need to walk the boat out as far as we can, otherwise we'll be sitting on the road when we get in it.'

Dixon nodded and began wading along the road, pushing the boat ahead of him. The water was almost up to the top of his boots before Watts stopped.

'This should do. In you get.'

Dixon and Louise climbed into the boat and then Watts began pulling it still further along the road.

'I've got a wetsuit on,' he said, grinning.

The water was up to his waist before he jumped in, dropped the outboard motor into the water and switched it on.

'Where to then?'

'Into Moorland, then left opposite the church,' replied Dixon.

The wind was whistling across the Levels and the water was choppy, even in the confines of the road, although the hedges on either side provided a little shelter. The boat bounced over the waves, sending spray into Dixon's face. It was his second boat trip in as many days and he had spent much of the last one being sick over the side. He was determined not to do the same again.

'Can you slow down a bit?'

'Yes, Sir.'

The water was up to the letter boxes of the first houses they passed on their way into Moorland. Furniture was piled up on the ground floor of each of the bungalows, the owners of the two storey houses at least having an upstairs to store their sofas and chairs.

Off to the right and set back from the road was a large red brick house with a huge earth wall around it.

'King Canute, according to the newspapers,' said Louise.

Watts followed the road around to the left, opposite the church.

'That's Grafton's place,' said Dixon, pointing at the first bungalow on the left. The water was level with the bottom of the windows. Grafton had been right. The sandbags were a waste of time. 'And that's Mrs Freeman's. I want to have a look at it on the way back.'

Louise nodded.

They followed the lane towards the river and Waterside Cottage.

'How deep is it here?'

'About twelve feet,' replied Watts.

Dixon looked across at the cottage. The water was lapping just below the first floor windows and the ridge of the tiled roof on the porch was just visible.

'Can we get closer?'

'I'll need to watch the propeller on the gate, but we can have a go.'

Watts tilted the outboard motor up until the propeller was just under the surface of the water. Then he edged the boat forward in line with the top of the porch and between two bushes that were sticking out of the water. It seemed a good guess for the line of the garden path.

Dixon leaned over and peered in through the first floor window. The water was level with the mattress of a single bed, presumably in the spare room, and various items were floating around it. Dixon noticed a small suitcase and several jigsaw puzzles, still wrapped in their cellophane. The door was open and he was able to look through to the landing, but all he could see was water lapping against the bannister at the top of the stairs.

'I've seen enough.'

Watts turned the boat and headed back along the lane.

'Is that a field gateway?' asked Dixon, gesturing towards a break in the hedgeline on the right.

'Looks like it, Sir,' replied Watts.

'Can we go in?'

'I'll give it a try.'

Watts turned the boat into what had once been a field and was now a lake. He switched off the engine, allowing the boat to drift towards the hedge.

'What're you thinking, Sir?' asked Louise.

'That this would be a good place to wait, assuming you're on a bike and waiting in the dark for Stanniland to do the necessary. Tucked in behind this hedge. Let's see if they got any photos of tyre tracks. We're, what, a hundred yards from the cottage?'

'More like seventy, Sir,' said Louise.

'OK. Let's head back, Sergeant. I want to have a look at that house on the right though.'

'Yes, Sir.'

Dixon was sitting in the bow of the boat, watching the water pass by on either side. It was murky, with a thick brown sludge floating on top and, in places, oil. The clean up operation was going to take months.

'This is the one,' he shouted, waving at Watts. The boat slowed to a stop outside Moorland House.

'Can we go in?'

'The gate's closed. And we're only in four feet of water. I've not got clearance.'

Dixon took his jacket off and rolled up his sleeve. Then he leaned over the front of the boat and reached down behind the gate, which was visible just below the surface, feeling for the latch in the freezing cold water.

'Got it.'

Then he pushed open the gate.

'Can you get me over to that window?' he asked, flicking the water off his arm.

Watts took the boat forward, towards the window to the right of the front door. Dixon knew it had once been Mrs Freeman's dining room and was now her bedroom. He could just about make out a bed through the net curtains. Then he tapped on the glass. Single glazed metal framed windows. He grinned at Louise.

'What is it, Sir?'

'How far is it to the lane from here?'

'I dunno. About ten yards?'

'They're not double glazed,' replied Dixon. 'She could've heard a bike.'

'Seen enough?' asked Watts.

'Yes. Let's get out of here.'

'Good. It's going to be pissing down in a minute.'

Dixon dropped Louise back at Express Park and then drove down to Musgrove Park Hospital. He parked behind Roger Poland's car and walked into the pathology lab.

'Can I help you, sir?' asked the receptionist.

'It's all right. I know where I'm going, thanks,' replied Dixon, disappearing through the swing doors.

He watched Poland at work from the safety of the anteroom for several minutes before summoning up the courage to tap on the window. He knew that Poland would insist he go into the lab and he could see that his current subject was unusually gruesome. He winced when he got the dreaded wave.

'What the . . . ?'

'The Ilminster Bypass,' replied Poland. 'Head on. They really need to do something about that road.'

Dixon turned away and walked over to the window.

'I need to have a word with you about Elizabeth Perry.'

'They've let you loose on an unsuspecting public again, have they?' asked Poland.

'My disciplinary proceedings have been concluded satisfactorily, if that's what you mean, and thank you for asking.'

'What you mean is you got away with it?'

'I did,' replied Dixon, with a wry smile.

'Good. Calls for a curry that, I think,' said Poland. 'I thought the Perry case was Janice Courtenay's though?'

'She's gone on holiday.'

'My notes are in my office.'

Dixon did not need to be asked twice. He disappeared through the swing door on the far side of the lab and was sitting on the corner of the desk in Poland's office by the time he caught up with him.

'What do you want to know?' asked Poland, pulling Elizabeth Perry's file from the bottom drawer of his filing cabinet.

'Tell me about the knives.'

'The main one was pink. Probably looked something like this,' replied Poland, handing a piece of paper to Dixon.

It was a colour printout of a web page featuring a set of Colourworks kitchen knives in bright pink.

'The smallest one,' said Poland. 'The blade's an inch or so across the base and three inches long. Slightly curved, as you can see. It could well have been one of those.'

'But this isn't the knife that killed her?'

'No. That's more your ordinary steak knife. Longer. Thinner. Not tapered until the tip. More serrated too.'

'How can you tell?'

'We've got the wounds made by the pink knife. There are several of those, much the same and easily identifiable. Then one of them extends a further two inches into her chest cavity and penetrates the heart. It's made by the second blade. Narrower and turned around the other way so the cutting edge is on the opposite side to the initial injury.'

'So, the second knife was carefully inserted into the existing injury?'

'It was,' said Poland, nodding.

'OK. So, we've got an elderly man who hears a diesel engine and a suspect, Stanniland, who drives a diesel van. Then we've got an elderly woman who hears a motorbike and a second knife wound.'

'You think it was two people?'

Dixon nodded.

'Could've been, I suppose,' said Poland.

'I'm thinking Janice was blinded by the DNA. One profile equals one person. Therefore, the elderly woman must be wrong. Add to that the fact that Stanniland drove a diesel van and you could be forgiven for thinking it was case closed.'

'You could.'

'So,' continued Dixon. 'Was it one person or two?'

'That's your dep . . .'

'If you "that's your department" me again, I'm gonna order you a vindaloo and watch you eat it,' said Dixon.

'Yes, it could've been two,' replied Poland, grinning.

'More likely, I'd have thought.'

'Why?'

'Why else would he bother to hide the fatal injury inside an existing stab wound? Stanniland would've just stabbed her again, surely?'

'Possibly.'

'All right, ask yourself this. If it was Stanniland, why would he suddenly take so much care when he's been dropping cigarette butts on the landing and puking up in the garden?'

'True.'

'And why is he murdered by the Albanians a few days later?'

'Really?'

'We fished him out of the sea on Saturday.'

'Bloody hell.'

'We've got no DNA trace in a pile of vomit and the man we are supposed to believe it came from had Barrett's oesophagus . . .'

'Stomach acid.'

'Exactly,' said Dixon. 'So, if the vomit was kept for any length of time the DNA trace in it would've disintegrated.'

Poland nodded.

'How long was it between the initial stab wounds and the one that killed her?' asked Dixon.

'I'd say about ten minutes, judging by the blood loss.'

'Would she have died anyway, without the second knife wound?'

'Depends when she was found. She wouldn't have lasted more than a few hours, at best, but the milkman at 6 a.m. may have been in time to save her.'

'But she would've appeared dead, wouldn't she?'

'You would've felt a pulse but to all intents and purposes she'd have looked dead.'

'So, Stanniland leaves thinking he's killed her. Our Albanian motorcyclist then goes in to drop the cigarette and the vomit, finds her still alive and does the necessary. It all fits, Roger.'

'Why though?'

'To make sure Stanniland gets caught. He wouldn't dare talk and it keeps it clean and simple.'

'But, why did the Albanians want her dead?'

'Money's my guess,' replied Dixon. 'They were paid.'

'Who by?'

'Don't know yet.'

'You were sticking your neck out a bit on the TV, weren't you? Ruling out the husband . . .'

'I'm paid to use my judgement,' replied Dixon. 'I used it. Is there anything you can tell me about the second knife wound? Was he left or right handed, perhaps?'

'Impossible to say. She was lying face down on the floor when the knife was inserted slowly and then pushed straight down. The markers we use to determine that just aren't there.'

'We need to know, Roger.'

'I'll open her up and have another look then, now that I know where you're going with this.'

'Thanks.'

'You owe me a curry.'

'A vindaloo?'

'Piss off.'

Chapter Twelve

Dixon arrived back at Express Park just after 4 p.m. His old windscreen wipers had only just kept up with the volume of water out on the M5 as he drove north and it had been a relief to get off the motorway. He parked on the top floor of the car park, ran across to the staff entrance and was still shaking the water off his coat as he walked along the landing to the CID area on the first floor.

Jane and Mark Pearce were sitting side by side at workstations in the window. Louise was on the telephone and Dave Harding was staring at his computer screen, although he had the look of a man whose eyes had glazed over some time ago.

Dixon waited until Louise had finished her call.

'What've we got then?'

'Mrs Freeman's staying with her sister in Langport.'

'Good,' replied Dixon. 'What about you, Dave?'

Dave Harding sat back in his chair and pointed at the screen in front of him.

'Timed at 2.27 a.m. Christmas Eve. Junction 24, on the southbound slip road.'

Dixon walked over and stood behind him. The image was grainy and taken from an overhead camera, but it clearly showed a motorcycle travelling down the southbound on slip. The rider was wearing black from head to toe: black leathers and a full face helmet.

'Can we get it enhanced?'

'High Tech are working on it now,' replied Harding.

Dixon nodded.

'What about the number plate? A577 RYB is it?' asked Dixon, squinting at the screen.

'Registered to a Volvo 340 in the name of Edith Rosemary Craven. She died in 1989.'

'See if those plates crop up anywhere else in the system.'

'I'm on it, Sir.'

'Not exactly a modern bike, is it?'

'Possibly an old Triumph, something like that.'

'What about further down?'

'We've got this timed at 2.39 at junction 25,' replied Harding, clicking on another photograph. 'Then this one at Taunton Deane services five minutes later.'

'He's not travelling very fast,' said Dixon.

'It's dark, the roads are wet and it's raining in this one,' replied Harding.

'Any more?'

'Just looking now.'

'Keep at it then, Dave. Well done.'

Dixon watched Harding maximise a second window and click 'Play' on the camera footage. The time stamp told him all he needed to know; 'CAM 1335 M5 (J27) 0255'. The camera was looking north and the motorway was dark, illuminated only by the lights on the off slip. Dixon paused, wondering when the next vehicle might appear, but nothing seemed to be moving in either direction.

Harding spoke just as he turned away.

'There we are.'

Dixon turned back to the screen to see a single headlight travelling in the nearside lane, straight towards the camera. He watched it pass underneath the camera and disappear from view.

'On to junction 28,' said Harding.

'Cullompton,' said Dixon. 'Sing out if you get anything.'

'Will do.'

'What about you, Jane? What've you got?'

'We've looked at all the campaigns Tom Perry's been involved in since he was selected last year. There's Hinkley C, but he's just one of a number of voices in favour of that. He's proud of his green credentials too, according to his website. He's against the pylons that'll go north from the new reactor to Avonmouth, saying they should go under the sea or underground, and is in favour of the tidal lagoon in Bridgwater Bay.'

'He's in favour of solar power too,' said Pearce. 'But in the right place, so he's supporting residents opposing the solar panel farm at Brent Knoll. He seems to be a bit of a sceptic when it comes to wind turbines though. He's campaigning against the wind farm between East and West Huntspill.'

'What about housing developments?'

'The only contentious one is on the edge of Burtle,' said Pearce. 'That's five hundred houses.'

'We're compiling a list of the players in each case, on both sides of the argument, and can let you have it later today,' said Jane.

'Anything else?'

'He's a big supporter of the Flooding on the Levels Action Group, or FLAG, but then everyone is. It's why he rented in Northmoor Green. To be among them.'

'To feel their pain,' said Harding, without turning away from his screen.

'I think he's done that, don't you, Dave,' said Dixon. 'It's a body and crime scene to us, but it's his wife and his home. And he's lost them both.'

'Sorry.'

'Anything else?' asked Dixon, turning back to Jane and Mark Pearce.

'His selection seems to have been a bit of a nightmare. Not sure I can make head or tail of it, to be honest. I printed off this from the *Bridgwater Mercury*,' said Jane, handing a piece of paper to Dixon. He looked at the headline.

'Bridgwater and North Somerset Tories Ignore Primary Vote.'

Dixon read aloud.

'Last night a meeting of the executive council of Bridgwater and North Somerset Conservatives refused to ratify the selection of Tom Perry as prospective parliamentary candidate for the party in the forthcoming general election, despite his selection having been made by local people at an open primary. The meeting was attended by Somerset County Councillor Rod Brophy, one of the candidates defeated by Mr Perry at the open selection. Mr Brophy declined to comment.'

'Is there anything else?'

'I didn't see anything,' replied Jane.

'It says here, "The selection is expected to be rerun behind closed doors." Perry must've won again though, mustn't he?' asked Dixon.

'I suppose he must,' replied Jane.

Dixon folded the piece of paper and put it in his jacket pocket. 'I'll take this. You concentrate on the campaigns.'

'All right.'

'You got anything, Dave?'

'Stayed on at junction 28, so I'm watching 29 and 30 now. Exeter.'

Dixon was making a cup of coffee when Harding shouted over to him.

'Stayed on at 29 and 30, Sir.'

'So, what does that leave?'

'A30 west to Okehampton, Plymouth on the A38 or Torquay on the A380.'

'Louise, see if we can go and see Mrs Freeman tomorrow morning, will you?'

'It's New Year's Eve.'

'I'm sure she won't mind.'

'And if she does?'

'Remind her it's a murder investigation.'

'Stayed on the M5 at the A30 intersection,' said Harding. 'Watching the roadworks at Splatford Split now.'

Dixon walked over and stood behind Harding, drinking his coffee.

'There he is,' said Harding pointing at the screen. 'Just going into the fifty limit.'

The motorbike stayed in the nearside lane.

'That's Torquay then, isn't it?'

'Or Newton Abbot,' replied Harding. 'The next camera will be at Pen Inn roundabout. Should take him about fifteen minutes.'

'Good.'

'Here's the email from High Tech. It's a bit sharper. Shall I forward it to you?'

'Print it, will you, Dave.'

'Mrs Freeman is expecting us at 9 a.m. tomorrow, Sir. Is that all right?' asked Louise.

'Fine,' replied Dixon, walking over to a printer that was churning out a piece of paper. 'Yes, that's better. Let's identify the make and model then. Get it over to Traffic and see if they can tell us what it is.'

'Yes, Sir.'

'Anything at Pen Inn, Dave?'

'Nothing yet. I started ten minutes after he passed the last camera so it should be about right.'

'What's between Exeter and Newton Abbot on the A380?' asked Dixon.

'Chudleigh on the right, Teignmouth. Kingsteignton. Loads of villages.'

Dixon waited, watching Harding's eyes scanning the screen.

'No, nothing,' said Harding. 'I'll check the town cameras in Teignmouth.'

'You won't be able to do that until tomorrow now,' said Dixon, checking his watch. 'It's gone five.'

'Shit.'

'You head off, Dave. Be back here at 8 a.m. for an early start. And you, Louise.'

'Yes, Sir.'

'What about you two?'

'Nearly finished,' said Pearce.

'I'll bring it with me and see you at home,' said Jane.

'OK,' replied Dixon. 'Feed Monty if you get there first, will you? I need to have a word with Tom Perry.'

The front door of the bungalow opened as Dixon reached up for the bell and he lurched back just in time to avoid the large golf umbrella that sprang open in front of him.

'Sorry!' The voice came from behind the umbrella, which was lifted up by a tall man with dark curly hair, greying at the sides. He wore brown corduroys and a sleeveless padded jacket over a brown check shirt. He stepped out onto the garden path, holding the umbrella over himself and Dixon.

'This is Inspector Dixon, Barry,' said Tom Perry, from his position in the doorway. 'Inspector, this is Barry Dossett, our area campaign director.'

Dixon and Barry Dossett shook hands.

'I saw you on the TV, Inspector. And you were right, the electorate would take a dim view of us if we tried to deselect him.'

Dixon nodded.

'You should go into politics,' continued Dossett.

'No, thanks.'

'I'll be on my way then, Tom,' said Dossett, turning back to Perry. 'I'll await your call on Thursday.'

'Fine,' replied Perry.

Dixon watched Dossett stride down the garden path and across to the new Land Rover Discovery parked on the other side of the road, in front of his old Defender.

'Did you want something?' asked Perry.

'A word, if you've got a minute,' replied Dixon, wiping the raindrops from the end of his nose.

'You'd better come in.'

Perry closed the door behind Dixon.

'Tea?'

'Thank you.'

'We'll go through to the kitchen. My parents are watching the news in there.'

The living room door was open and Dixon recognised the familiar jingle of the BBC News Channel as he followed Perry along the passageway into the kitchen.

'Take a seat,' said Perry, gesturing to a small table against the wall, just inside the back door. 'Sugar?'

'No thanks.'

'Are you here to ask questions or tell me what's going on?'

'Questions,' replied Dixon.

'Best get on with it then.'

'What's the significance of Thursday?'

'I've got until then to decide if I'm going to fight the election.'

'Was there a move to deselect you?'

'There was but Central Office got involved and put a stop to it. I'm told I have you to thank for that.'

'Me?'

'What you said on the telly.'

Dixon smiled.

'What are you going to do?' he asked.

'I don't know yet.'

Dixon watched Perry stir the tea and then throw the teaspoon into the sink.

'I can't get it out of my head that someone killed Lizzie to stop me standing,' said Perry, placing a mug on the table in front of Dixon. 'What would you do?'

'If someone tries to stop me doing something it tends to make me more inclined to do it.'

'Me too.'

'And you said it's what your wife would want you to do?'

'It is.'

'Do it then.'

'What about *them*?'

'You leave them to me.'

Dixon watched Perry staring into his tea and waited.

'You had some questions?'

'How did you get into politics?' asked Dixon.

'My parents brought me up with a very strong sense of duty and . . .'

'I'm not a journalist,' said Dixon.

Perry smiled. 'No, of course not.'

'Give me the real answer. Just between us.'

'An old fashioned notion about wanting to help people, I suppose,' replied Perry. 'And it's got to be better than working for a living. I've always hated being an architect.'

'Isn't it well paid?'

'Not as well as you might think, and certainly not in a small firm on Richmond Green. I can't even pretend that I'm terribly good at it either.'

'Really?'

'Yes, I'd much rather be out and about, meeting people. The corridors of power and all that, too,' replied Perry, shrugging his shoulders.

'Is that it?' asked Dixon.

'Vanity and ambition played a part, if I'm being brutally honest.'

'You are.'

'Everyone'll tell you they go into politics to represent people and help their communities but that's bollocks. You don't go into politics to represent, you go into politics to govern.'

'That confirms what I've always thought,' said Dixon, smiling.

'What?'

'That those who seek elected office are the last people who should hold it.'

'You're probably right,' replied Perry, laughing. 'But don't quote me on it.'

'I won't.'

Dixon loosened his tie and undid the top button of his shirt.

'Are you all right?' asked Perry.

Dixon was fumbling in his jacket pockets. He sighed. 'Have you got a biscuit or something I could have. I seem to be out of fruit pastilles.'

'Blood sugar, is it?' asked Perry, getting up and walking over to the kitchen cupboards.

'Yes.'

'Lizzie was diabetic, so I know the signs.' Perry placed a large biscuit barrel on the table in front of Dixon and took off the lid. 'Help yourself.'

'Thanks.'

'What insulin are you on?' asked Perry.

'Betalin,' replied Dixon, through a mouthful of digestive biscuit.

'Is that a human insulin?'

Dixon nodded.

'Are you all right on it?'

'When I remember to eat.'

'No side effects?'

'No.'

'It didn't agree with Lizzie. Damned near killed her . . .' Perry closed his eyes and took a deep breath. 'Sometimes I forget. Just for a second.'

'I understand,' said Dixon. 'What happened?'

'She switched to animal insulin and was fine after that.'

Dixon was watching Perry. His eyes had glazed over and he was breathing deeply, so Dixon banged the lid on the biscuit barrel, as loudly as he dared without breaking it, and slid it across the table.

'Here, you'd better take these away before I eat the lot.'

Perry sat up with a jolt.

'Done the trick?' he asked.

'Yes, just in time, thank you.'

'Good.'

'Tell me about Lizzie,' said Dixon.

'God, where do I start?' asked Perry, shaking his head. 'She was beautiful, funny, loyal, kind. Why she picked me I'll never know.' His eyes welled up with tears.

'Tell me about the process then. How did you get selected?' asked Dixon, changing the subject.

'The first thing you have to do is join the party and get involved. Deliver lots of leaflets and go canvassing, that sort of thing. Show willing so you get a good reference from your association chairman when the time comes. I stood for the council in my local ward too. That always looks good on a CV.'

'Did you win?'

'God, no. I wouldn't have done it if there'd been a chance of me winning. The last thing I wanted was to become a bloody councillor.'

Dixon nodded.

'Go on.'

'Then I applied to get on the Approved List. You have to be on the list before you can apply for a parliamentary seat.'

'And what does that involve?'

'The Parliamentary Selection Board. A day of psychometric testing, speaking tests and other hoops they make you jump through. Mine was held at Boreham Hall.'

'And you passed?'

'I did. First time, oddly enough. I had to speak for five minutes on the use of genetically modified crops. Easy.'

'What then?'

'Well, then you're on the Approved List. You pay your eighty quid and become a member of the Approved Conservative Candidates Association, which enables you to apply for a parliamentary seat when a constituency advertises a vacancy.'

'And you applied to Bridgwater and North Somerset?'

'I did. And got lucky. Well, I thought it was lucky at the time.'

'Why?'

'I got on the list late and most of the other seats had already selected so there were only a few of us left when North Somerset advertised. It's a safe seat too. Thirty years an MP and then retire to the House of Lords. Lizzie used to joke about it. Lord and Lady Perry of Northmoor Green, she'd say. Or something like that. And a pension to die f . . .'

'What happened when you applied?' asked Dixon, trying to distract Perry.

'The selection committee met to sift through the CVs and I got through to the first round. Eight of us did. Then it's a ten minute speech about why I was the right candidate for North Somerset and twenty minutes of questions from the selection committee. That took place at the Bridgwater Con Club.'

'And who's on this selection committee?'

'Two representatives from each ward in the constituency is the usual rule, I think. Barbara Sumner, the old association chairman, was there. And the agent, Lawrence Deakin. Barry was there too, but just as an observer. I don't really remember who else was there.'

'What does the agent do?' asked Dixon, shaking his head. 'I don't really . . .'

'He's a paid employee of the Association. It's his job to ensure we comply with the party constitution and the law,' replied Perry. 'Not an easy job. I wouldn't want it.'

'And Barry Dossett?'

'The area campaign director. He's like a senior agent or regional sales manager, I suppose. He covers Bristol, Avon and Somerset, Devon and Cornwall, I think. Possibly Gloucestershire too.'

'Must've gone all right then, the selection committee?'

'Yes, it did. Someone gave me a hard time about green policy, or tried to, but I handled them OK.'

'Who was that?'

'I can't remember who asked the initial question; how green are you or something like that; but the follow ups came from Liam

Dobbs, now I come to think of it. He was the deputy chairman political.'

'Was?'

'Yes, he resigned after the final selection meeting.'

'Tell me about the final selection then.'

'There were three us. Me, Rod Brophy and Jenny Parker. She's since been selected for one of the Bristol seats, but the General Election is not for another sixteen months, don't forget. I'm the only one with a by-election.'

Dixon nodded.

'It was an open primary at the Hollingsworth Hall, down at Canalside in Bridgwater . . .'

'What's an open primary?'

'The meeting was open to any registered elector in the constituency, not just party members. Not sure of the point of it, really, apart from making for a bit of extra publicity.'

'And what happened?' asked Dixon.

'I won. At the first vote too. No need for second preferences.'

Dixon raised his eyebrows.

'It's an odd voting system,' continued Perry. 'Alternative Voting, or something like that. They rank the candidates in order of preference.'

'What happened then?'

'That's when it all got a bit messy. The executive council refused to ratify the outcome of the primary and so the selection process had to start again. Only this time they held it behind closed doors. Party members only. Central Office went berserk. Hold an open primary to include local electors and then ignore their democratic vote. It was a PR disaster.'

'But you won again?'

'I did,' replied Perry. 'Didn't expect to, but I did.'

'Who was behind it?' asked Dixon.

'Rod Brophy and his cronies, from what I can gather. You've got to remember that I was just the new candidate at that time so I didn't have any real idea who anyone was. I knew the chairman, the ACD and the agent but that was it, really, so I'm getting all this second and third hand. But it was a small group of Brophy's supporters. They stuffed the executive council meeting and tried to do the same when the final selection was rerun, only it didn't work. Politics is a dirty business, Nick,' said Perry. 'Can I call you Nick?'

'You can, Mr Perry.'

Perry frowned.

'Tom,' said Dixon.

'Too many vain and ambitious people, jostling for position.'

'What's the executive council?' asked Dixon.

'All powerful,' replied Perry. 'They have to approve all candidates, the accounts. They're basically the scrutiny committee overseeing what the management committee do.'

'And who's on it?'

'There'll be a list of attendees kept at each meeting.'

'And the management committee?'

'That was Brophy's power base, I think, and they all resigned after the final selection. Barbara Sumner's three years as chairman were up at the next AGM anyway. Not sure she was in on it, though. Both deputy chairmen resigned immediately, as did the treasurer and the two co-opted members.'

'Names?'

'Liam Dobbs was deputy chairman political, and Gail Mackay was membership and fund raising. Patricia Taylor was the treasurer and the two co-opted members were Iris Warner and Bob Cartwright.'

'What happened to them?' asked Dixon, scribbling down the list of names on his notepad.

'They're still around, I think. Don't see 'em. I've got a feeling that a couple of them have joined UKIP, but I may be wrong about that.'

'And what about Rod Brophy?'

'He's still around. He's Conservative group leader on Somerset County Council. Sits on Sedgemoor District Council too, so he's not going anywhere in a hurry.'

'Where's his seat?'

'Burnham North. He lives in Rectory Road,' replied Perry. 'Do you know it?'

'I do,' replied Dixon. 'What about this attempt to deselect you?'

'It hadn't really got off the ground. Dobbs was trying to engineer an emergency executive council meeting, apparently. Ringing around trying to muster a bit of support.'

'He's still on the executive council?'

'Yes. He resigned from the management committee but stays on the exec because he's ward chairman in Highbridge.'

'Who is he?'

'Young fellow. Runs a small graphic design business in Bridgwater, I think. Fancies his chances at being an MP one day too, I expect.'

'It hadn't got very far then?'

'No. They were doing it out of concern for me, they said. I might be a bit distracted from the campaign, need time. You can just imagine it, can't you?'

'You were going to think about the campaigns you're involved in at the moment?' asked Dixon.

'There's nothing,' replied Perry, shaking his head. 'The only one that's remotely contentious is the wind farm at East Huntspill. I suppose you could call it contentious.'

'Is it likely to go ahead?'

'It's early days. I hope not.'

'And your involvement?' asked Dixon.

'I galvanised local residents, got them organised into an action group. We got 'no to the wind farm' signs produced, petitions, letter writing campaigns. That sort of stuff. I spoke at a public meeting in the village hall too. Westricity were livid. Refused to send a rep to the meeting.'

Dixon nodded.

'They did an exhibition of the plans and I organised a demonstration outside. They were furious.'

'Did Lizzie go?'

'Yes, she did,' replied Perry, smiling. 'I was standing on a wall outside the hall with a megaphone. It was great fun.'

Dixon was scribbling in his notebook.

'Wind farms have their place,' continued Perry. 'Offshore, for example. But local residents don't want it and I'm there to represent them.'

'What about the other campaigns?'

'Hinkley C,' replied Perry, 'but I just jumped on that bandwagon, really. Everyone's against the pylons to Avonmouth. I'm in favour of the tidal barrage in Bridgwater Bay even though it'll never happen in my lifetime. Got to appear green, these days,' said Perry, shrugging his shoulders.

'Isn't there a planning application at Burtle?' asked Dixon.

'That'll never happen either.'

'Why not?'

'It's not in the local plan for a start. And how big's Burtle?' Fifty houses? It'll destroy the place. It's pie in the sky and the developer knows it.'

'Who is the developer?'

'The local farmer, but no doubt there's a house builder behind him ready to go if permission's granted. He'll keep reducing the number of houses until he gets it, even if it takes twenty years.'

'Wasn't there one about solar panels?'

'East Brent. That'll go through. Sad, isn't it, when a farmer's most profitable crop is solar panels.'

Dixon closed his notebook and slipped it back inside his jacket pocket. 'One last question.'

'Fire away.'

'What will happen if you don't stand?'

Perry shrugged his shoulders.

'There won't be enough time left before close of nominations to rerun the selection, so they'll probably hand it to Brophy.'

Chapter Thirteen

'Working with Louise now, is it?' asked Jane, before Dixon had closed the back door of the cottage.

'Are you jealous?'

'I'm just kidding.' She put her arms around him and kissed him. 'How'd you get on with Perry?'

'Surprisingly honest, for a politician . . .'

'He's a Tory,' protested Jane.

'He is,' replied Dixon, smiling. 'Anyway, he's hardly your stereotypical Alan B'Stard, is he? And more's to the point, he's lost and bewildered. His wife's dead and he has no idea why.'

'You'll find out,' said Jane.

Monty appeared from behind the table in the corner of the kitchen and started jumping up at Dixon.

'Finally managed to tear yourself away from your food bowl, have you?'

'Yours is in the microwave,' said Jane. 'I've pierced the lid, so all you've got to do is switch it on.'

'Thanks.'

Jane sat on the sofa and began flicking through the channels on the TV remote control.

'Did you bring that stuff home?' asked Dixon, shouting from the kitchen, over the noise of the microwave.

'I've got it here.'

Dixon waited for the ping and then dragged the plastic container out of the microwave and onto a tray. Then he picked up a spoon and walked into the lounge.

Jane rolled her eyes.

'You could've . . .'

'What's the point?' interrupted Dixon. 'It tastes the same and saves washing up.'

Jane dropped a green file onto his lap. 'That's what we've got so far.'

'Anything stand out?'

'Lots of press interest in the wind farm between East and West Huntspill.'

'That's the one that Perry said was the most contentious. Westricity, isn't it?'

'Yes,' replied Jane. 'They're behind the solar panel application at East Brent too.'

'Have you done a company search?'

'No.'

'Do one. Let's see who the directors and shareholders are.'

'What'd he say about the selection?' asked Jane.

'You wouldn't believe me if I told you.'

'Try me.'

'It was an open primary they call it, so you get local people to select your candidate for you. Then you ignore them. Brilliant!'

'Who are these people?'

'I don't know. But, I'm bloody well going to find out.'

Dixon flicked through the file of papers while he waited for his chicken korma to cool down. One member of the wind farm action group had an ancient conviction for assault but that was hardly likely to be relevant. Otherwise it was a catalogue of newspaper articles, profiles of those involved on both sides, and a report of an incident at a public exhibition in West Huntspill Village Hall. The leader of the action group had been cautioned for a breach of the peace after ripping down parts of the display. Tempers had got a bit frayed, according to the witnesses.

Dixon finished his curry and took Monty for a walk, leaving Jane watching the TV. It had stopped raining, so they kept going past the Red Cow and turned left up the hill. Monty was sniffing along the hedge on his long lead and taking the chance to paddle in every puddle he came across, but Dixon was miles away, trying to tackle the case from both ends at the same time.

Start with the murder and work back. John Stanniland had almost killed Elizabeth Perry and then the mystery motorcyclist had finished the job and seen to it that Stanniland got caught. Only they hadn't banked on PGL contaminating the DNA sample leaving a loose end to be tied up, Albanian style. It made sense and they were closing in on the motorcyclist.

Coming at it from the other end was turning up lots of possibilities but nothing with any substance to it. Feelings run high in politics and it wouldn't be the first time that an unwelcome planning application in someone's back yard had led to murder, but that still didn't explain why Elizabeth Perry had been murdered rather than Tom. Dixon was missing something. He knew that.

'What time did you come to bed?' asked Jane. 'Coffee?'

'Must have been about twoish. Yes, please.'

'You weren't out walking all that time?'

'No,' replied Dixon, handing Jane a piece of paper.

'What's this?'

'A list of names. It's the ringleaders in that selection fiasco. The ones who tried to get rid of Perry. I want everything we've got on them. Company directorships too. Let's see if any of them are connected with Westricity, or anyone else for that matter.'

'OK,' said Jane. 'What're you up to?'

'I'm going to see Mrs Freeman then we'll ruffle a few feathers at the Conservative office.'

'We?'

'Yes, me and Lou . . . are you winding me up again?'

Jane smiled.

'Just be careful. Remember, the Albanians are in the mix.'

'I know, I know,' replied Dixon.

Dixon thought about his last encounter with the Albanians as he walked across to his Land Rover. He remembered the feeling of a gun barrel in the small of his back and the words of their leader, Zavan.

I hope our interests never conflict.

'What's the address?'

'Flat 2, Fisher's Bridge Mill,' replied Louise. 'It'll be a converted mill. Down by the river, I suppose.'

'Langport hasn't flooded, has it?' asked Dixon.

'No.'

Louise was peering over her shoulder, watching Monty, who was standing with his front paws on the back of her seat.

'He's fine. Just likes to see where we're going, that's all,' said Dixon.

'Does he go everywhere with you?'

'Pretty much.'

Dixon could handle an arson attack on his cottage. It was rented, after all. But not if his dog was home alone. And the Albanians knew where he lived.

'Why are we seeing Mrs Freeman again?' asked Louise.

'I want to see just how deaf she is,' said Dixon.

'Take the next left,' said Louise. 'Whatley Lane. It's a dead end.'

A large four storey converted mill was visible at the far end. It was built of grey stone, with the top two floors clad in timber, and had retained its large oval doors on the ground floor, although these were now glazed and looked like patio doors. The front entrance was at the side. Dixon parked in the visitors' parking space, walked over to the low wall on the far side of the car park and looked down at the river.

'Difficult to imagine it's caused such bloody havoc lower down.'

'There's more rain to come, according to the forecast last night,' replied Louise.

Dixon shook his head.

'Let's get this over with.'

Dixon rang the bell for flat 2 and listened at the small speaker.

'Yes.'

'Inspector Dixon to see Mrs Freeman.'

The lock in the glazed front door buzzed so he reached up and grabbed the handle, wrenching it open before the buzzing stopped. The hallway was dark but Dixon could make out a figure at the far end silhouetted against a window. She was waving to them.

'Mrs Freeman?'

'Joyce. You want Edna. She's in here.'

'Thank you.'

'She's not too good at the moment. It's all been a bit of a shock for her, I'm afraid,' whispered Joyce.

'Was she insured?' asked Dixon.

'Yes, and her neighbours were very helpful. Got everything they could upstairs.'

'They've got the pumps working now,' said Louise. 'And . . .'

'She'll never go back. Not now. Not unless they dredge the river. She'd be too frightened it'd happen again.'

They followed Joyce into her flat and along the corridor to a lounge with a large window overlooking the river. Edna Freeman was sitting in a chair, with a blanket over her legs. The television was on, but she was watching the water swirling past the old mill. Joyce leaned forward and spoke into her left ear.

'The police are here, Edna.'

She looked up and smiled at Dixon. He fumbled in his pocket for his warrant card.

'There's no need for that,' said Edna, waving it away.

'Do you think we might turn the television off?' asked Dixon.

'Yes, of course,' replied Joyce. 'Would you like a cup of tea?'

'No, thank you,' replied Dixon. 'This won't take long.'

'I'll leave you to it,' said Joyce.

Dixon turned to Edna. 'You gave a statement to my colleagues about Christmas Eve?' he whispered.

Edna Freeman smiled.

'You're testing me, aren't you? If I was ten years younger I'd put you over my knee.'

'You heard me though, didn't you?'

'I did. If there's no background noise I'm fine.'

'When you heard the motorbike on Christmas Eve, did you have the telly on?'

'No.'

'Radio?'

'No. I'd been asleep. It was deathly quiet.'

'What woke you up?'

'I don't know.'

'Tell me about your husband,' said Dixon.

'He loved his motorbikes. I used to ride pillion in the early days but then he had to get a sidecar for me. We went all over Europe once. That was on a Triumph Bonneville.'

'What other bikes did he have?'

'It was a BSA 500 when we met, then the Triumph and two Nortons. I've still got the last one. He never sold it. It's in the shed.'

'All British,' said Dixon.

'Of course,' replied Edna, smiling.

'Did you ride?'

'No. Only ever pillion or in the sidecar. I never learned to drive either.'

'So, the bike you heard that night, was it British?'

'Yes.'

'You can tell from the sound of the engine?'

'Oh, yes. They're distinctive, like a Rolls Royce Merlin. Not high pitched or tinny like the modern rubbish. And definitely not a Harley Davidson.'

Dixon reached into his inside jacket pocket and took out four folded pieces of paper. He unfolded them and then flattened them over his thigh. Then he passed the top one to Edna.

'Do you wear glasses?'

'Yes, they're here, dear,' she said, picking a pair up off the coffee table beside her. She put them on and looked at the piece of paper.

'It's a Norton Commando. Do you have any other photos of it?'

Dixon handed her the other photographs. She stared at them one by one.

'Yes, there we are. Exhausts on both sides. That makes it the SS type. If they're on one side it's the S type but high level exhausts on both sides is the SS type. The one in my shed is a 1970 Fastback, if it's not rusted away by now.'

'Will you be going home?' asked Dixon.

'I'd like to see them stop me.'

'Only your sister said . . .'

'If she thinks I'm going to sit here staring at that bloody river for the rest of my days, she's got another think coming!'

'They don't make 'em like that anymore,' said Dixon, walking across to his Land Rover. He was holding his phone to his ear.

'No, Sir,' replied Louise.

Dixon turned away. 'Yes, fine. Put Dave on, will you?'

'What've you got?'

Dixon nodded.

'Good. Right, Mrs Freeman has identified it as a Norton Commando SS type, so get onto DVLA. You know what we need. For the whole of Torbay. Then contact all of the Norton parts suppliers and local garages. Get a list of everyone they supply parts to. All right?'

'Well done, Dave.'

Dixon rang off.

'He's got it on a number plate recognition camera in St Marychurch, then it disappears,' said Dixon, climbing into the Land Rover.

Louise was already sitting in the passenger seat.

'Torquay?'

'Yes. Fancy a trip to the English Riviera?'

They looked more like residential barn conversions than offices, but the signs on the car parking spaces confirmed that Dixon was in the right place. Four of the spaces were marked 'Bridgwater and North Somerset Conservative Association' so he parked in one of those, next to a grey Vauxhall Astra. All of the other spaces were empty.

'Well, it is New Year's Eve, I suppose.'

'They probably got drunk at the Christmas party and left it here,' said Louise.

'There's a light on in the office,' said Dixon, peering over his shoulder. 'Let's go and try our luck.'

They were walking across the car park when the light went out and a tall figure appeared behind the frosted glass of the front door. A small black umbrella opened and the figure then stepped out into the rain. It was a man and he kept his head down as he turned to lock the door behind him. He turned when he heard footsteps walking up the steps behind him.

'I'm sorry, we're closed.'

'I'm surprised to find anyone here at all,' said Dixon, holding his warrant card in front of him. 'It is New Year's Eve, after all.'

The man leaned forward and squinted at Dixon's warrant card.

'We're in the middle of a by-election campaign, Inspector.'

'And you are?' asked Dixon.

'Lawrence Deakin. The agent.'

He was tall, thin and bald. Dixon reckoned he was in his late forties, or possibly his early fifties, but it was difficult to tell without a measure of grey hair. He was wearing jeans and an orange raincoat.

'May we have a word, please, Mr Deakin?'

'Well, I was just . . . yes, of course.' He turned back to the front door and opened it. 'Come in.'

Dixon and Louise followed Deakin into a small open plan office on the ground floor. There were four desks on the right, opposite a line of large printing machines.

'All of that stuff that gets pushed through your letter box gets printed here, Inspector,' said Deakin. 'We've even got a machine to fold it.'

Dixon nodded.

'The only bit we can't automate is delivering it. We rely on volunteers for that.'

'Not the postman?'

'Too expensive. Every candidate in a parliamentary election gets one leaflet delivered. That's the Election Address. But we like to deliver more than that.'

'So I've noticed,' said Dixon.

'Sorry about that.'

'You haven't asked why we're here.'

'I rather assumed you were going to tell me,' replied Deakin, sitting on the corner of one of the desks.

'How well did you know Elizabeth Perry?'

'I thought . . . wasn't her killer found washed up at Brean Down?' asked Deakin.

'He was. How well did you know her?'

'Well, I'd met her several times. First at the selection . . .'

'Selections,' interrupted Dixon.

'Yes, selections, then at dinners and such like, when Tom was speaking. She was always out campaigning with him too. Full of energy, she was. And great for the association, really brought everyone together.' Deakin sighed. 'Everybody thought she was lovely.'

'And Tom?'

'The same,' replied Deakin, nodding. 'I can't begin to imagine how he must be feeling . . .' His voice tailed off.

Dixon walked over to the window and looked at the fields behind the office block.

'Nice office,' he said, nodding. 'How long have you been the agent?'

'Six years.'

'So you know the membership fairly well?'

'I do. The active ones. I meet them at coffee mornings, dinners.'

'And the management committee. You work closely with them, I imagine?'

'Yes.'

'How well do you know Rod Brophy?'

'Very well. He's a past chairman of the association, councillor.'

'And Liam Dobbs?'

'Not so well. He's been a member, say, four years or so.'

'How involved were you in the selection process?'

'Very. It's my job to make sure it's done right. In accordance with the constitution and the party rules. I don't have a vote or a say in who is selected. That's for the members.'

'And the open primary?'

'We followed the correct procedure,' said Deakin.

'Whose idea was it to hold an open primary?'

'Central Office suggested it. The selection committee were reluctant but went along with it. I think they took the view that 90 per cent of the final audience would be party members anyway so what did it matter?'

'Why the reluctance?' asked Dixon.

'Fear of something new. The risk that the opposition stuff the meeting and select someone unsuitable . . .'

'But surely someone unsuitable wouldn't even make it through to the primary?'

'That's the counter argument, yes.'

'So, who was behind the move to reject the open primary selection?'

'Behind it?'

'Yes.'

Dixon waited, watching Deakin's eyes darting around the room.

'Look, I don't think it's any great secret that Rod Brophy regarded the seat as his when Ken stood down.'

'Or died,' said Louise.

'Yes, or died, as it turned out.'

'Was Brophy on the Approved list?' asked Dixon.

'No. But where there's a particularly strong local candidate an association can select them anyway.'

'So, was Central Office's insistence on an open primary an attempt by them to ensure Brophy didn't get it?'

'I don't think so. Look, what's this got to do with Elizabeth Perry's death?'

'You tell me,' replied Dixon.

'I don't know.'

'What happened after the primary?'

'The executive council met to ratify the selection, only they didn't.'

'Was that a surprise?'

'Yes.'

'How many people attended the meeting?'

'Thirty or so.'

'And how many people usually attend a meeting of the executive council?'

'Twenty perhaps.'

'And what did you think when you saw a full house?'

'I don't remember,' said Deakin, standing up. 'It was an important meeting. Look I really need to be . . .'

'How did Central Office react?'

'They weren't happy about it. Threatened to put the constituency on special measures.'

'Which are?'

'Basically, they step in and take over running it.'

'But that didn't happen?'

'No.'

'So, tell me about the final selection. How did Tom Perry win if there was an orchestrated effort by Brophy to stuff the meeting, as he had done the executive?'

'I didn't say he had.'

'You didn't have to.'

'It's the nature of politics, even in the same party when we're all supposed to be on the same side. For every supporter you've got, there's another who hates you,' said Deakin. 'Or supports someone else.'

'So, the stop Rod Brophy brigade had time to get their act together?' asked Dixon.

'They did.'

'What about the ballot at the executive meeting?'

'Secret. All I've got are the numbers.'

'Can I see the minutes?'

'They're confidential,' replied Deakin.

'And what d'you think confidential means in the context of a murder investigation?' asked Dixon.

'Look, what has this got to do with Elizabeth's murder?'

'You let me worry about that, Mr Deakin. All right?'

Deakin sighed.

'I'll get them.'

'Thank you. For that meeting and for the previous three as well, please.'

'You certainly know how to rub someone up the wrong way.'

'Thank you, Louise,' said Dixon, smiling.

They were sitting in his Land Rover, listening to the rain hammering on the roof. Dixon was flicking through the minutes of the executive council meetings.

'What it gives us is a list of those who turned up just to block the primary selection.'

'And one of them may have killed Elizabeth Perry.'

'Had her killed is a more accurate description, but yes, one of them may have done.'

'Why?'

'That's what we've got to find out, isn't it,' replied Dixon, reversing the Land Rover out of the parking space. Then he stamped on the brakes.

'What is it?' asked Louise.

'At least we know where to come to find Mr Dobbs,' said Dixon, looking in his rear view mirror. 'Dobbs Design. Not a very imaginative name for a graphic design company, is it?'

'Any sign of Unwin?' asked Dixon. He had done his injection in the Land Rover and was eating a sandwich bought from the canteen on the way to the CID area.

Jane shook her head.

'Where does he live?'

'Moorland.'

'Could be staying with friends somewhere then, couldn't he?' asked Louise.

'Either that or he's at the bottom of the . . .'

'How did you get on at the Conservative office?' asked Jane, cutting in.

'Good,' replied Louise. 'The agent was there and . . .'

'Get a boat over to Moorland to have a look,' said Dixon.

'They've been,' replied Jane.

'What've we got then, Dave?' asked Dixon, turning to Harding.

'Thirteen Nortons registered with DVLA in the TQ postcode area. That was the simplest way to do it, but it takes in Newton Abbot and Totnes too, so we can disregard some of them.'

'Are these the SS type?'

'The registration isn't that specific, sadly, so this is all Nortons.'

'How many in Torbay itself?'

'Seven.'

'What about off road notifications?'

'They're included.'

'And the parts suppliers and garages?'

'They add another three to the list. One was a PO box but I got the address from the post office,' replied Harding, handing a piece of paper to Dixon.

'Well done.'

Dixon looked at his watch. It was just after 1.30 p.m. 'Torquay anyone?'

'Er, I was due off at four, Sir. Got a party to go to tonight,' said Pearce.

'It's New Year's Eve, Sir,' said Harding.

'What about you, Louise?'

'I'll come. I'll just ring my husband and let him know.'

'I might as well come too,' said Harding, with a heavy sigh. 'I'll only be sitting at home watching Jools Holland and feeling sorry for myself.'

'Billy no mates,' said Pearce, grinning.

'Right, you and me, Louise. Dave, you go with Jane. We'll split the list and be back by six.'

'Yes, Sir.'

'There are three in Torquay and two each in Paignton and Brixham,' continued Dixon, looking at the list. 'We'll take Torquay, Louise. Look for a roadworthy SS type with the high exhaust pipes on both sides.'

'Yes, Sir.'

'And remember, if you find one and I'm right, you'll be talking to someone who kills people for a living, so no heroics. A few general questions, eliminating from enquiries, the usual flannel, then get the hell out of there. All right?'

'Yes, Sir.'

'Mark, if you could just ring the Devon lot and let them know we'll be on their patch, that'd be great. If you can fit us in before you go off partying, that is?'

Chapter Fourteen

It was just before 3 p.m. when Dixon parked in Henbury Close, a modern development of terraced town houses set back off the main road, just along from Torquay Football Club at Plainmoor. The floodlights were visible over the rooftops, but they were off and all was quiet.

'Bet it's chaos here on a match day,' said Dixon. 'Number 16's in the far corner over there.'

The garages and parking spaces were some distance from the houses themselves, which fronted onto a communal garden area. Louise followed him across the grass and waited behind him while he rang the doorbell.

'Mr Treadwell?'

'Yes.' He was in his late sixties and was wearing a dressing gown and pyjamas.

'My name is Detective Inspector Dixon and this is PC Willmott. We understand you're the registered owner of a Norton motorcycle.'

'I did a SORN thing, the off road notification. You can't do me for not renewing the road tax.'

'It's not about that, Mr Treadwell. May we see the bike, please?'

'Why?'

'A Norton motorcycle was involved in an incident a week or so ago and we're just eliminating bikes from our enquiries at this stage.'

Treadwell nodded. 'Hang on,' he said, closing the door. Dixon could see him through the pane of glass rummaging in the pockets of a coat hanging on the wall behind the door. 'Here you go,' he said. He handed a set of keys to Dixon, holding it by the smallest key.

'That's the garage key. It's that block over there. Third one along. Just push the keys through the letter box when you've finished.'

Dixon watched the door slam, looked at Louise, and raised his eyebrows.

'Takes all sorts, I suppose.'

'What's his problem, I wonder?' asked Louise.

'Did you see the cannula in the back of his left hand?' asked Dixon. 'C'mon. Let's go and have a look at this Norton.'

The number 16 painted in large black letters on the white garage door confirmed that they had the right garage and Dixon inserted the key in the lock. Then he lifted the up and over door, holding it up in one hand while he peered underneath it.

'Is there a light?'

Louise ducked under the door and felt along the wall for a light switch.

'Here it is.'

The garage was full of old furniture and boxes but they could just about make out a motorcycle leaning against the wall at the back. The fuel tank was missing and the seat cover had rotted away, revealing the cushioning underneath.

'Come and hold this a sec,' said Dixon. 'If I let go it'll drop.'

Louise took hold of the door from Dixon and he stepped into the garage. The door lowered a little, which added to the gloom, and it didn't help that the light bulb was covered in dust and cobwebs.

There was no way through to the back to get a close look at the bike, but, more importantly, no way to get the bike out either. Dixon looked at the floor in front of the pile of furniture. None had been moved in ages, judging by the dust.

He stepped up onto a dining chair and leaned over. The tyres were flat, the rubber perished and the layer of dust on the mudguard confirmed it had not been disturbed in a while too. Shame.

Then he checked the exhaust. There was only one.

'This isn't it. Let's go.'

Dixon dropped the keys through Treadwell's letter box and shouted 'thank you' after them, before striding across the grass to his Land Rover.

'Where next?' he asked, jumping into the driver's seat.

The Grosvenor House Hotel had been painted bright pink, presumably to match the Bentley parked outside the front door, and was in Grosvenor Road, just behind the seafront.

'This is the one that was in that programme on the telly,' said Louise.

'What?'

'They did a fly on the wall documentary.'

Dixon parked his old Land Rover next to the Bentley. 'I must be in the wrong business,' he said, frowning.

'The bike's registered to Paul Jonathan Hollingsworth.'

'I only hope he hasn't painted it pink,' muttered Dixon, getting out of the Land Rover.

The receptionist pointed them in the direction of the manager's office.

'Where's the staff car park?' asked Dixon.

'Out through the double doors at the end of that corridor.'

'Good. Find Mr Hollingsworth and tell him we'll be there, please.'

'Yes, sir,' replied the receptionist, reaching for the telephone.

The staff car park was a small courtyard behind the hotel. It was large enough for vans to deliver to the kitchen door, one Ford Fiesta, a bicycle rack and one Norton motorcycle. Dixon walked over to it, leaned over and looked at the number plate. It had a layer of grime on it but the murder of Elizabeth Perry was almost a week ago now. More than enough time for the number plate to have been changed and a fresh layer of dirt to build up. Then he flicked off the yellow plastic caps and took a photograph of the screws that attached the number plate to the bike. It was clear they had not been touched in some time. He shook his head. Single exhaust too, and no sign of a dummy one being attached to the off side of the bike.

Dixon was taking a photograph of the tyres when he heard footsteps behind him.

'Can I help you?'

'And you are?' asked Dixon.

'Paul Hollingsworth. The manager.'

'I'm . . .'

'I know who you are,' interrupted Hollingsworth. He was wearing dark trousers and a white shirt. The receptionist had been wearing a pink jacket so the pink tie was no doubt part of the staff uniform.

'We're eliminating Norton motorcycles from our enquiries, Mr Hollingsworth. Can you tell us where you were on Christmas Eve?'

'Here. I was on duty until midnight then went to bed. I live in.'

'And this is your bike?'

'It is. It's a Fastback.'

'D'you keep it garaged usually?'

'No. I've got a cover for it and there's a carport round the side I can use if I'm not going to be riding it for a while. Can you tell me what it's all about?'

'No,' replied Dixon, shaking his head. He turned to Louise. 'Constable Willmott here will take details of anyone who can vouch for you on Christmas Eve.'

'My alibi?'

'Something like that.'

Dixon waited until Louise had finished writing down the names and addresses of two members of staff who would confirm Hollingsworth's movements on Christmas Eve.

'Where d'you get it serviced?'

'I do most of the work myself but there's a garage in Babbacombe that does anything tricky.'

'Name?'

'Babbacombe Motors.'

'And where do you get the parts?'

'The owners' club are pretty good. eBay sometimes. And there's nortonparts.co.uk.'

'Thank you very much, you've been very helpful,' said Dixon.

'Happy to help,' replied Hollingsworth.

'Can we get round to the front that way?' asked Dixon, pointing to the service road around the side of the hotel.

'Yes, you can.'

'Thanks.'

Hollingsworth turned to walk back to the kitchens.

'One last question.'

'Yes.'

'D'you see any other Nortons about? On your travels?'

Hollingsworth smiled.

'There's one Paignton way I've seen on the seafront a couple of times. Always give them a wave. And a nice one in Wellswood, I think it must be. I've seen it turning out onto the Babbacombe Road.'

'Where?'

'There's a parade of shops. Ilsham Road.'

'Thank you, Mr Hollingsworth.'

'We'll get the local boys to check his alibi but there's no sign of anything on the bike,' said Dixon, climbing into the driver's seat.

'One more to go,' said Louise, opening her notebook.

'Give me a minute to ring Jane.' Dixon was holding his phone to his ear.

'What've you got?'

'Not a lot, really,' replied Jane. 'One wreck and then another that's in showroom condition. It's only done 170 miles.'

'A speedometer can be disconnected, don't forget,' replied Dixon.

'It's in an air conditioned garage with a BSA 500 and two I'd not even heard of.'

'What about the tyres?'

'Dave checked it over. There's no sign it's been ridden at all. The tyres even had the stickers still on them.'

'It's a 1978 model. Very rare,' shouted Dave.

'He's driving,' said Jane. 'We're on the way back from Brixham.'

'How many left?' asked Dixon.

'Just one then we're done. What about you?'

'Nothing. One left though. See you back at Bridgwater.'

Dixon rang off.

'Where next?'

'Parkhill Road,' replied Louise. 'Number 31A.'

Dixon had driven up and down Parkhill Road three times before they spotted the faded 'Private Road' sign on what they had thought was the entrance to Vanehill House. That sign had been brand new.

'Who'd be a bloody postman,' he said, turning into the narrow lane.

There was a high stone wall on the right, with overhanging trees, so Dixon switched his headlights on.

'That's better.'

The ground on the left sloped steeply away to the harbour below, which was visible between the houses on the left, the lights of the harbourside restaurants and boats twinkling in the darkness. The houses had been built below the level of the road and Dixon counted five rooftops visible in front of him.

'Can you see the numbers?'

'No,' replied Louise, peering out of the passenger window.

Dixon drove to the end of the lane, which opened out into a large car park in front of Vanehill House. Judging by the signs, it was used as offices but it was closed. Dixon turned the Land Rover and slowed to a crawl back along the lane, switching his lights to full beam.

'There it is,' he said, pulling up across the drive. 'Looks like the Bates Motel.'

'What's that?'

'Not you as well.' Dixon rolled his eyes. 'Doesn't anyone watch the classics anymore?'

'Which one?' asked Louise.

'*Psycho*,' replied Dixon, getting out of the Land Rover. A floodlight on the corner of the garage came on, triggered by a motion sensor, no doubt. 'Thank God for that.'

The garage was on the right, sideways on to the wide drive, with an empty carport next to it. A small path then led to a flight of stone steps down to the front door. A footbridge also went across to a door at first floor level. A second path then ran along the side of the carport before turning down the side of the house and round to the back. Or was it the front?

'We're at the back, aren't we?'

'Looks like it,' replied Louise. 'That's the kitchen down there.' She was pointing to the window on the right of the door at the bottom of the steps.

Dixon noticed the letter box in the door across the footbridge.

'Let's try that one,' he said.

'No lights on,' said Louise.

'We'll try it anyway, just to make sure. Then we can have a snoop.'

Dixon walked across the footbridge and pressed the doorbell. He heard it ring and listened for the sound of footsteps.

Nothing.

'There's a torch in the glove box,' said Dixon. 'And wave your hand in front of that light.'

Dixon leaned over the handrail and looked in the window to the right of the door. It was a bathroom. On the left was a bedroom. Then he walked back along the footbridge and down the steps. He was halfway down when the floodlight went out.

'Louise!'

'Yes, Sir.'

He watched the beam of the torch waving about in the dark like an old searchlight and then the floodlight came back on.

'Spooky, isn't it?' said Louise, handing Dixon the torch.

'The overhanging trees don't help.'

He shone the torch in the kitchen window. Then the window to the left of the door. It was the dining room, although the table itself was only just visible beneath a large collection of porcelain figurines. The mantelpiece and the shelves either side of the fireplace on the far wall were also covered in figurines.

'An antique dealer?' asked Louise.

'Could be,' said Dixon, nodding. 'What's the name?'

'Dale Reed.'

Dixon crouched down, opened the letter box and shone the torch into the hall.

'It's the back door.'

'What can you see?' asked Louise.

'Shelves on the left. Cleaning stuff. Kitchen on the right. Coats and boots hanging up. Usual sort of stuff.'

'Shall we try round the front?'

They followed the path along the back of the house and then around to the front. The path opened out onto a large patio, giving a grandstand view right across Torbay to Berry Head.

'That explains it,' said Dixon.

'What?'

'The attraction. It's a bit of a dump from the back, isn't it?' He was shining the torch through the large patio doors into the living room.

'Oh, shit,' said Louise.

'What?'

'The light's gone out again.'

'C'mon, let's see if we can find that bike.'

They walked up the second flight of steps to the garage. Dixon tried the door. It was locked. He shone the torch through the frosted glass window at the back of the garage but could not see a motorcycle, or anything much for that matter.

Louise had managed to get the floodlight to come back on and was looking down the side of the garage.

'Here,' she said. 'What's this?'

Dixon handed her the torch, which she shone down the side between the garage and the front wall. Then she reached in and began pulling at a tarpaulin.

'It's a bike.'

The gap was narrow. Just wide enough for a bike and the tarpaulin slid off to reveal a Norton, or rather the skeleton of a Norton. The headlight was smashed and the fuel tank had gone. Not only that, but there was no exhaust pipe at all, let alone one on either side.

'This hasn't moved for years,' said Louise.

'Can you see a number plate?'

'There is one, but I can't read it from here.'

Dixon took the torch and walked around to the back of the garage. Then he shone the torch down the side.

'B83 ERD,' he said.

'That's it,' replied Louise.

'C'mon, let's get out of here,' said Dixon.

They stopped to give Monty a run on Babbacombe Downs and arrived back at Express Park just before 6 p.m. Jane and Dave Harding had caught them up on the M5 at Taunton and followed them the rest of the way.

'Anything interesting?' asked Dixon, as they walked across the car park.

'No,' replied Harding. 'The last one was at Marldon, just off the ring road. A roadworthy SS type. The two exhausts and everything.'

'Really?' asked Louise.

'Yes,' replied Jane. 'We got quite excited until we found out the owner died of cancer in November.'

'Who did you speak to?' asked Dixon, holding open the door.

'His wife. Pancreatic. Took six weeks.'

'And no one else rides the bike?'

'No.'

'Did you check it over?'

'I had a quick look,' replied Dave. 'Couldn't see anything.'

Dixon nodded.

'You two might as well head off,' he said. 'Enjoy what's left of New Year's Eve.'

'Thank you, Sir.'

Jane waited until Dave Harding and Louise had gone.

'Bit of wild goose chase then?' she asked.

'That's a good idea,' replied Dixon, smiling.

'What is?'

'A bottle of wine and watch *The Wild Geese*.'

'You have got to be kidding.'

It had been a long night. Jane had insisted on sitting up until midnight and then fireworks had kept Dixon and Monty awake for another half an hour after that. Jane had slept through them, of course, and was still asleep now, despite a prod in the ribs.

It was just after 8 a.m. on New Year's Day and Dixon was standing in his kitchen watching Monty eating his breakfast. His walk in the field had been curtailed by rain and it looked set for the day, judging by the thick blanket of grey cloud. Still, it offered plenty of time for some background research into Perry's political campaigning.

Dixon was waiting for the kettle to boil when he heard his phone ringing. He fumbled in his back pocket and then looked at the screen, recognising the number straight away.

'Yes, Sir.'

'We're getting reports of a body in Moorland. It's in the garage of a bungalow. A lad was out in his canoe and looked in the window.'

'Canoe?'

'Yes. The dive boat's on the way but it'll be a while before we can get out there.'

'Address?'

'It's 17 Church Street.'

'Do we know who lives there?'

'Harry,' replied DCI Lewis. 'Harry Unwin.'

Chapter Fifteen

Jane was tying her hair up in a ponytail as Dixon turned out of Brent Knoll and sped south on the A38. It was less than five minutes after DCI Lewis had telephoned and it was not the start to New Year's Day she had been hoping for.

'Do we know if it's Harry?'

'Not yet,' replied Dixon. 'Some kid was out in his canoe and saw a body hanging in the garage. That's all we know.'

'If it is Harry . . .' Jane's voice tailed off and neither of them spoke again until they were going over the M5 at Huntworth.

'When does the tenant move into your flat?' asked Dixon.

'End of January. But we've got to clear it first.'

'Might be an idea if we stayed there for a while.'

Jane nodded and turned back to the passenger window, watching the fields on the nearside disappear under the floodwater.

Dixon turned into the farm gateway on the bend just outside Moorland. It had been dry on his previous visit but was now under two or three inches of water. He spotted Roger Poland's Volvo and two police Land Rovers, neither of them fitted with snorkels. He pulled up next to Poland and a group of uniformed officers that included PC Cole.

'How long till the dive boat gets here?' asked Dixon, winding down the window.

'We were told about two hours, Sir,' replied Cole. 'But that was half an hour or so ago.'

'That's no bloody good.'

Cole shrugged his shoulders.

'You got here quick, Roger,' said Dixon.

'It's only one junction on the motorway.'

'Hop in then,' said Dixon. 'Let's see if I fitted this snorkel properly.'

Poland walked around to the back of the Land Rover and opened the door.

'And you, Cole. The rest of you can stay here.'

Monty jumped over the seat and sat on the front seat next to Jane. Dixon leaned over and put his lead on, then he opened the door and let him jump out.

'I'll put him in the back of one of the Land Rovers, Sir,' said Cole. 'This lot'll keep an eye on him. Won't you?'

'Yes, Sir.'

Dixon waited until Cole had jumped in the back of the Land Rover and then turned out of the car park.

'Who fitted the snorkel?' asked Poland.

'He did,' replied Jane.

'You did use silicon, didn't you?'

'Yes.'

'Well, we'll soon find out,' said Poland.

'This is the second time you're going to get wet on my account, Cole. Thank you.'

'You'd have done the same for me, Sir,' replied Cole.

'Right, here goes,' said Dixon, accelerating along the lane. The water rose up in front of the Land Rover and the bow wave was soon washing over the bonnet.

'Slow down,' said Poland.

'We need a bit of a bow wave,' replied Dixon. 'It keeps the water away from the doors.'

He eased off the accelerator and the bow wave receded but the water was getting deeper fast. They were no more than two hundred yards from the field gateway but it was almost level with the top of the front wing and well over the air intake. Then it began bubbling up under the back door.

'What's the worst that could happen?'

'We get rescued off the roof by the dive boat,' replied Poland.

'And you get the piss taken out of you for weeks, Sir,' said Cole.

'Thank you, Cole,' replied Dixon, accelerating again. The bow wave was washing over the bonnet now and dirty water was trickling into the passenger compartment.

'What's that smell?' asked Jane.

'Slurry.'

'Mixed with oil,' said Poland.

'If it gets much deeper we'll start to float,' said Cole.

'It gets shallower as you go into Moorland, I'm sure it does,' said Dixon.

'He's making it up as he's going along,' said Poland.

Dixon felt the steering becoming lighter and the Land Rover began turning sideways. He turned the wheel to the left, trying to straighten it up, and gunned the engine.

'We're floating,' said Jane.

'We'll have to let the water in to sink us,' said Poland.

'No bloody fear.'

Suddenly the wheels hit the road surface again and the Land Rover lurched forward. Dixon eased off the accelerator and straightened it up, before accelerating again. They felt the Land Rover beginning to rise up and the water level started to drop away. Bungalows appeared on either side of the road.

'We're in Moorland,' said Cole.

'How deep's the water?' asked Poland.

'A couple of feet,' replied Dixon, looking out of the driver's side window.

Poland opened the back door of the Land Rover, allowing the small amount of water still in the passenger compartment to drain away.

'We didn't even get our feet wet,' said Dixon. 'Right, let's find number 17.'

'It's the other side of the church,' said Cole. 'On the right hand side.'

Dixon crept forward, but the water was no more than knee deep now. It was up to the level of the wooden seat in the lych-gate and seemed to shallow off still further beyond the church. He stopped across the drive of number 17 and Poland opened the back door and jumped out, carrying his bag.

'Is the exhaust clear of the water, Roger?' shouted Dixon.

'Yes.'

Dixon revved the engine several times and then switched it off.

'I'll go back in the boat,' said Jane.

The water was over their wellington boots.

'My trousers are soaked anyway,' said Cole, splashing up the drive. 'This way, Sir.'

They followed PC Cole along the side of the bungalow to the garage, which was set back, adjacent to the garden. Dixon looked in through the window. The body was silhouetted against the light from a window at the back of the garage, the head tilted to one side, but the figure was unmistakeable. Dixon turned to Jane.

'It's Harry.'

He put on a pair of latex gloves and then tried the side door. It was unlocked but needed a firm push to open it against the water on the inside. Cole followed and reached up for the light switch.

'I wouldn't, if I were you,' said Dixon.

Cole nodded.

What little light there was came from the small window at the back of the garage and the open door. Dixon stood still for a moment, allowing his eyes to adjust to the gloom. Harry Unwin was hanging from a ceiling rafter near the front of a small red car, his feet dangling in the water. The bonnet of the car was dented, presumably where he had been thrashing about on the end of the rope, kicking out as his life drained away. Poland and Jane waded into the garage and the movement of the water started Unwin's body swinging backwards and forwards.

Unwin's facial features were visible to Dixon, now that his vision had adjusted to the light. Unwin's eyes were wide open, bulging even, and his tongue was hanging out. He was fully clothed, and his hands were at his sides. Not bound.

'Over to you, Roger.'

Poland stepped forward and shone a torch in Unwin's face. Then he looked at his hands and wrists.

'Can't see any sign of restraint or other injury.'

'Time?' asked Dixon.

'Days certainly.'

'Who checked this place?' asked Dixon, shaking his head.

'Someone came out in a boat, Sir,' said Cole, 'but it couldn't get down the side here.'

'The water's hardly deep . . .'

Poland was feeling about in the water underneath Unwin with his foot.

'Here it is,' he said, picking up a small plastic kick stool. 'This is what he stood on.'

'How the hell did he get here?' asked Dixon. 'Look at the trouble we had.'

'He'd never have got through in that car,' said Cole.

'That's not his car,' replied Jane. 'He had a VW like mine.'

'Run the plates. See what we get,' said Dixon.

'My guess is it'll be his daughter's,' said Jane.

'He's got kids?'

'Two.'

'Wife?'

'Divorced.'

They stood listening to the rain falling outside and watching Poland examine Unwin. His body was turning on the rope now. Spinning.

Dixon turned away when PC Cole's radio crackled.

'Dive boat's on its way, Sir. They're about an hour away.'

'Good.'

'And the car is registered to Dawn Unwin. This address.'

'That's the daughter,' said Jane.

'Why on earth would he kill himself?' asked Cole.

Jane looked at Dixon, expecting an answer but none came. He was looking around the garage, deep in thought, and she knew better than to disturb him. Then he turned and waded across to the back door of the bungalow. It was open. He checked every room, with PC Cole close behind him.

'What're you looking for?' shouted Jane. She was leaning against the sink in the kitchen.

'I don't know.'

'I didn't see a suicide note,' said Cole.

'There won't be one because he didn't commit suicide,' said Dixon, watching Jane opening the kitchen cupboards one by one.

'How d'you know that, Sir?' asked Cole.

'Dunno,' replied Dixon, through gritted teeth.

'Shall we ask Mr Poland?'

'He'll tell us it's a suicide.'

'How . . . ?'

'Because it looks like one, Cole,' said Dixon. 'Just like Georgina Harcourt. Remember her, Jane?'

'The racing stables?'

'That's it. The overdose . . .'

'You had no evidence of foul play,' said Jane.

'Still haven't.'

Poland appeared in the back door.

'My feet are freezing.'

'Well?'

'Looks like a suicide but I'll know more when I cut him down and get him back to the lab.'

'Shall we get SOCO over here?' asked Jane.

'Better had,' said Dixon, 'but they won't find anything.'

Dixon moved his Land Rover forward to allow the large black boat into the drive. It was flat bottomed and resembled a large skip, but the water was still too shallow so the outboard motor had been lifted clear. It was being pulled along by two members of the underwater search team wading either side of it. They were wearing wetsuits and bright orange lifejackets. Sitting in the boat were the scientific services officer, Donald Watson, DCI Lewis, two mortuary technicians from Musgrove Park, and DCS Collyer from the organised crime team in Bristol known as Zephyr.

'I've just been hearing about your stint as a trainee teacher, Dixon,' said Collyer, stepping over the side of the boat. He was wearing a pair of fishing waders, which Dixon eyed with a sense of envy, all feeling in his feet having left him over an hour ago.

'Yes, Sir.'

'My offer of a place on Zephyr still stands.'

'Thank you, Sir,' replied Dixon, noticing Lewis glaring at him.

Collyer's presence confirmed what he already knew. Deep down. Harry Unwin had been mixed up with the Albanians and he'd paid the price.

Dixon followed Lewis and Collyer along the side of the garage and waited outside while they went in.

'No way for him to die,' said Collyer, blinking as his eyes adjusted to the daylight.

'He was . . .'

'It's not what you think, Nick,' said Lewis.

'He gave the Albanians my home address.'

'No, he didn't,' said Collyer. 'He was feeding them false information.'

'What?'

'He gave them an empty property in East Brent. Took a huge risk.'

'The Albanians found you anyway, Nick,' said Lewis. 'But it wasn't Harry.'

'But you said . . .'

'I know what I said,' snapped Lewis.

'He didn't know,' said Collyer. 'Nobody outside Zephyr did.'

'And Harry was part of Zephyr?' asked Dixon.

Collyer nodded.

Dixon looked past Collyer and through the open door at the body of Harry Unwin, silhouetted against the back window of the garage and swinging slowly from side to side. Seldom had he misjudged anyone more. He prided himself on being an excellent judge of character and could count on the fingers of one hand the number of times he had got it wrong. But this time he had got it spectacularly wrong. He looked at Lewis, who shook his head, and then back to Unwin. Pride comes before a fall, as his mother had always reminded him. And this felt like a long fall.

'He gave them the wrong address?'

'He did,' replied Collyer.

Dixon waded past Lewis, into the garage and stood looking up at Unwin. He wondered how and why he had misjudged him. And why Harry had never said anything. He couldn't, of course he couldn't.

'Are you all right?' asked Jane, from the doorway.

'No,' replied Dixon. 'I'm bloody well not all right.'

Jane waited.

'I was wrong about him. He . . .'

'Lewis told me,' said Jane. 'C'mon, let's leave them to it. There's nothing you can do now.'

'Oh, yes there is,' muttered Dixon. 'Catch his killer.'

'Looks like a suicide, at this stage,' said Poland. He was standing outside the garage with Lewis and Collyer. Donald Watson was setting up an arc lamp inside so that he could photograph the scene.

'Remember Georgina Harcourt, Roger?' asked Dixon.

'Owned the racing stables?'

'Yes.'

'You're not still banging on about her, are you?' asked Lewis.

'Overdose, you said?' asked Dixon, turning to Poland.

'There was no evidence of . . .'

'Did she have children?'

'Yes, I think so,' replied Poland.

'Yes, she did,' said Jane.

'She was murdered and so was Harry,' said Dixon.

'Who by?' asked Lewis.

'Ask him,' said Dixon, pointing at Collyer.

'We know there's someone. A professional. But we don't know who or where or even how they communicate. No one's ever got close.'

'How though?' asked Poland.

'You've got children and grandchildren, haven't you, Roger?'

'Yes.'

'So, you know who I am. My reputation,' continued Dixon. 'I'm holding a gun to your head and I tell you I'll kill you, your children and your grandchildren unless you take these pills. It's your one and only chance to save them. What're you gonna do?'

Poland hesitated.

'Or how about I tell you I'll take your children, one by one, and dump them in the Bristol Channel. Alive. Unless you hang yourself. Now. One chance to save them. The clock's ticking. What're you gonna do?'

'We get it, Nick,' said Lewis.

'So did Harry.'

'This car stinks,' said Jane, sitting in the front of the Land Rover.

'I thought you said you were going back in the boat?'

'I'm going with you.'

'All right then,' said Dixon. 'But don't blame me if you get wet.'

'Go slowly and let it fill up with water. That'll stop you floating.' That had been Roger's advice, but Dixon ignored it. Letting the water in was a last resort.

It seemed to take longer on the way back to the farm gateway and Dixon wondered whether the water was getting deeper or whether it was just because he had been going slower. Either way, it wasn't long before they were picking up Monty.

'Where to now?' asked Jane. She had slid across to the driver's seat while Dixon had been putting Monty in the back.

'Express Park, then home.'

'Express Park? You can't go in there looking like that. You're soaked.'

'I'm not. You are.'

'But . . .' Jane sighed. 'What are you after?'

'The photos of Georgina Harcourt's bedroom.'

'The file'll have gone off to the coroner by now.'

'Yes, but the photos should've been scanned onto the system. Print them off then it's home for a shower and what's left of New Year's Day.'

'Are you sure they were both murdered?'

'As sure as I can be without any real evidence.'

'You'll find it. You're always right.'

'That'll come back to haunt you one day.'

'You'll see to it,' said Jane, smiling.

'I will. And besides,' continued Dixon, 'I was wrong about Harry.'

It took Dixon twenty minutes to hose down the inside of the Land Rover. The floodwater had left a thin layer of brown silt on everything and Dixon shuddered to think what it was. A mixture of mud, oil and slurry was being optimistic and if he was to stand any chance of getting Jane in it again, the Land Rover needed a damned good clean and a potent air freshener. And so did he. Monty would need a bath too.

Dixon was standing in the shower wondering how on earth he was going to prove that two people had been murdered without any evidence. Unless the killer confessed, it was going to be a challenge. But now he owed it to Harry. And then there was Georgina

Harcourt, who had been trying to contact him the night of her murder. And Elizabeth Perry. And John Stanniland. The list went on. How many more were there? And how many more would there be before Dixon caught up with him? Or her.

So many questions and, standing there in the shower covered in foam, it felt as though the only thing he knew for sure was that Jane had been at the shampoo and shower gel bottles again. All of them facing front on the shelf. He smiled. She was the same with the jars and tins in the kitchen cupboards.

He stared at the bottle of shampoo in his hand. It was a compulsion and Jane had no choice. An obsession. He dropped the bottle and leapt out of the shower. Then he wrapped a towel around his waist and ran downstairs, leaving the shower running.

'You're dripping water everywhere,' said Jane. She was kneeling on the floor, drying Monty with a towel. 'And you're still covered in shampoo.'

'Where are the photos?'

Jane reached over to her handbag, which was on the floor next to the sofa, took out a plastic wallet and handed it to Dixon. He began flicking through the photographs of Georgina Harcourt's bedroom.

'I printed the lot,' said Jane, watching Dixon. 'What's going on?'

'What did you notice about the kitchen cabinets at Harry's place?'

'Oh, they were all over the place. It was all I could do not to tidy them up.'

Dixon grinned.

'Ring your folks, will you? See if they'll have Monty. Then pack a bag. We'd better get over to your flat.'

'Why?'

'Because we're about to start rattling cages.'

Chapter Sixteen

'Get off here,' said Jane, as they raced south past the off slip at junction 23 on the M5. 'You've missed the Bridgwater turn . . .' She spun round in the passenger seat of her car and looked over her shoulder, watching a patrol car speeding down the on slip, with a blue Ford Focus right behind it. 'That's Dave, isn't it?'

'It is,' replied Dixon. 'And that's armed response. I lined them up while you were dropping Monty off.'

'Torquay?'

'Yes.'

'Let's hear it then.'

'Obsessive compulsive disorder. I like to think I know quite a bit about it, living with you.'

'Me? I haven't got it.'

Dixon raised his eyebrows.

'I just like things tidy, that's all.'

'Think about Georgina Harcourt's bedroom,' said Dixon. 'Her make-up on the dressing table, perfume bottles.'

Jane switched the internal light on in the car and took the photographs out of her handbag.

'They're all neat and tidy,' she said.

'Now compare that to her drinks cabinet.'

Jane leafed through the photographs until she found the right one.

'It's all over the place.'

'And what about Harry's kitchen cupboards?'

'All over the place.'

'And the shelves in the garage?'

Jane hesitated, then looked at Dixon.

'Neat and tidy.'

'So, the killer's waiting for the overdose to take effect. What's he gonna do? What's he compelled to do?'

'Straighten the jars and perfume bottles.'

'Now he's waiting for Harry to die. It wasn't a long drop so it would've taken a few minutes. What's the killer gonna do?'

'Tidy the shelves,' replied Jane.

'And we know it wasn't Harry because . . . ?' asked Dixon.

'The kitchen cupboards were a mess.'

'And so was Mrs Harcourt's drinks cabinet.'

'Where are we going then?' asked Jane.

'The last house Louise and I went to,' replied Dixon.

'The Norton was a wreck, wasn't it?'

'The one we saw was, but I'm guessing there's another.'

'Two?' asked Jane.

'Why not?' replied Dixon. 'Yes, I've got a Norton but it couldn't have been me, officer, it's a wreck. Look.'

Jane nodded, slowly.

'No one was in and we didn't get a look in the garage. Only I looked through the letter box, didn't I?'

'Well?'

Dixon smiled. 'Made your OCD look like a mild case.'

'It's a bit of a long shot, isn't it?' asked Jane.

'Hollingsworth said there was a Norton in Wellswood, didn't he?'

'According to Louise's notes.'

'Parkhill Road. Past Meadfoot beach and up Ilsham Road,' said Dixon. 'Avoids all the CCTV on the harbour and the cameras on the lights at the bottom of the hill.'

'How d'you know that?'

'I looked at the map. It is traditional.'

'You cheeky . . .'

'Thank you, Constable,' replied Dixon. 'Better let the Torquay lot know what's going on. If this guy's who I think he is, it might turn nasty.'

Dixon listened to Jane's conversation with the duty officer at Torquay but his mind was elsewhere. He was watching the headlights flashing by on the northbound carriageway but the silhouetted vision of Harry Unwin's body hanging in the flooded garage, spinning slowly on the end of the rope, was right in front of him. It would stay there and haunt him. He knew that. Then he saw him stepping up onto the kick stool and thrashing around, his legs flailing, kicking his daughter's car.

Dixon blinked. He could picture Harry's face in front of him, his hand around Harry's throat pinning him to the vending machine. There had been no fear in his eyes then and Dixon now knew why. And it explained why Harry had made no formal complaint about him.

'Fuck it,' muttered Dixon, through gritted teeth.

Jane looked at him and frowned, her phone still clamped to her ear.

Dixon shook his head.

Jane rang off and put her hand on his knee.

'Harry?'

'Yes.'

'You weren't to know.'

'That doesn't help.'

They drove the rest of the way in silence until Dixon turned into a large lay-by on the tops of the cliffs, just outside Torquay. The lights of several boats anchored in the bay were visible in the distance and the moonlight shimmered on the water. On another night Dixon might have stopped to enjoy the view.

'I suppose we should be grateful it's not pissing down with rain,' he said, getting out of the Land Rover.

Dave Harding and the patrol car had pulled into the same lay-by and parked either side of him.

'What's going on?' asked Jane.

'Did you bring the body armour, Dave?'

'Yes, Sir,' said Harding, opening the boot of his car. He handed a set each to Dixon and Jane.

'Do we . . . ?' asked Jane.

'Yes, we do,' said Dixon. 'Put it on.'

The two uniformed armed response officers had got out of their car and were standing either side of Harding.

'Right then,' said Dixon. 'The house is down a lane. It's a cul-de-sac and there are offices at the far end with a large car park, so we'll turn and park in there.' Dixon turned to the armed response officers. 'Follow me on foot. It's only twenty yards at most and it'll keep the cars hidden.'

'Yes, Sir.'

'The Torquay lot are sending some backup and they'll be waiting for us in the car park. Dave, you wait out in Parkhill Road and be ready to block off the lane with your car. All right?'

'Yes, Sir.'

'Right. Let's get on with it. There'll be several other cars in the area in case we need them.'

'Do we need this body armour?' asked Jane, getting into the passenger seat of her car.

'I've got a song going round and round in my head,' said Dixon. 'Spear of Destiny. Remember them?'

'Before my time,' replied Jane. 'What's it called?'

'Never Take Me Alive.'

Dixon waited for the armed response car to turn and park just inside the entrance to the car park, next to the patrol car that was waiting for them. The drive was empty but lights were on in the house this time.

'There's definitely someone in there, Sir,' said the uniformed officer. 'We got here ten minutes or so ago and a woman arrived in a Range Rover. It's in the carport at the side of the garage.'

Dixon nodded.

'You've been briefed?'

'Yes, Sir.'

They were wearing body armour so had got that message, at least.

'There's a floodlight on the corner of the garage,' said Dixon, looking down at the house. A light was on in the kitchen and an upstairs bedroom, although the curtains were closed. Then he saw movement in the kitchen window. 'Right, down the steps it is then.'

Dixon looked over his shoulder at the armed response officers, who were waiting behind the Range Rover. Then he stepped forward, triggering the floodlight. The woman in the kitchen leaned forward over the sink, looked up at him and then disappeared from view.

Dixon ran down the steps and rang the doorbell.

'Who is it?' It was a woman's voice, shouting, and it came from some distance behind the door.

'Police.'

'Oh, hang on then.'

They could hear keys jangling behind the door.

'Maybe she was expecting someone else,' whispered Dixon, taking his warrant card out of his pocket.

She was tall, perhaps in her late thirties and was wearing a white dressing gown.

'We're looking for Mr Dale Reed,' said Dixon, showing her his warrant card. 'Is he in?'

'No.'

'But he does live here?'

'Yes.'

'Where is he?'

'Out on a job.'

'What sort of job?'

'He's a lift engineer.'

'And your name is?'

'Andrea Parks.'

Dixon looked past her at the shelving unit to his left. It was set in to the wall and extended a full seven feet or so from the floor, each shelf covered in an array of cleaning products. All of the labels were facing the front. Several pairs of shoes were lined up under the bottom shelf, all side by side and all perfectly straight.

'May we come in?' asked Dixon.

'Er, yes.'

'Thank you.' Dixon stepped into the hall. 'We'd like to take a look around, if we may. It may help if you got dressed . . .'

'But, we're going out later. I was just getting ready.'

'Detective Constable Winter will go with you.'

'Why are you wearing that?' asked Andrea, pointing to Jane's body armour. 'Where's Dale? Is he all right?'

'I was wondering when you were going to ask me that,' said Dixon.

'What's he done?'

'C'mon, let's go and get you dressed,' said Jane.

Dixon turned to the uniformed officers and nodded. They began checking each room in turn, while Dixon rang Dave Harding.

'Doesn't look like he's here, Dave. Back off a bit, keep out of sight and block the lane if he appears.'

'Yes, Sir.'

Dixon noticed a set of car keys in a small bowl, just inside the kitchen door. One had the Range Rover logo on it and the other was a blank remote control. He pointed it at the garage door and pressed the open button, listening for the sound of a roller door opening.

'Bingo,' he muttered.

He found the light switch on the wall, just inside the door, and switched it on. It was empty, apart from a motorbike paddock stand. Then he looked along the shelves against the wall, before stepping back and closing the door.

'Whose is the car, Andrea?' She had changed into jeans and a green Hollister sweatshirt and was sitting on the edge of the sofa.

'Dale's.'

Dixon turned to Jane. 'Run a check with DVLA, will you?'

'Registered in my name, all right?' said Andrea.

'And the house?'

'The same.'

'What does he do for a living?' asked Dixon.

'I told you. He's a lift engineer.'

'Big house, Range Rover.' Dixon paused. 'Norton.' He watched Andrea's eyes darting around the room. 'I must be in the wrong business,' said Dixon.

'He works for Kone.'

'What about the porcelain?'

'Mine. I do a bit of dealing. For fun, really.'

'How long have you been together?'

'Fifteen years.'

'How'd you meet?'

'I worked in a club. Look, it suits me. All right. And I ask no questions. It's none of my business.'

'I bet it isn't,' said Dixon.

He walked back along the corridor and stood in front of the shelves just inside the back door. Then he turned and followed the short passageway around to the left, into the dining room. This was the room directly behind the shelves and yet the dividing wall on his left was adjacent to the door frame. Dixon frowned. It had been at least four paces along the passageway to the dining room. He walked back to find Jane standing in the hall.

'What's up?' she asked.

Dixon looked at the kitchen door. It was the exact same height as the shelves. Then he tapped the back wall of the shelving unit with his knuckle. It was chipboard. Hollow chipboard. That settled it.

'What d'you notice about this house?' he asked.

'I dunno,' said Jane, shaking her head.

'No ground floor toilet. A house this size with no ground floor loo. Very odd.' Then he winked at Jane, stepped back, brought his left foot up and kicked the third shelf as hard as he could.

'What are you do . . . ?'

The force of Dixon's kick sent the shelf through the panel at the back. Jars and bottles came crashing down, some of them smashing on the floor.

'Look,' said Dixon, pointing to the top of the unit. 'It's buckled in the frame.'

'Frame?'

'Door frame,' said Dixon, kicking it again.

This time the whole unit buckled and the top half fell forward, sending Dixon stumbling back to avoid being hit by the last of the bottles that hadn't fallen at his first kick.

'A secret room,' said Jane, peering in.

Dixon dragged the two halves of the shelving unit into the kitchen and then stepped over the bottles on the floor.

'It's the downstairs loo. Or it was,' said Dixon, pulling the cord to switch on the light.

'Bloody hell,' said Jane.

'For downstairs loo, read armoury,' said Dixon. 'The tools of his trade.'

The lavatory had been removed and replaced with shelves. But this time it wasn't cleaning fluids lined up on them. It was guns and ammunition. Handguns, automatic weapons, shotguns and lots of ammunition. Dixon pulled back the shower curtain to reveal two sets of body armour. There were also several boxes of latex gloves, overshoes and paper overalls.

'Fuck me.'

Dixon turned to see one of the local uniformed officers staring at the guns.

'We'd better . . .'

'Wait,' said Dixon. 'We haven't got the owner yet.'

'Is that a grenade?'

Dixon nodded.

'Let the armed response boys know. And arrest her for perverting the course of justice.'

'Yes, Sir.'

'Then bring her upstairs.'

'Yes, Sir.'

'Let's have a look up there, Jane,' said Dixon, bolting the back door from the inside.

At the top of the stairs the corridor split. One ran along the middle of the building, with doors to either side, and the other led straight ahead along a short passageway to another back door, presumably accessed via the footbridge. The bathroom was the last door on the left, before the back door. Otherwise, Dixon counted four bedrooms, two of them en suite, and yet another bathroom.

He followed the corridor to the end and into the bedroom on the left. Then he checked the bedroom opposite. This time the long wall inner wall was covered by a large wardrobe. Long inner wall? Dixon stepped back out into the corridor and looked at the end wall. It finished just beyond the bedroom doors.

'Are you seeing what I'm seeing?'

'Yes,' replied Jane.

Dixon flicked the rug away from in front of the wardrobe with his foot.

'Looks like this wardrobe moves,' he said, looking at scuff marks on the carpet underneath.

He sat down on the floor and placed his feet on the skirting board. Then he placed both hands on the back edge of the wardrobe and pulled, moving the wardrobe a foot or so away from the wall.

'That's far enough,' said Jane. 'I can get in there.'

Dixon watched her shuffle along the wall and then disappear into what had once been a built in wardrobe perhaps.

'What've you got?'

'Hang on, there must be a . . .'

A light came on.

'What can you see?'

'Maps, paper mostly. And cash. There must be thirty grand. Photographs on the wall,' replied Jane. 'And pills. Lots of pills.'

'Restoril?'

'Yeah.'

'I knew it.'

'Georgina Harcourt?'

'Yes.'

'Oh, shit.'

'What?' asked Dixon, trying to squeeze along the wall.

A latex gloved hand appeared around the corner and passed Dixon a photograph. He held it up to the light and looked at it.

'Shit indeed,' he muttered.

'When was it taken?' asked Jane.

'Looks like last weekend when we were walking back from the Red Cow. Are there any more?'

'Not of us.'

Dixon stepped back out into the corridor. The two uniformed officers were waiting there with Andrea Parks, who had been handcuffed behind her back.

'Is there anything else we need to know about?' asked Dixon.

She turned away and looked at the floor.

'What about the loft?'

'Fuck you.'

Dixon's phone started ringing. He answered it before the second ring.

'Yes, Dave.'

'He's here.'

Dixon rang off and ran along the corridor to the back door. Jane followed.

'Keep her out of sight,' said Dixon, pointing at Andrea.

He waited behind the door until the floodlight on the corner of the garage came on. Then he opened the door and stepped out onto the footbridge.

Dale Reed was sitting on his Norton motorcycle in the middle of the drive. He was dressed head to toe in black leather with a full face black helmet. He stared at Dixon.

'Dale Reed?'

No reply.

Reed sat back and unzipped his leather jacket.

'Police.'

Suddenly, Dixon heard a scream behind him. He turned to see Andrea Parks running along the corridor towards him. He watched one of the uniformed officers catch up with her before she reached the door and bundle her into the bathroom.

'Run, Dale!' she screamed.

Dixon turned back to Reed just in time to see him draw his gun from inside his leather jacket.

'Armed police. Drop your weapon!' The shout came from the carport to Reed's right.

Dixon looked at the gun. It was silenced and pointing straight at them. He stepped in front of Jane.

'No,' she gasped.

'You must've known it would end this way, Dale,' said Dixon.

'Armed police. Drop your weapon!'

Reed looked down at his fuel tank and then back to Dixon. Then his arm jerked to the right and he fired twice. Dixon heard no sound except breaking glass. He spun round. Andrea Parks was falling backwards in the bathroom, blood spraying across the tiled walls.

Then four shots rang out in quick succession. Reed was thrown into the stone wall, landing in a heap at the base behind his Norton, which had toppled over on its side.

Dixon watched the two armed response officers edging forward, their guns aimed at Reed.

'Get an ambulance!' shouted Dixon.

He turned to see Jane emerging from the bathroom.

'She's dead.'

Dixon closed his eyes.

'Two shots to the head,' said Jane. 'What about him?'

One of the armed response officers was pumping Reed's chest.

'Dead,' said Dixon.

Dave Harding was shouting at local residents further down the lane to stay indoors but his voice was soon drowned out by the sirens coming from all directions.

'The Americans have got a name for it,' said Dixon.

'What?' asked Jane.

'Suicide by cop.'

'Where to now?'

'What time is it?' asked Dixon. He was sitting in the passenger seat of Jane's car, watching fireworks going off on the far side of Torbay.

'Just before midnight,' replied Jane.

'Someone should tell 'em New Year's Eve was last night.'

Jane sighed.

'Gits,' continued Dixon. 'Every dog within five hundred yards of that lot is going to be shitting itself.'

'And cat.'

'Yes, and cat. Look at Monty. Big lad, doesn't take any crap, but he's terrified of the bloody things.'

'Have you finished?'

'They should be banned.'

'Can we go now?' asked Jane.

'There's a Travelodge at junction 27,' replied Dixon. 'We can't go home.'

Dixon was deep in thought as they drove north out of Torquay. The forensic examination of the house would be going on through the night but he had got what he wanted, and three boxes of papers, Reed's computer, iPad and phone were on their way to Express Park. Devon and Cornwall Police could keep the rest. Andrea Parks and Reed were in the mortuary at Torbay Hospital and their post mortems would be taking place the next day, or later that day, given that it was after midnight, although the cause of death would not be unduly taxing in either case.

He felt sorry for the firearms officers who had killed Reed. They had saved his life. And Jane's. But now they would be suspended pending a formal investigation. And for what? Doing what they had been trained to do. Still, the likely outcome was a commendation. Dixon would see to that.

And Harry? Died in the line, as the Americans would say. But the vision of his body spinning on the end of the rope still lingered.

'Where are we?'

'Just north of Exeter,' replied Jane.

Dixon looked up at the stars, only this time no one was looking back. He noticed Jane watching him.

'Fran?'

'She's gone now.'

'What do we do about the Albanians?' asked Jane, changing the subject.

'Depends what Reed's stuff tells us, but I'm not holding my breath. I'm tempted to pay 'em a visit.'

'Are you mad?'

'No.'

'Reed had a photo of us and who d'you think he was working for?'

'It may have been on his own account. Perhaps he thought we were getting too close?'

'How would he know?'

'Well, now that's another question.'

'Here we are,' said Jane, allowing her car to drift onto the off slip. 'One room or two?'

'One,' replied Dixon. 'I think we're what's called an open secret, these days.'

Chapter Seventeen

Dixon switched on the radio as they sped north on the M5 the following morning, catching the tail end of the local news.

'Meanwhile, Tom Perry, the Conservative prospective parliamentary candidate for Bridgwater and North Somerset, has today announced that he will be standing in the forthcoming by-election. He is defending the Conservative seat vacated on the death of the former member of parliament, Sir Kenneth Anderson. There had been some speculation that Mr Perry, whose wife Elizabeth was murdered in the early hours of Christmas Eve, would stand down. Police are yet to make an arrest in connection with Mrs Perry's murder.'

'That's not right,' said Jane.

'Back to the flooding now, three pumps have arrived from the Netherlands and are being installed . . .'

Dixon switched off the radio.

'You like him, don't you?'

'Yes,' replied Dixon.

'He's a Tory.'

'I know what he is. And I know what he stands for.'

'I never thought I'd end up living with a Tory voter,' said Jane, shaking her head.

'I didn't say I'd vote for him. When did I say I'd vote for him?'

'You didn't.'

'That's right, I didn't. Now, concentrate on the road, Constable,' said Dixon, smiling.

They turned into Express Park just after 9 a.m. and parked under cover. Dave Harding ran across from the staff entrance to meet them, opening the passenger door of Jane's car before Dixon had taken his seatbelt off.

'You'd better come quick, Sir.'

'What's going on?'

'Zephyr. They're taking everything.'

'Everything?'

Harding nodded.

Dixon and Jane, with Harding following, ran across to the staff entrance and up the stairs.

'In here, Nick,' shouted Lewis, as they ran along the landing. He was standing in the doorway of meeting room two and Dixon slowed to a walk when he spotted DCS Collyer sitting at the table.

Dixon paused in the doorway and watched four officers in dark suits carrying the boxes and Reed's computer along the landing towards the lift.

'Don't tell me,' said Dixon, slamming the door. 'There's things going on . . .'

'Shut up and listen,' said Lewis.

'Let's be quite clear, Inspector,' said Collyer. 'I do not have to explain myself to you.'

Dixon's eyes were closed while he counted to ten.

'We're making significant progress and are on the brink of a major . . .'

'Bollocks.' Dixon could contain himself no longer.

'I'm sorry,' said Lewis.

'It's fine,' said Collyer, standing up. 'I like a man with fire in his belly. But the fact is, Dixon, we're taking it and there's bugger all you can do about it. All right?'

'DCS Collyer has agreed to let us know if they find anything relevant to Elizabeth Perry's murder,' said Lewis.

'Really,' said Dixon, opening the door. 'They had a tap inside those racing stables and never said a thing, so you'll forgive me if I'm not overly optimistic this time.'

'We're all on the same side,' said Lewis.

'Are we?'

Dixon slammed the door behind him.

'Looks like a transfer to Zephyr is off then,' said Jane.

'Car keys,' said Dixon, holding out his hand.

'Where are we going?'

'I'm going to Bristol. You're staying here.'

'No bloody way,' said Jane, picking up her handbag.

Dixon was staring out of the large windows at the front of the police centre, overlooking the visitors' car park, watching the boxes and computer being loaded into the back of two black cars.

'Louise.'

'Yes, Sir.'

'Get me everything you can find on Dale Reed.'

'Yes, Sir.'

'We'll be back later.'

'Steady on. It's a new car,' said Jane, watching her speedometer as Dixon raced past the Burnham junction on the M5.

'Sorry,' he replied, easing off the accelerator.

'Are you sure you should be doing this?'

'No.'

'Turn around then.'

'We're after the money. And only the Albanians can tell us who it is.'

'Yes, but they might . . .'

'I'll be fine. Zavan and I have an understanding, don't forget.'

'And what d'you think he's gonna tell you?'

'I don't know. Probably nothing. But he may say something I can use. Anything will do. We've got nothing at the moment, have we?'

Dixon was watching a car in his wing mirror.

'Bloody hell,' he said, frowning, 'this guy's in a hurry.'

Jane looked over her shoulder.

'There's another in the middle lane.'

Dixon slowed down and pulled across to the inside lane, glancing in his rear view mirror at every opportunity.

'Oh shit.'

'Who is it?'

'Collyer.'

Suddenly, a third car sped up behind him, just as the others pulled across sharply, one taking up position on his offside and the other in front of him. Dixon was boxed in. Then the car in front started braking.

'We're being T-packed.'

'Brent Knoll Services,' said Jane.

'We don't seem to have a lot of choice.'

Dixon waited until the last minute, hoping to veer off into the service station and then use the back road to get clear, but the Zephyr cars had other plans and began moving over, forcing him off the motorway. If he had been in his old Land Rover it might have been different, but this was Jane's car and it was brand new, as she kept reminding him. Once on the slip road, the lead car indicated right and turned into the lorry park. Dixon followed.

The lorry park was empty apart from one car at the far end, its boot open, the driver exercising his dog under the trees. Dixon watched Collyer walking back towards him and wound down the window.

'Get out,' said Collyer.

Dixon followed him across to the grass area.

'Where the fuck d'you think you're going?'

'Panto at the Hippodrome.'

'Don't give me that.'

'You know full well where I'm going and why, so . . .'

'Wind your neck in,' said Collyer. 'For the first time in years, we've got someone on the inside and we can't have you wading in with your size tens. All right?'

Dixon was sucking his teeth and breathing hard through his nose.

'We play our cards close to our chest because we have to,' said Collyer. 'But this is close and when we've got them all, you'll get your chance. Until then, you'll just have to wait.'

'Yes, Sir.'

'We want them thinking it's business as usual. And besides, as far as we can tell, they played no part in Elizabeth Perry's death.'

'As far as we can tell?' asked Dixon.

'They just made the introductions, that's all. But we don't know who, why or when.'

'Someone will.'

'They will. And when the time comes you can ask them. All right?'

'And what about Stanniland? They killed him.'

'They did,' replied Collyer.

'Reed had photos of us,' said Dixon.

'Nothing to do with the Albanians. We'd have known if they were targeting a police officer.'

'But would you have said anything?'

'Credit me with some . . . look, just get back in your car and fuck off home. And if I see you in Bristol I'll nick you for obstruction.'

'What'd he say?' asked Jane.

Dixon ignored the 'No Entry' signs and used the back lane to get out of the service station.

'They've got someone on the inside and don't want us rocking the boat.'

'Is that it?'

'The Albanians made the introduction to Reed, but Collyer doesn't know who, why or when.'

Jane shook her head.

'Oh, and they weren't behind Reed targeting us either, apparently. He'd have known.'

'But would he have said anything?'

'I asked him the same question,' said Dixon.

'And what'd he say?'

'Something along the lines of "fuck off before I nick you for obstruction".'

'Nice.'

'Let's go and get Monty. We can find a dog friendly B and B later.'

'But we're safe to go home, surely? If the Albanians aren't after us?' asked Jane.

'You want to take the chance?'

'I'll ring my folks.'

It was lunchtime when they arrived back at Express Park to find Dave Harding, Mark Pearce and Louise sitting in silence in the corner of the otherwise deserted staff canteen.

'Did they tell you anything?' asked Louise.

'Never got that far,' replied Dixon.

'We were intercepted,' said Jane.

'That was me, sorry.' DCI Lewis was standing behind them, in the doorway. 'People don't tend to like it when you make them look foolish.'

'Foolish?'

'Reed had been on the radar for years but they'd never got close. Then you come along and, bang, you've got him.'

'Literally,' muttered Jane.

'Yes, literally,' said Lewis. 'It makes them feel uncomfortable.'

'Tough sh . . .' said Dixon.

'And you didn't exactly make it easy for him either,' continued Lewis.

'What happens now?' asked Louise.

'Back to the drawing board?' asked Jane.

'Not quite. And besides, there isn't one,' replied Dixon.

'Will a flipchart do?'

'Reed and Stanniland were the foot soldiers and the Albanians were just the intermediaries, according to Collyer.'

'That can't be right though because who else could have put Stanniland up to it?' asked Pearce.

'And he had a belly full of their national dish,' said Louise. 'Tavë whatsit.'

'That's right,' said Dixon. 'But we can't take that much further, for reasons beyond our control, so we'll have to come at it from the other end.'

'Find the motive,' said Jane.

'Someone paid the Albanians, or at least asked them, to set up Elizabeth Perry's murder. Not Tom's. Elizabeth's. That's the key to this.'

'It's not going to be easy,' said Lewis.

'It isn't, Sir,' replied Dixon. 'So, we keep looking until we find it. We'll start with the selection fiasco and the wind farm at East or West Huntspill or wherever it is. Something about those two things stinks. We can move on to the other campaigns if we need to.'

'What does Perry say?' asked Harding.

'He has no idea why anyone would want to kill Elizabeth, which makes two of us at the moment.'

'Yes, Sir.'

'Dave, Mark and Jane, you focus on Westricity. I want full background checks on the directors and shareholders. And minutes of Sedgemoor District Council's Development Committee and the County Council's Scrutiny for Policies and Place Committee.'

'That's a bit of a mouthful,' muttered Mark.

'Get the minutes of all meetings where the wind farm has been discussed. Let's see who lines up on both sides of the argument, shall we?'

'Yes, Sir.'

'No doubt we'll find Councillor Rod Brophy in the mix. He sits on both committees and there must be a reason why he's so keen to be elected the local MP.'

'Ambition? Greed?' asked Harding.

Dixon ignored him.

'We'll focus on the selection, Louise.'

'Yes, Sir.'

'Right then,' said Dixon. 'Let's go canvassing, shall we?'

'She's down the sailing club.'

Dixon just managed to get his foot in the door, as it was slammed in his face.

'What the . . .?' The voice came from behind the door.

Dixon held his warrant card up.

'Oh,' said a teenage boy, opening the door.

'And Mr Sumner?'

'They're both down the sailing club.'

'Who are you?'

'Their son, James. I'm home from uni.'

Dixon nodded.

'Shall I tell them you're looking for them?'

'No need,' said Dixon, as he turned and walked back down the garden path.

He knew the Burnham-on-Sea Sailing Club, not that he had ever considered himself blessed with sea legs. His one and only sailing trip to the Solent had left him vomiting over the side of the yacht, much as his recent trip in the lifeboat had done. Still, each to their own.

The tide was out and two lines of motor cruisers and yachts were sitting on the mud banks of the River Brue, their pontoons lying flat on the mud. Dixon was listening to the rigging rattling in the wind.

'Never understood the attraction,' said Louise.

'Me neither,' replied Dixon, holding his hand out in front of him. 'C'mon, let's get in there before it starts raining again.'

The front door was open but the lounge was deserted, so Dixon rang the bell on the bar.

'Hello?'

'Mrs Sumner?' asked Dixon, spinning round.

'Yes.' She was in her early fifties with short dark hair. Deck shoes and a Musto jacket over a cable sweater told Dixon he was in the right place, but then he knew that. He smiled. It was rather like plus fours and a Pringle sweater. Golf club? Every time.

'I was just leaving,' continued Mrs Sumner.

'May we have a word, please?' asked Dixon, his warrant card in his outstretched hand.

'Er, yes, of course. Shall we sit in the window?' Dixon watched her eyes scanning the lounge, checking it was empty, no doubt.

'Why not.'

Mrs Sumner sat with her back to the window. Dixon sat down opposite her. Louise sat down at the table to his left and took out her notebook.

'I was surprised to find the club open today,' said Dixon.

'We wouldn't usually be. My husband's the treasurer and he's come in to do the accounts. Easier when it's quiet.'

'I wanted to ask you about your time as chairman of the local Conservative Association.'

'I gave that up last year.'

'Are you still a member?'

'Yes,' replied Mrs Sumner. 'I'm still on the local Burnham branch committee too. Look, what's this all about?'

'Your parliamentary candidate's wife has been murdered, Mrs Sumner,' said Dixon.

'Yes, of course she has. Sorry. Such a crying shame. I feel so sorry for Tom.'

'Did you know her well?'

'Not really. I stood down not long after Tom was selected. She came with him to a dinner once. Seemed very pleasant.'

'Tell me about the selection process then.'

'Oh, that.' Barbara Sumner rolled her eyes. 'What a mess.'

'Start at the beginning.'

'We advertised the vacancy when Ken died. Consulted with Central Office in the usual way. Got the CVs in and then followed the . . .'

'Whose idea was the open primary?'

'That came from Tim Spalding, the head of candidates.'

'And when did Rod Brophy say that he wanted to stand?'

'Early on. We had to delay the start so he could get on the list.'

'How long have you known him?'

'Ten years or so. He was already a member when I joined.'

'Did any other local candidates put their names forward?'

'No.'

'So, he got on the list and put his CV in?'

'He did.'

'And got through to the next round?'

'Yes. It's difficult to ignore such a strong local candidate.'

'Is he popular then?' asked Dixon.

'With who?'

'Let's start with the electorate,' said Dixon.

'He's elected to both the district and county councils, if that's what you mean.'

'And what about members of the association?'

'Mostly yes, I suppose. But we have our factions like any political organisation.'

'When did you first learn about the plot . . .'

'Plot?'

'Yes, plot,' replied Dixon, 'to stuff the executive council meeting with his supporters.'

'There was no plot.'

'I've seen the minutes and there are nine people there who hadn't been to a meeting in over a year.'

'About a week before,' said Mrs Sumner, with a heavy sigh, 'Liam Dobbs was ringing around.'

'And what did you do about it?'

'Nothing.'

'Why not?'

'Look, we felt that Central Office had forced an open primary on us. It's our candidate and it should be our choice. The electorate get their say at the election, don't they?'

'So, you agreed with Dobbs?'

'Yes. But not for the same reason. I wanted association members to decide, which they did in the end.'

'And Dobbs?'

'He wanted Rod.'

'Why?'

'You'd need to ask him that. Thick as thieves those two. Always have been.'

'What about Lawrence Deakin?'

'It was his job to see to it that we did it by the book, which he did. He's a good agent.'

'And Barry Dossett, your area campaign director?'

'He didn't seem keen on an open primary, but then it was a lot of extra work for him and the Bristol selections were just getting started at the same time.'

'What did Central Office do when all this kicked off?'

'Two members of the Party board came down to an emergency management team meeting. Barry Dossett was there. They threatened us with special measures, but we stood our ground and they backed off in the end. There'd already been too much damaging publicity, I think.'

'So, you rerun the selection and end up with the same candidate?' asked Dixon.

'We did. And a damned good candidate he is too. He'll make an even better MP.'

'What about this recent attempt to deselect him?'

'I don't know anything about that. I stood down at the AGM last year, don't forget.'

Dixon nodded.

'You don't seriously think this has anything to do with Elizabeth's death, do you, Inspector?'

Dixon was watching the rain running down the large conservatory windows, and the boats beyond, which would soon be afloat on the incoming tide that was just reaching them.

'I . . .' Dixon stopped when his phone bleeped in his pocket. 'Excuse me,' he said, reading the message.

wind farm protest meeting east huntspill village hall tomorrow 7pm J x

'Just routine enquiries, at this stage, Mrs Sumner,' said Dixon. 'Thank you for your help.'

It was dark by the time Louise dropped Dixon outside Express Park.

'You head off,' said Dixon. 'Eight o'clock sharp tomorrow.'

'Yes, Sir.'

'Where's Louise?' asked Jane, stepping out of the canteen into the corridor behind Dixon as he walked past.

'I sent her home.'

'Oh, right.'

'What've you got?'

'Plenty of stuff on Westricity. The council minutes will take a bit longer. Should have them by the end of tomorrow.'

Dixon nodded.

'The file's on my desk,' continued Jane. 'And Lewis was looking for you earlier.'

'Collyer'll have bent his ear so he's got to bend mine. That's the way these things usually work.'

'The chain of command,' said Jane, grinning.

Dixon let Dave Harding and Mark Pearce go home early and then sat down at a computer to check his emails. He looked up when he spotted the reflection of DCI Lewis standing behind him.

'Didn't know you were a fan of panto,' said Lewis. 'You should join Bridgwater Amateur Dramatics. It's *Aladdin* this year.'

Dixon sighed.

'I can just see you as Widow Twanky,' continued Lewis.

'Am I allowed to tell a senior officer to piss off?'

'No, you're not.'

Dixon sighed again, louder this time.

'And what were you gonna do?' asked Lewis. 'Steam in there and ask them . . .'

'Something like that.'

'You'd be at the bottom of the channel by now.'

'I doubt it.'

'Anyway, how far have you got?'

'It must be connected with politics somehow,' replied Dixon. 'Perry's selection was a shambles, so we're looking into that. And the various campaigns he was running.'

'Anything interesting?'

'Not yet. And the big question still bugging me is why kill Elizabeth and not Tom? If it's politically motivated, that is.'

'It may not be,' said Lewis.

'Then we really are back to the drawing board.'

'Find the motive and hope it'll lead you to the killer,' said Lewis, shaking his head.

'It will.'

'If you can find it.'

Dixon never slept well in a strange bed, although neither Jane nor Monty appeared to be having any trouble. It was almost 2 a.m.

and Dixon had read the file on Westricity twice. There had been no mention of Tom or Elizabeth Perry, but that would have been too easy, and the names listed in the shareholders register meant nothing to him. One would require further investigation, Welmore Holdings Limited, but that was it. It had been a nice evening though. A meal in the Farriers Arms, followed by a few beers in front of the fire. It was the only bit of good news Dixon had had in recent days.

'The B&B's opposite a nice pub, apparently.'

And it was. The only downside was the lack of Wi-Fi.

What struck him as even more unusual was that they hadn't mentioned the case once in the entire evening. Unusual, that, in the heat of battle. But then some things are more important, perhaps, and even police officers are allowed a private life.

Jane had talked about finding her birth parents, although she hadn't yet discussed it with her adopted parents. That had been Dixon's first suggestion, although he had to admit he was not exactly an expert in this situation. She must have been watching too many episodes of *Long Lost Family*.

'See what they say,' had been his advice. 'You never know, they may even know who they are and just never told you.'

'Wouldn't they be hurt?'

'Not half as much as they will be if you just do it and they find out.'

Jane had agreed with that one.

Dixon switched off the reading light on his side of the bed and slid down under the duvet. He knew that when he closed his eyes he would see the picture of Harry Unwin's body swinging on the end of the rope. Only this time it was the body of Wendy Gibson that appeared, lying on her back in the field gateway. Dixon could tell from the angle of her feet and the zip on her coat. He opened his eyes and she was gone.

He thought about the one person he had kept in touch with from college, now a solicitor in Swindon dealing with wills and probate, complaining that his life revolved around death.

'You wanna try seeing it from my end,' had been Dixon's reply.

Chapter Eighteen

'It's UHT milk,' said Dixon, dropping the small pot back into the bowl.

'I'm sure they'd give you some . . .' Jane's voice was lost in a yawn, 'proper stuff, if you asked.'

'Haven't got time for that,' said Dixon. 'C'mon, we said we'd be down for breakfast at 7.30 a.m.'

'You don't eat breakfast.'

'I do when I've paid for it. And it's a fry up.'

They arrived at Express Park just before 9 a.m. Dave Harding and Mark Pearce were leaning against the filing cabinets, talking to Louise Willmott, who was sitting at a computer.

'Morning, Sir,' said Louise.

'Has anyone spoken to Elizabeth's friends yet?' asked Dixon.

'The Met did. Briefly. Didn't find anything relevant.'

'Let's speak to them again then. Dave, Mark, that's your job. I want them all spoken to. All right?'

'Yes, Sir.'

'Ask them about the politics, people she may have met, anything unusual she may have said. All right?'

'Will do,' replied Harding.

'What about her phone?' asked Dixon.

'High Tech have got it. They checked her calls,' replied Jane.

'What about her iPad?'

'They've got that too. Nothing on it except photos. We looked at her Facebook . . .'

'Look at it again.'

Jane nodded.

'And I want a company search for Welmore Holdings Limited. Then background checks on the directors and shareholders. All right?'

'OK.'

'Who's Welmore Holdings?' asked Louise.

'It's a holding company that owns 20 per cent of Westricity,' replied Dixon. 'You're with me again, Louise. Just give me twenty minutes.'

Dixon switched on a computer and fetched himself a cup of coffee while he waited for it to start up. Then he sat down, opened Google and typed 'probate find' into the search field. Seconds later he was on GOV.UK learning about finding a will for people who died in or after 1858. He clicked on 'Start Now'.

On the next page he selected 'Wills and Probate 1858–1996' and entered Gibson under surname and 1994 for year of death. There were thirteen pages of the Probate Calendar returned for Gibson in 1994. A lot of Gibsons died that year.

They were listed alphabetically so he jumped forward to page ten, then twelve.

'There you are,' he muttered.

GIBSON, WENDY MAY

OF STICKLAND BARN MUCHELNEY BRIDGWATER SOMERSET

DIED 25 MARCH 1994 PROBATE BRISTOL 12 DECEMBER £411308 9451764579C

He entered the details in the required fields on the right of the page, clicked 'Add to basket' and then reached for his wallet.

Barry Dossett was just coming out of the Bridgwater Conservative Association office when Louise turned into the car park and parked in a vacant space in front of Dobbs Design.

'Will he be all right in here?' she asked, glancing over her shoulder at Monty.

'Yes, he's fine,' replied Dixon. 'He doesn't chew cars.'

Dossett saw them getting out of Louise's car and waited by his own. Dixon walked over to him.

'Lawrence has gone, Inspector. If . . .'

'Actually, it was you I was looking for,' replied Dixon.

'I'm afraid I'm due at a meeting in Bristol, then I'm off home.'

'Where is home?'

'Ascot. I do the weekly thing and stay in digs during the week. I'll be back tomorrow though. We've got an action day.'

Dixon frowned.

'The environment secretary's coming down to see the floods and support Tom's campaign. Plus we've got several coachloads of supporters coming down to knock on doors.'

'How involved were you with the open primary?'

Dossett looked at his watch.

'This won't take long,' continued Dixon.

'I was just overseeing it, really. I cover a large area and several other constituencies were selecting at the same time so it was pretty hectic. Lawrence ran it.'

'Is there a lot of extra work with an open primary?'

'Some. My own view, if you must know, is they're a complete waste of time,' replied Dossett, shaking his head. 'I can't think of one election we've won after going through this charade that we wouldn't have won anyway.'

'Why hold them, then?'

'I just do what I'm told, Inspector. That's the lot of us staffers. They'll tell you it's the publicity.'

'Who will?'

'Our political lords and masters.'

'So, how did you react when the executive council ignored the result?'

'I warned them what would happen but they went ahead and did it anyway,' replied Dossett, shrugging his shoulders. 'It was my first real involvement with the association, so I didn't know any of them that well. There'd always been a sitting MP before so we never had candidate selections to worry about. Anyway, they avoided special measures. Somehow.'

'Were you aware of the plot to . . .'

'You think this has something to do with Elizabeth's murder?'

Dixon ignored the question.

'Lawrence filled me in,' replied Dossett, with a sigh. He opened his car door. 'But it was no big deal. Every association has its factions. And they got the right result in the end.'

'Was Tom under pressure to stand down after Elizabeth's murder?'

'God, no. We just needed to know so we could get on with finding another candidate, that's all. Thankfully, we didn't have to. He's a good lad, is Tom. He'll go far. And he's got guts.'

'How well did you know Elizabeth?' asked Dixon, holding the car door while Dossett climbed into the driver's seat.

'Hardly at all, really. I met her briefly at the primary. Then again at the final selection. That's it, I think. It's rare for me to go to association social events.'

Dossett switched on the engine.

'What time does the action day start?' asked Dixon.

'Ten.'

'Where will you be?'

'Moorland to begin with then canvassing in the Burnham area for the rest of the day.'

'Thank you, Mr Dossett,' said Dixon.

He waited until Dossett had driven off before turning to Louise.

'Remind me to make sure I'm out tomorrow.'

'What now?' asked Louise, smiling.

'Let's go and see what Mr Dobbs has got to say for himself, shall we?' said Dixon, nodding at the light in the window of Dobbs Design.

The front door was open, so Dixon followed Louise into an open plan office area, with one light on at a workstation in the far corner. Dixon coughed, expecting to see a head pop up from behind the partition. Nothing.

Louise tiptoed over and peered around the partition, then she walked back towards Dixon, shaking her head.

'He's busy.'

'Doing what?' asked Dixon.

'Watching a film.'

'What sort of . . . ?'

'Don't ask,' replied Louise, rolling her eyes. 'He's got headphones on.'

Dixon tiptoed forward and dropped his warrant card over the partition onto the desk in front of Dobbs. He sat up sharply, fumbling for his headphones.

'We're looking for Liam Dobbs,' said Dixon.

'Er . . . yes . . . that's me.'

'We won't keep you long, Mr Dobbs. I can see you're busy.'

It was an interesting shade of red. Anger, fear, embarrassment, Dixon had seen it all. But seldom had he seen anyone go as red as Liam Dobbs. He was tall, even sitting in an office chair, and had the look of someone who spent far too long in front of a computer.

'How can I help?'

'Well, you can get rid of that, for a start,' said Dixon, pointing at the computer screen.

'Sorry,' replied Dobbs, reaching for the mouse.

'We're investigating the murder of Elizabeth Perry.'

'I thought you'd caught . . . ?'

'We have all sorts of leads we have to follow up. I'm sure you understand.'

'Yes, yes, of course.'

Dixon picked his warrant card up and put it back in his pocket.

'Why were you so keen to see Rod Brophy selected?'

'I wasn't.'

'Really?'

'No.'

'Then why did you stuff the executive council meeting with his supporters?'

'I didn't.'

'We've seen the minutes and the attendance register.'

Dixon watched Dobbs flicking the mouse from side to side, his eyes following the cursor around an empty screen.

'I thought we needed a local candidate.'

'As opposed to a candidate selected by local people?'

'Yes.'

Dixon turned to Louise. 'I wondered how long it would be before we encountered this, Constable. They call it "spin". But you and I would call it lies.'

'Hang on a . . .'

'Lying to police in a murder investigation is a serious business, Mr Dobbs.'

Dixon watched the beads of sweat appearing on Dobbs' forehead. He was swallowing hard too. Always a good sign.

'Perhaps we should get High Tech to have a look at Mr Dobbs' computer, Constable. See if there's anything on there that shouldn't be.'

'No, there's nothing. It's all legal.'

'I'm sure it is. Now where were we,' said Dixon. 'Oh yes, why were you so keen to see Rod Brophy selected?'

Dobbs hesitated.

'It wasn't just any local candidate, was it?'

No response.

'It was Rod Brophy? Why?'

Dixon waited.

'He's a friend of mine. Gives me a lot of work. And he lent me some money when I got into trouble.'

'What sort of trouble?'

'Business trouble. Things got a bit tight when the recession hit.'

'How much money did he lend you?'

'Thirty thousand pounds.'

'Have you paid it back?'

'Not yet.'

'Tell me about the work then?'

'What about it?'

'How much does he give you?'

'Whatever he can. Logo design, websites, search engine optimisation. He puts a lot of work my way. Friends of his. Acquaintances. He knows a lot of people.'

'And as an MP he'd be able to put even more work your way?'

'Yes,' replied Dobbs. 'That's what he said, anyway.'

'Has he asked for his money back?'

'No.'

Dixon nodded.

'Have you done any work for Westricity?' asked Louise.

Dixon looked at her and raised his eyebrows.

'We did their website,' replied Dobbs.

'We?' asked Dixon.

'I employ three staff. There are four of us here.'

'Where did the referral to Westricity come from?' asked Louise.

'Rod,' replied Dobbs. 'Look, you don't seriously think any of this has anything to do with the murder, do you?'

'A group of people, of which you were a ringleader, make a deliberate, orchestrated and failed attempt to get rid of Tom Perry,' said Dixon. 'And then his wife is murdered. You can understand our interest?'

'Really, it's . . .'

'Well, that's all for now. I suggest you keep quiet about this conversation. Is that clear?'

'Yes,' replied Dobbs, wiping away the tears that were rolling down his cheeks.

Dixon and Louise turned to leave.

'You're not taking my computer?' asked Dobbs.

'I understand you want to be an MP one day. Is that right?'

'Yes.'

'You'll go far.'

Dixon shook his head and continued walking.

'What was all that about the computer?' asked Louise, switching on the engine.

'When you've got them on the ropes, keep hitting 'em,' replied Dixon. 'I learned that watching Frank Bruno.'

'I didn't know you were a boxing fan.'

'I'm not, but everyone was rooting for Big Frank. It was back in the days when it didn't cost you an arm and a leg to watch it on the telly too.'

'Are we gonna take Dobbs' computer?'

'We've got no evidence he's committed any offence, have we?'

'I suppose not.'

'Where did that Westricity bit come from?' asked Dixon.

'I looked at their website. In tiny letters at the bottom of the 'About Us' page, it says, "Website by Dobbs Design".'

'Well done,' said Dixon, smiling.

'Where to now?'

'Brent Knoll. My Land Rover should've dried out by now.'

He was unlikely to get another chance for the foreseeable future, so Dixon could justify it. Almost. Just an hour, then he would catch up with Louise at Express Park. At least, that was what he told himself as he parked in the car park at Berrow Church. It was overcast, with a cold north wind blowing and the beach would be deserted. Perfect.

He opened the back of the Land Rover and watched Monty jump out and disappear up through the churchyard towards the beach. He followed him, pausing on the edge of the thirteenth fairway to allow two golfers to tee off, despite never having seen one reach the path. Then he stopped at the edge of the reeds to put Monty's lead on. Ahead lay a narrow sandy track that twisted and turned through the reed bed and out onto the dunes, and you never knew who or what might be coming in the opposite direction. The prospect of Monty terrifying an elderly lady with a chihuahua was not worth the risk, not that he would have done anything, except perhaps lick it to death.

Once out onto the beach, Dixon zipped up his coat, turned up the collar and then thrust his hands deep into his pockets. Monty would have to make do with his ball kicked along the beach today. The tide was out and dry sand nearer the dunes was being blown along at ankle height in small but fierce sandstorms, so Dixon walked further out on the wet sand to keep it out of Monty's eyes. They turned north towards Brean Down. Not a single car was parked on Berrow Beach; it was one advantage of a walk on the beach on a weekday in foul weather. And it would give him a chance to think.

He thought about an episode of *Long Lost Family* ending with the adopted child finding his or her birth mother and then blowing her head off with a .410 shotgun. It would not make good TV, but at least Wendy Gibson's cold case had some sense of direction now, for the first time in over twenty years, even if it turned out to be the wrong direction.

Would Jane react in the same way when she found her birth mother? Dixon hoped not. And it would be his job to see to it that she didn't.

Liam Dobbs. Harmless prat was the conclusion Dixon had arrived at. Although there was clearly more to Brophy's apparent enthusiasm to get selected, and then elected, than pure ambition and greed, to use Dave Harding's phrase. He expected to find a connection between Brophy and Westricity but was still no nearer finding a motive for the murder of Elizabeth Perry. Why kill Elizabeth if you wanted rid of Tom? The best he had come up with so far was that to murder Tom might be too obvious in that situation.

Laughable.

He was sitting on one of the old wooden posts that stopped cars parking too near the dunes, watching Monty digging, when he heard a large engine behind him, on the beach road. It was accelerating hard and getting closer. A large automatic, possibly a V12. Dixon stood up and turned to see a black Range Rover with tinted windows roar onto the beach, almost taking off as it came over the ramp. Once out onto the beach it turned towards him, sending sand spraying from wheels that were spinning on the soft ground. Dixon stepped back behind the line of wooden posts.

'Monty, here, boy.'

Monty ran over and Dixon put his lead on. Then he watched the Range Rover slide to a halt in front of him. He was about to find out whether he really did have an understanding with the Albanians.

Dixon waited, listening to the Range Rover's engine revving.

A small man got out of the front passenger seat and opened the rear passenger door. He was wearing black, exactly as he had been when they last met; when he had pressed a gun barrel into the small of Dixon's back.

'Get in.'

Dixon stepped forward.

'Leave the dog.'

'No.'

Dixon watched the man reach inside his jacket and pull out a gun, which he pointed at Monty's head.

'I really wouldn't do that,' said Dixon. 'If I were you.'

A shout came from inside the Range Rover. Dixon recognised Zavan's voice but didn't understand the language, although he could guess what order had been given. The small man put his gun away, shut the rear door and climbed back into the front passenger seat. Then the Range Rover reversed and turned so that the offside rear passenger window was facing Dixon. He watched the tinted window go down, to reveal Zavan sitting in the rear passenger seat, also dressed in black, as he had been last time.

'I have never understood the English love of dogs,' he said, in a strong eastern European accent.

'Get yourself one,' said Dixon.

'I intend to. When I retire,' said Zavan, smiling. 'I understand you wanted to see me.'

'I did.'

'You want to know who killed the politician's wife?'

'I do.'

'But they are already dead, are they not?'

'The foot soldiers are. I want to know who paid the money and who gave the order.'

'No one gave the order. So our interests again do not conflict.'

'If you say so.'

'I will emigrate straight away, if you ever join Zephyr, Mr Dixon,' said Zavan. He grinned, revealing a line of yellow teeth.

'Maybe I'll consider it then.'

'It would be good sport, would it not, Nick? May I call you Nick?'

'Football, cricket, rugby. They're good sports.' Dixon ignored his last question.

'Now, football I understand.'

'Who paid the money?' asked Dixon.

'Do you believe in insurance, Nick?'

'I do.'

'You house was repaired?'

'It was.'

'Good,' said Zavan. 'You must always have insurance.'

'What sort?'

'In this great country you can insure against anything and everything, can you not?'

'You can.'

'I always have insurance.'

'I bet you do,' said Dixon.

Zavan barked an order in Albanian, then he turned back to Dixon.

'I doubt we will meet again, Nick. Ustau çatinë e vet e le të pikojë,' said Zavan, waving his index finger at him.

Dixon watched the Range Rover accelerate away and turn back onto the beach road. Then it disappeared behind the sand dunes.

'Now we've both had a gun pointed at us, old son,' he said, squatting down next to Monty and scratching him behind the ears. 'C'mon, let's get back.'

They walked back along the beach to the path through the dunes and across the golf course, Dixon deep in thought.

Insurance. What was that all about? And he needed to get to a computer before he forgot the Albanian that Zavan had spoken to him. That must have been significant. Either that or Zavan had been telling him to take a long walk off a short pier.

Dixon ran along the landing and sat down at the first vacant workstation he came to. Then he switched on the computer and waited.

'Everything all right, Sir?' asked Louise.

Dixon nodded. He saw Jane's head pop up from behind a partition.

'Is he back?'

'Yes,' replied Louise.

Jane got up and walked over. She stood behind Dixon, watching his computer screen as he opened Google and typed in 'ustau catine meaning'.

'What's that?'

'Albanian,' replied Dixon.

'Have you seen them?'

'They saw me.'

'Are you all right?'

'Fine. Monty's a bit traumatised though. It's not every day you have a gun pointed at your head.'

'Is he . . . ?'

'He's fine. I don't think he noticed, to be honest.'

'Where were you?'

'Berrow Beach,' replied Dixon. 'What the hell's all this about?'

They were looking at the search results, which offered definitions of 'canteen' from freedictionary.com and lots of websites about wine.

'That can't be it,' said Dixon.

'It's including other results, look. Try that.' Jane was pointing at the top of the screen to a link 'Search only for ustau catine meaning'.

Dixon clicked on it and waited.

'What'd they say?' asked Jane.

'I'm not sure, really. He said something about insurance, this phrase in Albanian and then buggered off.'

'That's not it either, is it?' asked Jane.

'Can't be.'

This time it gave a definition of 'utsav'; a small cafeteria, as on a military installation. Dixon sighed. Then he typed the word 'Albanian' on the end of the search string and hit the 'Enter' button.

'That's more like it.'

The first result came from Wikiquote. Dixon clicked on it and was soon looking at an alphabetical list of Albanian proverbs. He scrolled down.

'The shoemaker goes barefoot.'

'What does that mean?' asked Jane.

By now Louise and Mark Pearce were standing either side of her.

'What's going on?' asked Louise.

'He's had another visit from the Albanians,' replied Jane.

'The English translation is "working hard for others one may neglect one's own needs or the needs of those closest to him",' said Dixon, sitting back in his chair.

'Who may?' asked Jane.

'Tom Perry.'

'And the needs of those closest to him will be Elizabeth?'

'It will.'

'What about the insurance thing?'

Dixon was still staring at the computer screen.

'Means we can go home, though, doesn't it?' continued Jane. 'If they'd wanted you dead they'd have done it there and then, wouldn't they?'

Dixon smiled. For a moment there, he had thought they were going to.

Chapter Nineteen

They had dropped their bags and Jane's car back at the cottage in Brent Knoll and driven to East Huntspill in Dixon's Land Rover and, while Jane had been impressed by the three air fresheners dangling from the rear view mirror, she had still grumbled about the smell.

The wind farm meeting got under way at the East Huntspill Village Hall at 7 p.m. sharp. Dixon and Jane were standing at the back watching the stragglers taking their seats in front of them. It had been a boring afternoon, reading through the documents that Jane and Mark had produced on Welmore Holdings; boring, that is, until he had come across the shareholders register. It would be an interesting interview with Mr Brophy the following morning.

'Right then, let's make a start, shall we?' said the meeting chairman, standing up behind a trestle table on the stage at the far end of the hall. 'As you know, Sedgemoor District Council have refused planning permission but Westricity have appealed. This will be going before the planning inspector shortly and we'll come on to what we do about that in a minute. First though, given that we are in the middle of a by-election, I have invited all of the candidates here tonight to tell us what they intend to do about it.'

He waited for the murmuring to subside.

'First, Mr Tom Perry, Conservative.'

Perry had been sitting at the front of the hall with the other candidates. He stood up and turned to face the audience, wearing a bright blue rosette. He reminded them that he had been instrumental in the campaign against the wind farm thus far and that he would continue to be so, if elected their member of parliament. Then he added that Conservative Party policy was to end the government subsidy for onshore wind farms, an announcement that was greeted with a round of applause.

'There has to be a balance between sustainable, green energy supplies and the impact on the environment. I would only ever support wind farms offshore.'

Another round of applause.

'Now Liberal Democrat candidate, Vanessa Hunt,' said the chairman, although that was obvious from the yellow rosette.

Dixon leaned over and whispered in Jane's ear. 'Janice looked at the other election candidates, didn't she?'

Jane nodded.

Mrs Hunt was a supporter of onshore wind farms, and solar power, but in the right place, and this was not the right place, due to the visual impact on the flat landscape and the risk to the unique biodiversity of the Levels. Her statement was greeted with more applause, as was the Labour candidate's, who said much the same thing. The largest round of applause went to the UKIP candidate, who was less than complimentary about wind farms.

'Hideous monstrosities that kill birds and generate enough electricity for fifty people to make a cup of tea in the advert break on *Coronation Street*. A complete waste of time and money.'

'He doesn't pull any punches, does he?' whispered Jane.

'He doesn't have to,' replied Dixon, smiling.

Jane frowned.

'He's not going to win,' continued Dixon. 'You can say what you like if you're not going to win. People can't hold you to it later.'

'How d'you know that?'

'There was an opinion poll in the *Bridgwater Mercury*.'

'Who's going to win then?'

'It's between blue and yellow.'

'Right then,' said the chairman. 'Let's . . .'

'Where's the Green candidate?' The shout came from the floor.

'She declined my invitation to attend. She didn't think that attending a wind farm protest meeting was appropriate during an election campaign.'

'Thought she'd get lynched, more like.' From the floor again and greeted with more murmuring.

'There's no Monster Raving Looney,' said Jane.

'Are you sure?' replied Dixon, grinning.

'Settle down, settle down,' continued the chairman. 'We need to get letter writing again. This time to the planning inspector. I've looked at the guidance, which says that original objections will be taken into account, but there's no harm in writing again. All right? There was a leaflet on every chair giving the address and reference number.'

'What do we say?'

'Make the same objections as last time. Visual impact, noise and shadow flicker. Remember these are large and close to dwellings. And the environmental damage, don't forget. One letter each. One signed by two people counts as one objection so everyone in the household must write separate letters. Got that?'

'What's the point if they take into account the letters we wrote before?

'The alternative is to do nothing and hope for the best,' replied the chairman.

'We can't take that chance.'

'No, we can't.'

More voices from the floor.

'Will the inspector do a site visit?'

'He will,' replied the chairman. 'So, it's important we have a huge poster campaign for him to see when he comes. I want a "No Wind Farm" poster in every window.'

'What about arranging a demo when he comes? Show him the strength of feeling?'

'I've taken advice on that and the general feeling is that would be counterproductive. We will be represented at his site visit. And have the opportunity to tell him what we think and why. But a mob following him around, shouting at him, is likely to have the opposite effect.'

'Who will be there then?'

'I will. And our newly elected MP, whoever that is. Maybe two others, but the committee will decide on that.'

'What about Westricity?'

'They will be there, of course, they will. It's their appeal.'

'Wankers.'

'Whatever we think of them, this is a planning process and if the appeal is to be thrown out, it will be on planning grounds. It's emotive, of course it is, but we must keep emotion out of it. Planning objections. Visual impact, that sort of thing. All right?'

'Did you see that piece in the papers, calling us NIMBYs?'

'May I?' asked Tom Perry, catching the chairman's eye.

'By all means.'

Perry stood up and turned to face the audience.

'"Not in my back yard" is a shabby accusation. Ignore it. I'm sure I speak for all of the candidates here tonight when I say that it is my back yard, and I'm proud of my back yard. I love it. And, no, I don't want a wind farm in my back yard.' Perry waited for the applause to subside. 'And what's more, anyone who says they do want a wind farm in their back yard is a liar.'

'Let 'em have it in their back yard, then.'

Perry smiled and sat down.

'What about Rod Brophy? You were at the planning meeting. What do we do about Brophy?'

'Nothing,' replied the chairman. 'He sits on the committee and is entitled to his opinion. But the committee made the right decision anyway so what does it matter what he thinks?'

Dixon leaned over and whispered in Jane's ear.

'I've seen enough.'

'What did you make of that then?' asked Jane, as she drove back towards Brent Knoll.

'I'm not sure I've learned anything new,' replied Dixon. 'Although Brophy's enthusiasm for the wind farm seems to be common knowledge.'

'Do they know why?'

'I doubt it.'

'And the relevance to Elizabeth's murder?'

'None. It sheds more light on Brophy's enthusiasm to get selected, perhaps, and the concerted effort to get Tom's selection overturned, but that's about it. And I'm not sure even that is relevant to Elizabeth's murder.'

'Why not?'

'If you wanted rid of Tom, you'd kill Tom, not his wife, surely?' asked Dixon.

'So, what happens now?'

'We speak to Brophy tomorrow, as planned. We have to follow that through, but I'm not sure we're any nearer finding the motive for Elizabeth's murder. Not that I'd tell anyone that.'

Jane sighed.

'Put your foot down and we can get to the Red Cow before they stop serving food.'

Jane tiptoed down the stairs to find Dixon fast asleep on the sofa, with Monty curled up beside him on a pile of papers. Dixon's laptop had shut down and the only light came from the credits on an old black and white film that was just finishing.

She tapped him on the knee.

'What time is it?' he asked, yawning and stretching his arms.

'Fourish,' replied Jane. 'What have you been doing?'

'Research,' replied Dixon. He closed his laptop and put it on the arm of the sofa, then he began pulling various documents out from underneath Monty.

'What's the film?' asked Jane, switching the light on.

'*The Train*. Burt Lancaster. Haven't you . . .?'

'No, I haven't,' replied Jane. 'Are you coming to bed?'

'Too late now. I'll take Monty for a walk, I think.'

'It's pissing down out there.'

'I've got a brolly and he's got a coat.'

'Suit yourself.'

Jane was right, it was raining hard. Cold too. But it was a chance to think. He was missing something. Where the killer has done the killing, more often than not you could place them at the scene, have some physical evidence, but here there was none. The true killer, the money, was removed, one or perhaps even two steps removed, from the killing itself. The physical evidence had led them to the foot soldiers and the only thing he was going to get from the go-between was some ramblings about insurance and 'the shoemaker goes barefoot'.

Perry probably had neglected Elizabeth's needs, if his statement was anything to go by. But he had been focussed on the election campaign and could, perhaps, be forgiven for that. It was the nature of a political marriage, although Elizabeth hadn't known she was getting into one until it was too late. It was a long and detailed statement and Perry's guilt shone through. Guilt that he had been dedicated to his political career, which had gathered a momentum of its own at the expense of his marriage, and guilt that Elizabeth might have died because of it.

Dixon had spent hours trawling through all of Perry's political activity since he had been selected to stand for parliament. Much of the legwork had been done by Jane, Mark and Dave, and it made for a thick file on each of the major campaigns. He had been through the wind farm file three times and yet nothing leapt out at him. Yes, Elizabeth had been there throughout, supporting her husband, but she had played no active part in any of the campaigning.

The cold case had more sense of direction. Or at least, it felt like it. It may turn out to be the wrong direction but he felt as if he was making progress, although that could probably be explained by self-delusion. As for Elizabeth Perry, what direction the investigation had was gone, despite Zavan's riddle. Dixon hated riddles as much as he hated cryptic crosswords.

He watched the rain bouncing off the parked cars, as he walked along Brent Street towards open countryside. He turned left at the end of the road, heading towards Berrow, folded up his umbrella and tucked it under his arm. Maybe the rain would wake him up.

'Shouldn't you be going with Louise?' asked Jane.

'I'm not driving all the way to Bridgwater and back again just to collect Louise,' replied Dixon.

He was driving along Rectory Road, looking up at the house numbers. They were large houses, set back from the road down private drives, but most had the name or number on the gatepost. He slowed down outside a large house with a huge tree in the front garden. Jane leaned across him and looked up.

'The Vicarage?'

'Picture a ten year old boy playing cricket in the drive,' said Dixon, smiling.

'You?'

'We must've missed Brophy's place. I'll turn round.'

They drove back along Rectory Road, peering at the house numbers. Jane was looking out of the passenger window and Dixon, the windscreen. Not easy, despite his wipers on full speed.

'That must be it,' said Jane, pointing to a house with high wooden gates and an entry phone on the gatepost.

'Wait here,' said Dixon, parking across the drive. 'I'll see if he's in.'

'We should've made an appointment.'

'Much rather catch him on the hop,' replied Dixon.

He ran around the front of the Land Rover and rang the buzzer.

'Yes.'

'Detective Inspector Dixon to see Mr Brophy.'

'I'm just going out.'

Dixon waited. A loud sigh came over the intercom, then the gates began to open. Jane jumped out of the Land Rover.

The house was large and modern, with a new Mercedes and a BMW X3 parked outside a built in double garage. It was difficult to tell whether the fountain was on, it was raining that hard, but the koi carp were obvious; large orange and white fish circling just below the surface of the pond in the middle of the front lawn.

Brophy was waiting on the doorstep. He was in his early fifties, with greying hair and an obviously dyed moustache. He'd put on a few pounds too and Dixon hardly recognised him from his photograph on the Somerset County Council website.

'You'd better come in.'

'Thank you,' replied Dixon.

The lounge was best described as minimalist. Almost austere. Two white leather sofas, a red rug in front of a white tiled fireplace and nothing on the mantelpiece. No television either. And no pictures on the walls.

'We're investigating the death of Elizabeth Perry . . .'

'I know.'

'How well did you know her?'

'Not very. Look, I'm sure you know that Tom and I were opponents throughout the selection process and when he was selected I took the deliberate decision to step back. Let him get on with it, as it were.'

'Tell me about the selection process.'

Brophy sat down on the edge of one of the sofas and gestured to Dixon and Jane to sit on the other.

'It was unfortunate.'

Dixon nodded.

'Central Office imposed an open primary on us. Bloody waste of time that was. There was a suspicion that Perry stuffed the primary with his supporters and skewed the result.'

'Where did this suspicion come from?' asked Dixon.

'I don't know.'

'How could he have done that though? He doesn't even live in the constituency, does he?'

'He was campaigning in advance of the meeting . . .'

'So were you,' replied Dixon. 'And that's allowed under the rules. I checked.'

'Well, I . . .'

'Did none of your supporters attend?'

'They did, of course they did.'

'Not enough though.'

'No.'

'So, whose idea was it to stuff the executive council meeting?'

'Now, steady on . . .'

Jane smiled. How to win friends and influence people, by Nick Dixon. Essential reading.

'How did you react when Perry won the primary?' asked Dixon.

'I was disappointed.'

'Is it true that you regarded this seat as yours when Kenneth Anderson stood down?'

'Who told you that?'

'Is it true?'

'I very much hoped that the local party would recognise my long standing track record of work as a councillor and select me, yes.'

'And you made no secret of that?'

'I suppose not.'

'So, how did you feel when Tom won?'

'I felt let down, I suppose,' replied Brophy. 'Look, I don't understand your interest in this. The selection was done and dusted last year.'

'A concerted effort is made to get rid of Tom Perry, when he's won the selection fairly and squarely,' said Dixon, standing up. 'And then his wife's murdered.'

'You can't seriously think . . .'

Dixon was standing in the front window, looking out at the fish still circling the pond.

'Let me ask you again, whose idea was it to stuff the executive council meeting?'

Brophy sighed. 'Mine, but it's a perfectly legitimate tactic. I just made sure that everyone who supported me and was entitled to be at the meeting went to it and voted.'

'And Liam Dobbs organised it?'

'He did.'

'What then?'

'Dobbs suggested that I be selected as an emergency measure. At an extraordinary meeting of the executive council.'

'A shoe in?'

'If you must.'

'And that's when Central Office stepped in?'

'They did. Perry's supporters tipped them off.'

'Perry's supporters or your opponents?'

'We make enemies, Inspector. It goes with the territory.'

'So, leaving aside vanity and ambition . . .'

'I beg your pardon.'

'My understanding is that most politicians are motivated by vanity and ambition,' said Dixon. 'Is that not true?'

'Some perhaps.'

'But not you?'

'No.'

'What are you motivated by then?'

'A desire to serve my local community. A sense of duty.'

'Not money?'

'I'm not sure I . . .'

'Tell me about Welmore Holdings Limited.'

'I've never . . .' Brophy's voice tailed off. He closed his eyes and took a deep breath through his nose.

'Never what?' asked Dixon.

Silence.

'Never disclosed your financial interest in the company?'

'No.' Brophy was staring at the floor in front of him.

'It was a rousing speech in support of the wind farm you made at the planning committee meeting. I've seen the minutes. They even remarked on it at the protest meeting last night.'

'We have to invest in sustainable . . .'

'We do. Particularly when your sister owns 50 per cent of a holding company that owns 20 per cent of Westricity.'

Brophy was pulling at a thread on the rug in front of him.

'And who owns the other half?' asked Dixon. 'I don't recognise the names, so I'm guessing they're trustees?'

Brophy nodded.

'And the beneficiaries of the trust?'

'My children.'

'So, did Elizabeth Perry find out about this, perhaps?'

'No,' snapped Brophy, jumping up. 'She . . . the two things are completely separate. She couldn't possibly have known about this.'

Dixon turned to Jane.

'It used to be called obtaining a pecuniary advantage by deception, Constable. That'll be before your time, though. Now it's just section 3 of the Fraud Act. Failure to disclose information that you are legally obliged to disclose. Dishonestly, of course.'

'But the planning application was turned down,' screamed Brophy.

'I'm sure the Crown Prosecution Service will take that into account, Mr Brophy,' replied Dixon.

'Am I under arrest?'

'Not yet, sir,' replied Dixon. 'But don't leave the country. We'll show ourselves out.'

Dixon paused on the front doorstep, watching the rain bouncing off the pond.

'Shall we check his phone and the cars?' asked Jane. 'See if either pop up in Bristol or Torquay?'

'Better had. But it wasn't him.'

'What if Elizabeth had found out and been threatening to expose him if he was selected?'

'Check his bank statements too,' replied Dixon.

'Will the CPS prosecute him for fraud?'

'I doubt it. But one thing's for sure.'

'What?'

'I can feel a resignation coming on.'

'Aren't we going home?'

'No fear. They're out canvassing today, don't forget. We'll be safer at Express Park,' replied Dixon, turning onto the M5.

And it had been safer. At least until lunchtime, when DCI Lewis caught up with them in the staff canteen. 'Meeting room two in twenty minutes' had been the order, which gave Dixon just enough time to give Monty a run in the field behind the police centre.

'I've had the chief super on the phone. Have you been hassling Rod Brophy?'

'I interviewed Mr Brophy in connection with Elizabeth Perry's murder, yes,' replied Dixon. 'And we explored possible motives. Such as his failure to disclose his financial interest in the wind farm at the planning committee.'

'He says you threatened him.'

Dixon laughed.

'It's not a laughing matter.'

'Yes, it is,' said Dixon. 'He was behind a determined effort to get rid of Tom Perry, only a matter of weeks before Tom's wife is murdered. Then we discover he's got his fingers in the till. Are you telling me we shouldn't explore whether those two things are connected?'

'No.'

'There you are then,' said Dixon, sitting back in his chair and folding his arms.

'He says you were aggressive.'

'Was I aggressive,' asked Dixon, turning to Jane.

'No, you . . .'

'You took Jane?' asked Lewis. 'What did I tell you about working with Louise?'

'Brophy's just up the road from me. I'm hardly gonna drive all the way to Bridgwater to pick up Louise and then drive back again, am I?'

'Well, you bloody well should've done. For this very reason.'

'And anyway, Louise has got the day off,' said Dixon.

Lewis shook his head. 'He's threatening to sue us if this gets out.'

'Look, we're doing some checks but we've pretty much ruled him out of the murder investigation.'

'Why?'

'The only way it works is if Elizabeth found out about his financial interest in Westricity and threatened to expose him. And how likely is that?'

'Unlikely,' replied Lewis.

'It is. Tom won the selection easily when it was rerun,' said Dixon. 'There's more to this than that.'

'Where does that leave us with Brophy?'

'Someone'll have to decide whether to prosecute him for fraud, but even that's unlikely. I expect when he calms down he'll just resign quietly and that'll be that.'

'What about Elizabeth Perry?' asked Lewis.

'No nearer,' replied Dixon.

'I gather the Albanians came to see you?'

'Some bollocks about insurance and the shoemaker goes barefoot.'

'Make the most of it because that's all you're gonna get from them,' said Lewis.

'What's that supposed to mean?'

'Zephyr went in there last night and they've gone. Cleared out.'

'Where?'

'No idea. Tirana, probably.'

'What about Collyer's mole?'

'Disappeared.'

'Bloody marvellous,' said Dixon, shaking his head.

'Did you send a copy of your statement to Collyer?'

'Yes.'

'So, what happens now?' asked Lewis.

'We start at the beginning and go right back through everything,' replied Dixon. 'You don't pay to have someone killed without good reason. It'll be there, we just have to find it.'

'Well, you'll have to do it without Mark Pearce and Dave Harding, I'm afraid. They're needed elsewhere.'

'You're taking people off the case? Now?'

'No choice.'

'What do I tell Tom Perry?'

'You could try reminding him about the budget cuts?' replied Lewis, shrugging his shoulders.

Dixon looked at Jane and rolled his eyes.

'And there's a memorial service for Elizabeth next Friday at St Mary's.'

'We'll be there,' replied Dixon.

Chapter Twenty

Friday 10 January

The water levels were dropping, there was no doubt about that. It may have had something to do with the pumps Dixon could see off to his left as he drove past Huntworth and out towards Moorland. Large plumes of water were spouting from four huge steel pipes, taking the water off the fields and back into the River Parrett. Another eight had been installed at Dunball on the King's Sedgemoor Drain, all of them brought in from the Netherlands.

How long it would last was a different story. Another band of Atlantic storms was due to sweep in over the weekend. It was still only mid-January, after all. But today the sun was shining, offering a little hope that things might improve. Now all Dixon had to do was find Tom Perry.

'He's gone home,' his father had said. 'He said he'd be back in time for the funeral.'

Dixon forked left at the bend and drove along the farm track. The road to Moorland was still under water and beyond the village it was still over ten feet deep. Eleven at Northmoor Green. He passed a blue Honda Civic, which had been left in a field gateway just before the track disappeared into the water, much like a jetty at high tide. Perry must have continued on foot.

The line of the track was easy to follow, assuming it was midway between the hedges on either side, and beyond the farmyard it continued up the earth bank and then along the River Parrett behind the farm, curving away towards Northmoor Green. The fields in between were all under water, the lines of the hedges marking their boundaries, and a lone figure was visible in the distance, standing on the riverbank, staring down at Waterside Cottage.

Dixon accelerated along the track. The water was shallow, which was evident from the debris hanging in the hedges on either side; an assortment of plastic bags, a bucket, what was left of several bales of hay and eight dead rabbits. He suspected that the farm slurry tank had overflowed and possibly also the septic tank too. The Land Rover would need another hose down.

He glanced across at the farmhouse as he drove past, the water gently lapping at the letter box, and thought about Mrs Freeman and old Mr Grafton. God knows what would be left of their houses when they eventually got back to them.

The gate at the back of the farmyard was closed but not on the latch, so Dixon edged forward, shunting it open with his bumper rather that than getting wet feet. Once it was clear of the front, he accelerated through the gap, listening to the gate bouncing down the side of the Land Rover. A few more dents to add to the many. Adds a bit of character to the old bus, he thought, as he accelerated up the track, clear of the water, and onto the top of the riverbank.

He watched a dead sheep float past in the current, just visible beneath the waves being whipped up by the wind. Then he accelerated along the track, glancing at the water on either side, to his left the river and below and to his right, submerged fields.

Tom Perry was on his hands and knees by the time that Dixon reached him, his tears leaving tracks in the mud on his cheeks, his fists clenched in the muddy puddle in front of him. Dixon ripped off his black tie and threw it in the back of the Land Rover. Then he jumped out.

'C'mon, Tom, get up,' he said, helping him to his feet. 'You're wet through.'

'I tried to get in,' replied Tom. 'The water's too deep.'

Dixon glanced down at the cottage. The high water mark, a line of brown sludge, was a foot or so above the water, making it eleven feet deep and still over first floor level. Several windows on the first floor were broken.

Suddenly, Perry bent down, picked up a stone off the gravel path and hurled it at the cottage, this time shattering a roof tile.

'I just can't do it anymore,' he screamed, dropping to his knees. 'I just can't do it.'

'Yes, you can,' said Dixon, squatting down in front of him. 'You can do it for Lizzie.'

'Putting on a brave face, all the time. You were at the wind farm meeting. I don't give a toss about the fucking wind farm. My wife's been murdered, for God's sake.'

'You don't care about the wind farm, Tom, you care about the people. And Lizzie cared about you.'

Perry began to sob, his head bowed. Dixon put his hand on his shoulder.

'Let it out, Tom. Let it all out.'

Dixon watched Perry sobbing, the sound of the River Parrett swirling past, the wind and the waves drowning out all but the loudest of his screams. He knew how Perry felt. He had been through it seventeen years ago and then again only a few weeks before, when he had finally found Fran. He'd let it out all over again, one quiet afternoon on the beach and with only Monty for company, and now the box was back on its shelf.

Perry would get there too. Dixon would see to it.

'We can't even bury her,' stammered Perry, between sharp intakes of breath. 'The churchyard's under water.'

'You will, Tom. When you're good and ready, there'll be a time for that.'

Perry stood up and turned to the river, his back to Waterside Cottage. He was breathing hard and watching the water racing past.

'Every day I wake up. Then I remember. And I go through it all over again. Every bloody morning.'

'Here's what you do,' said Dixon. 'You put all the memories in a box, close it and put it somewhere safe. In a corner at the back of your mind. Then when the time's right, and you can face it, you open the box.'

Perry nodded and did his best to raise a smile.

'Whenever you feel like it,' continued Dixon. 'Privately and when it's just you. These are your memories and yours alone.'

'What about the rest of the time?'

'You put on your brave face and make Lizzie proud of you.'

'What about your box of memories?'

'It's safely tucked away.'

'D'you open it?'

'Sometimes,' said Dixon, nodding. 'Sometimes.'

Perry smiled.

'I'll need to tell my landlord about the broken windows.'

'Bollocks,' said Dixon, shaking his head. 'Vandals everywhere these days. The insurance'll cover it.'

'What did you want?' asked Perry. 'You never said.'

'It can wait,' replied Dixon. 'C'mon, let's get you home.'

Dixon followed Perry to his parents' bungalow and then drove back to Express Park. He had a couple of hours before the memorial service at 2 p.m.

'This was floating around, Sir,' said Louise. 'Is it yours?'

She handed Dixon a brown envelope marked HM Courts and Tribunal Service.

'What is it?'

'A grant of probate for a Mrs Wendy Gibson.'

'Yes, that's mine, thanks.'

Dixon sat down at a vacant workstation next to Jane.

'All right?'

'Yes,' replied Jane. 'How was he?'

'Not good.'

'You were ages.'

'I found him on the riverbank at Northmoor Green. Soaked to the skin. He'd tried to get into the cottage.'

'What for?'

'Not sure he knew. Anyway, I took him home.'

Jane smiled.

'Anything interesting?' asked Dixon, watching Jane staring at her screen.

'No.'

He slid the grant of probate out of the envelope while he waited for his computer to start.

'IN THE HIGH COURT OF JUSTICE

The District Probate Registry at Bristol

Be it known that WENDY MAY GIBSON

of Stickland Barn Muchelney Somerset TA10 2HE

died on the 25th March 1994

domiciled in England and Wales'

Dixon glanced down at the executors, both at the same address and probably solicitors. Then he turned the page and looked at the will. It was short at only three paragraphs and dated 1991, over three years before her murder. The partners at the date of her death in the firm of Dolley & Freer Solicitors, 10 Market Place, Somerton, were appointed her executors and her entire estate was divided equally between the Royal Society for the Prevention of Cruelty to Animals and the Friends of Bristol Horses Society. The will had been signed in the presence of two witnesses, both of whom gave their occupations as clerks and their address as 10 Market Place, Somerton.

'What's that?' asked Jane.

'Just something on that cold case.'

'Didn't you hand that back?'

'No,' replied Dixon, opening a web browser. A quick search of Google confirmed that Dolley & Freer were still there, although only one of the executors named on the grant of probate was still a partner in the firm.

'A word, if I may?'

Dixon looked up from his screen to see DCI Lewis waving at him, so he followed him to a seating area at the end of the landing, overlooking the atrium.

'Getting anywhere?' asked Lewis.

'At the moment we're sifting . . .'

'Cut the flannel.'

'No.'

'Only the chief con is getting a bit jumpy.'

'Aren't we all.'

'Questions are being asked, Nick, and we can't answer them because of the news blackout on the Torquay end. That leaves us with our only suspect washing up dead at Brean Down. We're not looking too clever, are we?'

'I'm not sure I can . . .'

'And the longer it goes on the worse it gets,' continued Lewis. 'The press are having a field day.'

Dixon sighed.

'I know you wanted to speak to the Albanians,' said Lewis.

'They wouldn't have told me anything more than they already have done, even if Zephyr'd got 'em in custody.'

'Have you got anywhere with the insurance thing?' asked Lewis.

'No. I'd like to have a look around the bookmakers though.'

'It'd been cleaned out,' said Lewis, shaking his head. 'Nothing. Not even a fingerprint.'

'We'll just have to take a bit of bad publicity on the chin then, won't we, Sir?'

'Vicky Thomas is keen to do a press conference.'

'We need some news for that, surely?' asked Dixon.

'Talking of news,' said Lewis, 'I thought you might like to see this.' He handed Dixon a rolled up newspaper. 'Today's *Bridgwater Mercury*.'

Dixon looked at the headline.

'Councillor Brophy resigns.'

'Twat,' muttered Dixon, dropping the newspaper into a rubbish bin as he walked back along the landing.

Louise dropped Dixon and Jane off in St Mary's Street, Bridgwater, just after 1.30 p.m. and they waited just inside the churchyard, sheltering under an umbrella beside a large fir tree.

'Do we have to wait out here?' asked Jane. 'It's freezing.'

'I want to see who files past, their faces, and I want to hear what they're saying.'

'You don't think her killer will come, do you?'

'Yes I do.'

'Really?'

'It's someone close. Someone who has to come, because it would look odd if they didn't.'

'What makes you say that?'

'We've spent days going through all of Tom's political campaigning and come up with nothing. None of it explains why Elizabeth was killed rather than Tom. So it must be something else.'

'You mean we've wasted . . . ?'

'Of course we haven't,' said Dixon, glancing over his shoulder. Louise was parked in Cornhill, photographing all of the mourners arriving at the church.

'What else then?' asked Jane.

'No idea,' said Dixon, looking up at the church spire. 'I was hoping for some divine intervention.'

A group of twenty or so people, led by Barbara Sumner, filed through the ornate iron gates. She saw Dixon and turned to her husband, whispering in his ear. Behind her, Dixon recognised the agent, Lawrence Deakin, and the area campaign director, Barry Dossett, Liam Dobbs and most of the Conservative councillors on Sedgemoor District and Somerset County councils.

'That's Tom's local ward committee,' said Jane, pointing to a smaller group following behind. 'Moorland and Northmoor Green. You've seen their statements.'

'No sign of Rod Brophy,' said Dixon.

'Are you surprised?'

'No.'

Behind them came several people Dixon had seen at the wind farm protest meeting, including the chairman, then Tom Perry's opponents in the by-election, Vanessa Hunt, and the Labour candidate, Ben Holland. Nice touch that.

'Shame to miss a photo opportunity,' said Jane.

'When did you become such a cynic?' asked Dixon.

'It's living with you.'

'C'mon, we'll wait inside,' said Dixon, gesturing towards a large white van that had pulled up on the other side of St Mary's

Street. It had a large satellite dish on the roof and two men were unloading cameras from the back.

'Is nothing sacred?' asked Jane.

'Nothing,' replied Dixon.

They sat down at the back of the church and watched the families filing along the aisle. His and hers, Tom Perry at the back of the group, with the vicar.

'He's holding it together well,' whispered Jane.

'It's an act,' replied Dixon. Then he felt Jane holding his hand.

'Welcome to this memorial service when we celebrate the life of Elizabeth Grace Perry, beloved wife, daughter and sister.'

Dixon spent much of the next fifteen minutes or so watching the congregation, singing 'All Things Bright and Beautiful' and then in prayer. Some sang, some didn't, some knelt to pray and others leaned forward, pretending to kneel, either because they didn't believe or perhaps they just suffered from arthritis. It was a familiar scene and one that Dixon would have to face again soon, when Fran was laid to rest at long last. And he would put on an act, just like Tom Perry was doing now. After all, it's what you do, isn't it?

'And now Tom would like to say a few words.'

Perry stood up. He hesitated and then turned to his mother, sitting to his left.

'It's OK, Mum. Really. I want to.'

He stepped up onto the chancel and turned to face the congregation. Tears were streaming down his cheeks.

'She was my . . .' A sharp intake of breath. 'She was my life. All of you here knew her so I don't need to tell you what a beautiful, sincere, caring person she was, do I?'

'No.'

'That was her mother,' whispered Jane.

Perry smiled down at the front row of the congregation.

'We met at a friend's wedding twelve years ago and they have quite simply been the happiest twelve years of my life. It remains a mystery to me why she chose me, but she did and I will always be thankful for that.'

More sharp intakes of breath.

'We were never apart. When I broke my neck she never left my bedside. Six weeks that was. And when she was diagnosed with diabetes and we nearly lost her. But she was determined to live. She was a fighter.' Perry smiled. 'Then we realised it was her insulin and she . . . she lived life to the full after that. She was always doing something and it always seemed to be for someone else.'

Perry bowed his head and started to sob. The vicar stepped forward and put her arm around him.

'We did everything together and the prospect of doing everything without her is too horrible to contemplate, but as a man I now count amongst my friends said to me this morning, "Put on a brave face and make her proud of you." And that's what I'm going to do. I'm going to do it for you, Lizzie.'

Elizabeth's mother stood up and helped him back to his pew.

Dixon spent the next fifteen minutes thinking about his meeting that morning with Tom on the banks of the River Parrett, overlooking Northmoor Green. He had gone to tell him, to reassure him, that he was still looking for Lizzie's killer, but he never got the chance to say it. Perhaps what he had said would prove more useful to Tom.

Dixon and Jane had been first out of the church and had walked around the side to Louise's car, parked in Cornhill, avoiding the TV news cameras. They were back at Express Park ten minutes later.

'I'm just popping over to Somerton. I'll see you at home,' said Dixon, walking over to his Land Rover.

'What's in Somerton?'

Jane got a wave rather than the reply she had been expecting, but Dixon was not going to tell her his theory about the cold case. It was a little too close to home.

He parked in the loading bay outside Dolley & Freer Solicitors in Somerton just after 4 p.m. It was a grey stone terrace with flags fluttering from a pub at the far end. Each property had black painted railings outside and a stone entrance porch with pillars either side. There was even an entryphone, so Dixon pressed the buzzer and, to his surprise, it buzzed straight away.

'What's the point of an entryphone if you don't ask who it is?' asked Dixon, smiling at the receptionist.

'Oh,' replied the receptionist, 'we had a difficult client but he's dead now. Can I help you?'

'Is Mr Bulman in?'

'Who may I say is here to see him?'

'Detective Inspector Dixon, Avon and Somerset Police.'

'I'll be back in a second,' said the receptionist, getting up from her chair. 'Take a seat.'

She reappeared seconds later.

'This way, please.'

Dixon followed her along a dark corridor to a room at the back of the building, overlooking the garden.

'How can I help you, Inspector?'

'Stephen Bulman?' asked Dixon, holding out his warrant card.

'Yes.'

'You were an executor of the estate of the late Wendy Gibson.'

'I'm an executor of lots of estates, Inspector. When was it?'

'Probate was granted in 1995.'

'God, no, I can't remember that far back.'

'I hoped you might remember this case. She was murdered in a field behind her house in Muchelney.'

Bulman slumped back into his chair.

'I do remember that case, yes, of course I do.'

'What do you remember?'

'Not a huge amount. I was an executor with John Greenslade, but he's since retired. The administration would've been done by our probate clerk, Margaret Hall. She does three days a week. Whole lot went to charity, from memory.'

'D'you still have your file?'

'I can check but we usually destroy them after fifteen years.'

Dixon took the grant of probate out of his pocket and unfolded it.

'Did you make her will?'

'That was our clerk,' said Bulman, looking at the signatures of the witnesses. 'Ken Belworthy. Died now, I'm afraid. He was in his eighties then.'

'What about the will file?'

'Those we keep forever, but when someone dies the will file gets put with the probate file and is then destroyed with it. Should do anyway, but it doesn't always happen.'

'Can you have a look, please?'

'Yes, certainly. You hang on here,' said Bulman, getting up from his desk.

Dixon was standing in the window, looking out at the garden. Overgrown was the best word to describe it. The office was much the same, with every available space, including the mantelpiece, covered in piles of files, some of them covered in a thick layer of dust. Even the windowsill had a pile of files on it, the elastic band around each having perished in the sun and broken, the ends dangling down. He thought about the day he qualified as a solicitor; the same day he left to join the police. It had been a lucky escape. No doubt about that.

Stephen Bulman reappeared carrying two small index cards.

'These were in the archives,' he said. 'The probate file was destroyed in 2011, I'm afraid, and the will file went with it.'

'Shame,' said Dixon.

'It's not all bad news,' replied Bulman. 'This was in "deeds out".' He was holding up the other index card. 'It says the deeds came over from Lester Hodson in Bridgwater, so if they were holding the deeds when she died, they may have been holding an old will too.'

Dixon stopped to give Monty a run on the beach on the way home. The tide was out and the flashing lights from the amusement arcade cast just enough light to enable Dixon to pick out a large white Staffie in the darkness. That and the moonlight. A break from the incessant rain and a clear night sky. It was quite a novelty.

He took out his phone and sent Jane a text message.

on beach outside clarence fancy a bag of chips? N x

The reply came before he had put his phone back in his pocket.

on way x

He took his insulin pen out of his pocket and dialled up the correct number of units for his evening injection, using the light from his phone. Half an hour before mealtimes, even if it was just a bag of chips. Then he took the cap off and pressed the needle into his stomach through his shirt. He winced. Must have caught a nerve. An occupational hazard. When he pulled the needle out a tiny drop of blood appeared on his shirt where he had done it. He stared at it. Then he stared at his insulin pen, reflecting all the colours of the rainbow in the lights from the arcade.

Insulin.

Life saving for him, but it had nearly killed Elizabeth Perry. Those were Tom's words. But he was only half right.

Chapter Twenty-One

Dixon was halfway up the steps when Jane appeared at the top.

'I was just getting off the motorway,' she said. 'Where are you going in such a hurry?'

'I need to get to a computer.'

'I know that look.'

'You do.'

Dixon bundled Monty into the back of the Land Rover and then sped off north along the seafront. Jane followed. They arrived home in Brent Knoll in under five minutes.

'Shall I feed him?' asked Jane, letting Monty out of the back of the Land Rover.

'Yes, please,' replied Dixon, fumbling with his keys at the back door.

He ran in, switched on the lights and then slid his laptop out from under the television stand.

'What is it then?' shouted Jane, from the kitchen.

'Insulin. You heard him say it at the church.'

'He didn't say what, though.'

'He's mentioned it before. He said her insulin nearly killed her.'

'But he hasn't run any campaigns about insulin.'

'Give me a minute.'

Dixon opened Google and typed 'Tom Perry' into the search field. Then he hit 'Enter' and started scrolling through the results.

'Tea?' asked Jane.

'Yes, please.'

The sound of his heart pounding in his ears was drowned out by a metal food bowl being pushed around the kitchen floor.

'Did you do your jab?' asked Jane.

'Yes.'

'You'd better have something to eat.'

He had reached page ten when he noticed Jane standing next to him, holding a mug in each hand.

'I've seen it, only it never made any sense before,' said Dixon.

Then he added the word 'insulin' to the search string and hit 'Enter'. The very last result at the bottom of the page was the one he was looking for.

'There it is,' said Dixon. 'The fight to save my life, *Surrey Comet*, January last year. That's before Tom was selected.'

'Open it,' said Jane.

'A Surrey diabetic fears her quality of life will be devastated because the insulin she uses may not be available for much longer,' said Dixon, reading from the screen. 'Elizabeth Perry thought she was going to die when she had an adverse reaction to the human form of the medication.'

'That must be what he was talking about.'

'It must,' replied Dixon. 'In only a few months, Mrs Perry, 32, went from an active, outgoing woman, to a virtual bedridden recluse,' continued Dixon. 'But then she saw an advert in the *Comet* promoting animal insulin and realised there was a choice of medication.'

'Did you know there was a choice?' asked Jane.

'No,' said Dixon. 'I was just put on the human stuff. But then I haven't had any problems with it.'

'Scroll down,' said Jane. 'Now she fears the life-changing animal insulin will soon not be available.'

Dixon shook his head. 'Swedish company, Betalin Pharmaceuticals, has indicated that it is considering withdrawing supplies. The company currently supplies half of the 30,000 diabetics on animal insulin. The company has already stopped production for America, Canada and parts of Europe.'

'What's that all about then?' asked Jane.

'Money.'

'Scroll down. Maybe we should have a word with her,' said Jane, pointing at the screen. 'Penny Thurstan, from the Insulin Dependent Diabetes Trust, said, "It's bad enough having diabetes, but to live in fear that you may not have the medicine to keep you feeling all right, I think is beyond reason".'

'And her,' said Dixon, pointing lower down the screen. 'Dr Ann McConnell, medical director at Betalin UK, told the *Comet* that no decision had been taken.'

'Does it mention Tom?' asked Jane.

'Here. "Mrs Perry and her husband, Tom, are calling on the government to safeguard the supply of animal insulin . . ."'

'And he's on the brink of being part of the government.'

'Exactly,' said Dixon. 'Take away his reason to pursue it, just when it looks like he's gonna get elected.'

'There's a related story,' said Jane. 'Life saving insulin to be withdrawn.'

'February last year,' said Dixon, clicking on the link. 'A leading politician is taking up the case of a Surrey diabetic who fears her life is as good as over if the type of insulin she needs is withdrawn. Mrs Perry, whose husband Tom is hoping to be a Tory candidate at the next election, is being backed by health minister, Tim Sheldon.'

'There, look, you were right,' said Jane.

'What?'

'The company's medical director, Dr Ann McConnell, has already said that in the UK it works out cheaper for the NHS to buy animal insulin than human insulin. Dr McConnell refused to comment on how much it cost her company to manufacture human insulin, saying that it was commercially sensitive.' Jane frowned at Dixon. 'I don't get it. Why are so few diabetics on animal insulin, if it's cheaper?'

'It must be about the money,' said Dixon, slamming the lid of his laptop shut and standing up.

'Where are you going?' asked Jane.

'To see Tom.'

'But it was the memorial service today,' said Jane, frowning.

'Yeah, you're right. We can catch up with him tomorrow.'

'Are you coming to bed?'

'What time is it?'

'Twoish,' replied Jane. 'What's that you're looking at?' She was standing behind Dixon, peering over his shoulder. He was sitting on the sofa, with his laptop on his knee and Monty stretched out asleep beside him.

'When this is over, remind me to go and see my bloody doctor, will you?'

'Why?'

'It's not human insulin at all. It's synthetic, produced in a giant vat by genetically modified bacteria.'

'Sounds disgusting.'

'You're not the one pumping it into your system four times a day.'

'Rather you than me, Gunga Din.'

'Thanks.'

'What's that website?'

'The Insulin Dependent Diabetes Trust. None of this stuff was ever discussed with me. I was just told, "Sorry to tell you, old chap, you're diabetic. Here's your insulin."'

'Was that it?'

'Well, there was a bit more to it than that, but I was never told I had a choice of insulin.'

'Do they have to tell you?'

'They're supposed to.'

'What's the other stuff then?'

'Pork or beef insulin, extracted from the pancreas of animals slaughtered for meat and then refined.'

'Don't like the sound of that either,' said Jane.

'The point is people react to the different insulins in different ways. It says here that some people are allergic to the human stuff.'

'You're not though, are you?'

'No, but what about Elizabeth Perry?'

Dixon parked across the drive of the bungalow in St John's Road, Burnham, and watched Tom Perry talking to the elderly residents on the doorstep. It was an animated conversation, but then Perry must have known it would be. The 'VOTE UKIP' poster in the window was a bit of a giveaway. Nevertheless, they parted friends, Tom shaking hands with both of them before walking back along the garden path, his large blue rosette blowing in the wind.

Dixon reached over and pushed open the passenger door of his Land Rover.

'Get in.'

'Where are we going?' asked Tom.

'For a walk.'

'A walk?'

'Call it therapy,' replied Dixon. 'You got a dog?'

'No.'

'You should get one. There's nothing like a walk on the beach . . .'

'. . . in the wind and the rain,' said Perry.

'Away from prying eyes and ears,' continued Dixon.

Perry nodded.

'I should let my team know where I am,' he said.

'We'll only be half an hour,' replied Dixon.

They drove in silence along Berrow Road, then Coast Road, past the golf course and out onto Berrow Beach.

'This is where they found that burnt out car with the . . .' Perry stopped when he noticed Dixon looking at him. 'You?'

'Yes.'

'But you got who did it?'

'Got stabbed for my trouble but, yes, I got 'em.'

Dixon parked facing out to sea and then let Monty out of the back of the Land Rover. He set off south towards Burnham, Dixon following.

'Looks like we're going that way.'

'Aren't you going to lock the car?'

'No. Someone might nick it,' said Dixon. 'Be doing me a favour, but don't tell Jane that.'

'Jane?'

'Constable Winter. We're an . . . we're together.'

'I didn't think that sort of thing was allowed in the police?' asked Perry, running to catch up with Dixon.

'It's not. We've not been together long but seem to have got away with it so far.'

'What did you want to talk about?'

'When I was sitting in your kitchen the other day you said that Lizzie's insulin nearly killed her. Then you mentioned it again yesterday, at the memorial service.'

Perry stopped. Dixon turned and watched the water running down his face, only this time it was rain.

'God, that's not what this is about, is it?' asked Perry.

'I don't know yet,' said Dixon.

'But we . . . I haven't done anything about that for months. Not since I was selected.'

'Why not?'

'It's not exactly a local issue, is it? And I've been campaigning on local issues. I got one of our MPs to ask a couple of questions in the House, but that's it.'

'And when you're elected?'

'Then I'm gonna go after the . . .' Perry's voice tailed off. He turned and slumped down onto a tree stump that had been washed up on the high tide.

Dixon waited.

'That is what this is about, isn't it?' asked Perry, looking up at Dixon.

'How much money is at stake?'

'Millions.'

Perry took a deep breath, closed his eyes and turned his face skywards, allowing the rain to wash over him. Suddenly he jumped up. 'Well, they've picked on the wrong . . .'

'Not now,' said Dixon, stepping in front of him. He put his hands on Perry's shoulders. 'There'll be a time for that, but it's not now. All right?'

Perry sat back down on the tree stump.

'Yes.'

'The best thing you can do, for Lizzie and for everyone dependent on animal insulin, is get elected. The rest you leave to me.'

Perry nodded.

'Good,' said Dixon, sitting down on the tree stump next to Perry. 'Now, start at the beginning and tell me everything.'

'It was six years ago. New Year's Eve. We were in a furniture shop and she said she didn't feel well. Then she said she'd lost a stone, over Christmas. I mean, who loses weight over Christmas? Her doctor's surgery was closed so we went to the walk-in centre. They checked her blood and told me to take her to the hospital. Immediately. Her blood sugar level was 21 or something and her ketones were off the scale.'

'Sounds familiar,' muttered Dixon.

'Anyway, she was admitted and then we were told she was type 1 diabetic. They kept her in over New Year to get her stabilised and then sent her home with two insulin pens, one for day, at meal-times, and another for night time. No explanation. Nothing.'

'What happened then?'

'Various follow ups with the diabetic consultant and her doctor and she was fine to begin with. Then, after about six months, she started to feel tired all the time, had joint pains, couldn't stand bright lights. She became almost bedridden in just a few weeks.'

'What did her doctor say?' asked Dixon.

'He had no idea what was going on. She was tested for everything; MS, ME, you name it, she was tested for it. I thought she was dying, I really did. And all the time she was pumping the bloody stuff into her body that was causing it all.'

'Go on.'

'Then her memory started to go. She'd begin a sentence but forget what she was talking about.' Perry sighed. 'She really was bedridden by the end.'

'So, what happened?'

'I spotted an advert in the local paper. "Are you diabetic? Do you suffer from . . ." and it listed the symptoms. Lizzie had all of them. Every single one. Then it said, "It could be an adverse reaction to your insulin." So, I got her up, dressed and down to the doctor.'

'What'd he say?' asked Dixon.

'Didn't have a bloody clue, so he rang the diabetic centre at the hospital and made us an appointment for that afternoon.'

'And?'

'I had a copy of the NHS Charter with me and was ready for an argument, but when we explained it to the consultant he switched her to animal insulin straight away,' replied Perry. 'And the transformation was almost immediate. She had her first injections that night and the next day she was up and about before me. We even went to the cinema. Then the next day she came to watch the rugby. She hadn't been able to do that for months.'

'And she was fine after that?'

'Yes. No problems. Then when I got involved in politics, I decided to do something about it. I got in touch with Penny Thurstan at the IDDT and we went to see the health minister at the House of Commons. He assured us that the government was committed to preserving choice for diabetics and the supply of animal insulin was part of that, despite Betalin threatening to withdraw it.'

'And why are they doing that?'

'Money. Pure and simple. Animal insulin is more expensive to produce and cheaper for the NHS to buy, so the same profit margin isn't there for them, is it?'

'Hang on a minute. If the human stuff is cheaper to produce and they charge the NHS more for it, how do they justify it?' asked Dixon.

'It's the research and development costs. The old adage about the first pill costing four hundred million pounds and the second one costing four pence. They have to recover the R and D costs, don't they?'

Dixon leaned forward, picked up Monty's tennis ball and threw it along the beach.

'Oh, they'll tell you that synthetic insulin, I refuse to call it "human", is better at controlling blood sugar levels,' continued Perry, 'but there's a technical term for that.'

'What?'

'Bollocks. The only study done said there was no evidence whatsoever that it was better or worse than animal insulin.'

'The Cochrane Review?' asked Dixon.

'You've done your homework,' replied Perry.

'Couldn't sleep.'

'And choice is a joke. Were you given a choice?'

'No.'

'Of course you weren't. Money talks.'

'What d'you mean by that?'

'They incentivise the doctors and consultants to prescribe synthetic insulin.'

'Incentivise?'

'Pay.'

Dixon shook his head.

'There are about thirty thousand diabetics on animal insulin at the moment,' said Perry, 'and some of them just can't tolerate the synthetic stuff. Not to mention countless thousands on synthetic having all sorts of problems and thinking they're being caused by something else entirely. Look at Lizzie. First they thought it was ME, then MS.'

'What will happen to them if it's withdrawn?' asked Dixon.

'They'll die. Just like Lizzie would've done if I hadn't seen that advert. But that's a small price to pay for a profit margin.'

Chapter Twenty-Two

Dixon dropped Perry on the corner of St John's Road, where a group of Conservative activists were waiting for him, huddled under two large umbrellas. Then he sped south on the M5 to Express Park, arriving just before midday. Jane was standing by the printers in the CID area.

'Lewis was looking for you.'

'I sent him a text,' replied Dixon. 'What've you got?'

'A full company search on Betalin UK and anything else I can find on the directors and shareholders. There's only two of them, though. That Ann McConnell and Betalin AB. They're based in Gothenburg, Sweden. I'm assuming that AB is the Swedish equivalent of our "limited".'

'Must be,' replied Dixon. 'See if any of its directors live in the UK.'

'Will do,' replied Jane. 'Are we getting Dave and Mark back?'

'That's what I texted Lewis about.'

'Thank God for that,' said Jane, rolling her eyes. 'How'd you get on with Tom Perry?'

'Good. It's just as we thought. She had a bad reaction to the human insulin and switched to the animal. She was fine after that.

My impression is that he was going to make it his pet campaign if he got elected.'

'And the money?'

'Millions,' replied Dixon. 'Have we got Louise?'

'Not till Monday.'

The meeting lasted a little over ten minutes. Jane watched through the windows of meeting room two as Dixon became more and more agitated. Then the door flew open.

'And keep me posted,' shouted DCI Lewis.

'I'm assuming we're not getting Dave and Mark back then,' said Jane, as Dixon marched past her workstation towards the kettle.

'No.'

'Why not?'

'Not enough to justify taking them off their current investigation,' replied Dixon. 'Coffee?'

'Yes, please.'

'He tried to soft soap me with some crap about having absolute confidence we can do it without them.'

'He thinks you're on the right track then?'

'He does.'

'You need to have a word with Tom Perry about police budget cuts, if he gets in.'

'I might just do that,' said Dixon, handing Jane a mug of coffee.

The hotel had ticked all the boxes; cheap, dog friendly, and just off the M1 at Northampton. But Monty was the only one who had slept well. Dixon had spent most of the night reading the file on

Betalin UK and the sound of paper rustling at regular intervals had kept Jane awake too.

Dixon was sitting on the end of the bed, staring at his insulin pen.

'What's up?' asked Jane.

'I was just thinking about the side effects.'

'Every drug has side effects.'

'Yes, but they don't usually include getting stabbed to death.'

'I suppose not.'

Dixon dialled up ten units on the pen and then pushed the needle into the side of his thigh. He pressed the button and watched the dial turning, pumping the insulin into his leg. Without it he could look forward to rising blood sugar levels, a diabetic coma, organ failure and then death. With it he could lead a normal life.

He had never considered himself lucky when it came to his diabetes, not that he had wasted much time feeling sorry for himself either. His old climbing partner, Jake, hadn't let him.

'They're letting me out tomorrow,' Dixon had said, lying in his hospital bed after what had turned out to be a diabetic coma. 'My blood sugar levels are OK now.'

'Good,' Jake had replied, grinning. 'Pembroke on Friday, before some other bugger bags the first ascent of Suicide Wall.'

And that was that. No moping about at home for weeks; just straight out onto the sea cliffs as if nothing had happened, although it was only later that he realised the full extent of the favour that Jake had done him.

After that Dixon had just got on with it, having learned early on, and the hard way, that there was no alternative. Controlling his blood sugar levels had been easy, once he got the hang of it, and he had never suffered any side effects from his insulin. He was starting to realise just how lucky he had been after all.

'You can have my orange juice,' said Dixon, handing a tray to Jane in the restaurant. 'It's packed full of sugar.'

'Did you download the satnav app for your phone?' asked Jane.

Dixon winced.

'Whatever happened to the art of map reading?' he muttered, but it was lost in the noise of the coffee machine.

It took them ten minutes to find the Insulin Dependent Diabetes Trust office on a small business park on the edge of Northampton, although Dixon had checked the satellite image on Google Maps before they had left the hotel. He thought it best not to tell Jane.

The IDDT as it was known, according to the sign at the entrance to the business park, occupied the end of a terrace of modern two storey red brick offices set back from the service road. The block paved car park in front of the terrace was broken up into sections by box hedging, but the IDDT spaces were all occupied, as were all the visitors' spaces, so Dixon parked in a space marked 'Partridges Solicitors'.

'You'll get a ticket,' said Jane.

Dixon took a business card out of his jacket pocket and left it on the dashboard. 'That'll have to do,' he said, climbing out of the Land Rover. He stopped and looked up at the clear blue sky. 'It only rains in Somerset these days.'

'Seems like it,' replied Jane.

The door to the IDDT office was locked so Dixon rang the bell and waited.

'That's Penny Thurstan,' said Dixon, peering through the frosted glass window in the front door. 'Her picture's on the website.'

She was tall and slim, with very short grey hair.

'Must be her.'

'Inspector Dixon?'

'Yes, and this is Detective Constable Winter.'

'Come in.'

'We've parked in a space belonging to the solicitors, is that all right?' asked Jane.

'Hold the door a minute and I'll just go and tell them where you are,' replied Penny Thurstan, walking along the front of the terrace. 'Don't let go or we'll be locked out.' She disappeared into the office next door and reappeared a few moments later. 'That's fine.'

'Thank you, Mrs Thurstan,' said Dixon.

'Penny, please. Now, anyone for coffee?'

'Yes, please.'

Dixon and Jane waited in an interview room on the ground floor while Penny fetched three mugs of coffee.

'We're investigating the murder of Elizabeth Perry,' said Dixon, when she reappeared.

'You said that on the phone but I'm not sure I can help much. I'd met her a couple of times, and Tom, but I didn't know them that well.'

'When did you last see them?'

'February last year. We went to the House of Commons. We do a lot of lobbying, as you might imagine, but Tom gave us direct access to the health minister. It was great for a small charity like us and we were all holding our breath to see if he got elected. Then this happens. My heart goes out to him. I can't begin to imagine . . .' Her voice tailed off.

'So Tom was going to champion your cause?'

'They both were. Tom and Lizzie. They had real personal experience. Tom said he was going to do everything he could if he got in. Even a private member's bill, if he got lucky in the ballot.'

'Saying what?'

'That all diabetics must be given information about both types of insulin, alerting them to the risks, side effects, that sort of stuff. They're supposed to now but it doesn't happen. And guaranteeing the availability of animal insulin.'

'How could you guarantee it?'

'In 2002 the government bought a blood plasma supply company in America. It was when there was concern about Creutzfeldt–Jakob disease passing by blood transfusion. Tom's argument was if they could do it then, they can do it now. And there are 30,000 people dependent on animal insulin.'

'Would it have worked?' asked Dixon.

'I don't know. There's less money about these days, of course. But he was going to have a damned good go at it, I have no doubt about that.'

'Which company would the government try to buy?'

'Neither while the supply is still there, but it would have to be DK Pharma. Betalin's too big.'

'But Betalin are stopping production, aren't they?'

'It's under consideration, apparently. It's a very small part of their business, which is 90 per cent human insulin. That's where the bigger profit is.'

'Could DK Pharma cope with the extra demand?'

'No. Not straight away, anyway.'

'Why do the NHS put people on human insulin rather than animal if it's more expensive?'

'Is this on the record or off?' asked Penny.

'On,' replied Dixon.

'Then I'd best not speculate. But what I can say is that it's not based on any clinical evidence that it's any better. Have you looked at the 2004 Cochrane Review?'

'Yes.'

'Tom was going to do the speculating with the benefit of parliamentary privilege.'

'I think he still might,' said Dixon.

'Forgive me for asking, but I thought Lizzie was killed when she disturbed a burglar?'

'Is this on the record or off?' asked Dixon.

'Off.'

'We're looking at other possible motives for her murder.'

'Like what?'

'Tell me about Betalin.'

'They're a large Swedish pharmaceutical company. They produce 60 per cent of the world's human insulin supply, and the associated stuff, like pens and blood testing kits. They're aggressive in their marketing . . .'

'What about in the UK?' interrupted Dixon.

'Their UK arm is really just a small distribution company. They use the pharmaceutical wholesalers to get it out there. The company itself is part owned by the Swedish parent and part by Dr McConnell, who calls herself the medical director. She used to sit on the board of the National Institute of Clinical Excellence,' replied Penny.

'Friends in high places,' said Dixon.

'Precisely.'

'Is she medically qualified?'

'Oh, yes.'

'Let's assume that Tom and Lizzie had been successful in helping you raise awareness then, and tens of thousands of people wanted to switch to animal insulin, how much would that cost Betalin?'

'Millions,' replied Penny. 'It's not just the lost profit but the cost of scaling up their animal insulin production to meet the demand. Not to mention the lost bonuses.'

'Bonuses?'

'I said I wouldn't speculate, didn't I?' said Penny, slapping the back of her left hand with her right.

'Reading between the lines is a speciality of mine,' said Dixon.

Penny grimaced. 'Are you saying that someone at Betalin had Lizzie killed to stop Tom?'

'We're looking at a number of possible motives.'

'I never thought they'd go that far,' said Penny, shaking her head.

'It's just one of a number of possible motives that we're investigating and it is highly confidential . . .'

'Of course it is,' replied Penny. 'And what about you? Are you on human insulin or animal?'

'How on earth d'you . . .?'

'I've been around diabetics over thirty years, Inspector. And besides, there's a tiny drop of blood on your shirt.'

'Where to now?' asked Jane, climbing into the passenger seat of Dixon's Land Rover.

'Bracknell.'

'Betalin?'

Dixon nodded.

'We haven't got any evidence.'

'Well spotted.'

'But . . .'

'We're just making enquiries,' said Dixon. 'Besides, I want her to know we know. See what our precious Dr Ann McConnell does.'

'And what if we're wrong?'

'Then we've lost nothing.'

'What's a private member's bill?' asked Jane.

'Each year there's a ballot and the successful MPs get to place their own bill before the House. A few even get it made into law but that usually only happens if the government agrees with it and allows the time.'

'And Tom would've gone with the insulin thing?'

'I get the feeling he still will,' replied Dixon, nodding.

'Betalin won't like that.'

'D'you want to ruffle her feathers, or shall I?'

'You do it. You're much better at it than me,' replied Jane, smiling. She turned away when she heard the door being unlocked from the inside.

'Yes.'

'Detective Inspector Dixon and Detective Constable Winter to see Dr McConnell,' said Dixon, holding his warrant card up.

The door opened just enough to reveal a woman in her late fifties, wearing a two piece tartan wool suit.

'Do you have an appointment?'

'No.'

'You'll need an appointment.'

'Is Dr McConnell in?'

'Not today, I'm afraid.'

'And you are?'

'I'm her secretary. Muriel Dummett.'

'Well, Mrs Dummett, we have these marvellous little gadgets called automatic number plate recognition cameras. You may have heard of them?'

'Yes.'

'And mine tells me that's Dr McConnell's car,' said Dixon, pointing to a white BMW parked behind his Land Rover.

'Oh, yes . . . er . . . maybe she came back and didn't tell me. I'll just go and check.' Mrs Dummett tried to shut the door but Dixon stepped forward.

'We'll wait inside, if we may.'

Dixon looked at Jane and winked.

'You'll have to forgive Muriel, I'm afraid, Inspector,' came a voice from behind him. 'She's ever so protective of me. Cold callers, salespeople, you know how it is.'

'I do,' said Dixon, spinning round.

Dr Ann McConnell was older than he had expected. Maybe it was an old photograph on Google Images? Long dyed hair tied up in a bun and sickly sweet perfume. A touch of Botox too, perhaps. She was dressed casually, in black trousers and a black pullover, and looked a little bit too much like an Albanian gangster for comfort. It was only when Dixon stepped forward to shake her hand that he noticed fingernails stained yellow and the smell of stale tobacco, which explained the perfume.

'What can I do for you?' she asked.

'We're investigating the murder of Elizabeth Perry,' replied Dixon.

Dr McConnell was no poker player. Seldom had Dixon seen the blood drain from a face faster, but she did her best to compose herself with a loud cough and a shake of the head.

'Do I know her?'

'That was going to be my next question.'

'I don't think so,' said Dr McConnell, thrusting her hands into her pockets.

'Let me jog your memory. Her husband is the Tory candidate in the by-election. She was murdered on Christmas Eve.'

'Oh, yes. I've seen it on the TV. Tragic.'

'Three months pregnant,' said Dixon.

Dr McConnell turned away.

'And you gave a quote to the *Surrey Comet* last year.'

'Did I?'

'It was an investigation into the continued availability of animal insulin.'

'I give lots of comments to journalists, Inspector.'

'Mrs Perry suffered some very nasty side effects from human insulin. Does that ring any bells?'

'No.'

'And she went to see the health minister with her husband?'

'No, sorry.'

'Perhaps we could continue this in your office, Dr McConnell?' asked Dixon.

'Yes, of course, follow me.'

Dixon and Jane followed her along the corridor into a large office with a bewildering array of certificates on the wall, in amongst the watercolours. Dr McConnell sat down at one of the desks and gestured to Jane to sit down at the vacant desk opposite.

'Our PR consultant sits there when she's in. Freelance, one day a week at the moment, unless we've got something on.'

Dixon was looking at the paintings on the wall.

'When I was diagnosed with type 1, no one told me I had a choice of insulin . . .'

'I'm sorry, Inspector, but what has this got to do with the death of Elizabeth Perry? She was killed by a burglar. A robbery gone wrong, surely?'

Dixon turned slowly and fixed Dr McConnell in a stare Jane had seen only once before.

'Was she?'

'That's . . .' Dr McConnell hesitated, 'what it said in the *Telegraph*.'

'You shouldn't believe what you read in the newspapers,' said Dixon, turning back to the watercolour on the wall. 'Dartmouth?'

'Er, yes. We used to keep a boat on the River Dart.'

'We?'

'My husband and I. We divorced over twelve years ago now.'

Dixon nodded.

'When I was diagnosed, I wasn't told I had a choice of insulin. Why was that?'

'It's NHS policy to prescribe human insulin in the first instance.'

'But the NHS Charter says that patients are to be consulted and given the choice about their treatment. How can we have a choice if no one tells us there is one?'

'Well, I can't comment on an individual case and I'm sure you're not expecting me to, but human insulin is widely regarded as better at controlling blood sugars.'

'Widely regarded by who?' asked Dixon.

'The doctors and consultants who prescribe it.'

'But not the 2004 Cochrane Review. It said there was no evidence whatsoever that it was any better than animal insulin.'

'Well, it . . .'

'Why have there been no large scale clinical trials?' Dixon had moved on to another painting of the River Dart.

'That would have been taken into account by NICE before it was approved. Each new insulin has to . . .'

'But weren't you a director of the National Institute of Clinical Excellence?' asked Dixon.

'I'm not sure I like where this is going, Inspector.'

'Forgive me,' said Dixon. 'I get a little carried away sometimes.' He walked over to a larger watercolour above the fireplace.

'How much does human insulin cost the NHS compared to animal?'

'Animal is cheaper; about two thirds of the cost.'

'And more expensive to produce?'

'Yes.'

'So, just to be clear, human insulin is cheaper to produce and you charge the NHS more for it?' asked Dixon.

'Yes.'

'Which makes for a bigger profit margin?'

'This is commercially sensitive information, Inspector.'

'And politically, I should imagine?'

No reply.

'How much money changes hands for each patient prescribed human insulin?' continued Dixon.

'I don't . . .'

'Do you pay more for a patient switched from animal to human?'

'I'm going to have to . . .'

'We've been told about little bonuses. Is that not right?'

'No. We pay some consultants a retainer for research and . . .'

'That's what they call it these days, is it? A retainer.'

Dr McConnell stood up. 'Am I under arrest?'

'No,' replied Dixon. 'You're helping us with our enquiries, and we are most grateful.'

Dr McConnell sat down again.

'Tell me about the side effects of human insulin,' said Dixon.

'Some people report some minor side effects, but they're usually due to them not managing their diabetes properly.'

'And what about Elizabeth Perry?'

'There was probably some underlying condition or allergy to it in her case. A few people have reported symptoms similar to hers, but only a handful.'

'And what's to happen to them if you stop producing animal insulin?'

'DK Pharma will still be there. And they could try the analogues perhaps. We'll give everyone eighteen months' notice if we do stop production.'

'Eighteen months' notice or eighteen months to live?'

No reply.

'And what if a member of parliament was actively campaigning to raise awareness of the side effects of human insulin, not to mention the cost to the NHS?'

'I'm not sure I follow . . .'

'Well, it's hardly going to be good for business, is it?'

'So, you think we had Elizabeth Perry killed, is that it?'

Dixon walked behind Dr McConnell, still sitting at her desk, and looked at the painting on the wall behind her. She turned her head to follow him.

'Now that's Haytor, isn't it? On Dartmoor.'

'Yes.'

'Right, well, we'll leave you to it, Dr McConnell, thank you very much for your time.'

'Is that it?'

'For now. You've been most helpful, thank you again,' said Dixon, opening her office door. 'We'll be in touch if we need anything else.'

'How did you know that was her car?'

'I didn't,' replied Dixon, starting the old diesel engine. 'What's her home address?'

Jane took her notebook out of her handbag and flicked through the pages. 'Tulkeley Cottage, Englefield Green.'

'Find it on your phone, will you?' asked Dixon, turning the pages of his map book. 'We need to get there before she does.'

He turned out of the car park and headed east on the A329.

'It's right on the green,' said Jane. 'It's not far off the A30, you can't miss it.'

'Good.'

'Why don't we just follow her?'

'She'll spot us in this old heap and the chances are we'd lose her anyway. Remember, I needed the helicopter last time.'

'I'd rather not,' said Jane, rolling her eyes. 'We can park in the trees on the far side of the cricket pitch.'

They sped through the village and turned into Cricketers Lane.

'That's it there. Bloody hell. I thought cottages were supposed to be small,' said Jane, turning in her seat and pointing to a large green house set back from the road. 'The trees are over there.'

Dixon drove to the far end of the green and parked behind a small clump of trees. Despite the winter foliage it would be enough to hide them in the fading light. And he could make out Tulkeley Cottage in the far corner.

'How d'you know she's coming home?' asked Jane.

'She lied. And she's sensible enough to know we'll have spotted it, when she's had five or ten minutes to reflect on what she said.'

'Which is what she's doing now?'

'I should imagine she's on her way by now,' said Dixon, looking at his watch. 'She'll need her passport and . . .'

'There she is,' said Jane.

'That was quick.'

'Why aren't we . . . ?'

'We'll give her a couple of minutes to get comfortable,' said Dixon. 'Get her suitcase down off the top of the wardrobe, find her passport.' He was following the second hand ticking round. 'That's long enough.'

He spun the Land Rover around on the edge of the cricket pitch and raced back along Cricketers Lane, screeching to a halt across the drive, blocking in the white BMW. Then he ran up the gravel drive with Jane right behind him. The front door was ajar so he pushed it open and crept into the hall. He noticed a passport on the hall table, next to a brown leather handbag, so he picked it up. Then Jane nudged his elbow and pointed up the stairs. A light was on.

Dixon tiptoed up the stairs and peered into the bedroom, through the gap by the hinges. Dr McConnell was bending over a drawer and a suitcase was open on the bed. He turned to Jane and nodded, then he pushed open the door.

'Last minute packing is a dangerous business,' said Dixon, holding up the passport. 'I always forget something.'

Dr McConnell dropped the pile of clothes on the floor.

'Dr Ann McConnell, I am arresting you on suspicion of the murder of Elizabeth Perry.'

She slumped back onto the bed, put her head in her hands and started to sob.

'You do not have to say anything but it may harm your defence if you do not mention when questioned something you later rely on in court. Anything you do say may be given in evidence.'

'I didn't know she was pregnant. I swear I didn't know she was pregnant.'

Chapter Twenty-Three

'Where are they taking her?' asked Jane.

'Staines. She'll be transferred down to the custody centre at Express Park tomorrow morning,' replied Dixon.

They were standing in the living room window of Tulkeley Cottage, watching a police van turning out of the drive.

'And Dave and Mark?'

'On the way.'

'I should bloody well think so,' said Jane. 'What about forensics?'

'They're here, but they're wasting their time. What we're looking for will be on her computer, or in her bank statements. The Surrey lot are at her office now.'

'I've got her phone,' said Jane, holding up a clear plastic bag with a BlackBerry in it.

'What about the other one?'

'What other one?'

'There were two on her desk.'

'No sign of it,' said Jane.

'Muriel bloody Dummett,' said Dixon grimacing. 'Where does she live?'

'Virginia Water.'

'Get someone over there now and find out what happened to that phone.'

'Will do,' replied Jane. 'Where are you going?'

'It's stopped raining so I'm gonna give Monty a run on the cricket pitch. Then we'll have a look for her bank statements.'

It was just after 10 p.m. by the time that Dave Harding and Mark Pearce arrived. The search of Dr McConnell's house had been completed and several boxes of papers had been catalogued and were in the back of a police van on their way to Express Park. Her computer, iPad and mobile phone had already arrived at the High Tech Unit.

'We've finished here, Dave. Best get over to her office and sort that out,' said Dixon. 'You know what to look for?'

'Yes, Sir.'

'Good. Stay over and follow her down in the morning. We're gonna head back.'

'What's it all about, Sir?'

'Money, Mark,' replied Dixon. 'Lots of money.'

'Well done.'

'Thank you, Sir.'

DCI Lewis was waiting for Dixon and Jane on the landing when they arrived at Express Park just after 8 a.m. the following morning.

'Did she confess?'

'When I cautioned her she said she didn't know Elizabeth had been pregnant.'

'That's near as damn it then, isn't it?'

'We'll see when I interview her,' replied Dixon. 'But I'm not holding my breath. And we've got a lot of work to do before then too.'

'What time did you arrest her?' asked Lewis.

'Twenty-five past four.'

'Let me know if you need an extension.'

'Yes, Sir.'

'Louise has been in since five. She's made a start on the boxes that arrived last night. Room two.'

'I'll get some coffee and catch you up,' said Jane.

'What've you got?' asked Dixon, opening the door of meeting room two. The empty boxes were lined up along the wall and all of the documents were laid out in piles, covering the table.

'She's got three bank and three building society accounts,' replied Louise. 'There are statements for them all going back four years or so, but they stop last September. Nothing after that.'

'I wonder why,' said Dixon.

'Maybe she switched to online banking,' said Louise.

'Possibly. Or maybe she shredded them?'

Louise nodded.

'You know what to do?' asked Dixon.

'The requests have already gone in, Sir.'

'Well done.'

'Dave rang,' said Jane, from the doorway. She handed a mug of coffee to Dixon. 'They're about an hour away.'

'Good.'

'And Muriel Dummett's in custody at Staines. They found the remains of a mobile phone in her wood burner.'

'What about the SIM card?'

Jane shook her head.

'Tell 'em to keep hold of her until we've interviewed Dr McConnell,' said Dixon. 'She may give us enough for a charge of perverting the course of justice to stick.'

'Yes, Sir.'

Dixon spent the next hour thumbing through the bank statements that were neatly laid out on the meeting room table. There were also share certificates, dividend counterfoils, investment statements and a file marked 'old tax'. None of it particularly enlightening, although it did confirm what he already knew. There was a lot of money to be made out of insulin.

'Anything from High Tech, Jane?' Dixon shouted across to the CID area on the other side of the atrium.

'Just going through her phone numbers now. Nothing else yet.'

Then the lift doors opened and Dave stepped out with Mark right behind him, each carrying two archive boxes.

'In here with those, Dave,' said Dixon.

'She's downstairs, being processed. Her solicitor's here too. Followed us down in his car.'

'It's amazing what they'll do for a privately paying client, isn't it?'

'What's in the boxes?' asked Louise.

'Company stuff.'

'Nothing exciting, I don't think,' said Mark.

Dixon watched Louise check her phone and then run over to her computer.

'Just put them on the floor here,' said Dixon, gesturing to Dave and Mark to put the boxes against the wall behind the door.

When he looked back Louise was standing by a printer, picking sheets of paper off one by one as they came out. Then she ran over.

'Lloyds Bank. We've got five separate one thousand pound cash withdrawals, each a few days apart, starting 6 September,' she said, handing the copy statements to Dixon. He glanced down at the entries. The last withdrawal had been made on 25 September.

'Get the serial numbers.'

'Will do.'

'And for any others that come in.'

'Yes, Sir.'

'Anyone seen DCI Lewis?' asked Dixon.

'In the canteen,' said Jane.

DCI Lewis was reading a newspaper when Dixon sat down opposite him.

'What've you got?' asked Lewis, lowering the paper.

'Cash withdrawals. We're getting the serial numbers now.'

'And?'

'We found over twenty grand in Torquay,' said Dixon. 'It was pinched by Collyer. I need the serial numbers.'

'Leave it with me,' said Lewis, folding up his newspaper.

He had been looking forward to this interview, although it would take him a while to get used to the new room layout. He was sitting next to Dr McConnell, with Hugo Waters, her solicitor, to Dr McConnell's right. Louise was sitting to Dixon's left. Very odd. In front of them, against the wall, was a table with the recorder on it.

It began just after 2 p.m. Dixon introduced those present for the tape with Louise, Dr McConnell and Waters each acknowledging their presence in turn. Then he reminded Dr McConnell that she was under caution.

'Yesterday afternoon you told me that you didn't know Elizabeth Perry.'

'That's right. I don't know her.'

'Then, later in the same conversation, you told me about her symptoms, said she had some underlying condition or allergy.'

'I was confused. That's what's usually behind those sort of complaints.'

'What sort of complaints?'

'Side effects.'

Dixon opened a file and took out a piece of paper, placing it on the table in front of Dr McConnell.

'This is a printout of a newspaper article from the *Surrey Comet* in February of last year. In it Elizabeth Perry sets out her symptoms. Have you seen this before?'

'No.'

'But you gave a comment to the paper and it's included in the article.'

'I told you, I give lots of comments to journalists.'

'And we found it in a lever arch file in your office, marked "Press Cuttings".'

'That's maintained by Sarah, our PR consultant.'

'And you never look at it?'

'Rarely.'

'OK, so, just to recap, you told me that human insulin is cheaper to produce and more expensive for the NHS to buy than animal insulin. Is that right?'

'Yes.'

'What did you mean when you said you didn't know she was pregnant?'

Dr McConnell looked up and stared at Dixon.

'It never mentioned that in the newspaper reports.'

'The newspaper reports you've not seen before?'

Dr McConnell looked back down at her shoes.

'And where were you going in such a hurry?'

'Head office in Gothenburg.'

'You had no flight booked.'

'I was going to buy a ticket at the airport.'

'Of course you were. Odd though. I'd have thought a secretary as efficient as Muriel would've had that organised well in advance.'

'I forgot to tell her.'

'But you didn't forget to tell her to destroy your other phone.'

'I don't have another phone.'

'I saw it on your desk and we found the remains of it in her wood burning stove.'

Dr McConnell glanced across at Waters.

'She's currently being held at Staines on suspicion of perverting the course of justice,' continued Dixon.

'Not Muriel. You can't think . . .' Her voice tailed off.

'Tell me about Betalin UK,' said Dixon. 'It's part owned by you and the Swedish company?'

'Yes.'

'Only I had a rummage through the company accounts, not that I'm an accountant, you understand, and there were various bonus payments being made. What are those for?'

'Performance bonuses.'

'For increased sales?'

'Yes.'

'How does that work then? I mean, you can't make people get type 1 diabetes, can you?'

'No.'

'So, how d'you increase your sales?'

'We market to doctors and consultants. Make sure that Betalin is the brand they're thinking of when they are prescribing.'

'And where does animal insulin fit in with that?'

'There's no bonus payable for orders of animal insulin,' whispered Dr McConnell.

'You're gonna have to speak up a bit for the tape, Dr McConnell,' said Dixon. 'Can you repeat your last answer?'

'There's no bonus for animal insulin orders.'

'That's right,' said Dixon. 'And according to this memo, there's a penalty, isn't there? For the record DI Dixon is handing to Dr McConnell a copy of a memo from Patrick Sondgren dated 31 January last year.'

Dr McConnell took the piece of paper, glanced at it and then handed it to Waters.

'How much pressure are you under to wind down orders for animal insulin?'

'It's a business. You wind down the less profitable parts of your business and expand the more profitable.'

'But people depend on animal insulin . . .'

'I can't help that,' snapped Dr McConnell.

'What would've happened if Elizabeth and Tom Perry had continued their campaign to raise awareness of animal insulin?'

'I don't know.'

'I think you do,' said Dixon. 'Let's assume Tom became an MP and used parliamentary privilege to blow the whole thing wide open, that the NHS are buying the most expensive insulin, which costs you less to produce than animal insulin . . .'

'I . . .'

'And which, incidentally, is just as effective at regulating blood sugar levels.'

Dixon watched Dr McConnell's eyes darting around the room, first at Waters, then Louise, then back to him. She began picking at the seam of her jeans.

'I'm going to assume that's why you had her killed,' said Dixon.

'No.'

'A pregnant woman.'

'I didn't know she was . . .'

'To preserve your profit margin.'

'No.'

'And I suppose you thought Tom would drop the campaign if his wife was no longer around?'

'It wasn't like that.'

'What was it like then?'

Waters leaned over and whispered in Dr McConnell's ear.

'No comment,' she said.

'Just a week or so ago now we visited an address in Torquay,' said Dixon.

Dr McConnell looked up.

'And what d'you think we found?'

'I don't know.'

'Well, after the man had pointed a gun at me and been shot by armed police, we found a little over twenty thousand pounds in used notes.'

Dr McConnell shook her head.

'And the serial numbers of those bank notes match exactly the serial numbers of the cash you withdrew from your bank and building society accounts last September.'

'It wasn't . . .'

'You're on CCTV.'

Dixon watched Dr McConnell's face redden. She was breathing deeply now.

'You want to know who this man was, don't you?'

'No.'

'I'll tell you anyway,' said Dixon. 'He was the man who killed Elizabeth Perry.'

'And you can prove that?' asked Waters.

'We can.'

Dr McConnell looked up. Tears were trickling down her cheeks.

'You've no idea of the pressure I was under. They were threatening to shut us down. Animal insulin sales going up would've been a disaster.'

'So you had Elizabeth Perry killed.'

'She was the driving force behind their campaign. I had no choice.'

'How much did you pay?'

'Thirty thousand pounds.'

'How did you get in touch with her killer?'

'No comment.'

'You'll have to do better than that.'

'No comment.'

'All right, where did you meet him?'

'In a lay-by on the A303 just beyond Stonehenge.'

'When?'

'End of September, perhaps the beginning of October. It was before the clocks went back.'

'What car was he driving?'

'It was black.'

'Make? Model?'

'I don't know.'

'What did he look like?'

'I hardly saw his face.'

'What time was it?'

'Nine. It was dark.'

'And I suppose he didn't say anything either?'

'No.'

'Why did you ask Muriel Dummett to destroy your mobile phone?'

'Muriel is my employee. I instructed her to destroy the phone and she did as she was told. She knows nothing about this.'

'Why did you want the phone destroyed?'

'No comment.'

'What was the number?'

'No comment.'

Dixon sighed. He terminated the interview, closed the file and stood up. Then he took his insulin pen out of the top pocket of his jacket. Dr McConnell watched as he turned the pen until the Betalin logo was facing towards her.

'What exactly is human about it?' asked Dixon.

'Well, nothing,' she said, turning away and trying to wipe her tears away with the palms of her hands.

'I thought not.'

Chapter Twenty-Four

'So, that's it then?' asked Lewis. He was sitting on the corner of Jane's workstation in the CID area. Dave and Mark were sitting behind Jane, but had turned to face him.

'Not yet,' replied Dixon. 'I may need to interview her again. Let's get an extension. Another twelve hours should be enough.'

'What for?'

'I want to check that crap about the A303 at Stonehenge. See if she really went.'

'Why?'

'Because I don't think that meeting took place at all. Someone else set it up.'

'Who?'

'I don't know.'

'What makes you think that?'

'The other phone. You might buy a pay as you go SIM if you were setting up a murder, and then destroy it when the deal was done. But you wouldn't buy a whole phone surely? And then keep it handy, on your desk?'

Lewis nodded.

'She used that phone regularly,' continued Dixon. 'Why? And why was she so keen to get rid of it?'

'What d'you want us to do?' asked Jane.

'Check the number plate cameras on the M3 and A303 as far as Stonehenge. Her last cash withdrawal came from the . . .' Dixon looked at Louise and raised his eyebrows.

'Nationwide on first October.'

'And she said the meeting was before the clocks went back. So, that's the twenty-sixth.'

'She went to Sweden on the second and didn't get back until the twelfth,' said Jane.

'That's it then. From the twelfth to the twenty-sixth. Fourteen days. Check her diary in case we can eliminate any others too.'

Louise nodded.

'And get her mobile phone positioning. The one we do know about. Let's see if we can place it there. Just in case she hired a car.'

'Yes, Sir.'

'While you're about it, get the Surrey lot to speak to her neighbours at Tulkeley Cottage and her office. We're looking for any regular visitors.'

Dixon walked over to the large windows at the front of the police centre and looked out into the darkness. He watched the cars speeding around the roundabout at the entrance to Express Park and disappearing into the night. Commuters going home from work, probably. Lucky buggers. Yet another difficult conversation was coming, but Tom Perry had a right to know. What must it be like to have a nine to five job you leave behind when you go home? Watching CCTV at Tesco, for example?

He focussed on his reflection in the window and wondered whether it might have done him a favour, in the long run, if he'd been fired. Then he noticed DCI Lewis standing next to him.

'Let me know when you're ready to charge her and I can tell Charlesworth,' said Lewis. 'He'll want to do a press conference.'

'I'm more worried about telling Tom Perry his wife's life was worth thirty grand.'

The smell of coffee almost overpowered Dixon when he walked into meeting room two just before 3 a.m. Louise had been on the go since 5 a.m. the previous morning but had ignored all orders to go home. Dave, Mark and Jane were tired but still going strong. It was testament to the power of adrenaline. And caffeine. A potent mix.

He opened his mouth to speak but thought better of it. A flippant remark about thinking of the overtime, or something like that, hardly seemed appropriate when he knew that none of them were.

Louise yawned first.

'What've we got then?' asked Dixon.

'Nothing on the number plate recognition cameras,' said Dave. 'Doesn't show up on any of them.'

'We can't check the traffic cameras,' said Mark. 'It'd take days.'

'And the mobile phone?'

'There's a Vodafone base station at Amesbury, that's the London side of Stonehenge, and another at Winterbourne Stoke, this side. That's O2, that one,' said Louise. 'Doesn't register on either.'

'It'll take days to cover every base station along the M3 and A303,' said Jane.

'If we assume that she carried the second mobile phone with her then the number should appear wherever her first phone does, surely?' asked Dixon.

'Yes,' said Jane, hesitating. 'Amongst thousands of others.'

'So, if we get those records for her main phone, the second number will appear in the same listings. We did it before. Remember? And if we had the number it'd give us the calls.'

'Yes, but last time we knew the number we were looking for,' said Jane.

'We checked with the operators, didn't we?'

Jane rolled her eyes.

'Yes. Her only phone on a contract is the one we've got.'

'Well, we've got plenty of time,' said Dixon. 'I'll speak to Lewis about authorising it.'

'Good luck with that,' said Jane.

'Nothing from the neighbours,' said Mark. 'Her cottage isn't overlooked and she seems to keep herself to herself. Away most weekends and on business fairly regularly, but that's about it.'

'Where's her solicitor?' asked Dixon.

'He's at the Walnut Tree.'

'Better get him out of bed then. It's time for another word with Dr McConnell.'

'When you were interviewed yesterday, Dr McConnell, you said that you'd met Mrs Perry's killer in a lay-by on the A303 beyond Stonehenge.'

'Yes.'

Dave, Mark and Jane were watching the interview unfold on a television screen in an adjacent room.

'What time did you leave home to get there?'

'About sevenish. I went straight from the office.'

'So, it was a weekday?'

'Yes.'

'Which one?'

'I can't remember.'

'How long did it take you to get there?'

'About an hour.'

'Which way did you go?'

'Down the M3 and along the A303.'

'Where did you get on the M3?'

'Lightwater.'

'Where was this lay-by?'

'On the other side of Winterbourne Stoke. On the right.'

'The one with the snack van?'

Dr McConnell stared at Dixon, her head tilted to one side.

'Yes.'

'Was it open?

'No.'

'And the lay-by was empty?'

'Yes.'

'Did you fill up with petrol on the way there or back?'

'No.'

'So, you got there an hour early. What did you do?'

'I waited in my car.'

'Your own car?'

'Yes.'

'In the lay-by?'

'Yes.'

'Did anyone see you?'

'No.'

'Well, it's easily confirmed,' said Dixon.

'How?' asked Dr McConnell, turning to Waters, sitting on her right.

'From your office north of Bracknell south to the M3 then to Winterbourne Stoke in an hour, you'll be on every speed camera along the way.'

'Maybe I was wrong about the times. I said about an hour.'

'You did. And you said you were in your own car.'

'Yes.'

'Only that doesn't appear on any automatic number plate recognition camera either, Dr McConnell. Unless, of course, you're lying and you went by magic carpet.'

'I'm not lying.'

'We've checked every ANPR camera between your return from Sweden on twelfth October until the clocks went back. Nothing,' said Dixon, shaking his head, 'unless you were wrong about that too.'

'No.'

'We've checked the Winterbourne Stoke mobile phone base station too. No sign of your number either. Odd that, if you'd sat there for an hour as you say.'

Dr McConnell swallowed hard. She turned to Waters.

'Can you stop this?'

Waters leaned over and whispered in her ear.

'The mystery man in the black car. Who was he?' continued Dixon.

'No comment.'

'OK, let's talk about your second mobile phone. The one Mrs Dummett incinerated. Personal calls, was it?'

'No comment.'

'We will find the number and then we'll have all the calls made to or from that phone, so it'll save everyone a lot of time if you just tell us now.'

Dixon watched Dr McConnell shifting in her seat. She crossed her legs, then uncrossed them. She was watching the tape machine, avoiding eye contact with him.

'Who will we find on the other end?'

'No comment,' through gritted teeth.

'You see, I don't think you went to Winterbourne Stoke at all . . .'

'I did.'

'I think someone else did. And probably somewhere else entirely?'

'No.'

'You need time to think, I see that. No doubt Mr Waters can tell you how much time you're gonna have.'

'I think that's enough, Inspector. My client has answered . . .'

'Your client has lied,' replied Dixon. Then he terminated the interview. He paused in the doorway to watch Dr McConnell sobbing quietly, her head bowed, before he slammed the door behind him.

Dixon leaned against the wall in the custody suite and closed his eyes. He was careful not to touch the alarm strip at waist height, which meant arching his back, but it was far too uncomfortable even for a moment's rest. He opened his eyes just in time to see Dr McConnell being led to one of the counters. He watched the custody sergeant complete the custody sheet and listened as she was charged with the murder of Elizabeth Grace Perry on 24 December.

The decision to charge her would be reviewed by the Crown Prosecution Service before her first appearance in court, but Dixon knew he had got it right. Now all he had to do was find the person on the end of that phone. And tell Tom Perry. He wasn't sure which was going to be easier.

'What time d'you call this?' asked Tom Perry.

'What time is it?'

'Seven thirty. You look like you've been up all night.'

Dixon nodded.

'You'd better come in,' said Perry.

'Are your parents in?'

'They're asleep. What's going on?'

'Is there somewhere we can talk?'

'Er, yes. Come through to the kitchen.'

Perry leaned back against the sink. 'What's going on?' he asked.

Dixon slid a chair out from under the kitchen table. 'May I?'

'Of course.'

'You may want to . . .' said Dixon, gesturing to the chair at the head of the table.

'No, I'm fine standing.'

'At 4.30 a.m. this morning Dr Ann McConnell was charged with Lizzie's murder. She's been remanded in custody and will appear at Taunton Magistrates Court later this morning.'

'Dr McConnell?'

Dixon nodded.

'Betalin?' asked Perry.

'She has confessed to arranging the murder.'

'How much did she pay?'

'Tom, I . . .'

'I need to know. How much did it cost her?'

'Thirty thousand pounds.'

'Thirty fucking . . .' His voice tailed off. He threw his head back and stared at the ceiling, breathing heavily through his nose. Dixon waited for the tears, but they didn't come.

'How did you know?'

'Serial numbers on bank notes matching large cash withdrawals,' replied Dixon.

Perry stepped forward and held out his hand to Dixon. He stood up and they shook hands.

'Thank you,' said Perry.

'If you have no objection I think there's going to be a press announcement later.'

'Just give me till lunchtime to tell her parents,' said Perry.

'I can do it if you'd rather.'

'No. I want to do it.'

'Well, I'll be heading . . .'

'So, did she think I'd just forget the whole thing? After she killed my wife.'

'She thought Lizzie would be the driving force behind your campaign,' replied Dixon. 'And if she was killed by a burglar you'd soon find other causes to champion.'

'Easy mistake to make.'

Chapter Twenty-Five

Dixon arrived back at Express Park just after midday, after two hours' sleep and a walk on the beach. It was the best he was going to get, and he felt better for the walk rather than the sleep. Jane was already back at the police centre, having left after Dr McConnell had been charged earlier that morning. Dave and Mark were back too, but there was no sign of Louise.

'How are we doing?' asked Dixon, inhaling the steam off a mug of coffee that Jane had thrust into his hand.

'Lewis was looking for you,' said Jane.

'And Mr Charlesworth and Vicky Thomas are here too, Sir,' said Mark.

'Anything else from Surrey?'

'There's some trace DNA at Tulkeley Cottage. We'll know if there's a database match later.'

'Anything else?'

Dave Harding shook his head.

'And the cameras?'

'No.'

'What about her computers, iPad, email? Nothing in there?'

'Not that can't be accounted for,' said Jane.

'No photos?'

'No.'

'It comes down to that damned phone then, doesn't it? I'll speak to Lewis.' Dixon took a swig of coffee. 'Is that decaf?'

'It's all we've got left,' said Jane.

Dixon winced. 'Pinch some proper stuff from Professional Standards or something. We're gonna need plenty of caffeine.'

'You got ten minutes?' DCI Lewis was on the other side of the landing, shouting across the atrium.

Dixon turned to Jane and raised his eyebrows. 'Here we go.'

'Well done, Dixon,' said Charlesworth.

'Thank you, Sir.'

Lewis closed the door of meeting room two behind him.

'That's it then?' asked Charlesworth.

'No, Sir. There's no doubt the money was Dr McConnell's. She has the motive and she's confessed. But all that stuff about a meeting in a lay-by on the A303 was rubbish. There's someone else . . .'

'Ah, the mysterious phone.'

'Why incinerate it? Why lie?' asked Dixon. 'Unless she's hiding someone.'

'Look, we've got her, we've got the money and the motive. We've got the killers, the foot soldiers as you call them, and the Albanians have disappeared. I think that's it as far as I'm concerned.'

'Well, it's not as far as I'm concerned,' said Dixon.

Charlesworth peered at Dixon over his glasses, which had slid down his nose.

'What Dixon means, I think, Sir, is that he'd like more time to explore whether or not someone else was involved with Dr McConnell,' said Lewis. 'Whether it was a joint enterprise.'

'Is that right, Dixon?' asked Charlesworth.

'Yes, Sir.'

'And what about this afternoon's press conference?'

Vicky Thomas sat up.

'That can go ahead, Sir,' replied Dixon. 'I've spoken to Tom Perry and he's telling her family.'

'But we can't tell the press it's case closed?'

'I'd rather we did. Then, if there is someone else, he or she will think they can relax.'

'What if McConnell tips them off?'

'She wouldn't dare, Sir,' replied Lewis. 'She'll know we'll be watching for that.'

'Sounds good to me,' said Charlesworth. 'What about you, Vicky?'

'Fine.'

'What do we say about Betalin?'

'Nothing. It's just a straight statement of fact. Dr Ann McConnell has been charged et cetera, et cetera. We'll leave the press to speculate about the motive,' said Vicky.

'I think Tom Perry will have something to say about it too,' said Dixon.

'He mustn't prejudice her trial.'

'He won't, Sir. I'll speak to him.'

'What d'you need then, Dixon?' asked Lewis.

'We don't have the number of the second phone but if she carried it with her then it should register on the same base stations as her other phone. So, we get mobile positioning records for, say, five base stations where we know she was at a given time and then cross reference them. If we get lucky there'll be only two numbers that show up on all of the lists. Then we've got the number and the rest will fall into place.'

'There's a lot of speculation in that,' said Charlesworth.

'What if she didn't carry the second phone with her?' asked Lewis. 'She may have kept it in her office.'

'She may.'

'And there'll be thousands of numbers to sift through.'

'I'm sure there's a computer script than can do that for us.'

'It sounds very expensive too,' said Charlesworth. 'Is there really nothing else?'

'A trace DNA sample from her house. We don't know yet if there's a database match,' replied Dixon.

'Well, let's hope that comes through. We certainly can't sanction a mass trawl through mobile positioning records, and a speculative one at that. You'll have to think of something else, Dixon,' said Charlesworth.

'What about personnel?' asked Lewis.

'We may need extra help but . . .'

'You can keep Dave and Mark for a week to get this lot sorted. Then I'll have to take them off you.'

Dixon sighed.

'Are you and Constable Winter still an item, Dixon?' asked Charlesworth.

'Yes, Sir.'

'We need to do something about that too.' Charlesworth turned to Lewis and raised his eyebrows.

'Yes, Sir,' said Lewis.

False summits; he'd always hated them. It was the disappointment, his hopes dashed, and then the sickening realisation that he had to get up, dust himself down and keep going. It wasn't the end, after all. The worst had been the Dôme du Goûter on the way up Mont Blanc, but this one was right up there with it, and at least he had known the Dôme du Goûter was coming. He'd been warned about it, was prepared for it even. He closed his eyes and remembered the line of head torches snaking their way up the summit ridge above him in the first light of dawn. Then he had reached for his camera and the photograph was still hanging on his bedroom wall. It had survived the cull of his old climbing photographs when Jane moved in.

The soft ping of an email arriving brought him back to his computer screen. Yes, it was a false summit and yes, he would keep going. He had no choice.

He opened the email and grimaced. The DNA sample found at Tulkeley Cottage came from a brown hair found in the bedroom. No other information was given except that it was from an unidentified male not on the national database. He closed his eyes, but the summit ridge was shrouded in darkness now, the lights gone.

'What's up?' asked Jane. She was standing next to him with a mug of coffee in her hand.

'No DNA match.'

'Bugger.'

'We've got Dave and Mark for a week. And the mobile positioning is a non-starter.'

'Why?'

'Too expensive and too speculative, apparently.'

'So, what do we do now?'

'Well, she won't tell us who he is, so we've got to find him,' said Dixon. 'I think you and Louise need to have another word with Muriel Dummett. Where is she?'

'She was released on police bail this morning. The CPS say there's not enough to charge her.'

'Yet,' muttered Dixon. 'Have another word with the neighbours too, while you're up there.'

Jane nodded.

'We can go back through her bank statements. See if there are any payments to anyone interesting.'

Jane was making notes.

'And let's get her divorce papers. You never know, they may name a co-respondent. We can speak to the ex-husband. And holidays.'

'Holidays?'

'See if she's flown anywhere apart from Sweden recently. If so, who'd she go with? Check the seating plan on the plane.'

Jane frowned.

'I know. It's called clutching at straws,' said Dixon, shaking his head.

'We're still waiting for the full report on her computers,' said Jane. 'High Tech may still come up with something.'

'Let's hope so.'

'And the calls to and from her landlines.'

'Good.'

'It could be that she's lying because she doesn't want to drop the Albanians in it,' said Jane. 'They're dangerous people.'

'If that was right, why did she keep the phone?' asked Dixon. 'She'd have got rid of it last October when the deal was done.'

'Yeah, you're right. It doesn't add up.'

'We'll just keep digging until we find him, or until we've got enough to justify the mobile positioning.'

'Here's Louise,' said Jane. 'Nice lie in?'

'You are kidding?'

'Yes, I am. Coffee?'

'Yes, please.'

'What about you?' asked Jane, turning to Dixon. But he was miles away, on the beach at Berrow, listening to an Albanian gangster talking about insurance.

What the hell was all that about?

Chapter Twenty-Six

Thursday 23 January; Polling Day

Dixon was parked in the loading bay outside Lester Hodson Solicitors in Bridgwater, watching the traffic warden in his wing mirror. She peeled the back off a parking ticket and stuck it in the middle of the windscreen of the car behind his Land Rover. Then she stepped forward, reaching for her ticket machine, her eyes fixed on Dixon's number plate.

He wound the window down, held out his warrant card and was relieved when it had the desired effect.

'Sorry.'

'That's fine,' said Dixon. Then he turned back to Wendy Gibson's will file.

The solicitor had been reluctant to release it without seeing a death certificate, until Dixon pointed out that they must have seen both a death certificate and a grant of probate before they had released the deeds to Dolley & Freer in 1995. It was testament to the inefficiency of their deeds clerk perhaps that the file hadn't been marked for destruction at that time, but Dixon was not complaining.

The initial attendance note was what he was looking for. The notes of the first meeting between the solicitor and Mrs Gibson that he hoped might hold the key to his cold case. Not that he had wasted much time on it in recent days, as the hunt for Dr McConnell's accomplice dragged on, but he had found himself outside Lester Hodson's office and it had only taken him ten minutes to persuade them to release the file.

He slid the papers out of the faded brown envelope and unfolded them. They felt damp to the touch and he grimaced when a small cloud of either dust or mould spores exploded in front of him. He wound the window down again, despite the rain.

The will was held together by a rusty staple that had left a brown stain in the top left corner of the page. At least it hadn't been handwritten in quill pen. He glanced at the will, which was almost identical to her last one, except for the appointment of different executors. Then he turned to the correspondence pin; faded pieces of paper of all different sizes held together on a rotten treasury tag; the ink, once black, having faded to brown.

The last piece of paper was the one he was looking for, although sadly it was a page of handwritten scribblings made by the solicitor during the meeting. There was no detailed attendance note, as was the requirement these days. The note was dated 12 May 1985 and Dixon counted sixteen words on the page, all of them legible, just. 'Wendy May Gibson; executors Lester Hodson; residue to FoBH and RNLI; child (adopted 1954), leave nothing.'

It was short and to the point, but it told him what he wanted to know, although now he had someone else to find.

Jane was just leaving when Dixon turned into Express Park at midday. They each wound their windows down.

'Where are you off to?'

'She stayed at the Bishopstrow House Hotel last May, according to her credit card statements,' replied Jane.

'We looked at those, didn't we?'

'It's an MBNA account we didn't know about.'

'Did she go alone?'

'It was a double room.'

'And she paid?'

'Looks like it.'

'Where is it?'

'Near Warminster.'

'What time will you be back?'

'Fourish, I expect,' replied Jane. 'I'll send you a text.'

'OK.'

'And Louise has got her divorce papers.'

Dixon parked under cover and took the lift up to the CID area.

'Jane's gone . . .'

'I bumped into her on the way in, thanks, Louise,' said Dixon. 'Anything in the divorce papers?'

'Adultery but the co-respondent is unnamed. Seems to have been only one though and there's reference to dirty weekends in Blackpool, Bournemouth and at the Bishopstrow House.'

'A regular haunt of hers then?'

'Looks like it,' replied Louise.

'Ex-husband?'

'Seeing him tomorrow.'

'These them?' asked Dixon, picking up a plastic document wallet.

'Yes.'

'Do me a favour when you get a minute, will you?'

'Yes, Sir?'

'Wendy May Gibson. Here's my file,' said Dixon, dropping a folder onto the desk next to her. 'She gave a child up for adoption in 1954. Get onto the adoption agency and find out what became of him or her. And don't tell Jane either.'

'Why not?'

'It's complicated.'

'OK.'

Dixon sat down in the corner of the staff canteen and peeled open an egg and cress sandwich. Then he began flicking through Dr McConnell's divorce papers. Ten minutes later he had finished both, still felt hungry and had learned nothing that Louise hadn't already told him. Another dead end, unless Jane came up with something at the Bishopstrow House.

He trudged back to his desk, sat down and reached up for a green document wallet marked 'insurance'. It contained copies of all of Dr McConnell's insurance policies; office, public liability, house and contents, buildings, car and life insurance. There were also two life assurance policies, just in case Dixon had misheard the Albanian accent. He had been through it any number of times and had even searched for policies on the life of Elizabeth Perry. Nothing. But then Zavan had been referring to a different type of insurance. He must have been. The type of insurance that a criminal takes out when asked by another to commit a crime.

Dixon would ask him if he could but even that door had been slammed in his face. Much longer and Lewis would be winding down the investigation still further. And he'd already got one cold case on the go.

He was waiting for the kettle to boil when he noticed Louise waving at him.

'PC Cole's on the phone. Asking for you.'

Dixon walked over and took the phone from Louise.

'Yes.'

'PC Cole, Sir.'

'What is it, Cole?'

'I'm at the polling station in Brent Knoll. The parish hall. I think there's something you ought to see.'

'What?'

'A postal ballot paper's been handed in. A motorcycle courier rode up about an hour ago. The staff here called the returning officer and he rang us. There's something in the envelope.'

'Has it been opened?'

'No, Sir. It feels like a memory stick.'

'Whose ballot paper is it?'

'Harry Unwin's, Sir.'

'Harry's?'

'Yes, Sir. Not only that but it doesn't match the name written on the postal voting statement.'

'What's the name on the statement?'

'Nicholas John Dixon.'

Chapter Twenty-Seven

'Ring Jane and let her know what's going on, will you?'

'OK,' replied Louise.

She was sitting in the passenger seat of his Land Rover, but Dixon could hardly make out what she was saying over the noise of the diesel engine, as they raced north on the M5.

'She's on her way back. I told her to wait for us at Express Park.'

'Good.'

Dixon parked on the forecourt of the new Brent Knoll Parish Hall, right next to the 'Loading and Unloading Only' sign.

'You won't be able to leave that there.'

Dixon looked over to where the shout had come from. Three people were sitting on a bench by the front door, sheltering under two large golf umbrellas. One wore a blue rosette, one yellow and the other red. He shook his head. Perhaps political parties can cooperate with each other after all, he thought, waving his warrant card at them as he ran in the front door.

Two large tables had been set up in the foyer, with a black box on the end of the far table. Against the wall opposite were four timber polling booths.

'D'you have your polling card?'

'No,' replied Dixon, showing the clerk his warrant card.

'Through there,' she said, pointing to a door at the back of the foyer.

PC Cole was sitting on a stool in the kitchen, sipping a mug of tea, and jumped up when he saw Dixon.

'Sir, this is Robert Sampson, the returning officer.'

'You'll be Detective Inspector Dixon?' asked Sampson. He was short, with dark curly hair and was dressed casually in jeans and a blue pullover.

'Nicholas John,' said Dixon, shaking his hand. 'Where is it?'

'Here,' replied Cole, handing Dixon a plastic evidence bag. 'I bagged it up just in case.'

Dixon looked at his watch. It was just before 4 p.m.

'What time did it come in?'

'Just after lunch. Say twoish,' replied Sampson. 'The staff here rang me and it took me an hour or so to get here.'

'What made them ring you?'

'You can hand deliver a postal vote to a polling station on election day, Inspector, but the ballot paper must match the postal voting statement. It's in a sealed envelope, but the code on the front doesn't match the statement. It's not your ballot paper. You're not even registered for a postal vote.'

Dixon nodded.

'Not to mention what's in it,' said Sampson.

Dixon was squeezing the envelope between his thumb and index finger. 'It's definitely a memory stick.'

'It came in the blank envelope,' said Sampson, 'which is why they opened it. If it had been in envelope B then it wouldn't have been opened until the count.'

'So, when they opened the blank envelope they found the postal voting statement and a sealed envelope A with the memory stick in it?'

'Yes.'

'But they've not opened envelope A?'

'No.'

'So, let me get this right,' said Dixon. 'You put the ballot paper in envelope A, seal it and then put it, with the postal voting statement, in envelope B?'

'Yes.'

'Then you put it in the post.'

'You have to sign the postal statement and add your date of birth. The codes on both must match too. Otherwise it's rejected.'

'Why did you call the police, if that's not a daft question?'

'It was the memory stick in the envelope. That could be anything, couldn't it?' replied Sampson. 'And I recognised the name. Didn't he hang himself a couple of weeks ago? It was in the paper.'

'When were the postal votes sent out?' asked Dixon.

'Two weeks ago.'

'When did Harry register for a postal vote?'

'I checked that,' replied Sampson. 'He registered four years ago for the Europeans and ticked the "all elections" box. So, now he gets one every time. Got one . . .'

'And it would've been sent to his home address?'

'He probably had a redirect on his mail, Sir,' said Cole. 'What with Moorland under water.'

Dixon turned to Louise.

'I'll find out,' she said.

'What about the courier then?' asked Dixon.

'Black leathers and a full face helmet,' replied Cole, reading from his notebook. 'Said nothing, just handed them the envelope and left.'

'No markings?'

'None.'

'Did you speak to those three sitting outside?'

'Er, not yet, Sir.'

Dixon raised his eyebrows.

'I'll go and do that now, Sir.'

Dixon walked over to the small drawer to the left of the kitchen sink, opened it and took out a knife.

'Let's open it then, shall we?' he said, pulling on a pair of latex gloves.

He opened the plastic evidence bag and took out the small envelope. Then he slit it open with the knife and peered in.

'A memory stick and a ballot paper.'

Dixon took out the piece of paper and unfolded it.

'Well, that's one vote Tom Perry will have to do without.'

'The elector is deceased,' said Sampson. 'And even if he wasn't it would still be rejected because the postal voting statement is defective.'

'Well, it's evidence in a murder investigation, Mr Sampson, so we'll be hanging on to it.'

'Yes, of course.'

Dixon was holding the memory stick in the palm of his hand.

'I wonder what's on it,' said Louise.

Cole reappeared in the doorway.

'No markings on the bike, Sir. He didn't even switch it off, apparently. Just parked up, in, out and away again. They didn't get the number plate either.'

'Probably false,' said Dixon.

'What are they doing out there?' asked Louise. 'Sitting in the rain.'

'It's called "telling",' replied Sampson. 'They're finding out which of their supporters have voted so they can remind any who haven't.'

'It's your local polling station, Sir,' said Cole, grinning.

'Where to next?' asked Louise.

'The High Tech Unit at Portishead. Ring ahead and let them know we're on the way. And if they've gone home before we get there I'll arrest them for obstruction.'

'D'you want me to tell them that?'

'No.' Dixon was standing in his kitchen watching Monty finishing his supper. Then he took him for a quick run in the field behind his cottage. Five minutes would have to do.

'You'd better sit this one out, old son,' said Dixon. 'It's going to be a long night.' Then he locked the back door of his cottage and jumped in the Land Rover.

They arrived at Portishead just before 5 p.m. and Dixon parked on the grass verge outside a small single storey office block on the edge of the headquarters complex.

'Is this it?' asked Louise.

'It is.'

Dixon walked into the open plan office area. The tops of several heads were visible behind computer screens in amongst the vacant workstations, but none looked up. He tried coughing.

'Who did you speak to?'

'Kevin Hardy,' said Louise.

Dixon shouted the name and a head popped up from behind a screen at the far end of the office. The figure waved and then disappeared again behind his computer.

'Sociable lot,' said Louise.

'Are you Kevin Hardy?' asked Dixon, when he reached the desk at the far end.

'Yes.'

'We rang. We've got a memory stick and need to know what's on it.'

'I'll need to scan it for viruses first.'

'Fine.'

Hardy held out his hand.

'Gloves, if you don't mind. There may be fingerprints on it.'

Dixon and Louise watched while Hardy put on a pair of latex gloves and then inserted the memory stick in one of the USB ports on his computer.

'What d'you think is on it, Sir?' asked Louise.

'I can tell you exactly what's on it.'

'Really?'

'An insurance policy.'

'No viruses,' said Hardy. 'Just a wmv file. Windows Media Video. It's short too.'

'Odd file name,' said Loiuse.

'Sigurim. It'll be Albanian,' replied Dixon. 'Can we see it?'

'Yes. Stand behind me.'

Hardy clicked on the wmv icon launching Windows Media Player.

'It's a short clip, look,' said Hardy, pointing to the timer on the right, which was counting down from 1 minute 27 seconds. 'And there's a time stamp.'

'October 9, 0721,' muttered Dixon.

The camera was moving forward, as if mounted on a person, and he or she was walking through dense undergrowth. The sound was muffled; branches hitting a coat, a broken twig underfoot. Then the vegetation cleared, revealing the foot of a cliff.

Suddenly, the camera turned as a figure appeared from the undergrowth behind it.

Dixon was gritting his teeth and breathing through his nose. Hard. He clenched his fists, the keys and coins in his pockets digging into the palms of his hands.

'D'you recognise him, Sir?' asked Louise.

Dixon leaned forward and listened.

'Do you have the money?' An Eastern European accent.

'Yes.'

The figure held out a large padded envelope and a hand reached out from behind the camera to take it.

'It needs to be clean. An accident or a burglary gone wrong.'

'It will.'

'Is that it?'

'What do you want? A receipt?'

'No, I . . .'

'Go. Now. You will not hear from us again.'

The figure turned and disappeared into the undergrowth. Then a hand reached up in front of the camera and the clip ended.

'Can you email that to me?'

'What's your email address?'

'I'm on the Bridgwater list. Send it to DCI Lewis too. Mark it urgent and ask him to ring me when he gets it.'

'Will do.'

'There's nothing else on the memory stick?' asked Dixon.

'No,' said Hardy, dropping it back into the evidence bag. 'I'll catalogue it and let you have a witness statement on the email too.'

'Thanks.'

'You'd better drive,' said Dixon. 'I'm expecting a call.'

They were just turning onto the M5 when his phone rang.

'What d'you need?'

'Dave and Mark, Sir.'

'Fine,' replied Lewis.

'And a mobile positioning check. I know the where and the when.'

'OK.'

'Meeting room two, Sir. Half an hour. We're on our way now.'

'I'll get everyone together.'

Dixon rang off and opened a web browser. He entered 'translate' in the search field, then 'sigurim' in the 'Enter text' field.

'Gits,' he muttered.

'What is it?' asked Louise.

'Sigurim. It's Albanian for insurance.'

Jane, Dave and Mark were waiting for them in meeting room two when Dixon and Louise arrived back at Express Park just after 6 p.m. DCI Lewis was loitering in the CID area.

'I circulated the film so they've all seen it.'

'Good,' replied Dixon. 'Just give me five minutes and I'll be over.'

He sat down at a workstation and switched on a computer.

'Get me those divorce papers, will you, Louise?'

'Yes, Sir.'

'You know who it is, don't you?' asked Lewis, as Dixon closed the door of the meeting room.

'I do, but without the cameraman we're going to have a fight to use the film, so we need more.'

Lewis nodded.

'It was on a memory stick that was hand delivered to my local polling station. The postal voting statement had my name on it and the ballot paper is Harry Unwin's.'

'Harry's?'

'Yes, Sir,' replied Dixon. 'The postal votes were sent out two weeks ago, after Harry was murdered. So, someone must've broken into his temporary accommodation and stolen it. Louise checked with the post office and his mail was being redirected to . . . ?'

'His mother's flat in Bridgwater.'

'Let's get uniform over there to speak to his mother and the neighbours. Someone must've noticed.'

'Unless it was intercepted before it was delivered,' said Mark.

'Or delivered to a communal entrance. Some flats have easily accessible letter boxes,' said Dave.

'Well, let's check,' said Dixon.

'You said you knew where and when the film was taken?' asked Lewis.

'There's a time stamp which gives us the when: 0720 on 9 October. The where is the Avon Gorge at the bottom of the Main Wall.'

'How d'you know that?' asked Jane.

'It's at the foot of "Conan the Librarian". Don't ask,' said Dixon, rolling his eyes. 'It's a rock climb. Short, very difficult and I spent three days one summer falling off it. There used to be a bolt twenty feet up. That's gone now, but it's definitely it.'

'Mobile positioning it is then,' said Lewis. 'D'you have the number?'

Dixon slid a piece of paper across the table to Lewis. He looked at it and handed it to Jane.

'Expedite it, Jane,' said Lewis. 'I'll authorise it.'

'Dave and Mark, traffic and number plate cameras,' said Dixon, sliding another piece of paper across the table. 'Either will do, both would be better.'

Dave picked up the piece of paper and looked at it.

'Should be easy,' he said, grinning.

'What else?' asked Lewis.

'The divorce papers refer to weekends away with her unnamed co-respondent in Blackpool in October 2001 and Bournemouth in

October 2002. I want to check the hotels to see if she stayed with someone and, if so, who. We can start with the main ones and work down.'

'Will they still have records going that far back?' asked Louise.

'We'll soon find out.'

'What's the significance of Blackpool and Bournemouth in October?' asked Lewis.

'Party conference,' replied Dixon. 'Conservative Party conference.'

Chapter Twenty-Eight

'What time is it?' asked Jane, leaning back in her chair and yawning.

'Twoish,' replied Dixon.

'You did leave a light on for Monty?'

'I left the telly on. Thought it would keep him company.'

'Good,' said Jane, smiling.

Dixon looked up when he heard footsteps coming along the landing.

'Well?' asked Lewis, appearing round the corner of the canteen. 'You still here, Sir?'

'I've been home and come back again.'

'Well, we've got him on an ANPR camera in Clifton. It was a bit earlier than we were expecting so Dave's going back to look at the traffic cameras again.'

'What about the hotels?'

'Nothing from either Blackpool or Bournemouth, but that was a long shot after all this time anyway.'

'And the mobile positioning?'

'There's an Orange base station on the opposite side of the gorge at Oak Wood,' replied Dixon. 'We were promised an email around about now.'

'There you are, you bastard.' The voice came from a workstation behind Dixon.

'You got him, Dave?'

'Traffic camera on the A4176 where it joins the Portway, 0634.'

'That's enough, surely?' asked Lewis, 'even without a mobile fix?'

'Probably,' replied Dixon, 'but we'll give them another twenty minutes or so. He's not going anywhere.'

'How d'you know that?'

'The declaration's not due till three o'clock.'

Dixon double parked in the High Street outside the Bridgwater Town Hall, alongside a large van with a satellite dish on the top and BBC News written on the side. Dave and Mark pulled up behind him, blocking in the ITV News van. The Sky News van was parked further down the one way street.

One of the uniformed officers on the door stepped forward but then recognised Louise sitting in the rear passenger seat of Dixon's Land Rover and returned to his post under the entrance portico.

The town hall had recently been painted white and seemed to glow in the street lights. It was a three storey Victorian building with arched windows on the first floor and two stone entrance porches with square columns, access to one of them blocked by newly painted black railings. The doors of the other were open and light was streaming out into the night.

'We'll need to be discreet,' said Dixon. 'I don't want this plastered all over the news. We'll get him out of the auditorium first, all right?'

'Yes, Sir.'

Dixon turned to the uniformed officers on the door.

'You two, with us.'

'Yes, Sir.'

He stepped over the television cables laid across the pavement and in the front door.

'It's ticket only, I'm afraid.'

The man on the desk was in his late sixties, if not older, and would not have made much of a bouncer. But then the crowd at an election count tend to behave themselves, particularly when the television cameras are there. Dixon waved his warrant card at the man and kept walking.

He paused at the bottom of the short flight of stairs and checked his watch: 2.45 a.m.

'There are two ways out. A small door at the far end by the stage that leads to the back stairs. Dave, you can take that with Mark. Go inside then along the wall. All right?'

'Yes, Sir.'

'Just make sure you're between me and the door.'

'Yes, Sir.'

'Jane, you cover the double doors at the back with uniform, but keep them out of sight until you see me move in.'

'Right.'

'Louise, you're with me.'

Dixon turned and walked up the stairs. The double doors at the back of the auditorium were open and people were milling about in the hall, some carrying drinks. He walked along the back wall and stood in the middle, watching the scene unfold. Dave and Mark crept in and walked along the side wall to the front, taking up position behind the TV crews, just inside the door by the stage. Jane was standing by the double doors at the back.

All of the folding tables that had been set up along each side of the hall were empty and a group of casually dressed council staff were waiting on the far side, looking up at the stage. Counting had finished and the tables in the middle of the hall were covered in lines of ballot papers, all tied up in elastic bands in bundles of one thousand.

Tom Perry's line was the longest. Some small consolation, perhaps, but Dixon thought about what it had cost him.

'What's going on?' asked Louise.

'They're verifying the spoilt ballot papers,' replied Dixon. 'They have to check each one.'

A large crowd was gathered at a table in front of the stage. Dixon spotted the returning officer, Robert Sampson, this time wearing a jacket and tie, holding up one ballot paper at a time to allow the candidates and their agents to scrutinise it. Perry was at the front of the group, with Lawrence Deakin, looking relaxed and not taking much notice. Judging by the bundles of votes, there could be five thousand spoilt ballot papers all allocated to his nearest challenger and he would still win.

Four other groups of supporters were waiting at the front of the hall, each identifiable by the colour of their rosettes. Blue, yellow, red and purple. Dixon recognised some of those wearing blue rosettes, but not all.

'How d'you spoil a ballot paper then?' asked Louise.

'Voting for more than one candidate, putting your name on it, or just writing "fuck off" on it, I suppose.'

'I never thought of that.'

'There's always next time,' said Dixon.

'Can you see him?'

'No.'

'Where is he?'

'He'll be here.'

Dixon looked at Dave Harding, who shrugged his shoulders. Then he looked at Jane. She shook her head.

'Who's that talking to the TV cameras?' asked Louise.

'That's the MP for West Somerset. I forget his name.'

Dixon watched Tom Perry step back from the crowd still verifying spoilt ballot papers and speak to a young man with short dark hair.

'Who's that?'

'Don't know,' replied Louise.

'Go and ask Jane.'

Louise returned a few seconds later.

'It's Simon King, Lizzie's brother.'

'Not the marine?'

Louise nodded.

'Oh shit, that's all we need.'

'Who's that in the top hat?'

'That'll be the Monster Raving Looney.'

'There's even a white rabbit,' said Louise.

'They all come out for by-elections,' muttered Dixon.

Robert Sampson stepped back from the table and the crowd began to disperse to join their supporters as the candidates made their way onto the stage. Dixon watched Perry step back to allow the other candidates up the steps.

'We'll be live on *Newsnight* soon,' said Louise.

'There he is,' said Dixon.

'Where?'

'Sitting down at the front.' Dixon turned to Jane and nodded.

Louise stepped forward.

'Wait.'

Barry Dossett stood up, straightened his jacket and then made his way to the back of the crowd of Conservative supporters. He was unmistakeable, standing several inches taller than everyone else. The padded jacket had been replaced by a blazer and red tie. Odd that. There was no blue rosette either.

Dixon was distracted by the noise of Sampson tapping the microphone. Then Sampson glanced down at the TV crews and nodded.

'I, Robert Frederick Dunning Sampson, being the returning officer in the parliamentary election for the Bridgwater and North Somerset constituency held on Thursday 23 January do hereby give notice that the number of votes recorded for each candidate at the said election is as follows.'

'What do we do?' asked Louise.

Dixon glanced across at Jane and nodded. The two uniformed officers appeared in the doorway. Then he looked at Mark, who leaned forward and whispered in Dave Harding's ear.

'Follow me,' said Dixon.

'Abbot, Peter Benjamin Thumper, White Rabbit Liberation Party, thirty-nine.'

'Democracy is a wonderful thing,' muttered Dixon, but it was lost in the cheer of a small group of people to his left.

'Blythe, John Joseph, United Kingdom Independence Party, UKIP, seven thousand seven hundred and nineteen.'

'I'll go right, you go left,' said Dixon.

'Crowther, Lauren, Green Party. Three thousand and eighteen.'

Dixon walked forward, the noise in the hall masking his footsteps, and took up position on Dossett's right shoulder. Louise was standing to his left.

'Holland, Benjamin Michael, Labour Party, three thousand six hundred and ninety-nine.'

Dixon's heart was pounding. Much louder and Dossett would surely hear it? Even over the noise of the Labour supporters cheering.

'Hunt, Vanessa Milburn, Liberal Democrats, fifteen thousand four hundred and five.'

Dixon glanced up at the stage. Perry was smiling, but for how much longer?

'Jackson, Rupert Walter, Monster Raving Looney Party, three hundred and twelve.'

Jackson stepped forward and his wave was greeted with a loud cheer.

'Oliver, Marcus Ralph, Independent, seventy-seven.'

Another loud cheer, this time from the supporters of all the parties.

'Perry, Thomas James, Conservative Party, twenty-two thousand three hundred and forty-one.'

A louder cheer drowned out the few boos. Perry glanced down at his group of supporters in front of the stage. Then he spotted Dixon standing next to Barry Dossett, his area campaign director. The smile was gone. He looked quizzically at Dixon and shook his head.

'The total number of votes cast was fifty-two thousand six hundred and ten and I hereby declare that the said Thomas James Perry is duly elected Member of Parliament for the said constituency.'

Perry was staring at Dixon and appeared unmoved at the huge cheer that went up from his supporters. It took a nudge before Perry noticed that the Labour candidate had been trying to shake his hand. Perry then shook hands with all of the candidates before stepping forward to the microphone at the invitation of Sampson.

Perry hesitated, staring at Dixon. Dossett was clapping and cheering but stopped when he noticed Perry staring in his direction. Then he turned and saw Dixon standing next to him. He closed his eyes, bowed his head and made a half hearted attempt to turn for the door.

'We'll give him his moment of glory,' said Dixon, taking hold of his arm. 'You owe him that much.'

Perry was still staring at Dixon. He nodded.

'Er, ladies and gentlemen, can I begin by thanking the returning officer and his team here at the count for a very smooth operation? And for sitting up into the early hours counting votes. Whatever they're paying you, it's not enough.'

The council staff waiting at the back cheered.

'I'd like to thank my opponents for a most enjoyable and clean fight. I have made many friends during this election campaign, on all sides of the political spectrum, and for that I will remain deeply grateful.'

Perry paused to allow the applause to subside.

'I'd like to thank my agent, Lawrence Deakin, and . . .' Perry hesitated, frowning at Dixon, '. . . my area campaign director, Barry Dossett, for their support during the campaign.'

Dixon saw Simon King turn and look in his direction.

'And also my team of supporters, volunteers all, who have been out knocking on doors and delivering leaflets in all weathers. Thank you.'

Yet another loud cheer.

'I'd also like to thank the people of Bridgwater and North Somerset for placing their trust in me. Whether you voted for me or not, my door will always be open. And to the residents of the Somerset Levels I say simply this: dredge the rivers!'

Perry looked down at his feet and swallowed hard. Tears welled up in his eyes and he was fighting to hold them back.

'Finally, I'd like to dedicate this election victory to my wife, Lizzie. Without her I would not be standing here today and . . .' The tears began to stream down his cheeks. 'This is for you.'

Vanessa Hunt stepped forward and put her arm around Perry. He looked up and stared at Dixon, no more than thirty feet from the stage, holding Dossett by the arm. Dixon turned away, dragging Dossett with him.

'We'll take this outside,' said Dixon.

Dossett grimaced.

Once out onto the landing Dossett was handcuffed by one of the uniformed officers.

'Barry Dossett, I am arresting you on suspicion of the murder of Elizabeth Grace Perry. You do not have to . . .'

Dixon heard footsteps and turned. Too late. The blow caught him on the right side of his jaw, but he felt no pain until he hit the floor.

'Simon!'

It was Tom Perry's voice, coming from the double doors at the back of the hall. Dixon looked up. Dossett appeared to be leaning over backwards, with Simon King holding him up by the neck, Dossett's head under his right arm.

'Simon, stop!'

One of the uniformed officers stepped forward.

'One more step and I snap his fucking neck!' screamed King.

'Simon, think about Lizzie,' said Perry. 'Let him go.'

'He killed my sister.'

'And the police will deal with him. It's what Lizzie would want. You know that.'

King's nostrils flared as he tightened his grip on Dossett's neck, lifting him until his back was arched and only his toes were on the ground. Much further and Dossett's neck would break.

King glared at Dixon, then Jane, then the uniformed officers.

'I don't want to lose my brother-in-law as well,' said Perry, stepping forward. 'We've all lost enough already, haven't we? It's got to stop, Simon.'

King's breathing slowed. He looked down at Dossett over his right shoulder and back to Perry. Then he released his grip and allowed Dossett to slide to the floor. Dossett lay on his back, with his hands cuffed behind him, sobbing.

'I'm sorry, Tom,' said King.

Perry stepped forward and stood over Dossett, staring down at him.

'Why, Barry? Why Lizzie?'

'You were going to ruin everything,' stammered Dossett. He tried to sit up but slumped back to the floor. 'Everything!' he screamed.

Dixon stood up. He was holding his jaw between his index finger and thumb, moving it gingerly from side to side.

'Just get 'em out of here.'

'Yes, Sir.'

'And those bloody TV cameras!'

'Nick, about Simon,' said Perry, turning to Dixon as the two uniformed officers dragged Dossett to his feet. 'Will you . . . ?'

'I'll do what I can, Tom,' said Dixon. 'I'll do what I can.'

Chapter Twenty-Nine

Monday 27 January

Dixon dropped his file of papers onto a vacant workstation and walked over to the kettle.

'Jane gone?'

'Yes,' replied Louise.

He filled the kettle, switched it on and then leaned back against the worktop.

'I've had a reply from the adoption agency, Sir.'

'And?'

'A baby daughter. Born 7 January 1954. Mrs Gibson was nineteen.'

'Older than I expected. Does it give a name?' asked Dixon.

'Julia Rebecca.'

'What about a reason?'

'Her husband was killed in the Korean War. May 1953 at the Battle of the Hook. He'd only been out there a few days.'

'That doesn't explain why she gave up the baby, does it?'

'Maybe she couldn't afford it? Or perhaps it wasn't his?'

'Where's the child now?'

'She was adopted by a family in Bristol. Kept her Christian names and became Julia Rebecca Jameson.'

'Where is she now?'

'She got married in 1998. Julia Woodgates, she is now. Lives in Muchelney, would you believe it?'

'Yes, I would,' said Dixon, with a wry smile. 'Children?'

'Two, from a previous marriage.'

It was a small world, and it explained the flowers on the grave that had always puzzled the vicar. Perhaps the rage that drove her to obliterate her mother had turned to remorse over the years? Maybe it happened when she became a mother herself? Still, those were questions for another day.

'D'you know her, Sir?'

'We've met.'

'D'you want to go and pick her up?' asked Louise.

'No, you go. You've done all the legwork. It's not every day you get to solve a cold case and it'll help with your transfer to CID.'

'Thank you, Sir.'

'Check for a shotgun certificate before you go. Either her own or her adopted parents. And ring me if she denies it.'

'Yes, Sir.'

'Take Dave or Mark with you. I'm going home.'

'You never told me about the cold case,' said Jane.

They were sheltering in the porch at Berrow Church, watching Monty wandering around the churchyard in the rain.

'Louise has gone to pick her up now,' replied Dixon.

'Who?'

'Are you sure you wanna know?'

Jane nodded.

'The victim gave a child up for adoption in 1954. A daughter. Let's just say the reunion didn't go well.'

'It was the daughter?'

'The daughter no one knew she had, don't forget. There was no reference to her anywhere, except in some scribbled notes gathering dust in an old solicitor's will file. It wasn't even her last will; the one before that.'

'How did you know to look for it?'

'I am a solicitor, don't forget.'

'And you thought I'd . . .'

'No, I didn't think you'd blow your mother's head off,' said Dixon, smiling. 'I thought you might be upset. That it might put you off looking for her.'

'What frightens me more than anything else,' said Jane, sitting down on the bench, 'more even than finding out she's dead, is that she doesn't want to know me . . . wants nothing to do with me.'

'Her loss.'

'Doesn't feel like it.'

'Why not just take it one step at a time. Find the file and then you'll at least know why. Finding her is stage two and, if she's still alive, then you worry about whether or not to meet her.'

'I suppose so.'

'It's your decision, but whatever you decide, I'm right behind you. All right?'

'I know that,' said Jane, smiling. 'Idiot.'

'We really must talk about insubordination at your next staff appraisal, Constable Winter.'

Jane stood up and kissed Dixon.

'One step at a time, then. I'm just gonna get the file. Then we'll see if I can find her and if she's still alive. That's all.'

'Fine by me,' replied Dixon.

'Where the hell's Monty gone now,' said Jane, glancing around the churchyard. She stepped out of the porch, turned and looked up the path to the top of the churchyard.

'Can you see him?' asked Dixon.

'I think he's trying to tell us something,' replied Jane, grinning.

Monty was waiting for them at the gap in the wall, where the path veered off across the golf course to the beach.

'It's stopped raining,' said Dixon, holding his hand out in front of him.

They followed Monty across the golf course, out onto the beach, and turned north towards Brean Down. They were level with the wreck of the *SS Nornen* before Dixon spoke again.

'Why now though?'

'It just feels right, that's all,' replied Jane, staring at another raincloud that was heading straight for them across the estuary. 'Now that I'm . . . settled.'

Dixon knew not to press the point. 'Settled' sounded good to him. And he felt the same.

'I don't like the look of that cloud . . .'

Jane was interrupted by the loud blast of a horn and turned to see a car speeding towards them along the beach. It slid to a halt and Tom Perry got out.

'Thought I might find you here, only they said you'd gone home and you weren't there, so . . .'

'You should've been a detective.'

Perry smiled.

'I wanted to thank you.'

'No need,' said Dixon.

'Simon told me Dossett's not pressing charges against him?'

'No.'

'First decent thing he's done,' replied Perry. 'Did you interview him?'

Dixon nodded.

'What's his connection to Dr McConnell?'

'They were lovers,' replied Dixon. 'Have been for years. He was the unnamed co-respondent in her divorce, so that dates it to at least twelve years ago but they'd been seeing each other for several years before that. They met at a Conservative Party conference.'

'Is that it?'

'He'd put some money into her business in the early days and . . .'

'Money again!'

'McConnell was on the brink of selling out to Betalin AB.'

'And they didn't want me rocking the boat?'

'No.'

Perry leaned back on the front wing of his car.

'It was always going to be about the money, Tom,' said Dixon. 'We knew that.'

'I suppose we did,' replied Perry. 'Whose idea was it?'

'Dr McConnell's. But Dossett set it up. They both blame each other but that's the most likely scenario.'

'How did you know it was him?'

'A tip off.'

'Who from?'

'I really can't . . .'

'No, of course you can't.'

Perry picked up Monty's ball and threw it along the beach.

'I'm not going to rock the boat. I'm gonna sink it,' said Perry, watching Monty chase off after the ball. 'What about you? Simon hit you, didn't he?'

'Didn't feel a thing,' said Dixon, rubbing his chin.

'Thank you.'

'Really, it's all part of the . . .'

'I know it isn't,' interrupted Perry. He held out his hand. Dixon took it and they shook hands.

'And you, Constable Winter,' said Perry, shaking Jane's hand.

'Call me Jane, please.'

'I gather the water level's going down?' asked Dixon.

'It was,' replied Perry. 'Till some twit further up opened the sluice gates.'

'Some people . . .'

'We must have a bite to eat sometime,' said Perry.

'I hope you like curry,' said Jane.

'Love it. Anyway, I must go. I'm on my way up to London. I'm being sworn in tomorrow.'

'Good luck,' said Dixon.

'Thanks,' replied Perry, getting into his car. He wound down the window. 'And if there's ever anything I can do for you . . .'

Dixon waved and Perry sped off.

'You didn't mention the budget cuts,' said Jane.

'No.'

'You'll be telling me next you voted Tory.'

'No,' replied Dixon, smiling. 'He doesn't need to know that though, does he?'

Author's Note

Thank you very much indeed for reading *Dead Level* and I hope you enjoyed it. I wanted to say a few words about the plot, which was born out of bitter personal experience.

On New Year's Eve 2002 someone very close to me was diagnosed with type 1 diabetes. From that point on her experience mirrored that of Elizabeth Perry (except she wasn't murdered!). No advice was given about the choice of insulin available and you can guess the rest.

Mercifully, I spotted an advertisement in the local paper placed by the InDependent Diabetes Trust—a real organisation that very kindly agreed to appear in *Dead Level*—and once the switch to animal insulin was made her recovery was both immediate and, thank God, complete.

Who was it who said that 'fact is stranger than fiction'?

So, my message is simple. If you or anyone you know has been affected by any of the symptoms set out in this book following a prescription of human insulin, please seek immediate medical advice. Further information can also be found on the IDDT website at www.iddt.org.

Thanks again for reading.

Damien Boyd
Devon, UK, October 2015

Author's Note

[illegible] the plot, which was [illegible] of my personal experience.

[illegible]

[illegible]

Thanks again for reading,

[illegible]